OMEGA TRAIL

Max Sargent Corporate Espionage Mystery Thriller 2

BEN COLT

Max Sargent Corporate Espionage Mystery Thrillers
available in the series by the author BEN COLT
can be read in any order

1

'Sold for US$34 million to Samson'.

The simple white text message on the black screen didn't do justice to the enormity of the purchase. The Dark Web chat window was devoid of character or enthusiasm, plainly announcing the winner of the auction's bidding.

There was a pause for several moments and then another curt message appeared which closed the proceedings. 'That concludes our sale for today'.

Six bidders situated in different parts of Europe, Asia and India sighed or swore at their computers, as their screens then went blank with a small message now saying, 'Site Not Found'.

Two other bidders nodded with satisfaction. The first with a username of 'Samson' was the successful, winning buyer of the complete designs and specifications for the latest Stealth Silencer 50. The most effective, quietest silencer suppressor available. A breakthrough design, where the firing of a gun with this silencer attached was barely audible, at just 50 decibels. This was another winning bid for them, for cutting-edge military designs not yet released onto the market, nor even yet supplied to that country's armed forces. Expensive for a three-dimensional drawing of a small titanium tube, but worth it to have the highly effective design of the various baffles and chambers inside. The possibilities for an almost silent gun were endless and deadly.

Phil Landon in the UK was the other person smiling at the screen, but he hadn't won the Dark Web auction. He'd already got most of what he wanted at the start of the online event, when contenders were shown innocuous cuttings from the unnamed Stealth Silencer 50 designs. These were displayed to bidders as a teaser and proof of what they were competing for. They showed buyers it would be worth it. Phil Landon had worked hard to be included in this online sale and from the design snippets he'd seen, he now knew exactly what was being sold and could find out what he really needed to know. He didn't want to buy the plans for this new military product. He just wanted to find out where this design originated from and he had enough information to do that now. He wanted to know who was putting these secrets onto the black market.

Phil Landon could also see that the username of the winning buyer, 'Samson', was the same name he'd heard had apparently won several previous sales. That was the other piece of information he'd wanted, and his suspicions were now proven. A repeat buyer was voraciously buying up secret weapon designs. He would report back to his superiors that someone was obtaining otherwise unavailable ordnance designs on the black market. This was military design espionage, the hunt would now surely begin.

Max Sargent's career with the Royal Marine Commandos had not gone as planned. Having only just earned his green beret with this elite fighting force, at just nineteen, he was sent to Sierra Leone in 2000 to help evacuate officials and peacekeepers. But rebels were closing in on the British troop's position at Lungi airport and Max and his friend Pete's patrol got into a firefight with a gang of rebels. Many were killed on each side ending with Max, Pete and their Colour Sergeant 'Fifty' being taken. The rebels didn't want them as hostages, they wanted revenge for their comrade's lives. Max watched his friend Pete being murdered in front of him. He took his chance, grabbed one of their Kalashnikov guns from them and killed all six of the bloodthirsty rebels. He managed to escape and helping his injured superior 'Fifty', they made their way through deserted buildings and wasteland finding their way back to their troop's camp. The harrowing incident and death of his friend were too great a shock too early in his commission and he asked for an honourable discharge from the Marines. They didn't want to lose him, he was destined to be a formidable Commando. However, given his bravery and the exceptional circumstances, they agreed to his honourable discharge. He was also awarded the Military Cross for his actions saving the Colour Sergeant.

At just twenty years old Max locked the whole Marines episode away in the back of his mind and returned to 'civi' life and to his father's small business, happy to be away from the front line and settle into an impressive corporate career behind a desk.

At his father's plastics moulding business in Twickenham, he began looking more closely at the costs of materials being ordered and found he had a skill in negotiating better deals with the suppliers. He worked for progressively larger firms, working his way up through corporate procurement to become one of the UK's most sought after and highest paid Chief Procurement Officers while still in his late thirties. He had been paid well, invested wisely, been awarded large shares tranches, big bonuses and incentive schemes. Max had benefited from sign-on pay-outs and several mutually agreed redundancy pay-outs with long notice periods paid in full, when he'd persuaded his Chief Executive they didn't need someone at his level anymore.

He lived in one of the largest detached houses overlooking London's Clapham Common, alongside several other valuable houses down a private avenue. Max's home was now worth about £5 million and he had almost another £2 million sat in his garage with his treasured Ferrari F40 and exotic Vector W8 supercars.

But then Max Sargent's ordinary executive life had changed after he was caught naively thinking he could help out one of his old bosses, by giving him some information from the company he'd worked for. It was just a favour, but it was illegal and a tagging system on the contracts database had alerted the Technology Officer of the suspicious download. As he waited to find out what would happen to him, he was put on an 'Executives Pending' corporate espionage list which MI5 had access to. Si Lawson who headed up one of their Cyber teams had come to see him and offered to drop all charges of corporate espionage for Max, if he did one small 'observe and report' job for them. They knew something was amiss in a large company and needed someone to see what was happening, but from the inside.

Max had little choice, so applying for the vacant Chief Procurement Officer role he joined the target firm hoping to quickly discover what corruption, if any, might be going on there. The more he looked, the more he uncovered. The investigative exercise became more intense, and dangerous, as the stakes got higher and his cover was at risk of being blown. Various people had a lot to gain and lose, and Max found himself being the only person with any chance of thwarting what eventually became a potentially catastrophic global situation. People died.

If anyone had explained to him at the start what he would go through, he would never have agreed to the job. But like so many things in life, once you start something and it gradually gets harder, people rise to the challenge, they're hooked and want to see it through. That's what had happened to Max. He'd gone from just a bit of snooping around in a corporate office, his home turf, to putting himself in life-threatening situations in foreign countries for the good of the so-called assignment. Even though he had operated alone on the front line, Si Lawson's assurances, presence and guidance had swung the balance for him. With the might of the British Intelligence's formidable MI5 behind him, Max had felt protected and bizarrely found, mainly in hindsight, he'd enjoyed the excitement of it all. Perhaps it filled some small part of the void left behind these last twenty years from leaving behind the anticipated adventures he'd planned with the Marines.

MI5 protects the UK at home and overseas against threats to national security. MI6, otherwise known as the Secret Intelligence Services, gathers intel outside the UK in support of the UK's defence, security, economic and foreign policies.

When the job for MI5 had finished, Si Lawson was good to his word and all the pending corporate charges were dropped and he was let go by his company with full pay-off rights and a clean reference. Management and Human Resources were asked to sign a Non-Disclosure Agreement not to mention Max's operation for MI5 and to provide a clean reference whenever asked. Max was free to continue with his procurement career in large corporations if he so wished.

Max took a month off to think about what he wanted to do next, but all along he had a niggling suspicion that he would likely ask to find out more about continuing his corporate role for MI5. Si Lawson had mentioned to him several times that if he wanted to talk about a job with them, then he need only ask. Si had told him that during the single operation Max had helped them with, he had gone through more frontline experiences most field agents wouldn't amass in a whole career with the Intelligence Services. He'd carried out under-cover intelligence gathering, avoided detection, engaged with potential target subjects, and pieced together various leads and clues. Also, whilst unarmed himself, Max had needed to fight an assailant and work with armed MI5 agents, so had had some involvement with firearms. Though unintentional, Max was an MI5 Cyber corporate field agent in the making.

Max finally asked to see Si Lawson again and went back into Thames House at Millbank, MI5's base overlooking the River Thames at Lambeth Bridge, just down from the Houses of Parliament. He told Si he would consider another corporate-related job and whilst he didn't want to commit to a full-time position with MI5, they agreed to employ Max as an 'Associate Field Agent' to be called upon if something suitable came up.

Military Intelligence Section 5, better known as MI5, are the UK's security and counterintelligence agency working alongside the Government Communication Headquarters, the Defence Intelligence and its sister agency MI6 the Secret Intelligence Service, better known for its fictional star James Bond. MI5 is directed by the Joint Intelligence Committee and ultimately falls under the Cabinet Home Secretary, to protect British economic interests, Parliamentary democracy, and act as the lead counter-espionage and terrorism unit. Originally there were around ten Military Intelligence Sections which have over the years been absorbed into just MI5 and MI6. The work and operations now undertaken by them mainly consist of intelligence gathering, analysis and investigation. However, the word Military in their titles serves as a clear reminder of the other strands of more action-orientated work they handle in the front line battle against terrorism and espionage. They either have within their ranks or can call upon at any time from a huge wealth of specialists, military, police, tactical, ordnance, transport, equipment and field operatives.

MI5 has around four thousand staff under the Director General, who then has three main divisions working alongside a legal advisory team. There is a Director General of Strategy, a Director General of Capability involving technical operations, analysis and surveillance. Then lastly the number two of the organisation, the Deputy Director General heads up International Counter-Terrorism, Northern Ireland Counter-Terrorism and the division that Si Lawson's team worked in, being Cyber and Counter Espionage.

Max was paid a retainer salary to undergo some of the basic MI5 training to better equip him for future roles and give him a real insight into what happens at MI5. Given his albeit distant Commando training and the experience he'd already had with his last MI5 operation, he effectively jumped much of the basic training their recruits usually underwent in the Academy. Si Lawson devised an extensive, customised two-month plan for Max, which dipped into all parts of the organisation covering both classroom theory and active duty in the field.

Max was already a well-rounded leader with superb communication skills, charm and negotiation abilities, all gained from his time in companies managing departments, dealing with management and suppliers, and attending many team-building and executive training days. MI5 took him through how to do more targeted research, where to find information on people and things normal individuals don't know where to look. How to effectively analyse data, information, theories, leads and gather evidence. This led to law, covering the rights of individuals and a whole list of regularly used legal arguments and parameters with everything that is and isn't allowed with commonly encountered incidents.

Max was given a complete breakdown of what MI5 does, alongside the services of MI6, the Government Communications Headquarters and the Defence Intelligence service. He then spent time in various departments including Si Lawson's own Cyber and espionage team, the Technology department, records, analytics and investigations. Having benefited from the services of the technology and ordnance teams for his previous operation, Max spent some quality time getting to know some of the characters that might help him in the future. They covered many tricks and enhancements they were able to do with mobile phones, computers and surveillance equipment including mini cameras, listening devices and motion recorders.

The hardware team worked on the specialised gadgets often used, the real-life James Bond accessories, built into everyday items or converted from something ordinary looking, disguising some wonderful gadget. With technology improving all the time, better, faster, smaller were constantly pushed for and these guys knew how to make a fantasy idea become reality.

At Si's request, Max also had a couple of days with the firearms division. Si knew that Max had experience from his stint in the Marines two decades ago, but felt a reintroduction would be useful to bring things up to date for him. This was not because he would be registered to carry a firearm, he was legally still a civilian, but after the previous operation, it was clear that knowledge about them would be useful.

The first day was spent in the classroom learning about a standard array of firearms. These included the Glock 17 and 19, and SIG Sauer P range of handguns, and various submachine guns such as the famous Heckler and Koch MP5SF and SIG516 semi and fully automatic machine guns. Also, the Heckler and Koch HK417 marksman rifle and the Remington 870 shotgun were covered. He learned about their effectiveness, how to load and fire them, bullet types and sizes, and their effect when used on various objects such as people, walls and trees. Max was reminded that despite many movie heroes hiding behind walls or say their vehicle for cover, most modern-day guns' bullets would pass straight through such objects. The hero may as well be hiding in a cardboard box for all the protection it would give them. Finally, Max was taken through some basic explosives and grenades including fragmentation, stun, chemical, high explosive and smoke variants.

The next day was then spent on the range with trained firearms officers demonstrating many of the guns Max had learned about the previous day. The officers loved giving someone these demonstrations as they could go through shooting a variety of these weapons, which kept their eyes in and broke the monotony of training regularly with just the weapon assigned to them. Max had been permitted to try out a few of the guns, much to his nervous excitement. He was shocked at the sheer destructive capabilities of some of these modern firearms. The spectre of the memory of shooting those rebels had flashed through his mind as he'd unloaded a magazine of one of the fully automatic machine gun's he'd tried.

Si Lawson started in the Met police where he worked his way up through the ranks specialising in the Fraud squad, then in particular corporate financial fraud. He worked closely with many of the large consulting firms who had their so-called fraud teams and were often the first point of call when company fraud was suspected. Once they had established that a criminal act had 'allegedly' been committed then his team would be called in to investigate and handle any prosecutions including the high profile arrests often surprising the perpetrator in their offices in front of all their staff.

Then the lure of more money from Ernst & Young to head up their global fraud team was too irresistible to refuse. After many good years there he simply grew tired of the constant demands upon him to suddenly be in New York, then off to a client in Dubai, then to come back to Paris. He was being pulled in too many directions and with the generous pay and rewards of being a partner, was expected to just drop everything when required and immediately go to the next case, whenever, wherever. It was simply not worth it to him, so when a contact recommended him to the MI5 Cyber Espionage unit, he jumped at the opportunity to be UK based again as one of several team leaders. Si was now sixty years old only betrayed by his silvering hair as he was still fit and maintained good trim with regular walks with his family.

His phone rang and it was Chuck Johnson, one of several assistants to MI5's Deputy Director General. "Si, can you pop up and see the Guv in ten minutes." It wasn't a request.

"Anything I need to bring," asked Si, wishing they'd just say so at the start, as anyone seeing the Deputy Director General would ask if they needed to prepare or come with anything.

"No, just yourself. See you in a mo." Chuck hung up before Si could even ask what it was about.

'Just 'cos you work for the boss doesn't mean you can treat us all like shit', Si thought to himself. Si was intrigued to know why the number two in MI5 wanted to see him, it always meant something serious, a new job, or something needing fixing. In his younger days, he would have got nervous about being called in by the boss when you didn't know what it was about. Si was too wise and long in his career to worry about such things now. His philosophy had often been 'what will be, will be'. He knew there was no point in worrying about something you couldn't control or change, you just go with it.

He came out of his office and checked with his own deputy Vince to make sure there was nothing that had come up out of the ordinary recently, but there wasn't. Si grabbed a quick coffee from the machine, quickly drank it, then made his way up to the eighth floor where the various senior officers and management staff were located.

He exited the lift in the middle of a long corridor off which lay a myriad of open plan floors, single offices, waiting and meeting rooms and several larger conference rooms. With so many senior staff over the years each with their different preferences of what type and size office they deserved, the top floor had become a clash of old and new. It was a jumble of modern, light, open offices with glass walls, mixed in with traditional, older wood-panelled suites with assistants seated in their adjoining offices, protecting and fussing over their bosses. At the far end lay a separate glass-walled office area with its own meeting room and large oak door, behind which was the office suite of the Director General of MI5, responsible for the entire intelligence organisation and everyone in the building and out in the field.

Si made his way towards the area adjacent to the hallowed office area at the end and entered an open, bright office with about ten staff, three of whom were the personal assistants of the Deputy Director General, whose office lay behind yet more glass walls. Chuck stood up as Si entered and simply gestured for him to sit in one of the waiting chairs outside the office, saying, "He'll wave you in when he's free."

Si watched the 'Guv' talking calmly on the phone. He couldn't hear a sound as the glass walls were especially soundproofed with extra thickness and surrounding trim. The DDG noticed Si and looked like he'd begun wrapping up the call, waving him in.

Si entered as he put the phone down. "Good morning Deputy Director General," closing the door behind him.

The DDG was second in charge of MI5, often stood in for the top man, the Director General and was responsible for international counter-terrorism, counter-espionage, counter-proliferation and Si's section in cyber. The enormous responsibilities and burdens of the role were fielded admirably by this seasoned, experienced veteran who had served his time in the police, armed forces and government. He was well versed in the ways of the world including the corridors of power and real-life operations out in the field. He'd been shot in the theatre of war, an unseen war, he'd been knighted and honoured many times and had earned the respect of all who worked for him, through his calm, clear and decisive demeanour. He would listen, often ask for views, assess and compute, then give his authoritative commands, and people would follow.

After a brief but genuine and polite catchup, the DDG got straight to the point, he had eight minutes.

"Si, Phil Landon one of our field agents has been working on a particular security leak we appear to have with one of our military manufacturers. Long story short, he managed to get himself accepted into a recent auction on the Dark Web to get visibility of what's going on. Ever heard of the Stealth Silencer 50?" the DDG asked.

Si shook his head. "No. Sounds interesting though."

"That at least is a good thing you don't know it," said the DDG. "No-one should know about it. It's not released, indeed it's still at the prototype stage after testing and modelling. It's basically the quietest gun silencer ever produced. I saw a demonstration video some while ago. Literally couldn't hear the damn gun going off at all, quite amazing. Something to do with the baffles design in the tube."

Si was eager to know what the issue was. "So what's the problem that Phil Landon found?"

"Well at this recent auction, no guesses as to what was being sold off. The designs for our Stealth Silencer 50." The DDG frowned. "That means we have a major security leak, and because we now know what item was being auctioned, we at least know it's originated from the makers, Empire Arms. One of their small subsidiaries designs these leading-edge technology hardware items. Then once tested and approved by all the usual people including the customer, being the Ministry of Defence, it's passed to another larger-scale manufacturer to make and knock out. Apollo Designs are the start point, they created this masterpiece."

"So why don't we go in there, take everything apart and question the staff?" asked Si.

"We can't rely on simply questioning suspects, the perpetrator will just clam up and we'll never find them. We have to catch the person or people taking these designs to the market. However, there's more." The DDG sat back in his chair. "We also need to find out and stop the broker selling these designs off on the

Dark Web. Christ, he's running an eBay for Arms secrets, which makes us look stupid. This will all hit the Prime Minister's desk later this week and I want to include a plan of what we're going to do about it. Your plan."

Si agreed. "Give me a day with my team and I'll have something back with you for the PM."

The DDG leant forward and almost apologetically said, "There's one last thing." Si couldn't help thinking about the famous TV detective Columbo played by Peter Falk, who would always have just one last question as he left, then just one more again.

The DDG continued. "As well as finding the thief at Empire, and tracing the broker and shutting them down, we also need to find out who the repeat buyer is that's spending tens of millions on obtaining these design secrets."

Si was usually an optimist but had already gathered the complexity of tracing all three links in this chain. "That will be tricky Sir, we'd have to somehow draw out the broker and then the buyer to find out who they were. All these things are done using the web and Swiss bank accounts, everything's hidden these days, nothing's face-to-face anymore."

"You're right Si, this is a tricky one, but that's why you're sitting with me talking about it and not someone else from the floors below." He smiled at Si and started to look behind him at his team, signalling he was ready for his next scheduled appointment. "Have that plan back to me by close of play tomorrow Si."

Si Lawson walked back along the top floor corridor to be met by the Director General himself, coming out of the lift deep in conversation with his Director General Capability. Behind them their three lead directors in that division for Technical Operations and Surveillance, Technology and Analysis bustled along vying for position behind their two superiors.

Si stood to one side and nodded to the Director General who looked up briefly from his conversation. "That matter the Deputy's spoken to you about Si, I need that all tied up in the next month." He half-smiled at Si then returned his attention to his followers and was gone.

Si didn't have any opportunity to acknowledge the demand, nor discuss it. He'd been thinking as he left the DDG that an operation such as the one just dropped on him would probably take four to six months, maybe three at a push. That had all just gone out the window with the head of MI5 giving him just one month.

Si had to marvel at the immense capacity the Director General had to take in everything his team and staff told him. The amount of information he held was impressive. He needed to be in the position of understanding pretty much every operation, progress report, new intel, threats, technologies, threatening factions and anything else across MI5 that he could be asked about by the Prime Minister. When he had the answer, all was well, but if on the rare occasion he hadn't been updated suitably, everyone down the chain of command regarding that piece of missing information would hear about it and not in a positive way.

Si got back to the safety of his own open-plan offices and his team of twelve staff. He nodded to Vince his deputy who was anxiously waiting to find out how the meeting with the Deputy Director General had gone and what they were in for. Vince followed him into his office and closed the door.

"Well, boss?" Vince eagerly asked.

"It's a tricky one Vince, we'll need our four team leads in here for the rest of today and probably most of tomorrow. Before I tell you all about it let me just make three calls," said Si.

First, he looked up Agent Phil Landon in the MI5 intranet directory and getting straight through to him explained he'd been asked to lead the operation and could he be available later today and tomorrow to go through everything. Phil was delighted, this was the go-ahead he'd been waiting for on his case.

Next Si put in a call to the Chief Executive of Empire Arms plc, hoping the man was in the country, in which case nothing would stop him demanding to meet up that evening for a little heart to heart chat. He was available.

Lastly, Si had already started a thought process on how best to kick off this operation. He needed to get someone into Empire, someone who could then have unquestioned access into all parts of the company including the Apollo Design centre.

He needed a corporate plant who was well versed in obtaining intel, digging out corruption, avoiding discovery and could think on their feet if something flared up and got tricky. He had in mind someone who'd recently concluded a very successful mission with him. Someone he'd been most impressed by, who had coincidentally also just finished a couple of months' enhancement training.

He made his third call, to Max Sargent.

2

Sir John Tregar didn't like being summoned by anyone, but when Si Lawson of MI5 had been quite insistent that they met up tonight, his frustration had been replaced by anxiousness. 'What on earth could MI5 want with him?' he'd thought.

He had been the Chief Executive Officer of the medium-sized ordnance firm Empire Arms plc for about ten years. In his late sixties, with distinguished silver hair on the sides of his head and tanned skin from numerous and regular holidays to one of his villas in Spain, Italy or Florida. He managed to maintain a dashing six-foot-tall presence, despite a slightly over-weight body from far too many wonderful dinners and unhealthy foods, disguised in his favourite albeit dated dark blue pin-stripe suits.

Sir John had worked his way up through the accounting world starting with some of the large London private companies doing other people's numbers. He then realised that life in the corporate sector as a Finance Director and then onto Chief Finance Officer roles were far more lucrative. Some fifteen years ago he joined the growing and promising Empire Arms firm and guided them through floatation, with the considerable help of Deloitte's in London. With even higher plc salaries to keep up with their benchmarked peer corporations, share option grants, short and long term incentive plans, generous pension and huge bonus schemes, John Tregar hit the big money.

When the then Chief Exec retired he was in the prime position to take over the top role of the company he knew everything about, but he had competition. The Operations Director had been with Empire for two decades, was great at his job running the company, but simply didn't have time for boardroom politics and gossip. John Tregar was a master at the black art of corporate skulduggery and systematically got around each of the executive and non-executive board directors, selling himself with promises of what each of them had on their wish list, and putting down the poor Operations Director. John Tregar won the vote, was appointed the new Chief Exec and within a month had let the unfortunate and bewildered Operations Director go.

As one of the major innovation suppliers to the Ministry of Defence which included the Royal Navy, British Army, Royal Air Force Air Command, MOD Police and the Aircraft Carrier Alliance, it wasn't too long before the company's ideas and concepts were recognised with John Tregar's knighthood. The humble accountant had done well and with an impressive senior leadership team, ran a tight ship at Empire and was a stickler for respect and discipline.

One story that became recounted over the years throughout the firm's offices, was of a celebratory dinner in town Sir John had taken his fellow directors to, after winning a big contract. The wine had flowed and by dessert, the already excitable Marketing Director had become very slapdash with his pally comments and physical contact. When it was calmly suggested he should leave, he'd given Sir John a drunken hug and at the same time a sort of laddie kiss and a pat on the back of his head. Sir John had summoned the unfortunate chap up to his office the moment he got in the following morning and summarily dismissed him for bringing the company into disrepute. He was escorted off the premises by security with no pay or awards. He tried to take the firm to Tribunal, but the Empire lawyers had an easy task of proving negligent, inappropriate behaviour, witnessed in a public place, clearly bringing the company, represented by Sir John, into disrepute.

Sir John exited the offices of Empire Arms plc, occupying a vast area in Charlwood Surrey, right next to Gatwick airport. The main executive offices were surrounded by many of the subsidiary companies, each with their own offices, hangers, technology centres and warehouses. The whole complex was hidden away in the countryside with no passing traffic, with the entire perimeter surrounded by a high metal fence. A sizeable team of security guards patrolled outside and covered all main entrances and the approach, day and night. Among the many basic items they supplied mainly to various parts of the British Ministry of Defence, this was where weapons and tactical field advantages were born and designed. Live firearms and ordnance were tested here, security had to be robust.

Sir John's chauffeur waited for him opposite the main reception, holding open the rear door of the Marlin Blue new Bentley Flying Spur. He settled into the rear seat covered in Beluga black hide. The six-litre W12 engine was unique in design, having three banks of four cylinders, producing acceleration and top speed performance stats most Ferrari's would be happy with, whilst swathing its occupants in unbridled, luxurious comfort and technology. As the chauffeur started the engine, the Bentley's 'Flying B' emblem gracefully rose into view on the front of the bonnet, displaying its illuminated wings, a unique feature of this model.

"Simpson's in the Strand, thank you, Oliver," Sir John said to his chauffeur, thinking to himself that 'at least the MI5 man had booked them a decent dinner venue, surely it can't be too serious'. He settled back in his seat listening to Classic FM's calming symphonies and concertos. The journey to central London during the evening rush would take well over an hour, travelling up the M23 past Bletchingley, then the A23 past Croydon, Brixton and Lambeth.

Si Lawson could have hauled Sir John Tregar into MI5's Thames House at Millbank and put the frighteners on him, but had elected for the charm offensive using the 'steel gauntlet in a velvet glove' approach. He suspected the Chief Exec would appreciate the old fashioned, gentlemanly surroundings and if he needed to bring out the big guns and emphasise how serious this was for the man and his company, then he would.

He'd booked the table for eight pm and being a warm, clear evening, decided to treat himself to walking the mile and a half in a leisurely twenty-five minutes. Si exited the huge Thames House building opposite Lambeth Bridge, crossed the Millbank roundabout and proceeded past the Victoria Tower Gardens alongside the River

Thames. He passed the Black Rod's Gardens on his right, which was the end-most entrance to the House of Lords. Black Rod was responsible for controlling access to and maintaining order in the House of Lords, and for the State Opening of Parliament would summon Members of Parliament from the House of Commons to the House of Lords to hear the Queen's speech. The usher or yeoman of the House originates back to 1066 when a man called Ussier was the gatekeeper to the King, William the Conqueror.

On Si's left stood the imposing Westminster Abbey opposite the Palace of Westminster and the House of Commons. Passing Parliament square Garden Sir Winston Churchill's statue watched him, as he turned right and passing beneath the imposing Big ben clock tower, he crossed over to the river walkway under the Chariot statue of Boadicea. On the other side of the river sat the London Eye, the world's tallest cantilevered observation wheel, with its thirty-two capsules representing the thirty-two boroughs of London. Si could see the tourists inside each pod bustling in awe of the views they had across the City.

Riverboat cruises vied for position on the jetties, as office workers wanting to get home deftly slipped through the strolling tourists holding up their mobile phones, in a seemingly endless photo and video capture of all the sights around them. He continued past Whitehall Gardens and under the Golden Jubilee and Hungerford bridges that led into Charing Cross station to his left. In the distance among the many taller buildings Si could see the 310m ninety-five storey Shard and the domed top of St Paul's Cathedral built in 1675, representing the two vastly different spectrums of London's history, and now modernisation.

Opposite Cleopatra's Needle, an obelisk commemorating the British victory over Napoleon, Si walked through the Victoria Embankment Gardens and up Carting Lane where he emerged onto the busy Strand at the entrance of the Savoy Hotel.

Simpson's in the Strand was just to the left of its hotel owner and was established in 1828 as a gentlemen's smoking room, then a coffee house, before claiming its famous mantle of serving the finest traditional English foods, in particular its roast meats.

Si took his seat in one of the booths at the side of the large open high-ceilinged dining hall. The pianist in the corner of the large dining hall interrupted their classical tones and abruptly but softly played 'Happy Birthday' for the benefit of a large wealthy family table of diners. Just before eight o'clock, Si could see a dark blue Bentley pull-up in the Strand beside the restaurant's entrance and a distinguished gentleman got out, wearing a smart dark pinstripe suit and confidently entered.

As he looked around the room Si raised a hand and nodded at Sir John who allowed the staff member to escort him over to the table. Both men greeted one another cautiously and introduced themselves. They spent a short while talking about Simpson's and previous visits they'd both made to the establishment. Having perused the menus both ordered the lobster salad starter, followed by the aged Scottish roast beef to be carved off the trolley at their table. Both of them declined to order from the impressive wine list, opting for mineral water. Sir John would usually have been happy to try an expensive white wine with his lobster salad and red wine with his meat dish, but felt on this occasion he might need all his wits about him.

Si got down to business. "Sir John, you'll appreciate from the urgency of me needing to see you this evening, that I have a matter of grave importance to discuss with you. I thought perhaps a less formal dinner might afford us the appropriate candour required to deal with this matter. After all, we don't want boardrooms full of our staff watching this play out."

Si's opener had hit its mark and concentrated Sir John's full attention. "Good grief Mr Lawson, you're making this sound quite serious. Why don't you just come out and tell me what's happened and how it affects me?"

"Just checking, but I assume given your exposure to providing ordnance to the MOD, do all your staff sign the Official Secrets Act 1989?" Si asked.

"Of course they do, and our company non-disclosure and

data protection agreements. That's all locked down," bristled Sir John.

"Well promising to be good on a piece of paper is one thing." Si frowned for dramatic effect. "One of our field agents managed to infiltrate a Dark Web auction recently, which we believe frequently offers to the highest bidder various military ordnance plans and designs. Unfortunately, these are not items that are yet available on the market, let alone with our Ministry of Defence. They are being obtained and sold illegally."

Sir John looked angry at the thought that such vital secrets could be betrayed, but then realising that this problem must have something to do with his company, looking quite perplexed and concerned. "Good God, well how's this happening?"

Si continued. "We believe that someone is taking or copying the designs at source for these new technologies and then offering them to some kind of arms broker, who then organises the sale on the Dark Web. We also now know from the most recent design that was auctioned, where the source of the problem is."

"So what was this item, or rather the designs of?" asked Sir John, fearing the answer would be one of his products.

"I'm afraid it was the design for the Stealth Silencer 50."

"But that's one of our designs! It's not even launched yet," exclaimed Sir John, shifting awkwardly in his seat and looking around the room to check he wasn't drawing any attention to himself.

"Indeed. I believe your Apollo Designs firm came up with that particular item. Quite amazing I might add. But it's now been sold for a lot of money to a repeat unknown buyer," explained Si shaking his head to emphasise his displeasure at the problem they faced.

Sir John was dismayed, but then couldn't help but ask, "How much for?"

"Many tens of millions. And this isn't the first design from your company that has been sold." Si paused for dramatic effect. "Someone in your firm is selling sensitive military designs, to God knows who. Makes us all look pretty stupid. If this gets out, your Empire firm is finished."

Sir John was now panicking. "Hell and damnation, I'll get my security people onto this tonight, we'll find out who's doing this and hand them over. This is terrible."

Si was calm and resolute. "You will do no such thing Sir John. If you want any chance of getting through this mess, you will need to do exactly what I tell you, is that clear?"

Sir John's excitement stilled as he realised he'd lost any control over this matter and would have to now trust this Si Lawson from MI5, with his reputation, career and company. He sighed. "What do you want me to do?"

"We can't go blundering in willy nilly. I need to find out who in your organisation is doing this and catch them. To do that," explained Si, "I'm thinking of putting one of my people into your firm, undercover, with access to all areas. Hopefully, they'll hand us the person betraying you, and betraying the country."

"Who is this person?"

"I have someone in mind, still need to speak to them as I wanted to talk to you first. They're a corporate executive so will blend in fine, a Chief Procurement Officer by trade. They've done a job for me in the past and showed themselves to be completely able in these circumstances," said Si.

"I already have a CPO so how will that work?" asked Sir John.

"That's not a problem. You will employ my man as a consultant, you're bringing him in to review procurement, or top suppliers, or something like that. We'll sort the detail out, the good thing is that he can access every part of your company without raising any suspicion," outlined Si.

Sir John nodded. "Okay, I can do that. What else, I need to get this sorted."

"*We* will get it sorted. There's only one other thing I must ask of you at this point. You absolutely mustn't tell anyone what I've told you, or what we're doing here. No-one," insisted Si.

Sir John nodded.

"I mean no-one. Not your wife, your staff, security, driver, no-one Sir John. If you do, you'll be in breach of the Official Secrets Act yourself." Si wanted to ensure that if he put someone into Empire, the only people that knew about it were himself and Sir John.

At the end of the meal Sir John Tregar left Simpson's in the Strand quite shaky, he couldn't believe this was happening to him, to his company. That one or maybe more of his employees were daring to steal and sell off *his* designs. 'This bloke MI5 are going to put into my firm better be good' he thought to himself, as he settled back into the rear of his Bentley to go home. Sir John was loyal to his firm, and indeed his country, but uppermost in his thoughts, was how this whole sorry matter would reflect on him. He wasn't at all happy.

3

Max Sargent had got the call the previous evening from Si Lawson at MI5 asking him to come in today to discuss a potential new operation. That was it, no more details on the call, which had left him excited, but also anxious to know what Si had in mind for him. After his first operation followed by a couple of months of training, Max hadn't expected to be called upon for some while, assuming such tailored missions for corporate MI5 agents were far and few between. Not the case.

Despite kidding himself he should get a good night's sleep and go to bed early, he'd had a restless night and ended up coming back downstairs at one am to make a cup of tea. The last adventure had started quite innocently and ended up with people being chased and killed, with him in the middle of it all. 'What could Si have for him now?' he continued to wonder.

Late morning he walked across Clapham Common and took the five stops on the underground to Waterloo station, from where he walked over Westminster Bridge past Big Ben and the Houses of Parliament alongside the river to Thames House, MI5's headquarters.

Vince came down to collect him from reception and took him straight up to Si Lawson's office, where Max could see a few people already gathered in the meeting room. Si had been reviewing the case for the remainder of the previous day, straight after seeing the Deputy Director General and again all that morning. They'd pulled together a plan and were ready to talk it through with their unsuspecting star player.

Max sat in Si's office, who was genuinely pleased to see his young protégé again. "Well Max, I have to confess this has come round a bit faster than I thought, but we've got the perfect job for you."

"Perfect in what way, Si. The last job turned out to be a bit bigger than we all anticipated didn't it," joked Max.

"Indeed it did, but look what a fantastic job you did and that was before you'd had any training. Let's go into the meeting room and the team can take you through everything step by step," said Si.

They settled themselves in the meeting room and Si did the introductions. "You know most of the people in the room, Max. Vince my number two, Alan from technology, Josh and Ellie from our team. Finally, this is Phil Landon who is the field agent that has been working on this case alone up 'til now. Let's get started then. What we have in summary, before we get into the detail Max, is a requirement for you to drop into a Military Arms firm here in the UK and find out who there is stealing and selling off designs. You'll go in of course under the cover of a CPO consultant so you'll be quite at home in that respect. Once we have the thief then hopefully we'll take over to find the Arms broker and ultimately whoever it is buying up all these designs."

Max nodded in measured agreement to what sounded like an achievable assignment. He had a lot of questions but trusted the team to answer most of them during their briefing so let them continue.

Vince kicked off with a well-prepared slideshow of Empire Arms and Apollo Designs. He went through the directors, the history of the company and each of the subsidiary firms, the financials and the site layout near Gatwick.

When Sir John Tregar's picture came up Si interjected. "I met Sir John last night and he's primed and ready to employ you Max, as a Procurement Consultant. They have a CPO you'll need to work with. What's a good excuse for them wanting you to do a review in procurement," he asked Max.

Max took a moment remembering his consulting days. "A risk assessment's always a good one that no-one would bat an eyelid over. You know, checking governance, supplier contingency plans, potential risks to the business. Who's their CPO then?" asked Max.

Vince flicked the screen onto a LinkedIn profile showing a 'Margaret Fallon – Chief Procurement Officer, Empire Arms

Group'.

"Can you just scroll down the 'Experience' profile," asked Max.

Vince rolled the page down as Max quickly studied the list of previous roles this executive had posted on their page. "All okay?" checked Vince.

"Yes, all fine, seems we have someone in charge of procurement who isn't really a procurement expert, she has no real experience before her role at Empire. She started in the accounts and procurement back office. Let's hope she has some humility when I turn up there, nothing worse than someone who thinks they're amazing at their job, isn't and won't be told otherwise," said Max raising his eyebrows.

"Not an issue either way I'm sure Max. You'll have all areas access, I'll set that up with Sir John. He's the only person outside this room who'll know what's happening, he's as keen as we are to find out what's happening there, after all, it's happening on his watch," said Si.

Phil Landon added, "From the items being sold off we were able to trace them back to the maker's source and that led us back to Empire, in fact, more specifically back to Apollo Designs, part of Empire. That's where the designs originate from, so that's where they're also being stolen from, we assume. Don't make it obvious, but that's where you should focus when you get in there."

"What sort of weapons or designs are we talking about?" asked Max.

Josh had the summary for this. "We've been able to track back, with Phil's help, three designs from Apollo that have been sold online over the last eighteen months."

"Three," exclaimed Max, "so someone's been having a laugh for quite some time then."

Josh nodded and continued. "The first was a fairly straightforward battlefield helmet. Quite special though as it was made using a woven carbon fibre and Kevlar mix, amazingly strong and for smaller projectiles, bullet-proof. Most helmets barely do a damn thing, anyone shot in the helmet is usually dead, the bullet goes straight through them. Kevlar, titanium and Twaron have been used more widely, but Apollo's design was stronger and had reinforced ribbing in the design making it even stronger again."

"Why wouldn't this have all come to light when they were sold?" asked Max.

Si answered. "Unfortunately, unless we get to hear about the Dark Web sale, and we didn't until Phil here recently infiltrated an auction, then neither Empire nor us would get to know the design had been sold. It's not like it gets announced. It would be squirrelled away in some far-off country where the local military makers, or even underworld, would get to work secretly making these items and using them, again without us ever knowing. Maybe in a year or two, we might get intel of the weapon being used in the field, that's likely the first we'd have got to know about it, so no-one at Empire knows this is happening, except now for Sir John." Si gestured for Josh to continue.

"The next design coming onto the market from our Apollo friends was affectionately nicknamed 'APaRC' standing for Anti Personnel Room Clearer. They hadn't yet given it its military model name yet," said Josh.

"What on earth does that do with a name like that? Sounds like an anti-social vacuum cleaner," joked Max, managing to get a chuckle out of most of the audience.

Josh explained. "It's a disc grenade, about the size of an ice hockey puck. Once activated you have five seconds to slide it into a room across the floor, one way up. A fragmentation grenade is then shot up precisely six feet into the air and its high explosive charge detonates, blasting the entire room with ball bearings. It would kill everything in the room, hence the name Room Clearer."

"What about the person who's slid it into the room?" asked Max.

"Good question. One assumes that the destructive blast will kill everything inside, so I guess there's no need for the combatant to hang around near the doorway. They either scarper off or make sure they're behind a shield," said Vince.

"Sounds like it's too destructive for its own good. How much do these designs sell for then?" said Max.

Phil replied, "We don't know what those two went for but I'm guessing five to twenty-five million dollars each. We do however know what the third item sold for, as I was sat there watching the auction on my screen. Thirty-four million."

"Wow, that's not bad money for a simple design," commented Max.

Si added, "Well these aren't simple, that's the point, each one is ahead of the field, uniquely innovative, so if you don't have the expertise Apollo seem to have, it's easier to just buy the damn thing on the black market if it comes up. Phil, the last item?"

"So are these amazing designs coming from different inventors or a big team at Empire," said Max.

Vince replied. "From what I can see there are a few technology and design hubs at Empire, covering everything from tank parts, rocket launchers, field equipment, communications and weapons ordnance. Certainly, the Apollo Design firm consistently roll out new ideas. I imagine they have a team there but I couldn't find anything mentioning names. I guess they keep it quiet so staff can't be got at."

"And the third design?"

Phil spoke. "I managed to get an invite to the auction posing as a buyer for a certain small country, which had the latest Stealth Silencer 50 being sold off. A normal gun is about one-hundred-and-fifty decibels and is in the range that's harmful to human eardrum's. With most silencers that can be reduced to nearer one-twenty decibels, like a quiet thump. The SS50 is a masterpiece. They've got it down to nearer fifty decibels which is almost silent, incredible. Imagine being able to shoot someone, even in a busy street and no one knows where the shot came from. They wouldn't even know it was a shot!"

"So what makes it so quiet?" asked Max.

Josh replied. "It gets a bit technical with everything going on in such a small metal tube. It's all about suppressing and disseminating the gases. The crack of a bullet being fired is the shockwave, the thump of the hot gases escaping the muzzle. The SS50 uses a combination of metal mesh wipes throughout its expansion chambers and tunnels, some with frequency shifting gas chambers and a couple of high-frequency venting portholes."

"Okay, I get it, it's not a simple design," concluded Max. "So it's all about selling the design documents. Makes it easy to steal when it's just an electronic file doesn't it?"

Alan replied. "Yes, the old days of smuggling paper blueprint documents and handing over prototype models are gone. Would make the job much easier for us, but it's all now over the airwaves, under the cover of the electronic ether. That's why the sales are done over the Dark Web. Can't be traced like you can on the worldwide web, with computer internet protocol addresses, worms and the like."

"I've heard of this Dark Web but I honestly don't know anything about it?" said Max.

Alan elaborated. "The Darknet has websites like the world wide web but the networks are encrypted and IP addresses are hidden. You also need certain browsers to access it. Nothing is indexed by your usual search engines which see everything on the normal web, so you have to know the exact website address you're looking for otherwise you'll never find it. They're not like for example 'apollo dot com'. No, they'll be more like 'h57j8kjz4x5xx slash page one'. Effectively a huge, precise string code website, so unless you know exactly what it is and when it's online, you've got no chance of finding it. Once used for these auctions, it's discarded and like the so-called Dark Web 'onion' sites, any traffic on the site is bounced around the world through many servers. Phil here gave me the auction site address which was mumbo-jumbo and as soon as the auction ended it was gone, offline, couldn't be seen nor traced, a useless address once more."

Max pulled a face. "So how on earth are we going to find the broker selling these things, let alone the buyers?"

Si took over. "The first thing to do is find out who is stealing the design and passing them onto the auction broker. One lead gives us the next lead and so on. We start at the beginning of the trail, chase it along if we can and see where it takes us. As I mentioned Max, you're the key player at the start of this, we'll get you into Empire and you do your stuff stress testing the people there and find out what's going on. I'll set it up now with Sir John Tregar."

Alan reminded Max, "Don't forget if you want to call Si, use the encrypted ap I installed on your mobile in the 'Notes' ap. Just open it up and type in 'c a l l 2 2' and you'll get through to Si. If you need any other gadgets just tell me and I can see what we can do for you."

"Dig, observe and report," reminded Si looking at Max reassuringly.

"I seem to remember that's how the last operation started," frowned Max. "And that all ended up with me almost getting my head blown off!"

4

Margaret Fallon was fifty-two and not a happy person. She felt that life had passed her by, but life had given her every opportunity and she'd either squandered it or messed it up, usually by upsetting someone. She was a plainly attractive woman, now slightly overweight with short-cropped brown hair and matching brown eyes, deeply set in a severe, unwelcoming face. The good looks that she'd had in her youth had readily attracted a string of interested boys and men, however, each of them was rapidly driven away by her uncompromising and righteous attitude to them, herself and everyone else. Margaret felt she deserved so much more.

As a teenager, she had aspirations to become a doctor and although not naturally gifted academically, she worked hard at Durham University. The five-year degree course became a struggle and although she managed to get a first and start her post-graduate two years, the spark of desire had dimmed in her. She bailed out just before starting her specialist training which would have been some years more, working hard and not getting paid much. She deserved more and faster, and the resentment grew, of investing all those years towards a profession she now felt wasn't good enough for her.

The potential suitors came and went, but Margaret would not accept that perhaps it was she that needed to change her ways. No, none of them were good enough for her and why should she be the one that had to change.

She fell into an accounts job for a large insurance company, only because the naive woman interviewing Margaret, had mistaken her curt and arrogant demeanour to be that of a confident strong-willed professional woman. Margaret started selling insurance to corporate clients with some success. She managed to balance her negative characteristics with just enough charm for the length of a couple of one-hour meetings, often just enough to get the customer to sign up to a contract. Occasionally the more perceptive and sensitive customers would be immediately turned off the idea of having to deal with such a rude, aggressive saleswoman, that on several occasions the client brought the meeting to a swift close, asking her to leave. A couple of potential customers even felt so poorly treated by her, that they put in formal complaints to Margaret's manager, who continued to support her as long as the orders and commissions kept coming, though clearly, they could see now that Margaret was not the charming, persuasive salesperson they had once thought.

In the office, wherever Margaret went, conflict and negativity followed close behind. Most meetings she went to, or just conversations with colleagues, involved some kind of disagreement, put down, negative comment or conflict. Half the people she worked with in the office hated her, and half, mainly women, saw her as a strong female champion but not to be trifled with. Approaches from the opposite sex started to tail off and on one occasion Margaret found herself doing what she had never done before, asking a man for a date.

A new sales director, ultimately her boss's boss, had started with the company and was a highflying executive surely destined for bigger things. He was handsome, successful and single. He certainly had an interest in Margaret, at least initially, and his natural salesman charm and energy with her had unfortunately been mistaken for signals of flirtation and intention. Margaret had failed to notice that he was charming, positive and engaging with most people, so invested a huge amount of emotional energy and thought leading up to the big question.

She tried to engineer time with the sales director alone but didn't have the social and communication finesse required to accomplish this, without being awkward or obvious. The day finally came when most of the office staff were in the conference room for the weekly team briefing, but the sales director was in his office working on an important pitch for a client. Margaret had just returned from a customer meeting and they both ended up in the small photocopier room at the same time. As usual, the exuberant senior director was pleased to see Margaret and so she rolled the dice.

"Leonard," Margaret ventured, her usual confidence betrayed by her nervousness, "I wondered if perhaps you wanted to spend some time together?"

He completely missed the gravity of the question, continuing with organising his paperwork ready for the photocopier feeding tray. "There isn't anything we need to cover is there? But you know my door is always open, just pop in any time," he said, oblivious to her subtle intent.

Margaret pressed on. "No, you know what I mean, we get on well don't we."

At this point, Leonard perhaps realised there was more to the request than he had anticipated and instinctively wanting to buy a little time to gather his thoughts, but also double-check what exactly Margaret was asking, said, "Of course we do Margaret, we've always had a good relationship. What is it exactly you're asking?"

Margaret was now highly strung and trying to hide her exasperation at needing to spell it out for the man. Her flirtatious charm was quickly giving way to angry frustration. "I'm asking if you want to go out on a date with me, Leonard?"

On the other side of the office floor, the team meeting had come to a close and staff were filtering out, making their way back to their desks.

Leonard had never suspected that someone like Margaret Fallon would ever ask a man out on a date and certainly hadn't seen this coming *his* way. He suspected that he was damned if he did and damned if he didn't, and turned to look at Margaret with sincerity and calm. "Margaret, I had no idea that's what you were asking. I really do appreciate you…"

"But I thought you liked me," interrupted Margaret, not wanting to hear a rejection. Anger and embarrassment started to take hold.

Leonard continued. "I do appreciate you asking me and

apologies if you've misread my friendliness towards you, but I'm not interested in that way. Let's just keep it friends at work."

The rejection struck through Margaret like an axe. She felt humiliated and belittled. Unable to compose herself enough to graciously withdraw with a simple smile and apology for the misunderstanding, she simply couldn't stop herself from launching into the shocked, undeserving man.

"Misunderstanding! There is no misunderstanding." Margaret shouted, drawing the attention of everyone in the office who were now eagerly looking over to see what the commotion was about. "Who the hell do you think you are anyway. Strutting around the office as if you own the place. How dare you reject me like I'm a piece of trash."

Leonard was utterly surprised at the onslaught from one of his staff and held his hands up to Margaret and also the onlooking staff throughout the office. "Margaret, you need to calm down. I don't want to go out with you, but there's no need for you to start shouting at me and being rude. People are watching you."

Margaret pushed Leonard away from her dismissively, shouting as she turned to leave. "I wouldn't go out with you if you are the last man on earth. How dare you reject me, who the hell do you think you are." She stormed over to her desk, now shouting at the rest of the team. "What the hell are you all looking at. So the boss doesn't want to go out with me. Whatever." She grabbed her bag and left the office, leaving the bewildered Leonard to emerge, apologising to the team for the incident and explaining that he would never date anyone at work.

Margaret came in the following day with half a mind to resign. She was beaten to it when called up to Human Resources, where she found Leonard sat with the HR Director waiting for her. They explained to her despite her protestations, that her unprovoked outburst to the senior director in front of employees had made her position with the company untenable. They offered her the choice of being dismissed with no pay after which if she wanted to go to tribunal she had every right to do that, but they suggested under the circumstances she would not be successful. Alternatively, she could accept a generous compromise agreement which afforded her a leaving bonus, her notice paid as garden leave plus an inconvenience bonus, on condition that she agreed to it at the meeting and then immediately left the building not to return.

Margaret's rage at humanity and the injustice of the embarrassing situation, once again increased, but she took the deal with the final request that she be given a good reference.

She quickly got a similar role at the insurance company's competitor and without changing, had some staff and customers that went with her over-confident approach, and some who quickly disliked her. Margaret would create her leads through her network and also follow up on leads the telesales team had got her through their cold-calling efforts.

One such potential client persuaded to review their employee insurance scheme, was a large chain of car dealerships. The Orion group operated six sites selling cars throughout Sussex and Surrey, with licences from Ford and Kia. Orion was run by the Jones family with the father having just handed the business over to his son, Kevin Jones. As the young Managing Director of the firm, Kevin was a somewhat unwilling leader and manager of staff, who had been more at home quietly working in the dealership's back offices, arranging collections and deliveries, and handling customer test drives. But as the son of the owner, he was thrust into the role of leading the firm, which was not by choice or ambition. So the quiet, unassuming Kevin surrounded himself with great managers to carry the burden of leadership for him. He found the right people, they did well continuing to build on their successes, he paid them more, they did even better. Orion was very successful, making Kevin a relatively wealthy young man.

From the moment feisty, overconfident, take-charge Margaret Fallon walked into Kevin's office to sell him insurance, he was smitten. It was simply one of those inexplicable chemistry things. All along he just wanted someone else to take the lead and tell him what to do. Equally, Margaret was never going to hit it off with a strong alpha-male, she needed someone compliant, diminutive, but also successful and wealthy. He bought as much additional employee insurance as Margaret could sell him that day and being too nervous to ask her out, followed up with an email suggesting they celebrate the new deal with dinner, not expecting to even get a reply. Margaret was drawn to him and went to dinner, curious to further assess this potential partner. In their own ways, they hit it off with one another and started their relationship.

They married within a year and had their only child several years later. Margaret retired from work to look after the baby and enjoy her husband's reasonable fortune from the dealerships group. But Margaret was never going to be satisfied, always wanting and expecting more, and increasingly took her frustrations out on her hapless husband, who in turn became more downtrodden and unhappy. The banter and jokes, became quips then insults and plain rudeness, as Margaret's teasing and anger directed towards Kevin became relentless.

Their son was mid-teens when with the help of another kinder woman luring him away, Kevin walked out on Margaret and their son. Years of unhappiness had affected Kevin's judgement at work and Orion had slowly disintegrated into a small struggling three site dealership firm barely making a profit, with car sales such a highly competitive market to be in now. When they divorced because of the way Orion was structured and owned, Margaret got her fifty per cent of everything plus a single payoff for the few remaining years of childhood for their son, of just over a million pounds. The family house was sold and Kevin quickly disappeared off into the sunset with his new lady. Margaret bought a modest house in Lingfield Surrey near the racecourse and stayed home until her son was eighteen. He dropped out of education and decided to travel the world, picking up work to pay his way. He wasn't intending to come home anytime soon, to a mother who hated men and life.

By that time she knew she would have to do something for work, as retirement wasn't an option. A local Arms designer and maker, Empire, posted an ad for a vacancy running their back-office administration and accounts. She was interviewed by the then Finance Director a John Tregar and for once in her life forced herself to be compliant, courteous and professional, to get the role well below her experience and expertise. She came out as the clear top candidate and started at Empire just down the road in Charlwood.

Margaret was as content as she could be for some years, lonely, but content. She then became aware that the elderly Procurement Director was soon to retire and started her deliberate campaign with the now knighted Sir John Tregar and her outgoing boss, to win over the top Procurement role, despite no previous experience. She did know the company and had kept her nose clean all those years. She had a good knowledge of the suppliers as the accounts payable team fell under her remit, so she was able to quote products, costs and suppliers which seemed to impress the naïve management there. To her surprise, Sir John decided 'better the devil you know' and put Margaret into the Procurement Director role. After a few years she realised the British were adopting the American titles so successfully pitched to Sir John to upgrade her title to Chief Procurement Officer.

Margaret had a small team of about twelve staff in procurement. She was intimidating once more in her role of considerable power, not just over her staff, but internal stakeholders across the Empire business, and to suppliers. She quickly turned over staff in her team until she found an agreeable department makeup who either liked or tolerated her overbearing behaviour. She had at least learnt over the years that as long as you behaved professional with the top man, you could usually get away with things in the confines of your own team's office. Over the years her team settled into Margaret's way of doing things, mostly unchecked by professional procurement experts, such as Max Sargent. Margaret Fallon would not be happy about potentially being exposed by some highflyer putting her and her team under the microscope.

Sir John had asked her to pop in and knew full well that Si

Lawson's suggestion, or rather demand, to have one of his 'people' come in and do a procurement risk review, was going to go down with Margaret like a lead balloon. He reminded himself that he was the boss and had nothing to worry about. 'Just stick to your guns', he thought to himself as Margaret entered and sat opposite him forcing a smile.

"Margaret, we've known one another for many years now and I've always supported you haven't I?" said Sir John, who had intended to open with some reassurance for her. But his words began to unsettle Margaret as she shifted in her chair and looked concerned.

"You have been very good to me Sir John and I appreciate it. Equally, I've done a really good job for you here and saved the company millions of pounds. I hope that is also appreciated."

Sir John thought to himself that this was going to be harder than he'd imagined. "You have done a good job, and like all parts of the business, from time to time we must be seen to independently check that we are doing everything we should, to keep up with the professional standards expected of us." He waited a short moment for any reaction but got none as Margaret was trying to understand where he was coming from. "We've had external consultants come in over the years to help or review most departments across the business, except for procurement." Margaret's eyes narrowed on the Chief Executive, who thought now was as good a time as any to come straight out with it. "I've therefore decided to bring in a procurement expert, not to review you or your team structure, nothing like that, they will only be looking at how we mitigate procurement-related risks."

Margaret sat forward in her chair and pulled a face as she expelled air, then drew in a deep breath. "Sir John, you've got to be joking, of course bringing in someone to review procurement risk is bringing into question what I and my team do. How will that make us look? It's like we're being investigated for something. I'm not happy about this at all."

Sir John played it back straight. "I will make it clear to

everyone that this is routine due diligence to ensure that our risk program is indeed the very best it can be and stands alongside other large corporations. This is not about you Margaret, you need to understand that and get behind this. Please."

Margaret detected the finality in Sir John's tone and managed to channel the angry outburst she was about to make, down into her hands as she dug her fingers into the leather arms of her chair. She rose to leave.

"A Max Sargent will be here on Monday, probably only for a month or so. Margaret, it's in your interest to make him feel welcome and help him with his review," concluded Sir John.

"Of course, if that's what you want Sir John." Margaret walked out of his office not bothering to ask if he wanted his door left open or closed. She thought to herself, 'Like hell I'm going to help someone snoop around my business and tell me what I'm doing wrong. This Max Sargent won't know what's hit him when he meets me'.

5

Si Lawson had called Max to tell him to report to Sir John Tregar at the Empire Arms Charlwood complex Monday. Max had done what research he could on the company, products and those directors he could find with LinkedIn and Google. He drove his VW Golf GTI out of Clapham south on the A24, through Sutton, over the M25, past Betchworth and Leigh and within an hour he came into Charlwood. In the distance, he could see several aeroplanes lined up approaching Gatwick's runway flying low over the M23 before they touched down and another disappearing off into the distance having just taken off. Gatwick was the second busiest airport in the world only operating one main runway.

The Empire Arms estate was tucked away down a country lane with no signs for it until Max turned into the gated entrance, where he was greeted by several security guards. Whilst not armed with handguns, they each had clipped to their belts a sinister-looking black metal telescopic baton and a black polymer Taser X2 gun, capable of delivering two laser-targeted shots with 1400 volts to render anyone completely useless and stunned. Max could see the high metal fence surrounding the entire complex, with controllable CCTV cameras interspaced along its border, each on top of a fifteen-foot-high mast. Beyond he could also see other security guards casually strolling across the large grassy expanse between the fence and the start of any inner roads or structures. Buildings, sheds, warehouses and offices were scattered around the vast site.

Max gave his name as one of the guards pointed to a camera level with the car to the side of the entrance, wanting Max to look into the camera just for a second, long enough to capture his image.

"Ah yes Mr Sargent, here to see Sir John Tregar," the guard said looking at his clipboard. "Drive through to the main office in the centre and report to reception."

Max couldn't help but think to himself that for all the security they seemed to have, big tough guards, batons, fences, CCTV, they still had no idea someone was robbing them blind.

Max approached the impressive four-storey main office building, which seemed to sparkle with its mirrored windows, sat amongst the other grey, older blocks around the site. He parked up and reported to the reception in the main office building, where after a few minutes a secretary met him and escorted him up a floor to Sir John's large office suite. She introduced them to one another then quietly disappeared into her adjoining office, closing the door.

Sir John Tregar studied the young man sat before him. Max was impeccably turned out in his dark blue suit, crisp white shirt and a blue and red striped tie resembling that of the Guards Brigade. He noticed Max's steel Rolex Submariner watch and had already spotted his clean black shoes when he came in. Max had a laptop inside a black leather wallet case.

After some brief introductory chit chat Sir John asked, "So Max, you work for Si Lawson at MI5, what's that like then?"

Si had gone through everything Max would likely be asked and what he could and should not say. "Very interesting thank you Sir John. I've only been working with Mr Lawson a short while, helping them with corporate information gathering exercises like this one."

"And what exactly is your brief while you're here with us?" asked Sir John, wanting to ensure they were all on the same page.

"Per what Mr Lawson told you. I'll try to find out who in your organisation is stealing and selling your new technology and weapons designs. Then I'll hand back to MI5," said Max.

"I thought you were MI5?" asked Sir John.

"Well I am an Associate Field Agent working for MI5, so yes, I do. Combining my investigative skills with my Chief Procurement Officer role, I'm experienced in using my consulting role as cover."

"Ah yes, now about this role, are you clear about how to pitch it to my CPO here, Margaret Fallon?" asked Sir John.

"Very clear, I'll go through everything across procurement that represents any risk to the company, processes, suppliers, contingencies, governance, there's plenty to look at that I can almost guarantee most procurement teams won't be doing." Max wanted to check, asking, "What does Margaret Fallon know about this?"

Sir John gave a wry smile. "I've told Margaret that as with all departments, from time to time, we simply have to get independent reviews done to show we're following best practice, and that's what you'll be doing." He sat back. "You'll need to tread carefully with her Max, she won't take kindly to being questioned and God forbid that you tell her she should be doing better at something."

"Please don't worry Sir John, I've been doing this a long time and am used to handling, shall we say, tricky stakeholders. I'll couch any recommendations carefully, there's no blame here, we just want to improve things, for her. But all of this, let's remember, it's just the cover story. My main purpose is to find the thief, or should I say, spy."

"Sounds quite dramatic when you put it like that, but I guess that's what we're dealing with here," said Sir John rising to his feet. I still can't believe someone here has the cheek to be doing this. Or the know-how. Tell me if you need anything more from me and between you and Mr Lawson keep me updated won't you? I suggest I take you to Margaret myself, it'll carry more weight if they all see me introducing you to them. Then you're on your own."

"That would be great thank you," said Max, following Sir John out.

They walked through the offices where Max could see staff were intrigued as to who he was, that deserved being escorted through the offices by their Chief Executive. They entered a separate office area with a sign above the door saying 'Group Procurement'. Max could see about ten staff busying themselves around the open-plan office, a couple of small meeting rooms to the side and a single-walled office at the end, which he immediately assumed was for Margaret the CPO. They entered the office to find Margaret Fallon sat behind her desk, seemingly reluctant to get up at first. She rose as Sir John introduced Max. Her whole body language emitted negativity and unwelcome vibes towards him, it was so obvious she may as well have just said out loud 'I don't want you here'. Max was determined to be polite, professional and courteous, regardless of whatever he had to deal with from Margaret. Sir John left them with what sounded like a joke asking her to 'look after her guest'.

Max smiled at her and then to his utter amazement, Margaret sat back down at her desk and continued with the paperwork in front of her. Max thought perhaps she had something urgent so waited a moment, expecting her to then apologise and give him her full attention. She carried on with her document. Max got the message, this was going to be harder than even he expected.

"So Margaret," he opened with, "perhaps we can schedule an hour today for you to take me through everything you do here in procurement, so I can plan out how best to spend my time here. And a spare desk somewhere would also be great."

Margaret would have ignored Max all day if it were up to her, she'd made her point and gathered herself to finally acknowledge this *consultant*. "Mr Max Sargent. So what gives you the right to tell me how to run procurement here?" A strong, combative start.

Max took it as a positive she was at least speaking to him. "Well as you know Margaret, your Chief Exec just wants to give everything the stamp of approval, highlight all the good things you're doing here and maybe tweak some areas that could be improved. I won't know until I get across everything." Max stayed calm and knew she'd come back at him for what he'd said.

"I don't need a stamp of approval thank you, and what do you mean tweak areas that need improving?" she asked sternly, finally looking him in the eye.

Looking at her Max felt she was once an attractive lady, physically, but the overwhelming anger exuding from her face and demeanour cancelled out any good looks and portrayed a most unattractive person. "I've run many large procurement functions, getting them set up well is an ongoing process, you can never get it perfect, as you know there's always something to improve, it's the nature of the job. Let's work together and I'm sure you'll come out of this in a better position. I'm here to help, not criticise."

His reassurance seemed to help as Margaret sighed to herself as if to concede. She had looked up Max on LinkedIn and couldn't fail to be impressed with his two-decade career in procurement running and setting up teams for large corporations and winning the top individual procurement award from the Chartered Institute. She started to warm to Max's calm, consistent approach, just a little.

"Okay, why don't you find yourself any spare desk out there, introduce yourself to the team and pop back in here in say twenty minutes, then I can spend some time with you going through what we do here." Margaret gestured towards the open door and Max took his cue to leave.

He decided to address the whole room at once as it would be daft to go round each person repeating the same introduction. Finding an empty desk he addressed them all. "Excuse me, everyone, can I just introduce myself." The room quickly went silent in anticipation of wanting to find out about this visitor, as Margaret hadn't told them anything. "My name is Max Sargent, I've spent twenty years running procurement teams and Sir John has asked me to review potential risks and governance across procurement here." At this point, a few of the staff looked over to Margaret who was now standing in her doorway closely listening to what Max had to say. She showed no emotion but was impressed with the way Max was addressing the team openly. He continued. "I'm looking forward to working closely with Margaret and yourselves and only expect to be here a month or so. Thank you, I'm sure we'll be able to tell you more in due course."

Staff started to get back to work with the general feeling of appreciation to be told what was happening by this impressive consultant. They weren't used to Margaret being anywhere near as professional, nor addressing them as a team, nor frankly keeping them updated with anything going on.

Max familiarised himself with his desk, got out his laptop and notepad ready to talk with Margaret. Watching the team he could feel the hidden tension in the office. Staff were obviously repressed by their boss and fearful of doing anything wrong and then having to endure public humiliation and a dressing down from her.

Margaret came to the door of her office and nodded to Max that she was ready to see him again. He went back in and started to go through some of the areas he would be looking at. "Can I have a look at your supplier risk register?" he asked, knowing that hardly any procurement functions took the time to do this.

"What's a risk register?" asked Margaret crossly, embarrassed at having to ask.

Max explained. "You would go through each of your spend categories and suppliers, then rate each of them against criteria such as how critical their product or services are to you, do you have alternative suppliers, do they have disaster recovery plans in case something happened to them, like their factory burns down, that sort of thing."

"And what's the point of doing that pen-pushing exercise? I'm here to save money."

Her inexperience overflowed but Max hid his frustration well. "This is so you can identify what potential risks you have in your supply chain, then take action to mitigate the risks so that if say your supply is stopped, you have plans in place to prevent any damage or disruption to Empire. It's pretty standard stuff." Max realised the last comment was perhaps rubbing salt into the wound.

Margaret felt inadequate, but rather than wanting to learn from the expert, was more concerned with arguing as to why it was really necessary. "We don't have time to mess about with forms and surveys, we concentrate on making savings and doing the best deals," she pushed again.

Her remarks reinforced to Max he was dealing with an inexperienced procurement person. "Well, we also need to ensure the right governance is in place to support those greats deals you're doing. The last thing you want in procurement is for one of your critical suppliers to go out of business, your managers crying out for product, and you don't have a backup plan." Max was careful to use the word we, trying to engender some camaraderie as two procurement people both in the same game.

Margaret had previously experienced just the example Max had given. Years ago one of their uniform suppliers in China had closed overnight just before shipping an urgently required order to them for the Military Police. When it was found they didn't have any contingency plans in place, all hell broke loose as it took them six weeks to put in an emergency order with another supplier at double the cost. Despite the catastrophe, Margaret hadn't really learned the lesson nor done a risk register like Max was suggesting.

She conceded. "Okay, we can do one of your silly risk registers I suppose."

"Great," said Max feeling he was starting to make some progress, even if it was such hard work. "That's one thing we can get the team working on. Let's go through some other areas I have." Margaret raised her eyebrows deliberately in front of Max for him to see. He ignored it.

Max spent another two hours with Margaret in her office going through a long list of best practices, governance, control and risk areas across the procurement remit. Hardly any of them were being done here at Empire and Margaret was starting to realise that she would look pretty stupid if she didn't embrace Max's suggestions. He continued to reassure her that she would get the kudos for making the improvements, not only with management and her suppliers, but more importantly from her staff.

At the end, Max finally got to the matter he wanted to cover all along. "If you have some time Margaret, would you be able to give me a tour of the estate here at Empire? I'd be interested to have a look round the other buildings and subsidiaries."

Margaret didn't want to spend any longer with Max. "That's out of the question I'm afraid. I need to catchup up on everything having already spent so much time with you today. I'll get one of the team to take you around though." She popped out of the office followed by Max and went over to one of the young men. "Michael, could you show Max around the site, take as long as you need."

Max smiled at her constant rudeness, it was pathetic really.

Michael stood up nodding, pleased at the excuse to get out of the office and spend some time with the consultant. Michael was thirty years old, a little over-weight, about five-foot-ten with thinning hair and glasses. He'd fallen into procurement after attempting to become a top computer programmer, which he'd aspired to at University and managed to get a graduate job for one of the many gaming companies springing up. They'd been successful with a couple of driving games that had been sold to Electronic Arts, who were sweeping up most games for the gaming system firms such as Microsoft and Nintendo. They also churned out basic ap games, none of which made any money unless the advertising viewing went into millions, given everyone now expected all apps to be free.

Michael had been put onto their newly planned driver game to work with the computer graphic artists on 'improving the wheels'. They wanted the programming to better show the spinning wheels of the various cars in the new game, as the wheels hadn't been given much attention in their last games and visually were falling behind the precise look, feel and interaction with the road surface and drifting quality gamers now expected. He had to become an expert in how wheels, and more importantly, how tyres reacted to cornering, the grip and slide they gave depending on the speeds and angle of a turn on the tracks.

After four months of interpreting wheels and tyres' metrics into programming code to then compliment the car, suspension and steering programmers, Michael realised much to his disillusionment, that game programming wasn't for him. The exciting, glamorous finished game product, now often making more money than many big movies, belied the somewhat dull and intensively detailed programming behind the graphics, mostly taken for granted by the players. To the surprise of his manager, Michael quit and wanted nothing more to do with programming.

A friend of his happened to be a buyer for a supermarket chain in North London and recommended Michael. Such is the huge turnover of buying staff in the big retailers that he got a job and settled into dealing with suppliers, costs, products and services, a breath of fresh air compared to the programming job. After a few years, he wanted promotion faster than the retailer was ever going to give him and applied for a Senior Buyer's job with Empire Arms.

His hunger to learn and impress sat well with Margaret who brought him on board several years ago. Michael's character was by chance a good fit with his demanding, over-bearing boss and he absorbed her negativity and stress with his pragmatic and relaxed approach to everything. He didn't really like her and the way she treated people, but he didn't care either. He enjoyed the job, working for a relatively big firm and being out of London, had bought his first apartment in nearby Crawley Sussex, just on the other side of Gatwick to the offices.

"I'm in your hands Michael," said Max, as they left the procurement office. He waited until they'd left the offices then decided to see how deep Michael's loyalties lay for his boss, asking, "Quite a tough one your CPO, how long have you worked for her?"

Michael was relaxed about the question and quite open, figuring that Max wasn't a close friend or colleague by the way Margaret had treated him earlier. "Yes she can be, you just have to let it all ride over you I guess. I've been here a few years so am kinda used to it all. To some though it can be quite a shock, and many couldn't and don't put up with it."

Max felt he could have an ally so tentatively pressed on. "What do you mean? Staff turnover?"

"Oh yes, we've had people come and go, fallouts, rows in the office. It's always ended with them going or Margaret making their lives hell." Michael looked at Max concerned for a moment. "You won't repeat any of this will you?"

Max reassured him. "Of course not, just interested. I'm only here a month or so and just want to help by spotting a few things that can be improved. For everyone's good."

Michael relaxed again. "Thank heavens. Anyway, let's go round each of the buildings, that's a good way to cover off what happens here. We'll start with Hanger 1 over here," as he led Max towards the largest warehouse structure on the site. "Most of what we do here involves designing things, buying in gear for the MOD, some testing and some hardware fitting and alterations."

A security guard recognised Michael but still quickly searched them both before letting them pass. Inside the old aircraft hanger sat a large array of military equipment including several tanks, armoured personnel carriers, a rocket launcher, jeeps and field guns. Technicians purposefully dotted around the floor space examined, carried and dissembled equipment. Down one side a makeshift range sat quietly with a six-foot thick concrete wall at one end covered with many layers of sandbags. Remnants of some bullet-ridden targets stood dejected on several posts. To the other side were rows of metal shelving strewn with electronic equipment with radars, communications devices, aerials, monitors and mobile scanners and radio sets. Some were in pieces, some on benches being worked on.

Down the far end of the hanger enclosed with screening, there was a bustle of activity with about ten staff mostly in grey overalls or coats, all fussing around a jeep. Michael asked one of the men passing by, "Hey Simon, how's it going, what are you guys working on today? I'm just showing a procurement consultant round."

"Michael," nodding back. "We're fitting the jeep with distraction flares. Kind of Batmobile stuff," he simplified, for Max's benefit. Max looked puzzled so the technician elaborated. "It's a magnesium sixteen flare evasive halo that shoots up 360 degrees around the jeep to distract any fire-fight against the occupants. It'll blind snipers and hide the jeep with bright lights and a smoke curtain. The idea is they can get away to a safe distance, regroup, flee or fight back. Pretty cheap and simple, not sure it's a goer but we have to get it ready for a demo with the MOD commissioning team in a couple of days, at the Elizabeth Barracks up the road in

Pirbright Surrey."

Michael added, "They design stuff in here, test it out and add things to other things, like with the jeep flares. It's brilliant, like James Bond's 'Q' branch." The technician raised his eyebrows.

They left the hanger and walked across a large expanse of tarmac which from time to time got used to test various machines, trucks and radar. The next building was smaller with an office attached to a long hut. "This is Empire Technology," said Michael. "All the electronic wizardry happens in here. Communication devices, frequency jammers, helmet-cams. They're working on a new project that I've been involved with, buying some of the electronic components for them from Phoenix Arizona and China. I think you'll be impressed."

The security guard at the entrance knew Michael who often visited the offices of this building for technical meetings and briefings for sourcing items. They entered the offices and various staff looked up and waved at Michael, ignoring Max but accepting him with his friendly escort and also relieved it was Michael from procurement and not his boss Margaret. They passed a few open offices and Michael went into the end meeting room which had been requisitioned by the person working inside. Michael introduced Max to Jonathan and explained they were on a tour and could he tell Max what he was working on.

Jonathan happily stopped attending to several oscilloscope screens to explain to Max. "Has Max here signed the Secrets Act and NDA Michael?"

Michael didn't know but had assumed that had all been sorted with Margaret or Sir John. Max said, "Indeed I have," but was referring to the Official Secrets Act he'd signed back at Thames House for the MI5 and not anything he's signed for Empire Arms.

Jonathan continued. "We're developing a great little toy here for foot soldiers, it's called 'FIRM'. Well, that's my made-up name for it at the moment, no doubt someone in corporate or the MOD will give it some other name in due course." Not waiting for Max to ask what that stood for he continued. "It stands for 'Field Intel Radar

Mapping'."

Max was intrigued and already trying to figure out what the device could do with a name like that. Michael added proudly, "You'll like this Max."

Jonathan tried to hide a smile. "It displays an infrared radar map of your surrounding fifty metres or so, regardless of buildings or walls, showing everyone's position in relation to you, as well as any heavy equipment with a heat signal such as vehicles or ordnance." Michael and Jonathan looked at Max anticipating some praise. Max obliged.

"Wow, that's amazing. That's incredible. So you can see everyone around you." Max couched his first thought carefully. "But I guess that includes your own men?"

Jonathan nodded, "I'm already onto that where we can give each person a small transmitter the size of a button which will cancel out their mapping signal, so if the user only wants to see the enemy they can. Still working on making this remotely operated so they can switch from friendly to foreign or both on the radar. This is particularly helpful for say jungle or built-up terrain where the line of sight is poor. You can still see where everyone is around you."

Max took the opportunity to ask a more pertinent question to his mission here at Empire, as he seemed to have a friendly audience. "With such a brilliant design, how do you ensure its secrecy. What's to stop someone just taking the idea somewhere else?" Max hoped he hadn't alerted any suspicions with the question.

Michael and Jonathan didn't seem to mind the question and Jonathan replied. "Nothing I guess. We have good security here, it's not exactly cutting-edge technology, I'm just adapting what's already out there, just more effectively. It's just a mini radar, I can't imagine anyone would bother risking trying to steal it. The secret stuff is usually done by Peter over at Apollo."

"And the design is stored on a central library server, not on individual computers," added Michael, "they'd have to download it off Jonathan's pc while he was here using it."

'Interesting', thought Max, as he scanned the rest of the room, desk and computer for anything different looking. It all seemed standard. They thanked Jonathan and made their way out of the building.

Max now wanted to get into his main target being the Apollo building and hoped Michael was going to let him. "Michael, Jonathan mentioned the interesting stuff was made at Apollo, any chance we can go and have a look there. Maybe meet this Peter guy?"

Michael shrugged his shoulders, "You're kidding. There's no way they'll let us just walk in there. Even I don't know what they're working on, that's all high-level clearance stuff."

"Would Margaret have that clearance, maybe she could take me there?" Max asked.

"Yeah she probably would, don't know to be honest, never asked her about it. Come to think of it I'm not sure I'd want to, she'd probably tear me off a strip for being nosy," Michael laughed to himself. Max smiled back in agreement and sympathy.

"And who is this Peter chap at Apollo?"

"Oh Peter, Peter Kendrick. He's our mad professor here. He's a genius. He comes up with most of the new, wonderful designs we end up making here for the MOD and often America's Department of Defense."

"Have you seen anything Apollo have designed?" asked Max, hoping his barrage of questions wasn't going too far with Michael.

There was no hint of any suspicion from Michael. "I was lucky enough to see a testing of one of their grenades as I'd helped source the observation window the MOD bods would watch it through. Oh my God, it was awesome. They called it an APaRC. Still have to think what that stands for."

Max remembered MI5 telling him about this design which was one of those previously sold on the Dark Web auction, but patiently waited for Michael to work out what the abbreviation stood for.

"Anti people, no personnel," Michael struggled to get the words, "room clearer, that's it, Anti Personnel Room Clearer."

Max feigned interest though already knew exactly what this was. "What on earth is that?"

Michael stopped himself and frowned at Max apologetically. "I can't tell you, Max, sorry. It's top secret. I know you've signed the Secret's Act and all that, but I'd get fired if I told you about a design like that, it hasn't even come onto the market yet."

'That's what you think my friend', Max thought to himself, knowing full well that it had indeed come onto the market, but not to a legitimate military power, but to some dodgy, clandestine buyer on the Dark Web. "No problem Michael, I quite understand, I won't mention it again," he reassured his tour host.

They walked back towards the main offices as Michael pointed out the Apollo Designs building with adjoining large shed. Max was already thinking that he'd have to ask Margaret about seeing inside there and meeting this Peter Kendrick.

"As part of my risk review Michael, tell me about this central library server thing you mentioned earlier. Is that somewhere we can have a look at?" Max asked.

Michael hesitated to check with himself if he thought that would be okay and given the security the library had thought to himself there couldn't be any harm. Any excuse to delay having to go back to the procurement office. "Yeah, I think that's fine, follow me, it's in the basement of the main building. Lyndsey looks after it all."

6

Lyndsey Wyman had worked at Empire on and off for most of her life. She was truly one of the old hands there and was now solely in charge of the company's library and records database. These held all sensitive data, information, paper hard copy and electronic soft copy plans, designs, prototypes, patents and intellectual property for everything the group had done, was doing and had planned. An important job, but not the role she'd wanted.

Lyndsey was sixty years old and the years had not been kind to her looks. She'd gained a lot of weight through lack of exercise, sitting at a desk for decades and her love of home-cooked but unhealthy foods. She had grey hair which hung loose and usually unchecked around her head in an untidy bob, framing dark eyes and a weathered face portraying a motherly but unhappy sole. She'd never found the right man to settle down with but took solace in the company of her friends, her cats. She had seven of them and they were what kept her sane, gave her love and the companionship she needed. They were loyal, loving, followed her around the house, low maintenance, independent and never argued. To her, they were far better than any man could have been.

Lyndsey had started at Empire some forty years ago in the post room, a time when letters and written or typed memos were the forms of communications outside of conversation and calls. The single telex machine sat in the corner and had to be authorised for use due to its high cost to send words down the telephone line. Then the fax machine arrived, a marvel which could send a scan of a document down the line and reprint it out the other end. Her youthful and pretty looks soon got her noticed as she toured the offices twice a day handing out and collecting post, and one of the directors was looking for a new secretary and asked if she would like the position. Lyndsey only had basic typing skills and knew nothing of professional shorthand such as Pitman, but desperately wanted to advance herself, so took the role. Her new boss patiently suggested she practised her typing as much as possible in the office and she quickly became faster and more proficient. She also became very efficient at taking dictation by simply writing quickly the start of words and abbreviating the tail ends, then relying on memory of what was said to her when looking through her notes later.

She remembered her typewriter changing from the hammer arm letters to an electronic golf ball and also the day when white correction tape became available. Office workers would gather around her in wonderment to watch a demonstration of the magical tape being able to correct and hide any mistyped ink. The magical typewriter tape then became a magical correction fluid, white paper paint in a small bottle. Lyndsey had seen a lot of changes in the office environment in the last four decades. Typewriters to keyboards and computers, dial tone desktop telephones to fancy high-tech mobile phones, letters and memos to emails, directories and books to the World Wide Web.

She spent the next fifteen years as secretary and then as titles changed, personal assistant, to seven different managers across the business. Becoming tired of making tea and coffee and typing letters, Lyndsey moved into several junior to mid-ranking roles in marketing, then human resources, then accounts. During those fifteen years, she took a three-month sabbatical to travel the world and once left the company for all of two months, quickly returning having realised she was wedded to the company she'd spent her career with.

Lyndsey worked in the back-office accounts and administration team when a certain Margaret Fallon descended upon the company and became her new boss. Lyndsey very quickly saw through Margaret's temporary charm and good character, and the two women often clashed, forcing Lindsay to look outside of that department if she was to stay with Empire.

She'd worked for most departments across the company and was well-liked, though not thought of as highflying executive potential. The older gentleman running the Buying team had always had a soft spot for Lindsay and brought her into his department as a Buyer, where she worked for some years, happy to be away from Margaret Fallon back in accounts.

She knew her Procurement Director boss would be retiring soon and started to make a tentative play to be considered as his replacement. Whilst her record, attitude and loyalty were second to none, Lyndsey simply wasn't leadership director material. Then to her horror, she became aware of Margaret Fallon making a play with her boss to be considered for his replacement. She pleaded with her manager not to be taken in by Margaret's misrepresented demeanour and for the most part, he agreed that Margaret was not his first choice, but unfortunately left out telling Lyndsey that he didn't think she would be suitable in the role either.

Margaret, however, had another key ally in Sir John Tregar who'd employed her and although he liked and respected Lyndsey especially for her long servitude to the company, he believed that Margaret would make a tough, strong new Procurement Director. Margaret Fallon worked on Sir John, pleading her case, dropping hints and finally got the job.

Once more Lyndsey had to deal with her as the boss. It was then that after all those years of loyal service to the company, that she began to feel let down by them and unappreciated. She even went to see Sir John to explain that it was unlikely she and Margaret would see eye to eye on things and that she feared for her job. Whilst Sir John was empathetic, he suggested to Lindsay that she did everything she could to patch things up and get on with her new boss. She felt let down again, this company owed her for everything she had done for it.

Lyndsey did her very best to get on with Margaret, but unfortunately, their previous clashes had not been forgotten, nor forgiven by the newly titled Chief Procurement Officer. The underlying tension between the two of them got worse and Margaret had got to the point where she was ramping up the pressure and requests on Lyndsey, to manage her out of the business for poor performance. One of the usual key performance indicators for procurement staff is always that of savings and their delivery against targets. Margaret had set stretch and likely unachievable savings goals for Lyndsey who then, in a final effort to meet her numbers, started fabricating forecasted savings. Whilst surprising Margaret, she did not think to question the seemingly reasonable numbers that Lyndsey was submitting, and they became part of the overall reporting that Margaret was giving to the board of directors on Procurement's performance. In turn, the numbers then became part of the financial statements the company publicly declared.

Then one day, when Margaret was being grilled on her numbers by an overly keen young manager in finance, determined to ensure that each number was accurate and justified. It became clear that some of the savings were being grossly overstated. Margaret could see that the discrepancies were perpetrated by Lyndsey, but couldn't openly fire her because the ultimate overall responsibility for the incorrect savings numbers that had been given to accounts, lay with her as Procurement Director. However, she was determined to turn this misdemeanour to her advantage and tactically chose to summon Lyndsey to her office at five o'clock one Friday afternoon. The significance of this timing was not lost on Lyndsey, as this was usually when staff were let go by their managers at the end of the week, so as not to cause a fuss in the office and let things settle down over a weekend.

Lyndsey nervously sat down in front of Margaret but had no idea what the topic of conversation was going to be, but that just made it worse.

Margaret allowed herself to use her most serious tone. "Lyndsey, I know we've had our differences in the past, but a somewhat grave and delicate matter has been brought to my attention."

"What's that then, I've been doing really well lately and even hitting those rather ridiculous savings targets you set me," said Lyndsey.

"That's actually where we have a problem. It seems as

though you have been giving me inflated savings numbers?"

"I don't know what you're talking about. All my savings numbers represent accurate forecasts." Lyndsey now realised the game was probably up and she was in big trouble.

"The numbers you've been giving me all there in black and white, on reports, in your emails. They are incorrect. Indeed you have deliberately and repeatedly inflated these numbers to fraudulently meet your targets." Margaret was laying it on thick. "These numbers go into the company accounts. This is serious."

Lyndsey thought for a moment. She knew that everything Margaret said was true and it wouldn't take much to prove it to HR or a tribunal. "Well you are responsible for this team, you got the top job over me getting it, so the numbers become just as much yours as they are mine," challenged Lyndsey staring defiantly at Margaret.

"But they're your numbers, Lyndsey. This is a sackable offence you know. You have deceived the company." But Margaret knew what Lyndsey had said was correct, she was also liable for these errors, but now she had to bluff this out to her advantage. "We go back a long way and even though it's been up and down, and I should be firing you this evening, I've stuck my neck out for you, but only if you do exactly what I say." Margaret now wanted to gauge her reaction to the possibility of a way out of this and her not being sacked. She waited, watching Lyndsey closely.

Lyndsey had assumed she would be instantly dismissed and that was certainly not how she wanted her notorious service with Empire to end. She'd been here almost forty years and was not going to be kicked out. She had a huge pension waiting for her as part of her retirement fund, which she would lose if she was fired. "What are you proposing then?"

Margaret took in a deep breath. "I've had a quiet word with the powers that be," moving her eyes upwards as if to imply that she'd spoken with Sir John, which of course she hadn't, "and I've managed to save your job here at Empire, or rather a job, under two conditions."

Lyndsey couldn't help but let out a sigh of relief. Her

pension was safe. It sounded like she wasn't going to be fired. "What job and what are these conditions?" she asked.

"I think we can both agree that it would not be tenable for you to stay in procurement. I've put a word in for you with my successor in accounts and admin and managed to secure you the role in Records. In addition to that, you'll never speak of this again, if you do you'll still be fired."

"Records! You've got to be kidding. Down there in the basement by myself all day."

"It's an easy job but a really important one, you're looking after all of the company's IP. And let's face it Lyndsey, you only have a few years to sit it out there quietly to your retirement. With pension and all benefits." Margaret was persuasive.

Lyndsey didn't need to reconsider for too long. She didn't like Margaret, but it seemed she had saved her from being fired and more importantly saved her from losing her treasured pension and benefits. She'd also saved her from an embarrassing end to her long career here at empire. "Okay," she said simply.

As if reading her mind, Margaret pressed on with her final advantage. Nodding to Lyndsey and then gesturing towards the door for her to leave, the matter satisfactorily concluded, she said equally simply, "You owe me," as Lyndsey left the room.

'No, the company owes *me*', thought Lyndsey.

Michael took Max through the large reception area which had leading off it a couple of meeting rooms, a small staff canteen and the stairs and lifts. Behind the reception desks was a curved wall where a security guard sat in a chair, in front of a metal security coded door. The guard could protect the unmarked doorway as well as cover any presence or subtle protection required for the atrium as well. Michael nodded to the uniformed man and held up his ID badge. The guard nonchalantly turned and standing directly in front of the door keypad to obscure anyone seeing, punched in the four numbers, each accompanied with a beep. The metal door clicked open and Michael led Max down the well-lit stairway. Above them, as they came down the steps, a small cheap CCTV camera watched them.

"Quite impressive security for the basement," said Michael, "after all, it's where the group's designs and secrets are all held." He shouted out, "Lyndsey, anyone in? It's Michael."

A voice called out from across the large basement as they descended into view. "Hi Michael, yes I'm here. Saw you coming down the stairs on the TV. Come through then." Lyndsey came over to meet them and seeing Max said, "Who have you got here then?"

Michael introduced Max to Lyndsey explaining he was doing a procurement risk review for them. Max looked around the surprisingly large basement room which was well lit and fresh, with its air conditioning, despite not having any windows. There was one of those obligatory fire escape doors in the far corner which appeared to be overly robust and from the dust and boxes piled in front of it, apparently hadn't been opened in years.

The area was an Aladdin's cave of treasures and files. To one side there were rows of metal shelves and cabinets sporting an array of equipment including radars, radio sets, small cameras, helmets and bullet-proof vests. There was also a more interesting area of prototypes and samples of ordnance including handguns, rifles, telescopic scopes, strange-looking shotguns, tasers, net guns and a grenade launcher, each looking quite different from a normal device, having been modified or upgraded.

The centre of the basement was filled with rows of filing cabinets and cupboards, with some large, heavy-duty and rather old looking safes. This was the paperwork area where designs, blueprints, documents and even old microfiche slides were stored. Max noted that everything was in its place, carefully labelled and in order. On the further side of the room was what appeared to be a mixture of an office and household living room, which looked quite bizarre amongst the surrounding officious cabinets and weaponry samples. Lyndsey noticed Max looking at her 'lounge'.

"I bet you've not seen that in an office environment before eh Max?" Max shook his head smiling. Lyndsey continued, "Well my view was if I'm going to spend all day down here in the basement by myself, then the least they can do for me is allow me to have a little comfort. I've got my office over here," as she pointed to several large desks pushed together with two desktop computers on and a cheap CCTV digital recorder with a small screen showing the stairway entrance.

Lyndsey saw Max looking at the device and reminded herself, "Must get that hard drive fixed for the CCTV, loses all the video every now and then." Looking at a very comfortable looking leather chair, "My slightly less formal area for meetings, reading and downtime." Max surveyed the various un-matching armchairs and sofas surrounding a large coffee table. In the corner, there was even an old TV set, which he presumed allowed Lyndsey to have daytime television on in the background.

"Very nice, it all looks very well organised and comfy," conceded Max, who then noticed an empty cat basket in the corner.

Lyndsey picked up on it, "Oh that. When I started down here it was so boring I used to bring one of my beautiful cats in with me, to keep me company all day. The basket was her's, she loved it down here exploring and being with me. My boss came in a few days later and wasn't happy and that was the end of that. Shame, I love my cats, got six altogether."

Max sympathised with her, he also loved cats. "Michael tells me that all the new equipment designs are stored by you and not on the individual computers around the estate?"

Lyndsey enjoyed impressing visitors in her lonely job and warmed to Max's charm and interest. "Years ago Sir John, before he was knighted and when he was group Finance Director, was rightly concerned that Empire had all of its valuable designs and documents spread across different people, buildings and offices. It was a nightmare and would have been so easy for anyone to copy or steal our IP. So he brought in my predecessor to set up a central vault if you like, one single place, where the company's entire valuable documents, designs and samples would be held." She held her arms up and looked around the room proudly. "Of course I've made a load of improvements since I took over."

Max looked around again admiringly nodding. "I can see all the paperwork cabinets and hardware samples. So how do the electronic files get transferred to you?"

"They don't get transferred at all. Everything is held and worked on from the intranet and shared files that I hold on my closed network servers over there. One PC is linked to the servers and library, the other for normal email and internet use. Nothing in the library can be accessed from outside or via the internet as it's not connected to the outside world."

Lyndsey pointed to the large cabinet against the wall holding the racks of flashing lights from the various servers, databases and hard drives. "The IT guys have set it up somehow so that if any individual around the business, including the designers themselves, attempts to save the files on another device such as their computer or a memory stick, I get an alert. No one's ever done it while I've been in charge. It's a sackable offence you know. I back it all up each week onto a hard drive that gets locked in a safe here."

"Most impressive," said Max, who was thinking to himself that this all made his job a little easier, in that whoever was stealing the designs would have to be doing it from this room, unless it was the person responsible for actually coming up with an individual product. "And who has access to this room?"

At this point, Max could see he might have asked one too many a question as Lyndsey's expression turned to a quizzical look. "Why do you ask?" she said.

Max was quick with his reply. "Oh, simply part of my due diligence and risk review. I'd need to know you can't have any Tom, Dick and Harry just trot in here with so much valuable stuff lying around."

Lyndsey thought for a moment then perhaps reckoned that she'd been over-cautious with him. "I see, yes of course. As well as myself it's only the Head of Security who briefs the guards on the code and has access at night in case there was a problem, or fire, but he wouldn't know where to find anything anyway. Then there's my boss the Head of Accounts and of course Sir John."

"So that's the code for the entrance door for access to the room, paper files and samples, what about access to your computers and the soft copy files?" Max asked. Lyndsey gave him another look. "Last question I promise," said Max holding up his hands.

"I'm the only person who knows the log-ins for my PC's," said Lyndsey.

"What about backup if you forgot them or something happened to you?"

Lyndsey smiled triumphantly, ready with her answer to the probing question that might have caught her out. "Oh well, of course they're backed up. Any time I change them I write my new username and password on a card in a sealed envelope, which I give to Sir John's secretary for safekeeping. I get the envelope back when I give them a new one and it's never been opened yet."

'Not exactly hi-tech' Max thought to himself, but seemed to be effective and secure.

Max thanked Lyndsey for her time and left to return to the procurement office with Michael, much to his sadness. He'd enjoyed his tour of the site with the new consultant and quietly whispered to Max, "Back to Margaret eh," with a frown and feeling in a slightly mischievous gossip mood added, "Bit of history I gather, with Margaret and Lyndsey." Max looked puzzled. "I think they had a few clashes, both wanted the Procurement Director job. Don't know the detail but best not to mention it to either of them."

The following day Max went in to update Margaret on his progress and thoughts and they touched on his tour the previous day.

"We had a good look round the site but I was surprised we couldn't get into Apollo Designs. Michael said you might be able to help me with that one?" asked Max.

Margaret was visibly frustrated at the question, but Max just took that as the normal reaction now if he asked anything of her. "What's the special interest with Apollo?" she asked.

"No special interest, just that it was the only building we couldn't visit, it would just be good to meet everyone around the site, you know, get an understanding of what they do so I can understand if there are any risks involved."

"They don't really like strangers snooping around in there," challenged Margaret rudely.

"Completely understandable Margaret. But I'm not a stranger," Max decided to lay it on a bit and call her bluff. "I'm the person Sir John wants to undertake a risk review so I should have access to all areas don't you think?" He paused while Margaret was about to get angry. "But of course if you feel I shouldn't be allowed access then I'd have to accept your judgement."

Margaret stopped herself short of getting into a playground fight with Max, realising it would seem odd for her to prevent him seeing this one remaining office. Begrudgingly she replied, "Oh I suppose I can take you into Apollo for a quick look."

"I'd love to meet this Peter chap, your designer? Jonathan over in Empire Technology said he did all the new stuff," said Max.

"That won't be possible," replied Margaret protectively. "He'll be far too busy, and most of what he works on will still be confidential. You wouldn't be allowed to hear about those kinds of things."

Max felt he needed to press his remit given this was where the designs being stolen and sold were originating from. "I believe I do have full access Margaret, as agreed with Sir John and I've signed all the necessary NDA's."

Margaret was bristling now. "Well if you're going to quote names at me now why don't I call Sir John, who knows me far longer than you, and ask him?" She picked up the phone threateningly but waited for Max to tell her not to bother Sir John. But Max just shrugged his shoulders as if to say 'if you want to then go ahead'. Now she was committed, she couldn't back down, so she dialled Sir John's number and asked his secretary if she could have a quick word. Max waited patiently.

"Sir John. Sorry to bother you but we appear to have a misunderstanding about Mr Sargent's remit here. He's asking to view all operations including Apollo. I'm not sure he should be allowed in there let alone hear about what they're working on. It's top secret."

Sir John had been waiting for a call at some point in the next few days. He knew there was no way that even someone as professional and polite as this Max Sargent, wouldn't at some point get dragged into an altercation with Margaret Fallon. He also assumed from her tone that she was calling him with Max likely sitting there in front of her. She wanted to pull rank, but Sir John had assured Si Lawson at MI5 that Max would indeed have full access across the firm. He tried to let her down gently.

Max watched Margaret wistfully, avoiding a smile this time in case it was misinterpreted as a smirk. He anticipated that Sir John would be following Si's instructions on the call right now and explaining that he should indeed have access to Apollo. Margaret tried to interrupt whatever Sir John was saying with several protests, but to no avail. She ended the call with a huff and puff saying, "Alright then, if that's what you want Sir John." She put the phone down, glared at Max, then tried desperately to soften herself, failing visibly to hide her anger at being 'trumped' by Max.

"Well?" ventured Max, breaking the uncomfortable silence.

Margaret dismissed Max from her office with a wave, saying as he got up, "I'll take you over to Apollo tomorrow." She simply had to have the last word on it.

Once Max had turned to leave and Margaret couldn't see his expression, he allowed himself a smile. Margaret let him get clear of her office and quietly mumbled under her breath undeservedly, "Arrogant bastard".

7

Peter Kendrick was the top weapons and ordnance designer at Empire Arms, working in the Apollo Designs subsidiary. He was sixty-two and should have retired with a fortune, but instead continued to come up with amazing new design and technology inventions for the military, because he loved what he did. His thin, light frame of modest five-foot-nine height portrayed the nerdy academic that he was, topped off with spectacles, grey wispy hair and a face constantly showing concern and concentration. He was always thinking and solving problems, always getting onto the next thing on the long list of things needing doing he carried around in his head. That's why he was so good at his job, he was a relentless doer and in proclamation of it had a plaque on his desk given to him by his father saying simply, 'Do It Now!'.

Since he was a young lad, Peter Kendrick found he was happiest when building things. One of his favourite toys was his Meccano set, invented by Frank Hornby in 1901 which comprised a box full of metal construction pieces with holes in and a bag of small nuts and bolts to build such items as cars, tractors, planes, weapons and trains. He also had a large box of hundreds of pieces of interlocking plastic Lego bricks, which he built into towers, spaceships, houses and weapons.

Toy guns featured a lot in young Peter's life and before long he had quite a collection of them. Before the internet, television and electronic games, most boys were infatuated with Cowboys and Indians, and the Army. His father would take him every year to the Royal Tournament at Earls Court in London, which was the biggest British military show and display attended by members of the Royal family. Peter would clamber over tanks and jeeps on display, hold machine guns and rifles, sit on motorbikes and inside aeroplane cockpits. Then in the huge arena, he would watch in awe the military parades, mock battles, the bands and the motorbike stunt team. Then at the end, there was the famous Field Gun Race, where two elite Navy teams would disassemble and carry a massive field gun through an obstacle course, back again, reassemble and fire it.

He was destined to join the Army and being a clever chap went to the Royal Military Academy at Sandhurst Berkshire as an Officer Cadet, where he went through the officer's training program. Peter wasn't a combat soldier though he had many front-line stints, his ambition was always to be where the development happened. The gear, the kit, the guns. The Army still relied heavily on external firms such as Thales, British Aerospace, Vickers and other smaller ordnance makers and rarely brought such skills in-house. He passed out as an officer, with the Queen in attendance, and went into the then recently formed 3 Royal School of Military Engineering Regiment, based at the Gibraltar Barracks in Camberley Surrey. The site was shared with 8 Engineer Brigade and the Royal Engineers Warfare Wing.

At the RSME they provided training for many parts of the combat engineering regiments and also engaged in theatre support and weaponry provision. Peter was a model soldier and worked his way up through the Lieutenant ranks to Captain and finally was promoted to a Major. This was the highest rank he could attain without being a field operations officer, as he preferred to be with the supporting teams so he could look after, repair, supply and whenever possible have an input into the equipment specifications and design. He married a woman from the administration office and had a daughter. Life was acceptable and the benefits of being a married officer living on campus were good.

During the twenty-two years he served in the Army, Peter was part of the occupying forces in the nineties for Bosnia and Kosovo. Then towards the end of his service, he led an engineering team in Afghanistan in 2002, to ensure bridge-building equipment and upgraded radar kit were available to the troops when needed in the harsh terrains the country had to offer. Then just as he was preparing to leave the Army, Saddam Hussein decided to push the

West one step too far with his various threats and exploits, denying weapons inspectors unfettered access to his nuclear sites. NATO was fearful that he had 'weapons of mass destruction' capability and months before Peter was about to leave, he found himself as one of the most respected Major's of the engineering regiment's, travelling to Iraq and engaging in the most dangerous of wartime theatres he'd experienced in his career. Whilst the enemy were poorly trained and disorganised and sometimes gave up when overwhelmed, this bred inconsistency and surprise. The Army never knew whether to expect small or large resistance, untrained troops or their Special Republican Guard who might fight to the death or suddenly surrender.

Thankful to leave the Army unscathed after the Iraqi conflict, Peter was happy to get closer to the design and specification side of the weapons and was offered a senior role with the Ministry of Defence in London, where he acted as a Specialist Advisor to the procurement team there. This was a step in the right direction for him as he could recommend innovations and upgrades, however, these were then given to various suppliers and manufacturers to figure out and make. He found he was still not in the position of being free to design and invent such aspirations and also realised that the designers at the suppliers were being paid far more than Army Majors or MOD Weapons Advisors. After almost ten years with the MOD having been moved from central London down to a new MOD Procurement hub in Abbey Wood Bristol in 1996, finally, the perfect job came along for Peter.

One of the smaller suppliers to the MOD was a growing company called Empire Arms based near Gatwick. Peter wanted to come back to his Gibraltar Barracks roots near Surrey and was approached by the then Chairman of Empire over lunch, to consider joining them in a similar role to the one they saw him performing at the MOD. Peter said he would join, but only if he was given free rein to design and innovate whatever new weapons and upgrades he wanted to. The Chairman was hesitant, but when Peter told him of several ideas he already had, he was convinced that Peter could transform their New Products division and offerings to the market, and make them money, especially with his Army and MOD background and insights. Peter happily joined Empire for the largest salary and benefits he'd ever had and started a program of new technology and weaponry for the company.

After a few years of designing many improvements to existing equipment and some highly innovative and outstanding pieces of kit and ordnance, Peter again saw that he did not appear to be benefitting. He felt he should, from his multi-million-pound revenue items, all making huge profits for the company. He only had a few years before retirement and wanted a big payday for his efforts. Sir John Tregar did give him a sizeable raise and 'stay-on bonus', but he still felt unappreciated and underpaid. It was now only the love of the freedom of his job and the ability to do what he wanted whilst playing with ideas and inventions, that kept him at Empire, supported by the facilities he required from a large organisation.

Peter Kendrick didn't like jokes, he didn't like the employee social aspects of working for a company, but he did love to talk to fellow enthusiasts and designers to explore options, new ways of pushing the boundaries, overcoming challenges. He had a few other very capable designers in his team at Apollo and had a monthly meeting with Sir John to talk about everything he was doing. If Sir John sanctioned it, he would then present the update to the board, for their views, but mainly to approve the necessary funding for his idea explorations, design, build and testing. Other than these few opportunities to extol and discuss his thoughts, plans and progress, his job felt like a solitary one, shut away in his office and shed to get on with it.

So when Sir John had called him to say that Margaret would be showing around a procurement risk consultant with full authority access to all parts of the business, and plans being worked on, Peter hoped this rare visitor would genuinely be interested in his work.

Max had done his research on Peter Kendrick, knowing how important his visit would be to both himself and MI5. Apollo was where each of the valuable weapon designs came from, and were now unbeknown to them, being touted on the Dark Web market for anyone with enough money to buy, to steal. Max could see from this man's career that he had spent his life serving his country and promoting the development of the arms it used. This was his passion.

Margaret Fallon was still awkward about having to relent to showing Max around Apollo, that was quite clear from her body language as she led Max across to the Apollo Designs building. The guard standing inside a small foyer was more diligent this time, asking for ID's to be shown, checking their names on a computer under 'expected visitors' and asking them to sign in whilst looking up at a camera behind him on the wall, which took their pictures. He then called the office and moments later Peter Kendrick came through the doors and politely greeted them. Max could feel a tension between Peter and Margaret, but put it down to the negative, combative vibe she was giving out. Everyone on site knew how difficult she could be and after such a distinguished career in the military, Peter had as little to do as possible with someone like Margaret. He saw that Max had noticed their coolness to one another.

"Margaret and I go back a few years, don't we. Not seen you for quite a while though," thinking to himself 'Thank God'. "Hopefully you'll be impressed with what we're working on. Sir John says I can tell all, you must be an important guest Mr Sargent, come in both of you," offered Peter.

The layout was similar to other buildings, with two floors of offices and a large warehouse to the rear. Peter showed them around the offices and introduced them to various staff, then took them into the warehouse. Max immediately noticed the large area felt more secure than the other sheds and also far more comfortable, with wall panels, extra lighting, heaters and coolers, and a surgically clean, shiny concrete floor. There were only four other staff, all concentrating intently on their various projects, two at a large table assembling items and two moving around, collecting items off shelving. The racks held many parts, boxes and made-up devices, being either tested or completed prototypes. Max noticed a row of helmets and assumed these must be part of the Kevlar-Carbon-Weave project he'd heard about from MI5.

"This is where it all happens, where the magic is created," said Peter proudly, "sounds a bit like a Disney tour doesn't it?"

Max smiled, Margaret was still sulking and went over to the shelving and started examining a black solid disc shape. She was about to pick it up when Peter interrupted her. "Margaret, don't touch that please!"

Margaret pulled back with surprise. "What is it?"

"It's a floor grenade that jumps up into the air detonating a frag explosion. Guaranteed to clear the room. You don't want to be around when that goes off at eye level," said Peter.

Margaret withdrew despite being chastened, then quickly recovered her best-unimpressed look.

Max recognised his description as being the anti-personnel room-clearing grenade MI5 had mentioned to him. It was one of the items that had been stolen and sold off. He took the opportunity to ask, "Who keeps the designs for such a secret weapon?" Margaret looked over, frowning at his interest.

Peter replied, "Well apart from myself and any other designer here who invented and built it, no one. We work on the designs here, on the computers, but the files are all saved on Lyndsey's library servers."

Max was happy that the procedures at least seemed to be recognised and used by everyone and found himself wondering if indeed Peter himself could be the one selling off his own designs. Otherwise, someone would have to have access to them in the basement library. The list of potential suspects seemed to grow despite the tight security here. His thoughts were drawn back into the room by Margaret.

"There's no way anyone can access the library, didn't Lyndsey cover that when you met her yesterday?" The comment was either supportive of what Peter said, or maybe a little defensive, Max wasn't sure which. Margaret then asked Peter, "Are you able to tell Max here what you're working on at the moment?"

Peter looked excited. "Sir John says I can. I must stress absolute confidentiality, please. Only the board know about this and we're a few months off launching it properly. I've only just finished updating the designs so this is hot off the press." He waited to get a nod of agreement from both Max and Margaret, then started walking over towards a large object underneath a black cloth. "This really will change things," as he slowly pulled the cloth away and announced the name of the trophy kit beneath. "The Omega sixty-five-hundred!"

Max and Margaret stared at an oversized sniper rifle on top of a large tripod and the other four staff also looked over as their creation was being revealed to the visitors, wanting to take in their astonished looks. The extended length barrel was immediately apparent, being far longer than anything Max had ever seen of a rifle. He wasn't a gun expert but from what little he'd seen during the brief training on weapons in the Commando's and at MI5, he noticed the size of the barrel's diameter also appeared unusually large. Sitting prominently above the rifle was a big telescopic sight. The beautifully crafted matt black, long, sleek design combined with its huge size looked out of place in the workshop, like someone had got the measurements wrong and the whole gun was double the size it should have been.

Next to the gun stood another large tripod with what looked like a huge black twin-projector on top. The rear panel included a rubber eyepiece similar to a viewfinder or large binoculars and a cluster of lights, knobs and digital displays encircled the base. On the front, there were different large and small clear glass lenses. Finally. on the counter beside the two tripod devices, sat a medium-sized black metal closed case.

Peter Kendrick stood back with the others to admire his creation and proudly announced, "Imagine being able to shoot a target that was as far away from you as the horizon!"

From the statement Peter had uttered, they both took in the weapon in front of them and the possibilities of it. Max had some idea of a sniper's maximum range and had seen videos on YouTube claiming a supposed two-mile sniper shot record. "How far is the horizon then?" he asked.

Peter eagerly replied. "On a clear day a six-foot-tall person with good eyesight and an unobstructed view line can see about three miles before the earth's horizon curvature drops away. Of course, they can only see something accurately with the aid of a high magnification scope, but three miles is the line of available sight."

Margaret chipped in. "So this thing can shoot three miles?"

"Well, actually we reckon it can accurately shoot just over four miles, which is about sixty-five-hundred metres away. Hence the name, Omega 6500." Peter was nodding to himself with satisfaction. "Remember the sniper only has to elevate his firing position say twenty feet higher, in a building or on a hillside, and their line of sight to the horizon increases to around five miles."

"What do the Omega letters stand for then," asked Max. "Everything around here seems to have an acronym?"

His continued interest yet again visibly annoyed Margaret who grumpily shifted on her feet. Peter though was revelling in Max's interest.

"Oh, the letters of the word Omega don't stand for anything, it's the meaning of the Greek word Omega that seemed so fitting for this weapon."

"What's that then?"

"Omega means the extreme or final part, the end of something," said Peter. Margaret winced in puzzlement. "I named it that because whatever this thing shoots at, is finished."

"That's a bit dark isn't it?" said Margaret, then after thinking about it, "though I guess that's what guns do," shrugging to herself.

"But how can you ensure any accuracy over such a long distance? I thought snipers had lots of things to take into account for a bullet travelling so far?" said Max, hoping he hadn't given away too much with his distant military knowledge.

Peter's eyes lit up with the invitation to explain more detail about his unique weapon. "You're right Max. Snipers have to take into account many factors that will affect their shot and the bullet's path, such as altitude, wind speed, wind direction, even temperature and humidity. For a two-mile shot that bullet will take about six seconds to reach its target. That's a long time for it to get bounced around by the wind, air pressures and the bullet's shape aerodynamics. The maths and physics play a big part in setting everything up and that's before you need a top marksman aiming and firing the gun."

Peter walked over to the large rifle. "Firstly you need the projectile to be fired from a big enough rifle to allow the shell charge to have sufficient explosive power to get it to travel the distance. For this, that requires a ninety-calibre bullet and barrel. It's huge, that's almost twenty-three millimetres, point nine of an inch wide. It's unique. The discharge is so big we need this sturdy tripod to be fixed into whatever base is available so that no force is lost through the significant recoil this produces."

Peter then laid his hand carefully on the large scope on top of the gun. "Next you've got to have a scope powerful enough for the shooter to actually see with his own eyes what he's aiming at. Half the problem for snipers is that they end up targeting on a tiny dot in the distance, then once that bullet is off and away, there's nothing more they can do about it, but hope their aim along with all those calculations result in a lucky hit."

Max was fascinated. "So how does the Omega gun manage all those factors to ensure, as you say, the target is finished every time?"

Margaret had finally given up her bristling display and finally appeared to be interested in what Peter was telling them.

Peter was in a world of his own, taking in the questions without looking up from the device, infatuated with his own tour of this ultimate rifle. He moved over to the second tripod with the large lensed box sitting on top. "This is the brain of the system. In this device, you have everything you need to assess, measure, calculate and target the projectile. It incorporates a computer that will also take temperature, altitude and wind measurements. It also has a spotting scope similar to the one on the rifle, which will both have optional night vision optics and a laser range finder. This does all the thinking for you. It also has a laser targeting system." Peter looked up to see the reactions of his audience. Margaret looked clueless and Max was very intrigued.

"When you say laser targeting, that sounds like you're implying some kind of homing bullet. Surely not?" said Max.

"No, we can't yet get everything needed into a small shell to make it a homing bullet. Remember it's only travelling for a handful of seconds." Peter paused. "But what we can do is help the sniper's shot accuracy by adjusting the bullet's path minutely during the last couple of seconds of its flight towards the target. A fine-tuning of accuracy if you like." He pointed to the large box on the tripod. "As well as working everything out, this will allow the secondary sniper to aim the laser onto the target. Yes, this system needs two snipers. The riflescope is plugged into the brain box and laser targeting, which in turn is plugged into the final piece of this jigsaw, the projectile box."

Peter now patted the black case on the table, then opened it. "I say projectile because these are far more than a simple, dumb bullet which is just a piece of metal flying through the air. These are the Omega 'intelligent bullets'. I've not yet given them a name." He picked up one of the very large ninety calibre shells, almost an inch in diameter and about six inches long from tip to base.

It was the most extraordinary 'bullet' Max had ever seen, mainly due to its large size. The shell casing was clearly made of something stronger than brass and took up half the length of the whole thing. The actual bullet part had a tiny glass tip, a small dorsal fin and four small holes around the base of the projectile just above the casing. Max and Margaret looked completely flummoxed, much to Peter's delight.

Caressing it Peter explained. "The charge in the base of the casing shell will get the bullet the distance once this is fired from the rifle. Inside this, the tiny circuit board will be looking for the laser dot target through its minuscule lens on the tip of the bullet, connected by a hair wire down through the bullet core. As long as the sniper has fired the projectile with an accuracy of about five metres around the end target, the small stabilising jets have the few seconds they need to be fired by the system to tweak its accuracy right onto the target laser dot." Peter stood up straight puffing out his chest for a moment as if stretching.

Max and Margaret were speechless. To them, it was like listening to a mad professor dreaming about a weapon, in a fictitious movie. But this was real.

Peter continued. "Now I know you're thinking how on earth can a spinning bullet adjust itself in flight." Neither of them had yet thought that. Peter pointed back to the rifle barrel. "Most gun barrels have a rifled, spiral grooving down their length which spins the bullet to assist with its straight, longer flight. A bit like one of the American football quarterbacks throwing a long pass, with the ball spinning around its end to end axis. Well the Omega barrel, which is ninety centimetres long to give the bullet every chance of leaving the barrel as accurately as possible, has a smooth barrel bore."

He pointed to the projectile's fin. "The shell casing is loaded into the rifle here with this tiny fin slotting into a long groove slit down the length of the bottom of the barrel. So when the bullet leaves the gun it's not spinning, just for those vital few seconds. We want it flying flat with the fin on the underside. In that tiny time window of flight, the targeting system can fire any of the small charges which vent out of each of the four holes, each pointing at forty-five degrees to the rear, to minutely adjust the bullet's direction, but only by a few feet by the time it reaches the target. Like a final tweaking of accuracy given it's such a long shot for any human to make with certainty. Each flight adjustment porthole has a minute mixture of charge very similar to the solid fuel propellant rockets use, ammonium perchlorate with atomized aluminium powder, a catalyst, binder and curing agents. Each highly explosive charge sits in its own cavity within the projectile, about half the size of a pea, and packs a hell of a punch for the milliseconds it's required to make any small adjustment to its trajectory."

"That's quite incredible. Is there a battery in there?" asked Max.

Peter went back to the black case holding several of the impressive projectiles in a row, each embedded in a foam slot. There was a single empty slot for a shell casing to one side of the case surrounded in metal, not foam. "Each projectile is placed in this programming slot where it is readied for firing. It's activated, all the information is put into the circuit from the brain box, which is given a tiny electrical charge lasting long enough for it to be loaded into the rifle, fired and travel to its target. The transfer is done just like charging a mobile on a pad, through an electromagnetic field and data passing from induction to receiver coils."

Max was truly impressed and bubbling with excitement. Margaret looked pensive as if about to ask some questions, but then seemed to think better of it. They spent a while longer fussing over the devices Peter had shown them with Max taking up the slack from Margaret's apathy, by giving Peter and his team gushing praise and congratulations. The two of them eventually made their way back across to the main building and back up to the procurement office.

That evening Max got home and called Si Lawson at Thames House. Si was eager to hear how Max's first few days at Empire had been. "Well Max, anything to report yet?" he asked.

"Yup, been pretty busy and had a chance to gather my thoughts ready for you whilst driving home this evening. I've got quite a 'whodunnit' for you Si."

"Nice work Max, let's have it."

"Security at Empire is old fashioned but pretty tight in a strange way. Everything of value, designs, paperwork and soft files are kept in a single basement library, with restricted access by only a few people. Nothing gets saved around the site, it's all on their own servers in this records room, so anyone wanting weapons designs would have to access them from there. I can't see how else they'd be available," reported Max.

"Okay, that's good, limits the 'how it's being stolen' options doesn't it. What about any suspects Max?"

"Now that's a little more tricky Si, let me go through them. Got your pen and pad ready? Firstly we have the top designer himself, Peter Kendrick. He creates the designs so wouldn't need to nick them from the library, he's got everything in his head. But maybe some of his close team also understand the whole design projects they have there. Not sure."

"As you go through these people do you have any views yet on whether you think they could be our guilty thief?" asked Si.

"Honestly at this point, I don't suspect anyone more than the others. I'm just telling you who it could be, not who it might be." Max waited to get a grunt from Si then continued. "Then we've got Lyndsey Wyman who's in charge of the records library. There's a security guard, CCTV and only one door entrance. She's the only one with access to the servers. Apart from that, her sealed passwords are held, but not opened, by the head of security and Sir John's PA. That's kind of it for now."

"What about your Chief Procurement Officer there, how are you getting on with her?"

"Margaret Fallon," Max clarified for Si's note-taking. "She's fine apart from being constantly moody, grumpy and hates me being there. Otherwise, she doesn't have anything to do with new designs, nor have any access to them at all that I can see."

"Still sounds like a lot of people with potential access to these designs. I'll get Vince and the team to start checking backgrounds, assets, bank accounts, political persuasions, all the usual stuff we can do easily, just to see if anything obvious stands out as reasons any of them might want to steal plans."

"Money's a good enough reason for any of them I'd say," said Max. "I'd do it myself for thirty-four million," he laughed.

"That's not funny Max, don't joke around like that. Can't have you going rogue on me thank you," said Si, not seeing the funny side of Max's remark. "I'll also have a chat with the techy guys about ideas to potentially monitor their servers, logins and library access. Anything that might help show us the way to who's doing this. Anything else?"

"Re the servers, I think she said they were on a closed network or something, so not sure the guys can just hack into it I'm afraid," said Max. "There is one last thing, good for us as long as we're not too late. Some bait, for us to catch the fish with."

"What do you mean?"

Max continued with some excitement as he realised the game was on. "They are just finishing another new design. It's incredible. Peter Kendrick calls it the Omega 6500. Might just be what our thief will want to sell next," said Max proudly.

"What in God's name is an Omega 6500?" asked Si, his interest spiked.

"I can't remember all the technical details, it was a lot to take in, but basically it's a long-range sniper rifle system, with laser targeting, high-velocity shells and projectiles with the ability to make tiny adjustments to their path, ensuring the lasered target is hit."

"What do you mean by long-range? We already have sniper rifles that can do two miles, not highly accurate though," asked Si.

"How about four miles," proclaimed Max. "That's sixty-five hundred metres, hence the name."

Si was flabbergasted. "Four miles! That's amazing. With a self-adjusting targeting system. Oh my God, as long as we're not too late, that'll be worth a fortune on the Dark Web market. We need to move fast. Can you pop in say tomorrow evening after work, we'll have an update for you by then?"

"Sure thing."

"Max, well done, it sounds like we have ourselves a lot to be getting on with. If we get to find the thief we just might have a chance of getting to the arms broker and eventually the end buyer, if we can follow the path right through." Si was jubilant.

"What path?" asked Max.

Si nodded to himself as he said to Max, "We'll need to follow the Omega trail!"

8

Max spent the following day fussing around the procurement department, working on some draft slides he could potentially present in a week or so regarding the risks and improvements he'd likely recommend. He popped in to see Margaret to ask if he could interview some of the procurement team, knowing they would provide valuable insights into the many things her department should be doing but weren't. She begrudgingly agreed. Max had already seen a lot of areas for improvement, it was easy pickings when the person leading the procurement function had no real previous experience of managing and improving the vital area of supplier and cost control.

Whilst Max worked on his slides and even when he was sitting in front of procurement staff, listening to them desperately trying to impress him in the hope that he might offer them some job that would get them away from their boss, his mind was straying. Having read out the list of potential suspects to Si the night before, Max was finding that he couldn't help himself start to speculate as to who might be stealing and selling their precious designs. He kept coming back to the basement library and Lyndsey being the keyholder to all the company's secrets, 'surely she was involved somehow', he thought to himself. But a sweet old administration lady didn't strike him as being a corporate IP thief selling their wares on the Dark Web for tens of millions.

Max couldn't wait to leave a little earlier as he was keen to get home and then travel in to see Si Lawson at Thames House. When he left at 5:15 PM he predicted that Margaret wouldn't be able to stop herself making some snide comment as he left. He popped his head around her door to say that he needed to be off and was greeted with a curt, "Half-day?" He was getting to know her very quickly.

Max drove back up the M23, round the M25 past the Reigate and Leatherhead junctions and then up the A3 to his home on Clapham common. As he sat on the short underground journey he wondered to himself what Si and his team might come up with. They always seemed pretty efficient at sorting things out when they were able to. If he didn't have confidence in them supporting him as they did, he would never even consider being involved with what was effectively spying for MI5.

Vince led Max up to the Cyber team open office area and into the meeting room where Si was waiting, pleased to see him. Josh was also sitting at the table with a small box in front of him. Max took fifteen minutes to give them a rundown of everything he'd done, each of the visits he'd made around the Empire Arms site and then his views and observations on all of the people he'd met. They sat quietly listening, asking a few questions in particular about some of the individuals, while Vince diligently made notes on anything Max said that they hadn't already thought of. When Max had finished, Si handed over to Vince who referred to the documents and summaries he had in front of him and quickly went through each of the individuals that Max had mentioned to Si.

"At this stage Max we've done all the usual deep background checks on the names you gave us," said Vince. "Schools, parents, siblings, career history, any criminal record, their social media accounts, their bank accounts and investments, any creditors or debtors, you know Max."

"Anything funny come up?" asked Max.

"Unfortunately not, it's all a bit dull, no large sums of money being deposited in their bank accounts and no apparent motives for any of them to risk so much by stealing Empire's designs." Vince looked apologetic as Max frowned.

Si chipped in. "Come on guys, that's fine, we didn't expect it to be that easy finding a big red flag waving us to the guilty party did we. Max, we've been discussing it here today and have an idea. Thanks to your meeting with Peter Kendrick in the Apollo building and this brand new incredible Omega 6500 weapon you got to see.

As you said this could present the thief's next target to steal the designs for and sell. But we're going to have to move fast on this one."

Max nodded in agreement. "Yeah, Peter mentioned to me that the Empire board of directors knew about the project, but that he'd only just updated his files with the latest design details. So what are you suggesting? I'm guessing it's going to be down to me is it?"

Si smiled at Max sympathetically. "I'm afraid so Max, you're the one with access at the Empire site. I'm sure you've come to the same conclusion as we did. That basement room where all the designs are kept by this Lyndsey Wyman, is the key to us perhaps finding out what's happening."

Si paused and looked towards Vince allowing him to continue. "We need you Max to place a tiny camera somewhere in the library room that has a clear view of the computer that has access to the server holding all the soft copy design files." Vince waited for Max's reaction.

Max shifted a little in his chair but wasn't surprised. "Having thought about it today I kind of came to the same conclusion that something like this was probably our best option. Just another thought, is there some way I can get you remote access to Lyndsey's library network computer, the one that is not connected to the Internet?"

Josh replied. "Great idea Max, we'd considered that, but it's too risky. We'd have to either hardwire connect the server PC with the other PC on the desk that has Internet, or plug in a conspicuous USB transmitter dongle. Given both of her computers are on the desk it's not worth the risk of her or someone else seeing our cables or kit right in front of them." Josh opened the small box on the table.

"So what have you got for me?" asked Max.

Josh proudly held up a small black plastic cube about the size of a marble, a tiny clear lens was visible on one side.

"A spy camera," said Max, "I've seen these."

"Not one like this you won't have," Josh asserted. "These aren't available in the back of a magazine or from your online spy equipment shop." Max was intrigued. "The techie guys in the lab put this together for us this afternoon. This little spycam has a camera, individual infrared pickup scanner and circuit board, its own independent power supply with a tiny battery and also a micro Sim card."

"That's an awful lot of stuff in a tiny little box," said Max. "Can you now translate all that so I can understand what it does?"

"Sure. The infrared motion sensor will distinguish how many people are in the room, just like your mobile phone camera can pick out each face in a photo. Given that Lyndsey will almost always be in there, we might need to know when there's a second person in there with her. The camera will send everything to a mobile device using the Sim card it has, which can record it all anyway. That'll be your mobile Max."

"Why mine?"

"You're in the building so if we catch anyone looking like they're downloading the designs off that server-connected PC, then we need someone to either get in there as they do it, or at the very least see them leave the basement through the reception area. You can call us anyway if something happens."

"We'll have a field operative sitting in his car round the corner from Empire all day until you leave, Monday to Friday, so they can be with you in minutes if needed," assured Si.

"How long will its battery last for?"

Josh pondered, "Maybe a week, but we can simply give you another fully charged spycam to swap out after say five days."

"How do I test it's got the right view of the desk area?" questioned Max.

"Unless you're standing there with your mobile phone view open, you'll just have to use your best judgement eye line, it has quite a wide-angle lens so should be simple."

"You're all making it sound easy, but somehow I've got to get the damn camera in there in the first place."

Si put his hand on Max's shoulder, "You're a charming, clever chap, you'll think of something. Just do it tomorrow though, we need to find out who's doing this."

Max frowned and thought 'here we go again, always starts off easy then gets harder and harder'.

Josh asked Max, "Can I just have your mobile for five minutes, Max, I just need to sync them together so the spycam sends you the motion detector notifications and can receive the camera picture feed when you want to view it. It'll record what the camera sees whenever there's someone in the room anyway and as you won't have the time to view it during your office hours, I suggest you just send us the video file each evening and we'll get the guys here to view it overnight."

Max dutifully handed over his phone and ten minutes later was leaving Thames House clutching the small box with the precious spycam inside. He had a restless night at home trying to figure out a way of getting back into Lyndsey's basement and concluded it couldn't be done without her being there. He couldn't try to sneak in when she went off to the loo, that was ridiculous and too risky sneaking in anywhere. No, he needed a reason to go back to see her. An idea came to him. He would hunt through some of his old photos in the morning before he went into work.

The following day Max told Margaret he would be meeting some stakeholders around the business to get their views on procurement risks, much to Margaret's disdain as to why it mattered what other department's thought of procurement. The real reason was that Max wanted to be away from the procurement office today and passing through reception as much as possible. Ideally, he wanted to bump into Lyndsey coming in or out of her basement. He had arranged about six separate meetings and lingered as much as he dared in the atrium without looking suspicious, by talking to the receptionist, or the security guard. The day passed by and he was starting to wonder if he should just pick up the phone and ask to revisit the basement to have another look. That didn't feel feasible though.

By four o'clock Max only had a couple more opportunities to pass through reception and he was slowly making his way up the stairs, when he saw the basement door open and out came Lyndsey. He felt as though he'd won the lottery having waited all day to see her. She walked over to the canteen and bought a chocolate bar to have with her tea back in her office. Max quickly came back down the stairs and timed it perfectly to meet her as she walked back across reception towards her door. The security guard was near the main entrance talking to a visitor.

"Hi Lyndsey, fancy bumping into you again, I was hoping I might see you again," said Max enthusiastically.

Lyndsey was surprised to see Max. "See me again, what on earth for," she asked.

Max feigned embarrassment. "Well, it's a bit daft really, not about work at all." He hoped that by letting his professional demeanour slip, he would start to win her over. "You see I'm a bit of a cat lover myself, and I wondered if you'd had a few minutes to tell me about yours?"

Lyndsey's face lit up with joy. Her cats were the one subject she always had time for. "What a lovely idea Max, why don't you come and have a chat, I was about to have tea, would you like some?"

"I'd love to," said Max, as they went over to the security door and she punched in the four numbers to open it.

They descended into the large basement and as they passed by the shelves and racks to get to the seating area, Max was frantically searching for a good vantage point to place the spycam. When he'd arrived at the office earlier he realised that there was nothing on the tiny device to stick it onto anything, so he's got a small blob of Blu Tack and put it on the base of the little box ready. He spotted a potential location on the corner of a top shelf overlooking the desks, which conveniently had a lot of boxes and clumps of cables sitting on it, looking messy and dusty.

Lyndsey made them both a cup of tea and offered him chocolate as Max patiently sat with her asking all about each of her six cates, one by one, trying to think of some distraction to get her to look away long enough for him to place the camera. Time was running out and finally having told him every detail and story about her precious pets, she asked him what cats he had. He explained he was currently looking for a couple of British Blues, but pulled out his phone and proudly flicked through some pictures of his previous family cats, the ones he'd found the night before. Lyndsey adored them. However, the window of opportunity for Max was starting to close as he felt the conversation dwindle. His mind raced to find some sort of excuse to stay longer and distract her, then remembered the fire escape.

"Oh yes, before I go Lyndsey, it's not a procurement risk as such, but I couldn't help noticing your blocked fire escape. Would you like me to move those boxes for you?" he offered.

"The fire escape? Oh yes. It's been so long since that door was ever opened, I'd almost forgotten about it. I suppose we should clear it. How nice of you to offer," gushed Lyndsey.

Max had spotted that the fire door was in a corner of the room and wasn't visible from the end of the shelving units by the seating area. He just needed Lyndsey to come over there and not stay seated in her comfy chair. He got up and made his way over to the corner where a couple of large, heavy boxes sat neglected in front of the escape door. He looked round but she hadn't followed.

"Do you want to come over," he coaxed, "and have a look at these two boxes, then you can decide where you'd like me to put them?"

"Ah yes, good idea," said Lyndsey, who at last got up and came over to the corner. She had a look and suggested putting the first one on one of the racks in the middle of the shelving aisles. This was perfect for Max as it was hidden from view from where she was standing. He grabbed the box and went over to load it into the shelf she suggested. Turning round to see if he could see her confirmed that they were out of each other's sight. Max quickly grabbed the small camera out of his pocket and firmly placed it on the top shelf corner amongst the wires, aiming it to the desks as he squashed it down into the sticky Blu Tack. He hastily returned to Lyndsey who was waiting to instruct him on the second box, which he placed as she wanted. She thanked him as he left and returned to his office, where Margaret gave him a funny look.

"All okay Margaret?" he asked, expecting yet more grumbling about him seeing so many staff.

"What on earth have you been doing?" she asked.

Max missed a heartbeat, how could she know. "I'm not sure I understand?"

Margaret looked at his trousers. "You're covered in dust!"

Max's shoulders lowered in relief. "Oh that," as he brushed them clean, "It's nothing, just got roped into helping someone move something. Thanks for telling me," as he sat back down at his desk immediately looking busily into his laptop.

Fortunately, Margaret was equally happy not to continue the conversation as she called in one of the Buyers to then ask them why they hadn't got a better deal from a supplier. Max had time to settle down but couldn't wait to get home and see if the camera was working. He excused himself and went off to the men's toilets and settled himself in a cubicle, taking out his phone.

He opened up the app that Josh had installed and to his amazement, the small screen opened up with a view of the basement, good quality in colour, no sound. He could see Lyndsey to the side of the picture having another cup of tea it seemed, still in her chair and congratulated himself on having the desk with the computers more or less in the centre of the picture. At the bottom of the screen, a red recording light slowly flashed, next to a small outline picture of a head and shoulders, denoting that one person was in the room. Max smiled with satisfaction at his prowess to place the camera and the impressive technology of the little device, which was set up to send a single vibrate alert to his phone whenever the room became empty and movement or someone entering the space again was detected.

That evening he sent the video file across to Vince at MI5 to look through proving the spycam was in place and working, and also called Si Lawson to confirm that the camera was placed. They just had to wait now and hope they weren't too late.

The following day was Friday and as Max was parking his car in the Empire car park, his mobile vibrated once as it sat in its dash holder, like getting a nibble on a fishing line. Max eagerly grabbed the phone and opened the camera app in time to see Lyndsey arriving in her basement office for the day, with her coat on and dumping her bags onto the couch. He laughed out loud inside his car thinking again how amazing the little camera was, dutifully alerting him to someone coming into the space after a period of emptiness. He was going to find it hard to concentrate on work today with the temptation of wanting to watch the goings-on down in the basement. Max sent a short text to Si Lawson saying simply 'camera feed working well'.

Max busied himself continuing to draft out a report which he'd soon present to Sir john and perhaps some of the other directors. He had to keep up the pretence of actually being a risk consultant, to continue his cover, as he didn't know how long it might take to catch the thief if indeed they weren't too late or just barking up the wrong tree focusing everything on monitoring the basement.

He had several discussions with Margaret whose irritability had been replaced that day with a more contemplative demeanour. She seemed to be preoccupied with some other matter as she was forgetting to be her usual rude self. At one point he'd popped in, bracing himself somewhat, to begin gently taking her through some of his likely recommendations. He expected these to be taken as criticisms and receive an earful of chastisement, but instead, she listened and merely dismissed him with, "It all seems fairly reasonable, I guess you must report it as you see it." Coming from any normal person that would be a rude send-off, but Max felt quite relieved that was all she could muster, perhaps she was starting to see that his help would improve her team's profile and most importantly benefit her. Or maybe she had something more serious on her mind.

Max had never been one to work long hours for the sake of it or just to be seen to be looking as though you're busy. When he ran his own procurement departments he expected people to do their best job and achieve the goals they were set. He also knew that some people could get through double the work in half a day, that others could take all day to do. When he left the office himself at say 5:30 PM and there were still members of his team looking as though they felt they shouldn't leave until the boss had gone, he'd walk through the office telling everyone that unless they had something urgent, it was time to go home. However, after Margaret's comment a couple of days earlier about having a half-day, he was annoyed at himself for now thinking he would stay here this Friday evening until Margaret herself left.

One by one the rest of the procurement staff packed up and left for the weekend, soon leaving just Max and Margaret. Margaret kept looking up at Max to check if he looked as though he was leaving and to Max's surprise, finally came out of her office and said to him, "I've just got a final errand before I go, it's been a long week for you Max, why don't you head off now and I'll see you on Monday." She continued past him and left the procurement office. Max could see that she hadn't left for the day as her computer was still on in her office.

He sat there for a moment wondering whether to pack up, it had certainly been a long week for him and although it was only twenty past five, it seemed that most people left on a Friday around four-thirty. Max had always been happy to put in whatever time was necessary to get his jobs done, but he also looked forward every day to that point where he could just get into his car, away from everything and everyone, and just enjoy the simple pleasure of going back to the privacy and safety of his own home. There was nothing more he could do this week, so he closed down his laptop, gathered up his paperwork and made his way out of the procurement office.

At that moment his mobile phone vibrated once in his jacket pocket, sending an instant bolt of excitement through him. He quickly put his bag down on the floor and grabbed the phone instantaneously opening up the camera app. As the picture on the screen revealed itself his heart jumped into his mouth as he could see two people in the picture. As soon as the second person had walked into the room where Lyndsey had been, the alert had been pinged to Max's phone and at the bottom of his screen, there were now two small head-and-shoulder icons.

Max moved the phone screen closer to his eyes whereupon he could see Lyndsey sitting at her desk having swivelled her chair around to talk to the visitor. It almost looked like she was looking straight into the camera and Max's heart raced as he thought she might notice the small black object on the corner of the shelving. Lyndsey was talking to the visitor crossly and didn't look happy. Although the visitor had their back to the camera, the realisation of who the person was quickly descended on Max. The colour of the suit and the short-cropped brown hair matched someone he was now very familiar with. It was Margaret Fallon.

'What the hell is she doing down in the basement', thought Max, 'she doesn't have anything to do with Lyndsey or the library'. Conscious that he was still stood in the doorway of the procurement office, Max looked up to make sure no one else was watching him and decided to move back into the privacy of the empty department, closing the door behind him. Perching on the edge of a desk he stared intently at the screen, checking that the slowly flashing red light at the bottom was recording everything.

He could see the two women engaged in discussion, or was it an argument, as both of them were gesticulating at one another. To Max's astonishment, Lyndsey got up from her chair at the desk and moved aside to allow Margaret to sit in her place. She hovered for a moment until Margaret gently pushed her back and waved her away from the desk area, pointing for her to move further away. Lyndsey awkwardly and angrily moved to the side and then out of the camera view.

Max couldn't believe what he was watching and found himself wishing for Margaret not to touch the keyboard and if she did, please not the confidential computer on the right-hand side which had access to the closed network server files. Margaret was not a nice person and had made no effort to welcome him at Empire, but he didn't want her to be the person stealing their top-secret designs and selling them on.

Once Margaret seemed satisfied that Lyndsey had moved far enough down the room away from her, she turned to face the two computers. She pulled her chair in towards the computer on the left and for a moment Max was able to give her the benefit of the doubt. But as she settled herself into the chair Margaret then turned slightly to the right and began slowly and deliberately typing on the keyboard of the PC to the right.

It was at that point Max knew they'd caught their thief. "Oh my God, I can't believe it," Max said to himself out loud. He continued to concentrate intently on the picture, as Margaret summoned onto her screen what looked like to Max, a list of folders and files. She seemed to know what she was looking for and quickly took a small USB memory stick out of her pocket and plugged it into the desktop computer. Once the file she was looking for was saved onto the stick, she then closed the window and pulled it out, returning it to her pocket.

Max could see Margaret saying something to Lyndsey who was still out of view, she appeared to be talking in a threatening manner. Lyndsey came back into view as Margaret brushed past her and left, leaving a dejected-looking woman standing there helplessly. But as she awkwardly moved around Lyndsey, Margaret's shoulder knocked into the corner of the shelving unit in the middle of the room, dislodging the small entanglement of wires surrounding the spycam.

In Max's haste to press the camera onto the top of the dust-covered shelf, the Blue Tac hadn't been able to get a strong enough grip on the metal through the fine layer of dust. The wires and the spycam fell down a crack between the shelf units. The view on Max's screen changed from the office and desk area, to most of the picture being taken up by a view of the floor looking across the main aisle leading from the entrance to the office. Max cursed, but no matter, everything had been recorded on video. Moments later the phone in Max's hands vibrated once and the two head-and-shoulder icons changed to just one as Margaret had left the room. The spycam's infrared motion sensor was still functioning.

This suddenly jolted Max into the realisation that Margaret was probably on her way back up to the procurement office. For a moment, indecision gripped him and he couldn't make up his mind whether to pretend to be leaving, or still working at his desk.

Margaret made her way up the staircase through an almost empty office this late on a Friday and as she came into her department's area, was surprised, and a little annoyed, to see Max still working studiously at his desk.

"Crikey Max, you still here?" she said quietly and dismissively.

"Fraid so, I've just got a couple of things to finish, then I'm off," said Max without looking up. He didn't want to look at her for fear of betraying his incredulity towards her.

Moments before she came up the stairs Max had decided it was better for him to stay behind and to be with Margaret. As the saying goes, keep your friends close and your enemies closer. He was also unsure as to what to do next. Should he restrain Margaret and take the incriminating memory stick from her? Should he call security or call Si Lawson, or the police. His brief training at MI5 prevailed and he decided that the recording of her at Lyndsey's desk was not in itself enough to prosecute her, they now needed to catch her with witnesses holding the stick, or better still trying to sell it on to the broker.

Max figured it was very unlikely that Margaret would be looking to sell the plans on to this broker this evening, but felt that the least he could do was try to keep her here in the office for as long as possible, running down the evening's clock. He would stay here pretending to work until Margaret left first and was counting on her absurd competitiveness to wait for him to leave.

The clock slowly ticked on and the farcical stand-off between the two of them both continuing to work, went on and on. Margaret didn't come out and try to persuade him to go, nor did she pack up and leave herself. She'd made her mind up to leave after

Max had gone. For a ridiculous two more hours they both sat there finding things to do or just tidying up files, and even playing the age-old Solitaire card game on their computers. By eight-fifteen Max felt he had used up enough of the evening to be fairly certain that Margaret wasn't going to do anything with her memory stick that night, so he stood up to leave. He could detect the relief on Margaret's face as she subtly observed him packing up and started to close down her computer.

"Well that's me done, have a good weekend Margaret, see you Monday," said Max as he left.

Margaret wearily raised her hand in a farewell gesture. "Bye."

She waited briefly and left the office moments later, satisfied she had won the stand-off and relieved to be able to just get home and relax. Nervous exhaustion had caught up with her and she couldn't wait to have a quick snack and get to bed.

Max waited until he had driven clear of the Empire site to then eagerly call Si Lawson having just sent him the latest and revealing camera video file.

"Have you seen it Si? I've just sent you the file. Oh my God, we've got her. It's all there on film. We've done it," said Max excitedly.

"I got the file a few seconds ago Max, haven't had time to view it yet. What's happened?" Si was cautious but shared Max's enthusiasm. "You said *her*."

"About four-thirty Margaret Fallon, the CPO I'm working with in procurement, left our office and went down to the library basement. It's her Si. Margaret Fallon. She told Lyndsey to step aside while she copied a file onto a stick. You'll see it on the recording." Max was triumphant.

"It's almost nine o'clock Max, how come it's taken you so long to send me the file and call me? We might have to move quickly."

"I wasn't sure what to do next Si so I've been sitting there in the office all bloody evening keeping her there so she didn't have time to get home and do anything with the stick tonight," explained Max.

"Good thinking, you've done well. I can't believe we managed to get the camera in place just in time to catch this. Brilliant job Max. Let me call off now and view the video, then speak to the team here. We're going to have to move on this pretty quickly so stay by your phone and I'll call you back this evening." Si rang off, leaving Max in the silent vacuum of his car journey back home, bristling with anxious excitement.

Margaret Fallon walked through the door of her home in Lingfield and was thankful the day was over. She didn't like what she'd done and the way she'd used and threatened Lyndsey to get what she needed, but it would be worth it. She poured herself a fruit juice and grabbed a banana out of the fruit bowl and made her way upstairs, relishing the embrace of her bed. It was getting late, thanks to Max Sargent hanging around in the office for so long. She would get the file she now had sent off to the broker in the morning.

At ten-twenty Max's phone rang, it was Si Lawson at MI5.

"Max, we've all seen the video. Great job placing it in there. Thought you might like to be involved tonight, seeing as you're part of the team and everything. Hope you're not planning on a good night's sleep?"

"Why, what's happening tonight?" asked Max.

"Strictly speaking it will be tomorrow morning, at six AM. Meet us at the Star Inn pub car park in Church Road Lingfield. Don't be late, don't be too early, make sure you're there just before six. It's opposite Camden Road where Margaret Fallon lives. We've decided we have to pay her a visit before she wakes up. We can't have her doing anything with that stick in the morning. You can come along and observe." Si was clinical with his instructions.

"What do you mean, pay her a visit?" Max asked naïvely.

"Get a few hours' sleep, Max, big day tomorrow. We'll be doing a raid on Margaret's house!"

9

Max's alarm went off at four forty-five and he felt as though he'd only just put his head down to go to sleep. Five hours wasn't enough for any normal person. He had a light breakfast then jumped into his Golf GTI and made his way down to Lingfield, just North West of Gatwick airport on the opposite side of the M23. As he pulled into Church Road and approached the Star Inn, his car headlights illuminated a quiet but busy pub car park. There were a handful of normal cars, two police cars and an unmarked police van, from which the last of several heavily uniformed and helmeted police officers were emerging.

He pulled into the far end of the car park, watched by almost everyone there, and was grateful to pick out Si Lawson and his deputy Vince making their way over towards him. Max could see beyond the two men in the dawn light, the raid squad of policemen checking their equipment and casually talking to one another in hushed whispers. It seemed so bizarre, the sight of these dark blue silhouetted policemen with helmets on. One had a shield and another held a heavy-looking door ram, all going about their business in the middle of this deserted, quaint countryside village. Max then noticed two of the officers were armed, one of them had a Glock 17 fastened in a side holster and the other was protectively holding his Heckler and Koch MP5 automatic machine gun.

"Blimey Si, what are you guys expecting to find in her house? I thought she lived alone." Max was a little perturbed at the scale of the raid force preparing to enter the house of one middle-aged woman.

Si replied, "Do you know she will be alone? Do you know she won't have a firearm? You'd be surprised Max what people are capable of for a lot of money. This is serious stuff and for the protection of the officers, we have to be prepared for the worst. When they go through that door, they're never quite sure what's waiting to greet them on the other side. Not a nice feeling." Si had gone 'through the door' many times himself and come face-to-face with all sorts of situations and threatening hooligans. "Come over here and let me introduce you to some of the guys quickly, they've all been briefed and know the circumstances and what we are looking for inside."

"Do you need some kind of warrant to do this?" asked Max.

"Strictly speaking we don't, we can enter the premises to stop a crime in progress which is effectively what we are doing this morning. Don't worry Max, we are doing this all the time, we have access to Magistrates twenty-four-seven and got a search warrant at one AM this morning, just to be safe." Si was calm and reassuring as always.

He introduced Max to several of the senior police officers and got a knowing nod from the others. They'd all been briefed an hour before on how one of MI5's Associate Field Agent's had got the video recording they'd all seen, showing a major corporate thief stealing top-secret weapon designs from Empire Arms. The senior raid officer looked around his men to check that everyone seemed ready, then nodded for everyone to get into the van. Their target house was only three hundred yards down the road, but they needed to all arrive together by vehicle. The sight of six fully geared up police officers all walking down the street would be enough to frighten the living daylights out of anyone who happened to see them.

"Max, come with me and Vince in our car, stay close, it's our operation but we need to let the police get on and effect entry and lockdown." Si waived Max and Vince into his BMW.

The unmarked van had no side nor rear windows, hiding from view the ominous-looking police officers inside. It set off down the road, briefly pausing at a junction and then accelerated into the close before quietly but quickly coming to a stop opposite one of the end houses. Si followed close behind and pulled up his car as well.

Max had never seen six large policemen exit a van so quickly. Within seconds they were grouped around the front door waiting for the man tightly gripping the 'Enforcer' battering ram, a sixteen-kilogram steel tube with hinged handles capable of exerting three tons of force. With a single long swing, the officer brought the ram into the door where the two locks were positioned halfway up. There was a crack and splintering sound as the door slammed open bursting locks through brass retainers and the wooden door frame as if there was nothing there.

The second the door was open the enforcer quickly retreated allowing the first man to pass through holding up a shield, closely followed by the two armed officers both holding up their firearms. The final two policemen followed straight after. All five of them were in the house within a couple of seconds and quickly spanned out to their designated room areas. The lead officer with the shield downstairs and the first officer moving up the staircase, started shouting loudly and clearly as they moved. "Armed Police! Make yourself known, get down on the floor!"

Max waited just outside the front door with Si and Vince. He found the speed and ferocity of the raid squad's entry into the premises both impressive and frightening. It all happened so fast and so determinedly, he didn't have any time to think. If that was how he felt innocently watching, he imagined what it must be like if it's your house being raided so abruptly. His thoughts turned to Margaret Fallon.

Margaret had been fast asleep and when the impact of the enforcer smashing through her front door frame had shaken the house, the fright and adrenaline had instantly woken her up. Though the harsh and unbelievable reality of what was happening hadn't registered yet. After the crash of the door, she heard loud men's voices yelling 'Police!' and instructions being yelled throughout her house, along with footsteps and other men from various parts of her house shouting 'Clear!'.

She'd barely sat up in bed, terrified, when her bedroom door burst open to reveal a large man coming in wearing dark blue from tip to toe, a balaclava underneath a helmet revealing only the man's eyes and a gun thrust out in front of him at the ready.

Margaret Fallon screamed more loudly and longer than she'd ever screamed before.

As quickly as the brutal raid had started, with the entire house inspected by the officers, the commotion curtailed to calm. With the officers each entirely convinced there were no threats, dangers, traps or other people in the house, the tension and atmosphere could relax. Threatening burly policemen immediately became sympathetic professional law enforcement officers, mindful of the ordeal their target woman had just gone through. She would never forget that moment for the rest of her life and now they needed her composed and compliant.

The last officer to enter the house came into the bedroom and gently putting a hand on the man's raised handgun to lower it, removed her helmet and balaclava. It revealed to Margaret that she was a policewoman, a thoughtful concession from the lead officer. However momentarily reassured by this sight, Margaret then had to listen in horror as the policewoman spoke.

"Margaret Fallon, I am arresting you on suspicion of breaking the following;" Margaret looked horrified, the shock was too much and she started to cry. "The Official Secrets Act 1989, the Copyright and Patents Act 1988, the Proceeds of Crime Act 2002, the Data Protection Act 2018 and the theft of Empire Arms Limited intellectual property. Additional charges may be sought. You do not have to say anything. But it may harm your defence if you do not mention when questioned something which you later rely on in court. Anything you do say may be given in evidence."

Max could hear the rights being given to Margaret and her whimpering. He felt sorry for her. It was quite brutal for him to see the consequences of both her and his actions leading to such a condemning arrest in her bedroom. He then wondered if he should make himself scarce, but decided to wait for Si's lead on whether to stay or leave.

The officers were going through the house with a top-level search, collecting all computer equipment, separate hard drives, USB sticks, iPad, mobile phones new and old, anything with a hint of having a connection to the soft copy design theft, storage or transmission. They laid everything out in the living room.

The policewoman asked Margaret to get dressed and took her downstairs asking her, "We'd rather not turn your entire home upside down so would you be willing to verify that we have every item of your electronic devices, PC's and communication items here? I'd also ask you to point out the memory stick you used yesterday and any others that hold the Empire designs you took copies of?"

Margaret sorrowfully and slowly inspected each of the items on the floor in front of her, with four of the officers standing behind ready to take them to the van. Next to the large men in their raid fatigues, she looked small and pathetic, like a mouse before giants. Her head was in a blurry, surreal world and she had to strain to concentrate on the objects. She nodded at several of the items and pointed to one of the various USB sticks saying, "It's that one."

It was still only six-fifteen as Max turned round to see one of the marked police cars pulling up behind Si's BMW. Si added, "That's for them to take her to the large police station in Crawley for questioning. I'll be involved in that part." Max's heart sank again for the hapless Margaret, boy had they come down on her like a ton of bricks. Si could see Max was contemplative and added, "Just remember she was stealing this country's military designs and letting them be sold to God only knows who out there, terrorists, murderers, dictators."

"Okay, point taken," conceded Max.

He was then suddenly surprised to see the female police officer leading Margaret through the main door and out. Max was very aware of the black rubber covered steely handcuffs around Margaret's wrists, it was quite a shock. Si, Vince and Max all stood back to allow them to pass. Through her nightmarish blur, Margaret's eyes met Max's and for a moment she looked straight through him. Then she stopped. The policemen continued to pass her from behind carrying all the equipment out and began loading it into their van.

"Max?" said Margaret in disbelief. They all held their silence for a moment not quite sure what to say. "What are you doing here?" she asked simply shaking her head in disbelief, almost trustingly that this couldn't be so. Max was pretty good at knowing what to say for any occasion, but right now he simply couldn't find the right words.

Si interjected. "He's with us, Ma'am. MI5. I'm Si Lawson the lead investigating officer. I'll be speaking with you at the station in a short while."

Margaret looked at Si, then back to Max. "Is this some kind of joke! You're a procurement consultant for Christ's sake. Not MI5?" Margaret's bizarre world was getting nuttier by the moment.

Max just gave her an acknowledging smile but said nothing. The policewoman led Margaret over to the police car and put her into the rear, then got into the other side herself. The car drove off.

"Come on then guys," said Si, "let's follow them to the station."

Conversation in the BMW was limited during the short twenty-minute drive through Newchapel and Copthorne. Vince said, "Si, we should send one of the guys over to Empire to retrieve Fallon's office computer to check she hasn't copied it onto the hard drive there or sent it off somewhere last night, even if Max was there with her."

"Good point Vince, we can take care of that later, Max has an ID full access pass for Empire anyway, it'll save getting another warrant," said Si.

Crawley police station was one of the largest in the area with four floors above ground and a lesser-known floor below ground. The large buildings next to it were conveniently the Magistrates Court and the Coroner's Court. A seven-foot-high sturdy brick wall surrounded the entire police station complex, with the building's V shape shrouding the efficient yard to the rear, which could accommodate up to thirty-four cars, many of which at any one time or another would be marked police cars. Si's BMW pulled into one of the two entrances, each protected with strong steel barred gates.

Max and Vince followed Si into the building, who it seemed had been there before as he knew exactly where he was going. A couple of staff nodded to him as they passed by, word had got round that Si Lawson from MI5 was visiting to question a suspect after a raid. Max could see from the way officers were stepping aside for them in deference, that the uniformed police on the front line had huge respect for MI5 operatives. Maybe some of them aspired to one day join one of the two Military Intelligence Services.

Coming towards them down the corridor was a tall distinguished man, his shoulder epaulettes each sported a crown above crossed tipstave batons in a laurel wreath, denoting his high rank of Chief Constable. He was shaking his head in consternation whilst reading the document he was carrying and as he looked up and saw them coming towards him, he was immediately pleased to see them.

"Si Lawson, I don't believe it, you old rogue. I haven't seen you for, what three, four years. How is everything with Box 500." He heartily shook Si's hand and quickly shook hands with Vince and Max as well without yet being introduced. 'Box 500' was often how MI5 was referred to within the police force.

"Darcy, it's so good to see you too," said Si, equally pleased to see his old friend. Chief Constable Darcy Williams' mother had named her son after Jane Austen's Pride and Prejudice popular character Mr Fitzwilliam Darcy. He served with Si in the Metropolitan police.

Max and Vince politely waited for the two of them to briefly catch up until the Chief Constable went on his way with, "Anything you need Si, just ask."

The three of them made their way to one of the interrogation rooms, where Si gestured to Max and Vince to go into the next doorway which led into a small observation room behind one-way glass. He went into the room where Margaret Fallon was sat at a table looking thoroughly miserable, her life had just caved in on her.

The policewoman from the raid had dispensed with her fatigues, body armour and helmet, and was now standing smartly by the door. Si sat down and dealt with the usual precursors to an interview, asking if Margaret wanted a drink, going through more advisory warnings and dealing with the digital recording device and introductions. Margaret shook her head at the suggestion of getting legal representation, she just wanted to get on with it and had no intention of trying to get out of this. Once it was clear he was about to begin with his questions, Margaret spoke up first.

"Can I just say right upfront, I am so incredibly sorry about what I've done. I know it was wrong and really stupid. I guess I just got blinkered with the money being offered. I didn't realise it would all be such a big deal." Margaret did sound as though she was sorry as she gasped through her words.

"I'm afraid what you've done is a really big deal Margaret," asserted Si. "Surely you knew that stealing and selling intellectual property and designs from your company was illegal. Let me first ask about Lyndsey Wyman before we bring her in for questioning. What's her involvement?"

Margaret looked up. "Lyndsey? She's not involved at all. This has got nothing to do with her. I wouldn't want her to get into any trouble."

"But she let you access the designs on her library computer?" queried Si.

On the other side of the one-way glass, Max was watching closely and glanced at Vince, both wondering if sweet old Lyndsey the basement library and was part of this.

Margaret shook her head. "Lyndsey doesn't know anything about what I've done. Some time ago I saved her job. She was messing about with some numbers that would have been a stackable offence, but I managed to get her off. She used to be in procurement you see. Seemed to think that she should have had my job. All she cares about is seeing out her remaining time at Empire and getting her pension. She owed me, so I told her I needed access to the private server files for some old supplier contracts that were confidential.

She didn't even know what I was downloading."

Si nodded, Margaret was cooperating. Hopefully, this would be a clear open and shut case. "So you admit to downloading confidential designs that would compromise this country's Military?"

Margaret looked up and whilst she said, "Yes. It was wrong of me. But I don't think it was that big a deal," her face hinted some confusion.

Si gave a look of false puzzlement himself. "But I assume you were going to sell this design for many millions of pounds. Just like you did with the others you stole?"

Margaret now openly looked bewildered as if her interrogator had said something stupid. Si sitting opposite her, and Max and Vince behind the screen, all immediately knew something had changed. Margaret looked at the policewoman, back to Si, then turned to look at the mirrored glass knowing there was someone behind it watching, then back to Si again. All the while her face seemed to be asking 'what on earth are you talking about'. She spoke.

"Many millions of pounds? I wish. I'm getting eighty thousand pounds. Or would have." Margaret was wondering why Si thought she might have been getting so much money. "And what do you mean 'like the other designs I stole'? This is the first time I've ever done anything like this."

Max could feel the validity of the whole situation starting to crumble and pursed his lips waiting to hear the next couple of exchanges which sounded like they'd reveal what was going on here.

Si countered again. "The design you stole yesterday is worth significantly more than eighty thousand wouldn't you say?"

And then it all came crashing in.

"What, a lousy uniform design! You're kidding aren't you." Margaret was incredulous now and getting annoyed. She'd picked up that something wasn't gelling here and perhaps a misunderstanding had been made. What Si Lawson was saying didn't fit with what she'd done at all. Si, Max and Vince were all horrified, as the realisation that a mistake may have been made dawned on them with Margaret's last comment.

"What do you mean, *uniform* design," said Si with a lot of emphasis on the word in question.

"The design I copied yesterday," clarified Margaret. "That's what all this is about isn't it?"

"Go on."

"The new uniform design for the Gurkha regiment. It's top-secret, I know. One of the tabloid newspapers offered me eighty thousand if I'd leak them the designs. It's such an emotive topic their dress uniform. The current uniform's a bit dull. They're jazzing it up, but it'll cause a right hoo-ha. That's the only design I've ever copied at work. I'm really sorry."

Si looked at the mirrored glass and after some while, sighed. He couldn't see them, but Max and Vince were both frowning back into the interrogation room.

"So you haven't copied any other designs?"

"No. Like what?"

"Like the Kevlar-carbon helmet? Or the room grenade?" Si paused. "Or the Omega rifle system?"

Margaret blew up. It had been a long morning and it was only seven forty. The raid, her arrest, the charges, the journey in a police car, the interrogation. And these idiots had got it wrong? She wouldn't have minded being accused of something she'd done, but not all this other nonsense.

"Hell and damnation," she shouted. "I don't know anything about those things, other than hearing about that sniper gun thing this week when I visited Apollo with Max. You're bloody MI5 chap. God. I'd never copy, or steal, or sell designs for that kind of stuff. Wouldn't know how to. That would be criminal. It sounds like you're mistaking me for someone else?" Margaret stood there leaning on the table with both hands staring at Si. After a few moments, she gathered herself and realising the outburst wasn't a great idea, awkwardly sat down and asked for a cup of water.

Si stood up. "We appreciate your continued cooperation Ms Fallon. I'm going to handover to my deputy Vince Williams, he'll continue taking your statement. I think it would now be prudent for you to have legal representation which you can nominate, or the court can appoint for you. Just so you know, we'll be detaining you while we make further enquiries."

Si left the room with Margaret brooding at the table and went next door into the observation room. "Vince, all yours, find out everything you can about what she has done, the usual, we'll still charge her for the uniform design theft." Looking at Max, "but it seems we're back to square one with our weapons design thief. Bit of a mess now we've arrested Fallon. I'll have to have a chat later with Sir John and think how we deal with it Monday when people go back to work at Empire. We'll have to hold her now until we're clearer about what to do. We don't want to break cover and scare off the person we're still looking for by announcing Fallon's been caught by MI5. Come on Max, you and I will go to Empire now anyway and retrieve her PC, that'll all need checking as well."

Si and Max left the room and as they walked down the corridor Si popped his head round the door of the Chief Constable and explained what they were doing and could they borrow one of his uniformed men to take them to Empire just up the road. It was standard procedure and courtesy to have a uniformed officer with them from the jurisdiction they were operating in. Darcy willingly agreed and made a quick call to Sergeant Wilson in another part of the building, asking him to meet them out back and drive them there in a squad car.

Empire was only five miles away so the trip would only take fifteen minutes. In the car, Williams asked Si, "So what are we doing at Empire Sir?"

"It's a straightforward collection of computer evidence Sergeant, appreciate you coming along with us. We've apprehended someone stealing corporate information and just need to pick up their PC. That's all."

10

As they approached the Empire entrance gates Max asked, "Shall I use my ID or…"

Si cut in. "I'll get out with you Max, given we're turning up in a police car they'll probably wonder what's going on."

Max was amused that the large, tough security guard looked quite worried as the marked car pulled up alongside him and both he and Si got out. Si chose not to show his MI5 card as he knew the car and uniformed officer driving would be sufficient to get them in. "Police. I'm accompanying one of your employees," Max held up his pass, "just to collect something that we need for a case we're looking into. Trust that's okay, can you let us through please."

It wasn't a request and the security guard was thankful it had nothing to do with him and quickly opened up the gates without saying a word or asking for their names, which he kicked himself for once back inside his hut. He could get them when they left he thought.

As they pulled away from the entrance towards the large office building ahead of them, Max felt his phone vibrate once in his pocket. He pulled it out assuming it was a text, but realised as he brought the phone up to view he'd not set the vibrate for texts. He looked at the screen to see the spycam app flashing, signifying an alert.

Si turned round, "Everything okay Max?"

"Not sure," replied Max. "Bit strange. It's eight-fifteen on a Saturday," he opened the app, "and I've just got a movement alert from the spycam in the basement!"

"Well let's have a look then," said Si urgently.

Max passed the phone over shrugging. "Sorry, nothing to see. The camera got knocked off its perch last night when Margaret left the room."

Si looked at the screen which consisted mainly of a view of the floor.

"Mouse, spider maybe?" suggested Max. Then they both looked at one another. "Bloody hell," cried out Max, "could someone else be in there!"

"Sergeant drop us at the main entrance immediately! No sirens," instructed Si knowing how much police officers loved to put on the lights and siren at any opportunity.

As they drove alongside the car park they could see a surprising number of cars for early morning on a weekend. But that was quite normal with security guards, cleaning staff, deliveries and employees keen to crack on with a project or just get through an overload of work needing to be ready for Monday. Even Sir John's Bentley sat at the back of the car park area sign-posted 'Management', but with no chauffeur in sight, likely getting breakfast or a coffee inside.

They pulled up opposite the main entrance, Si and Max ran up the steps to the doors which, with no receptionist, were being manually opened by the guard in the atrium. When he saw the police car outside and two men running towards him he hastened to the doors and opened them without question.

Max then calmly said to the guard, "We're on police business. Has anyone just gone into the basement library?"

The guard still looked shocked at them both, then pulled himself together. "Er, not sure. I doubt it. It's the weekend, Lyndsey won't be in 'til Monday." Then added, "I've just got back from the loo." Max and Si looked at one another.

"I need you to punch in the code to the library basement right now. No questions," demanded Max, holding up his Empire ID badge again as if he needed to convince the man.

The man hit the four numbers hastily and opened the door to let them through. Max went first and raised his finger to his lips at Si, who didn't need to be told to go in quietly. They crept down the stairs. Max looked up at the small entrance wall camera, its operation light was off. At the bottom of the stairs, they had a view down one of the aisles between the shelving racks and could see Lyndsey's 'comfy' area, but not yet the desks. At the risk of both of them likely to make a noise, Max held his hand up for Si to wait there, while he crept along the aisle. They could hear the faint click of a computer mouse being used. Max's heart started pounding.

He knew another step would start to bring the desk area into view and as he continued forward now saw a figure sitting at the computer to the right. The private server access PC. His eyes widened in utter disbelief in recognising the person sat with their back to him, still unaware of his presence.

"Sir John?" whispered Max, more to himself than to the man himself.

Sir John jumped in his chair and swivelled around immediately, his hand moved to his chest at the shock of being disturbed.

"What the hell are you doing here?" asked Max, though he already suspected he knew the answer.

"Max! Jesus, you gave me a scare." Max could see he was churning round in his mind what excuse to give. "I was, I was just looking up some progress, on some of our projects. Always good to check what's going on in my company, via the library files." He started to swivel back round. "Let me just close this down first."

"Don't you bloody touch that keyboard!" ordered Si now coming into view and closing in on him fast.

He was then closely followed by the uniformed Sergeant Wilson who moved towards Sir John past Si and Max, holding one hand up and the other on his telescopic steel baton. "Do as he says Sir, step away from the desk and don't touch anything, or I'll be forced to use this," tapping the baton still in its belt holster. Any thoughts Sir John had of breaking the memory stick and trying to smash the computer on the floor immediately evaporated.

"Okay, okay," said Sir John, "just don't use that. This is all a terrible misunderstanding," as he moved away from the desk.

Si told Wilson to cuff Sir John while he quickly went over to the desk to have a look at what was going on. He instantly saw the small USB memory stick protruding from one of the ports on the front. The screen said it all, as it showed an open File Explorer window with hundreds of folders visible. Si could see the names of the folders correlated to either Empire departments, projects or other obvious titles, allowing easy navigation of them.

To the left was the Quick Access menu, he looked down the list until he came to the one called 'USB Drive (F:)' and clicked on it. The window then displayed the five files Sir John had just copied onto the memory stick, titled; 'Omega6500 rifle PK', 'Omega6500 riflesights PK', 'Omega6500 lasercomputer PK', 'Omega6500 projectiles PK' and 'Omega6500 notes PK'. The column next to each file labelled 'Date Modified' showed that they had all been opened and copied onto the stick in the last few minutes.

Sergeant Wilson was holding Sir John's arm with one hand and now calling back to the police station with the other, to ask them to send another squad car. At the same time he suggested to Si, "Sir, I'd advise you take a few pictures while we're all in here and have the evidence on the screen."

Max was impressed with this police officer's professionalism and efficiency and imagined if he hadn't followed them in, they might have had a bit of a tussle with Sir John who would likely have tried to destroy the evidence. Si already had his mobile phone out and was quickly taking pictures of everything and everyone, including some close-ups of the computer screen.

Si had a few moments to think and now said to Wilson, "Sergeant, I want to leave everything in here as it is, it's a crime scene now. That squad car you've ordered, ask for two officers to come here asap, I want one up in Margaret Fallon's office as we'll need her PC stuff shortly, but not yet, and the other down here. No-one comes in or out without my say so."

"Right you are Sir."

Si continued. "Max, you stay here until the officers take over, don't touch anything, then get a cab back to the Crawley station. Sergeant Wilson and I will take Sir John back now and I can get through all the preliminaries, charging and the like." Looking at Sir John, "And I'm sure he'll have an expensive lawyer with us in no time."

"Damn right I will," said Sir John quietly, frowning and shaking his head. He was well versed enough to know not to say anything until his 'brief' was there and was desperately now trying to think how he could get out of this mess. Unfortunately being caught red-handed by MI5 and the police didn't bode well for the knighted Chief Executive. The law was indifferent to grand titles, wealth and fancy executive positions. "What about my chauffeur and car, I should at least tell him he's not needed?"

It was Max who responded first, "That, Sir John, I think is the least of your worries now."

Wilson led Sir John through the basement and up the stairs, followed by Si. Sir John stopped on the stairs and looked pathetically at Si, then down to the steel handcuffs he had on. "There are staff working weekends, for the sake of the company, I'd request a favour please Mr Lawson?"

"In the spirit of cooperation Sir John, which I sincerely hope you'll contemplate reciprocating." Si nodded to Wilson, who then unlocked the steely manacles and removed them from Sir John's wrists.

"Nothing silly please Sir," Wilson warned, touching his steel baton again. Sir John nodded his head in agreement and they went out through reception to the police car. Si got in to drive while Wilson sat next to Sir John in the rear.

Max watched them disappear and decided it was best he waited at the doorway in reception rather than contaminate anything in the library. The security guard offered up his seat by the door.

Sir John brooded in the back of the police car with Sergeant Wilson watching him closely. Si Lawson glanced at his captive in the mirror at every opportunity whilst driving, trying to judge the man's mindset. From experience, he knew he had to make the most of the opportunity of speaking with him during the short car journey before process, jurisdictions and lawyers got involved, often frightening suspects into silence rather than persuading them to be truthful. Si felt he could detect regret and some trepidation from Sir John and knowing he only had less than ten minutes before they reached the station, chose his words carefully.

"You've presided over the growth of a successful Arms company Sir John. You're already a wealthy man, but I can understand the attraction of the huge sums of money involved with selling some of these cutting-edge ordnance designs." Sir John wasn't biting as he continued to stare at the back of the headrest in front of him. "Your lawyer may well want the sport and let's face it, the billing, to fight your case and try and get you off. Let me tell you now that when you're caught and witnessed perpetrating a criminal act, with the evidence we have on the computer, you will be prosecuted, shamed, embarrassed and go to prison."

Sir John's eyes briefly flicked up to meet Si's in the rear-view mirror. Si now had his attention. "For you Sir John, it's now all about damage limitation. I'm just having a friendly word with you now before your life changes forever, I've been through this many times before with others. You do have a choice here to do the right thing. It's quite simple really, the more you cooperate and help me get what I want, the less your punishment will be. Most sentences are reduced by a third for a cooperative party pleading guilty."

Si waited, hoping for Sir John to feel as though he had to fill the silence. After a few moments, Sir John looked up again and said quietly, "And what is it you do want?"

"I need to know who it is you're selling the designs to. The broker. Somehow I then need to find out who the end buyer is. I imagine you have no idea where these designs are ending up, but your assistance in helping us contact and find the broker will help you enormously. But I'm not known for my patience, so I urge you not to take too long to make your mind up. Once I've had enough of playing cat and mouse with you and your lawyer, you will be prosecuted to the full extent the law allows. I can help you Sir John, if you help me."

As the police car approached the station Si continued to check in the mirror for any reaction from behind and just for a moment thought he saw a glint of resignation in St John's eyes through his defiant default. Wilson had been listening and thought that Si Lawson had pitched his case perfectly to the suspect. He'd seen tough, resolute, argumentative criminals determined to fight their case by hook or by crook, then crumble into submission when faced with the reality of their impending punishment being watered down, just for a little cooperation. Wilson guessed that Sir John would end up being a 'crumbler', not a fighter.

Max had a chance now to settle down after the whole incident, his heart was still racing. 'Sir John, I can't believe it', he thought to himself. Max had previously assumed Lyndsey Wyman must have had something to do with it, and if it wasn't her then the designer Peter Kendrick was next on his list. But not Margaret, and certainly not Sir John. He took a moment to congratulate himself, after all, he had discovered the bait of the final draft designs of the new Omega 6500 rifle system, and set the trap by placing the spycam in the basement. Assuming Sir John was guilty and it certainly looked like it, they still only had the first link in the chain.

Somehow they needed to get to the next link along and how the designs were being sold. The broker. Then onto whoever was buying these military secrets. Max felt it was still a long way to go, but at least they were now at the start of the Omega trail.

Max arrived back at the police station an hour after Si who had started speaking with Sir John with his lawyer present. Vince was still talking to Margaret Fallon. They were both ensuring that the paths of their suspects didn't cross at the station. Max grabbed a coffee and went into the slightly darkened observation room overlooking Si and Sir John. It seemed they'd only just reached the point where Si had begun asking questions.

It quickly became clear to Max that the highly paid lawyer was hellbent on stringing everything out to buy more time and allow himself some space to figure out how on earth he was going to get his client off the charges. Because he knew this was going to be hard to do, he'd advised Sir John not to say anything. Si started with the simple questions and each time was met with a "No comment". Even when the questions were deemed to be non-incriminating like 'Are you the Chief Executive of Empire Arms Limited' Sir John would look to his lawyer who would shrug his shoulders in disdain. Si remained calm and continued asking questions, he was quite used to this game. He wanted to allow them to act out their nonsense because in the end, all it was doing was giving him the higher ground for if and when they got to a negotiation with plea bargains.

From Max's perspective, it didn't look good. The brick wall of silence being put up by Sir John was intensely frustrating, especially for Max who had been there when he was clearly stealing the designs right in front of his eyes. He started to wonder if Sir John's lawyer really could find some loophole or indiscretion to get his client off the hook. The questions continued with the 'no comment' replies and the lawyer occasionally chipping in with their usual remarks such as 'that's not pertinent to this investigation', 'you can't ask my client that question' or 'I hardly need to remind you, Mr Lawson, that my client does not have to answer that question if he so chooses'.

Max was not used to this process and found it maddening to watch. After about half an hour Si calmly stood up to leave, "I think that's just about exhausted my patience for now." He lingered a moment hoping that would remind Sir John of what he'd said in the car. After temporarily closing the interview on the digital recorder, as he left the room Max could hear him softly say to St John, "Damage limitation so far, zero."

Si exited and Max noticed Sir John shifting uneasily in his chair. He then turned to his lawyer and Max heard him say only the beginning of a harsh tirade, "This is a ridiculous tactic, they caught me, you're not looking after my best interests at all," after which his voice hushed to a faint whisper but from his body language and expression, Max could see him continuing to berate the confused looking lawyer.

Max left the observation room and saw Si at the far end of the corridor by the coffee machine, so went to see him.

"That was so frustrating," he growled to Si. "What was that you said to him at the end, you should have seen him have a go at his lawyer after you left."

Si smirked. "Really? Oh good. You just have to rise above it when they don't want to say anything and play silly games. It's always the lawyer that ends up making things hard for their clients. I had some honest advice for St John in the car and if we are lucky, things may change by the time I go back in there, from what you're saying about his reaction." He downed his coffee. "Come on, let's pop outside and get some fresh air. I'll make them wait 20 minutes before I go back in."

Ten minutes later Vince joined them outside in the rear car park of the station looking pleased with himself. "Fallon has given me everything I think we need. She's been completely cooperative and I'm positive that her taking the uniform design was her first and last criminal act. I've told her we'll be holding her here until further notice, to give you plenty of time Si to sort out how you want to play this with Sir John and Empire's management. Talking of Sir John, how's it going with him?"

"Just letting the casserole stew a bit longer," replied Si.

After another ten minutes they went back in, Max returned to the observation room and Si went back into the interrogation room. He could immediately see Sir John had a calmer demeanour whilst the lawyer was the one now looking angry and anxious. Wanting to showboat and retain some control, the lawyer opened up. "I've spoken with my client whilst you are out of the room and there's been a change. On condition of you guaranteeing a favourable report and consideration towards any court appearance or judgement that may or may not come about in the future, my client is willing to cooperate fully." Si played along and said nothing, giving no reaction. Now it was his term to have some fun with the arsehole lawyer. The man nervously continued. "So do we have a deal, that will perhaps help with any future plea bargain?"

Si shrugged his shoulders. "Now you know full well that I'm not in a position to give any guarantees or make any promises. I will file my report as I see it, so if your client chooses to be cooperative, then I'm sure that will help and count in his favour. It'll be up to the judge to decide how they want to weigh that information. And as for the plea bargain, you will also know that has absolutely nothing to do with me. That's up to the prosecutor, you and your client to agree to any terms and recommendations associated with a guilty plea."

Sir John frowned with dissatisfaction at his lawyer who tried one last time. "So it will be looked on favourably if my client cooperates fully?"

"That's more or less what I've just told you, but no guarantees," said Si looking bored with the conversation topic. He then glanced at Sir John and asked, "Are you happy to fully cooperate?"

Sir John breathed a sigh of relief. "Yes, I am. I'm placing my trust in you and what you said to me and will do whatever I can to help you. I have to warn you though that finding the arms broker I've been dealing with won't be easy, he doesn't know me and I don't know whoever he or she is. But we can get into all that later."

"Thank you Sir John, I appreciate your candour and willingness to help. I think we should start right at the beginning, don't you? Can I get either of you any food or drinks? We should settle down then for a long session so we can go through every single detail and if you're willing, start drafting a statement."

The lawyer was about to interject but Sir John raised his hand in front of him and stopped him in his tracks, nodding in agreement to Si. "Large black coffee for me please, and some biscuits would be great thank you."

Max settled down in the small adjacent room and for the next five hours, Si and Sir John systematically went through every detail. Sir John explained that it all started with a dinner meeting with industry representatives, where he overheard an unlikable but legitimate arms broker telling another guest about his trade and also the unscrupulous antics of the underground brokers he found himself having to compete with. Apparently, the dodgy brokers operated mainly on the Dark Web and would try to make contact with staff at weapons design or manufacturing facilities and carefully groom them to the point of offering large sums of cash, always visually a big incentive, in exchange for more innocuous and less important information to start with. Then once the first deal was made they would tempt the IP thief with more money for more important designs.

Many of these underground brokers would buy the stolen designs outright and could then take their time finding the right end buyer at a significantly inflated mark-up. Those brokers without huge funds or underworld cash backing, would agree to sell the designs and split the proceeds with the thief, usually keeping a very high percentage for themselves as a broker fee. The thief's proceeds would usually not be electronically transferred, as this would leave evidential tracing. Instead, arrangements would be made to pay the thief in cash or high-value items such as gold or diamonds.

Sir John had found himself being intrigued by this black market, cautiously existing and running alongside his own legitimate business, and curiosity got the better of him. He started tentatively exploring and learning about the Dark Web, helped ironically by his own Technology Security Manager at Empire Arms. He was unwittingly providing reports to Sir John as his Chief Executive, regarding any suspicious activity in the marketplace and online that they should be aware of. The unsuspecting manager had traced a temporary communication window for an encrypted email chat page, which had come across Sir John's desk. That evening Sir John's hunger for some excitement had got the better of him and he found himself anonymously starting to engage in a staccato conversation with an equally anonymous person that appeared to be one of these arms brokers. At the end of the chat before the window and page closed down, the broker would provide a new link and time for a chat window to be open again.

At the time Sir John was merely interested to find out more about this clandestine world operating within his business sector and intended to report the whole thing to his security manager and the board. However, he stopped himself short before doing this. He felt he wanted to find out more and play along with this mysterious, potential underworld broker. Assured by his IT man of total anonymity on the Dark Web, he was hooked. He hadn't intended for a moment to steal and sell any of his own company's plans, but when the person on the other side of the chat started tentatively enquiring what he might have of interest, Sir John's bravado kicked in.

He was able to reply that he was in a position to potentially access significant new designs and weapons technology. He wanted to show off. Then after many of these Dark Web encrypted and anonymous chats, the fateful and simple question came across the screen in front of him. It was the line that changed everything. 'Can you prove to me you have access to ordnance designs by sending me something simple? I can sell it on for you, could be worth millions.'

Max could see how easy it was for someone as important and wealthy as Sir John already was, to be slowly and carefully sucked into doing something they would never normally consider, with the lure of ego and the mention of vast sums of money at their fingertips. Max felt a little sorry for Sir John, who explained his story to Si eloquently and thoroughly. He'd let himself be groomed, pure and simple.

Sir John went on to explain that he had then gone down to Lyndsey Wyman's basement library to see what simple design he could copy, to prove to the broker he was able to access secrets.

Si had asked him, "How did you get access to the basement without Lyndsey being there?"

"I often work late or at weekends, nothing unusual about that," explained Sir John. "The security guard outside the door in reception would never question me wanting access to anywhere, this is my company, I'm the boss."

"But how did you access the login password for the private network server computer?"

"That was pretty straightforward. Lyndsey writes her password on a card inside a sealed envelope which is kept in my secretary's desk drawer. She always seems to use a thick black marker pen. I just held it up to a bright light and could see through to what was written on the card." Sir John allowed himself a smirk at the simplicity of it.

"And what about the CCTV camera above the basement staircase?" asked Si.

Sir John shrugged his shoulders. "Whenever I went down there I'd just reformat the hard drive of the CCTV digital recorder so everything on it got wiped, then leave it turned off when I went. Lyndsey probably hardly ever checks it anyway, so I assumed she'd never notice. It's a cheap nasty bit of kit so even if she did, would probably put it down to a dodgy recorder."

"Let's get back to you accessing the first design that you copied for this broker?" said Si.

Sir John continued to explain that, "Once in the system, I had a good look round the files for some small, insignificant product that I could use, just to show the broker that I could access such designs. I stumbled across the new Kevlar and carbon composite field helmet, but that hadn't yet gone through its rigorous testing and MOD sign off. I didn't make a copy of the file at that time as didn't want to walk around with an incriminating memory stick with the file on, nor did I want to start emailing it to my home PC leaving an electronic trail. I decided to use Lyndsey's other PC in the basement that was connected to the Internet for all his future communications with the broker."

"Clever," noted Si.

"It would also make it easy for me to copy a file from the library computer and then transfer it onto the normal computer right next to it using a stick which I then wiped before leaving. I even destroyed the computer I'd been using at home for the previous Dark Web chats, just in case there was some trail or evidence left on it. By doing all this, if anything did get discovered, then it would lead back to the basement and Lyndsey Wyman, and not to me. Jesus, I'm so ashamed of it all." Sir John hung his head tutting.

"So you then sent the helmet design specs to an unknown

person using the Dark Webchat they'd set up to communicate with you?" urged Si wanting to hear more. For someone claiming to have done all this on impulse, he was surprised at the detailed thought process that Sir John had put into all this.

"I'd saved the link for the next allocated chat time in a hidden password-protected file on Lyndsey's PC and sent off the helmet design file to the broker. They then gave me a link for the next chat for about a week later."

"You just blindly sent off one of your own company's designs over the Dark Web, to a recipient the other end who you didn't even know who they were?" Si didn't try to disguise his incredulous tone.

Sir John nodded, embarrassed. "Yes. Crazy isn't it. I simply cannot explain what on earth I was thinking at the time. I was still curious to see how this process worked and what would happen next."

"And what did happen on the next call?"

"The broker had obviously made the sale. I don't know how or who to, but they advised me on the chat that my cut was three million dollars, with instructions to collect the payment which would be made in the equivalent value diamonds and was waiting in a safety deposit box with a company based in Crawley, next to Gatwick airport. They gave me the password to access the box."

Sir John's lawyer started to ask if he was sure he wanted to continue and was waved off again.

"Yes, then what?" said Si.

"I went to the company with the safety deposit box, gave them the password and inside the box found a small black cloth bag with loads of small diamonds inside. It was unbelievable. It all seemed so simple," said Sir John as if he wasn't responsible.

"What have you done with these diamonds?"

Sir John sighed. "I took them to Hatton Garden in London and after getting a couple of the diamond dealers to give me a quote, sold them for two million pounds, half cash and half a bank transfer."

"Did you understand that you were breaking the law by stealing the design from your own company and selling it for your own benefit?" asked Si.

"I don't know. I guess I did deep down, but it didn't feel as though I'd done anything wrong. It didn't seem to affect anyone at the time. It was just a helmet design."

"What was the next design you copied and sold?"

"The broker then asked me what else I could provide the designs for and suggested something a little more significant," relayed Sir John. "To minimise my visits to the basement, I went down there one weekend just before one of the scheduled chat windows and had another look through the design files. I found the designs for another prototype weapon called the Anti-Personnel Room Clearer grenade which shoots up a low-level frag explosion."

"So you sent that specification file off to this mysterious broker did you?"

"I'm afraid so. Oh my God, what an idiot I've been. This is terrible." The reality of what Sir John had done was sinking in. He held his head in his hands for a moment.

"How much was your cut for that design?"

Sir John took a deep breath. "Seven and a half million dollars!"

"Sweet mother of God," exclaimed Si, who along with the lawyer in the room and Max sitting next door, was shocked at the staggering sum of money. "Same payment method?"

"Yup, the bag of diamonds was a bit bigger this time. I wouldn't know what to do with so many of them and that amount of money, so they are still in the safe back at my home."

"Any other designs Sir John?" asked Si wanting to affirm that it was him who was responsible for the Stealth Silencer 50 which his MI5 agent Phil Landon had seen being sold on the Dark Web auction.

Sir John looked thoroughly shameful and apologetically replied, "There was just one other design, I'm sorry, it was for some fancy silencer which made the gun firing almost inaudible."

"And how much did you get for that design," asked Si, knowing that the design sold for thirty-four million dollars.

Sir John obliged. "I got ten point two million dollars for that one. That's it Mr Lawson, those are the three I've passed on."

The lawyer had gone from being horrified at the large sums of money Sir John was talking about, to now looking quite impressed that such designs were worth so much and thinking to himself of Sir John, 'Cheeky bastard!'.

Max got out his phone and did a quick calculation from the numbers Sir John had mentioned. He worked out that if the silencer sale at auction was thirty-four million and Sir John's cut was ten point two, then it looked as though the broker was taking a seventy per cent fee and passing thirty per cent back to the original design seller. Quite a nice commission thought Max.

Sir John needed the loo and was also desperate to break off from his sheer embarrassment at having to relay what he'd done so asked, "Can we take a comfort break?"

Si agreed and was glad to have a break himself. Sir John was relaying so much information he needed a few moments to gather himself and refocus on some of the goals they were after. He popped next door to see Max while a police officer escorted Sir John and his lawyer to the canteen and men's room.

Max greeted Si. "I still can't believe what's been going on and that Sir John was the one doing it all. Unbelievable."

"I know, you couldn't make it up if you tried," said Si.

"How are we ever going to find out who this Dark Web broker is if the chat windows are encrypted and Sir John has no idea who the person is on the other end?" asked Max. "Is there some way the techy guys can trace him using the computer in the basement now we have access to it?"

"I don't think that'll work. From what little I know about the Dark Web and these temporary chat windows, is that they are heavily encrypted at both ends and the window is only activated and live for as long as the organiser wants it to be, then it's gone again. Let's see what Sir John comes up with that might help us find the broker, our cover that next with him," Si said determinedly.

Ten minutes later they settled back down again in the interrogation room and Si reopened with candour. "Firstly Sir John let me say how appreciative I am that you have decided to cooperate and if we continue in this vein, I'll be happy to positively report this back to the court when the time comes." Sir John nodded. "My main concern now is that we need to somehow find out more about this mystery broker you've been dealing with. Have you any ideas at all who it is or any information they've mentioned about themselves?"

Sir John shook his head but allowed himself some time to carefully think through a helpful answer. "I'm afraid I don't know anything about them. I don't even know if it's a man or a woman. Whoever it is has been very diligent in not giving away anything about themselves at all."

"Can the same be said about yourself Sir John? Have you told them anything about yourself?" asked Si.

Sir John thought again. "No, I don't think so. No, absolutely not. They've never really asked for any personal details. I guess that's the unwritten code with these sort of things is it?"

"Just take a few moments to go back over some of your interactions with this broker Sir John. Anything they've mentioned about themselves, where they are, what they call themselves, don't you have to have some kind of username or something?" Si was clutching at straws but from experience knew that pressing someone to remember some small detail often allowed them to dig up some small thing that might end up being useful.

Sir John frowned and whilst recalling in his mind the communications he'd had, continued to shake his head.

Sir John then sat up jubilant as if he'd just won a prize. "Ar hang on a moment. Yes. They did have a username. It was 'Water Spider'. Yes, that's it and mine was 'Blackbird'.

"Water Spider, well at least that's something I guess," Si conceded. "Why did you call yourself Blackbird?"

"No reason really, when the system asked me to create a username all I could visualise was the 'B' on the front of my Bentley and the first animal that popped into my mind was a Blackbird."

Max then suddenly had an idea and with no way of communicating to Si through the mirrored screen, left his room and hastily knocked on the door of the interrogation room. He then moved out of the doorway as Si came out, not wanting to be seen by Sir John and risk interrupting the flow of the conversation. Si looked at Max inquisitively.

"Si, I think I might have an idea. Sir John has mentioned several times he gets sent a Dark Web link and time for the next chat window to open. If we know when that is, the next one, maybe the techy guys can think of something to trace it back when it's live?" said Max eagerly.

Si nodded and disappeared back into the interrogation room closing the door behind him. Max returned to the observation room.

"Do you have a scheduled time and chat link for the next time the broker has offered to communicate with you?" asked Si.

The realisation hit Sir John that this might be another piece of useful information that would count towards a lighter sentence, he quickly replied. "Yes I do, it's tomorrow evening at eight PM. I couldn't tell you what the link is because it's always a scrambled list of numbers and letters. I will have saved it on Lyndsey's computer in the basement back at the Empire offices."

"Given we caught you Sir John copying the files for the new Omega sixty-five hundred long-range sniper system, are they what you were intending to pass on to the broker tomorrow? You haven't already sent them have you?" said Si.

"No, I haven't sent them over, I'd only just copied them across to the other PC when you lot came in. Water Spider had asked me for a big design this time and I'd already had the briefing from Apollo Designs that the Omega rifle was almost complete and the prototype was ready. I'm afraid I had already mentioned this to the broker on the previous chat, so they know that was my intention for tomorrow's communication. The broker had said they could probably sell such a design for even more than the others." Sir John was utterly remorseful and couldn't hold back a sob of despair.

Si now wanted to retreat from the onerous task and time commitment of interviewing Sir John, back to the brainpower and security of his team back at MI5 Thames House. He needed more heads than just his own to think about what options they had with this window of opportunity on Sunday evening. Tomorrow.

"Sir John, you've been incredibly helpful. You understand we can't release you given the pending charges and sensitivity of this case, so I'm afraid you will have to stay here in one of the cells for the time being until I can decide how we progress this. I'll ask the guys here to make your stay as comfortable as possible, the boss who is a friend of mine will ensure they look after you. We'll continue our conversation very soon." Si brought the interview to a close and handed over to the police officer in the room.

He and Max left their adjoining rooms at the same time and as they walked down the corridor, Si was already on his mobile phone to Vince who had finished with Margaret Fallon some hours earlier and was elsewhere in the building talking to several officers.

"Vince, meet us at the car, we've got some information that needs us and a few of the team to put our heads together and figure out what to do with it. Call Josh, Ellie and Alan the techie to meet us at Thames House in an hour. And make sure you have the contact details for the designer at Apollo, Peter Kendrick, we may need some help from him as well, but no need to drag him into London, I just need him available to us on standby. Keep your explanation to him brief, I don't want to upset him with everything we've got going on here today."

Max followed him out to the car where they waited for Vince to join them moments later. "You sound like you've got an idea Si?"

"Not yet Max, but I'm sure the team will come up with something, they always do," said Si confidently, re-energised.

"This is to figure out some way of using this next scheduled chat window tomorrow isn't it?"

"Yup, I think that's our one and only opportunity. We're going to try and catch ourselves a Water Spider!"

11

That Saturday evening everyone assembled in the meeting room of Si Lawson's MI5 Cyber offices at the Thames House building in Millbank, overlooking Lambeth Bridge on the River Thames. Around the table were Si, Vince, Max, Josh, Ellie and Alan from technology.

Si opened the meeting. "Thanks for being here on a Saturday, guys, we have a pressing window of opportunity, literally, given it's a Dark Web chat window that opens for us tomorrow at eight PM. We're going to use a computer in the basement library of the Empire Arms estate in Charlwood near Gatwick, just in case somehow the broker can check the IP address. The computer has the link for the chat window which won't exist or be online until the scheduled time tomorrow. Our corporate designs thief, using the name Blackbird, has passed on three separate ordnance designs across the chatline to our arms broker with the username Water Spider."

Everyone listened intently to Si as he continued. "Blackbird has recently mentioned that they can get hold of the designs for Empire's latest long-range sniper rifle, called the Omega 6500 and the broker is probably expecting to get these designs tomorrow night to then sell on. Having thought about it I propose that some of us here will be at Empire tomorrow posing as Blackbird the thief and somehow guys, we need to come up with a plan to track back to this broker and find out who and where they are." Si was satisfied with his opening summary to the team and sat back in his chair concluding, "Over to you guys, any ideas?"

The people around the room looked at one another, some had been taking notes, and all took a few moments to allow the information their boss had imparted sink in and process.

"Is there any way we are able to share any of the Omega designs with the broker or even say a sample?" asked Ellie.

Vince shook his head. "The Omega designs are top-secret and far too valuable to us, the military and this country won't allow them to get into the wrong hands. I can't see how we can possibly share them with the broker."

Si lent forward. "You're right, we can't exacerbate the problem by disclosing another design, especially not this one. Max has seen it at their Apollo company and it's quite a piece of kit. Unfortunately with us not being able to send its designs off, it rather limits our bargaining power with the broker."

Max had previously seen the amazing things MI5 Technology could do, so ventured, "Alan, I get that the whole idea of the Dark Web is anonymous and encrypted communication and transfer of information, but surely there's some way you guys can come up with a way of tracing the origin of the chat window?"

Alan was a younger guy and given he'd come in at short notice on a Saturday, was even more scruffily dressed than he would have been on a weekday. His expertise lay mainly with information intelligence, gathering and analysis, but he loved to also get involved with the technology hardware team who put together bespoke electronic devices and gadgets. In the past, he'd been involved with various modifications and upgrades to field operative's mobile phones including encrypted direct call facilities, a long-range directional listening device, wristwatch modifications and unique surveillance equipment. He was highly adept at anything Internet, app and software related, and had worked on several previous operations involving the infamous Dark Web.

Alan casually continued with the doodling on his pad in front of him that he'd begun at the beginning of the meeting. "The whole point of the Dark Web is anonymity. It's only accessible through specific networks in the first place, such as Onion Routing and the Invisible Internet Project. With the huge amount of encryption, it's almost impossible to track the location or device IP address of the user. Any data or communication gets bounced around numerous servers all over the place, I'm not aware of anything that can hack this yet."

Max observed, "You mentioned that it's *almost* impossible Alan, does that mean it could be done, a trace?" Everyone looked at Alan who stopped doodling.

Alan looked up. "Well, in theory, you'd need some kind of Seeker Trojan which could find the first transfer server down the line from your PC, jumping across and into that, then seeking the next portal to the next server, and so on until it reached the other end-user. Unfortunately, that's multiple encryptions and security to get through." Alan could see hope on the faces of the team around the desk, so explained further. "But then once the Seeker Trojan has got to the other end, if possible, maybe it can get some piece of information like the IP address of the device being used."

His audience had renewed hope which he spotted. "That's not it though. It then needs to make its way back down the line of servers and encryptions, and back to your computer to deliver the scrap of information it might have gathered." He added yet more problems. "And after all that, it has to be done whilst the dark web page or chat window is open. Once that's closed the game's over."

"So? Can you put together one of these Seeker Trojan's?" asked Si, then adding, "in the next twenty-four hours?"

"That would be impossible," said Allan defiantly.

"Well unless you've got another technology suggestion, and unless you've got anything pressing to do overnight and all day tomorrow, I suggest you get started on it right away?"

Alan looked as much shocked as he was excited at the prospect of the challenge.

"I'll probably need a couple of my guys in."

"Then get them in!"

He nodded quickly to Si then sheepishly got up and left the room to get on with his task. The next twenty-four hours for him would be a long haul and require him to draw upon every snippet of knowledge he had and could muster about writing a self-executing Seeker Trojan program.

Si continued. "I think before we go to the basement at Empire tomorrow evening we should drop in on Apollo and meet this designer Peter Kendrick. If we are going to impersonate the seller Blackbird, we need to at least be familiar with the Omega system. Even though we won't be sending files over to anyone, we might need to be able to talk about them with confidence. Vince, I suggest you contact Kendrick and ask him to meet us at Apollo tomorrow say seven PM to take us through his creation."

"If the Seeker Trojan thing doesn't work, we still need some way of luring this Water Spider broker out into the open. What about telling them upfront on the chat, that security on the Omega designs has just been upgraded and we're not able to access them anymore?" suggested Max.

"What's the point of that?" asked Vince.

Max elaborated. "Well, maybe we could tell the broker that even though we can't get the soft copy design files, we can provide a hardware sample of one of the pieces of kit from the Omega system. Maybe one of the sights or something, I don't know? It's just an idea. I'm just trying to think of ways of engineering a drop-off or even meeting with the broker."

Si was impressed with Max's thinking. "You know what Max, I like it, that's a really good idea. Sir John has already whet the broker's appetite by mentioning the Omega. If we pretend the designs are no longer accessible but that we can get hold of say part of the equipment, it would have to be a decent part, they're not going to turn their nose up at it. They'll still want it, surely, and any buyer can simply copy or reverse engineer it."

"Which piece of the Omega could you offer?" asked Max. "From what Peter Kendrick told me, much of the technology he's incorporated is already out there and available. He's just refined and adapted it to perform even better. I'm not sure offering the rifle would be of sufficient interest. It's just a really big gun after all and how would anyone be able to transport that to a meetup."

"What about the sights then, the ones on top of the rifle, or the second user's sites with the laser and computer you told us about?" suggested Vince.

Si wasn't convinced and shook his head, "It's a good idea,

let's have a think about it and revisit the topic when we are with Kendrick the designer. He can tell us which item is the most impressive, but shall we say, has the least new bespoke intellectual property involved. I do like the idea though of offering the broker a piece of kit that has to be handed over."

"Regarding the scheduled broker chat tomorrow," said Vince, "I think it would be prudent if you agree, for us to take Sir John along with us. As you say this is our one opportunity and we don't want any slip-ups, or to find ourselves not being able to log in. Also if the broker asks us any weird questions that only Sir John knows the answer to, then at least he's there with us to help out."

"I agree, you and I will be back down at the Crawley station tomorrow anyway to continue questioning him and Fallon, so he can come along with us when we leave to go to Empire." Si looked at each of them sat around the table. "Thanks guys for coming in, Vince I'll meet you at the station say midday tomorrow. We also need to organise the uniform guys to retrieve Sir John's office and home computers, and the diamonds from his home safe. Check-in with Alan before you leave and see if he's got anywhere with his Seeker Trojan, if he has then tell him to meet us at Empire at seven PM as well. Max, you've done well my friend. So well in fact that you can have tomorrow off!"

Max laughed, "Wonderful, and it's a Sunday as well."

"Not the whole day off though," teased Si, "you still need to be at Empire by seven PM."

Alan had spent the entire night working on trying to develop his Seeker Trojan program at Thames House. He'd got a couple of his fellow nerds to join him and spent many hours with them drawing out and correcting on a large whiteboard, the makings of a program design with all the operations it would have to be capable of to stand any chance of tracing the end user's location. Getting their IP address would just be part of the jigsaw puzzle as this would only tell them which Internet service provider was being used, which in turn might allow them to trace it back through the provider with the cooperation of that country's intelligence services.

They'd also discussed the possibility of activating the end user's device camera, if they had one that is, and taking a snapshot of the person which could then be checked with multi-country police records. They felt that was too much of a long shot. Then at about two AM, Alan had concluded that one of their best options to explore for the final execute program, if they could ever get to the end device, was to hope that the broker had enabled their Google location services.

Using HTML5 geolocation application programming interface, a JavaScript can capture your latitude and longitude which gets manipulated by a backend server and then transferred onto Google maps showing your position. Most computer users allow this so that if they utilise Google maps for directions or finding their nearest retail outlet for a shopping item, Google can automatically pinpoint you on its map.

Alan and his guys then worked through to the mid-morning, energised by their progress and the challenge they had, to create possibly one of the first programs that just might enable someone to be traced on the infamously anonymous Dark Web. The long session was interjected with high-five celebrations, arguments and lows where they almost gave up on the job and periods of silence where they each worked studiously on the parts of the programming code they had been allocated.

By the time Alan spoke to Vince who had just arrived at the Crawley police station with Si Lawson, he was able to report that he might have something that could be tried for the first time, for him to bring down to Empire for their evening meet up.

Si had praised the youngster for his hard work and ingenuity, but had also been clear that if Alan felt his Seeker Trojan program could be detected in any way by the broker on the other end, then they couldn't possibly risk using it. Alan had responded in his usual way with an attempt at mild humour and told Si and Vince he would only bring a program if it was worthy of the new name he would give it.

"I'm calling it ASS!" announced Alan. He was met by silence so continued to proudly explain its full name. "It's Alan's Stealth Seeker program."

Sir John Tregar and Margaret Fallon had also both been awake most of the night, having experienced their first time being temporarily incarcerated in an underground holding cell at the Crawley police station. The silence of the night had given them plenty of unwanted time to contemplate what they had done and what the consequences might be. Each of their rooms had nothing inside except a solid shelf with a thin mattress, for which they'd been provided with a blanket and pillow. These were holding cells, not imprisonment cells, so there were no other facilities in the room like a basin or toilet. This was where offenders would be temporarily held to either calm down, sleep off their intoxication, wait for investigating officers or lawyers to summon them for questioning, or be held until transferred to court or another location. They both hated it when the heavy steel door with a tiny observation shuttered window, were closed on them with an unforgiving bang, leaving them to their own shameful company and a taste of what might be to come should they be sent to prison.

There had been no dramatics, no swearing or shouting abuse at the police officers, no banging the door or threatening behaviour. They were both model detainees finding themselves in a world they'd only ever imagined or seen on television and neither of them liked it one bit. The two of them had only become aware of the other being detained at the same station, when coincidentally they both asked to go to the toilet and briefly spotted one another as one was returning to their cell and the other was leaving. Their utter shock and surprise at seeing one another was masked by their huge embarrassment of being there and what they'd done. Not a word was spoken by either of them.

Dawn was signalled with the arrival of a miserable metal tray of food and a mug of tea all trying to make itself look more appetising than it really was. Sir John Tregar and Margaret Fallon had both by this time reaffirmed their decisions to cooperate fully and do whatever they could to minimise the damage they had caused to their company. More importantly, minimise the inevitable punishment that awaited them in due course.

Max approached the Empire Arms complex just before seven PM. The different sized and irregular building shape silhouettes dotted around the estate, looked foreboding against the gloomy evening dusk. Their blackness was peppered with a few lights from a handful of weekend workers or security guards doing their rounds through every office on a regular basis, day and night.

Max had spent the entire day waiting to jump into his car and make his way down to Charlwood to meet the others, for what would be a defining moment in this operation. They all knew they only had one go at this with the invitation to the Dark Web chat from this elusive, mysterious arms broker. If the broker insisted on having the full plans for the Omega rifle system, or the MI5 team said something wrong on the chat exchange, the trail could go dead this evening and they wouldn't have any other way of ever catching up with the broker and certainly not the end buyers. Max had wondered to himself during the day who the broker could be and like people often do before they meet someone, had conjured up a fictitious vision of what the man might look like. He had wondered if it might be a woman, or a smart man in a suit operating for a foreign military organisation, but had opted for his made-up broker being a burly ex-military Russian. Of course, Max knew this would likely be a million miles away from what the broker really was, but that was his vision of him for now. So not to be trifled with.

As he approached the Empire Arms entrance he could see a brightly marked police car on the other side parked up waiting for him. In the front sat Si and Vince, with Sergeant Wilson accompanying Sir John Tregar in the back. Just as Max finished explaining who he was to the slightly bewildered security guard, who wasn't used to such officious comings and goings on a Sunday evening, a taxi pulled up behind him. Alan soon emerged from the rear of the car, mustering some relief at seeing Max there, through a tired sleep-deprived expression.

"Hi Alan, did you manage to come up with your Trojan program after all?" asked Max.

Alan carefully took out a USB memory stick from his jacket pocket and held it up pensively. "Here's ASS! Well, I've got something at least. In theory, it could do the job, but we haven't had a chance to test it, so unfortunately tonight will be its maiden voyage. We'll see anyway." He looked up at Max slightly concerned, knowing how important his program could be to the operation.

Alan climbed into Max's Golf GTI and they drove through the open gates to join the others. After a quick catch up through the open car door windows, Max led the way to the office building and warehouse of Apollo Designs.

Peter Kendrick arrived half an hour before them. He'd been quite perturbed when Vince had called him and asked him to meet them at his offices. Vince had left out that he was from MI5 and had merely told him that they'd like his help on a police enquiry which Sir John was also assisting them with. Unfortunately, the brief request for him to meet the police at his offices on Sunday evening had only made him anxious. After over two decades in the military, Peter liked everything to be just so and didn't like any surprises or to be kept in the dark. He was trying to think if there was anything that he had done recently that might have been brought into question. Sir John hadn't said anything to him by the time he'd left on Friday evening.

The security guard at the Apollo building entrance called out to Peter as he ushered the six visitors along a corridor towards his office, peeling off to return to the small reception area as the weapons designer emerged. Peter was quite put out at the sight of so many people visiting him under these strange and as yet unknown circumstances, with two men and a younger man he didn't recognise, alongside Max whom he'd recently met with Margaret, Sir John and a uniformed police officer.

"Good grief gentleman, quite an ensemble, what on earth is

going on here?" looking at Sir John for some reassurance and an explanation.

Sir John had already agreed with Si Lawson they would not yet mention his own indiscretions and pending charges, so that he still had sway over Peter. "It's okay Peter, there's a couple of things going on at Empire that I needed the police to look into. Nothing to do with you so apologies for the strange request and no need for you to be concerned about anything yourself."

"We are sorry to bother you at the weekend Mr Kendrick," said Si, "we just need you to give us a quick twenty-minute run-through of your long-range Omega 6500 rifle system, please? We are all bound by the Official Secrets Act and your chief executive here is also helping us with our enquiries."

Sir John nodded in agreement and gestured to the workshop doorway at the end of the corridor, wanting to avoid any more questions or explanations. They all trooped into the large adjoining shed where Peter Kendrick took them over to his prototype, hidden once again by a large dark cloth. Still a little unsure of the situation he now found himself in, he tentatively pulled away the covering to reveal his magnificent new weapon. His audience was once again impressed. He then proceeded to explain each part of the entire long-range sniper rifle system, with a slightly shorter version of the tour he'd given to Max that week. He went through the background of long-range sniper rifles and the challenges he faced as a designer wanting to push the boundaries of distance and accuracy even further. He then took the team through the top-level detail of each of the components being the computer unit with laser targeting, the rifle and sights, and lastly the self-adjusting projectiles.

The MI5 guys had agreed not to explain to Peter Kendrick why they wanted to find out more about the design. As they listened to him, each of them was ascertaining to themselves which parts of the whole system could potentially be offered up to the arms broker as a piece of hardware. Although the broker would want the proper designs, as long as what they had to offer had enough innovation and cutting-edge design built into it, then it could potentially be taken apart and examined to be re-engineered. This meant studying its makeup, components and hardware in precise detail to re-build the design specification starting only with a functional prototype.

"How many of these finished pieces of equipment do you have Mr Kendrick?" asked Josh.

Peter willingly replied. "At the moment the rifle and computer box that does the analysis of the variables, are unique prototypes. These are them. We have a couple of the rifle sights that we've been working on and a larger selection of the projectiles at various stages of readiness. Only a few fully functional."

Alan had the beginnings of an idea and similar to Si and Vince, was already starting to conclude that the item most suited to potentially be offered up as bait to the broker, was the projectile. The rifle, sights and targeting computer box were all modified and upgraded items already in the public domain. Making a larger rifle, longer more accurate sights and putting them together with a long-distance range finder, a laser and software to analyse the elements, where all entirely possible feats of another weapons designer. It was the projectile that was the unique selling point of this system.

Effectively a large bullet that could be shot out of a rifle with enough force to propel it four miles, that could then make small final adjustments to its trajectory within seconds, guiding it within a small tolerance onto its lasered target. That was what they had to offer up for an exchange. It also had the benefit of being small and portable, unlike the long heavy rifle or the large computer targeting system box, both needing to be attached to their large sturdy tripods.

Alan quietly whispered to Si Lawson, "I've got an idea about the big bullets we could use." Si nodded his acknowledgement and held up his hand at the same time gesturing Alan not to say anything else until they were out of the building.

At the end, Si thanked Peter Kendrick, as did Sir John and they left him to tidy up before he returned home, still none the wiser as to what exactly was going on.

All six of them made their way over to the main office building and were let through into reception and then into the basement entrance by the security guard. The underground library was fairly large, but with the racks of shelving taking up a lot of the first part of the space, the six men were rather cramped for space. Fortunately, they could spread out a little more once they got to Lyndsey's lounge and office area. Sir John felt a little sick as he viewed the desk area, it brought back memories of the previous day when Max and then Si had caught him copying the Omega designs.

He was brought back into the room abruptly as Si spoke. "Sir John and Sergeant Wilson, why don't you both make yourself comfortable on the sofa while we get on with things, we'll call upon you Sir John if we need you. I'm afraid you're just backup for when we start the online chat with the broker, in case you need to give us any pertinent information for our responses." Sir John nodded humbly.

Vince spoke to Alan. "Why don't you get set up ready with your program?"

Max explained that the PC on the left was the normal one connected to the Internet and the one on the right was the private network computer that had access to the server files and records. Alan clarified that the normal computer was the one that Sir John had been using for the Dark Web chats and after opening it up, with the help of Sir John providing Lyndsey's password, started to install his programme ready to hopefully invisibly attach it into the chat with the broker.

Sir John also pointed out his hidden file which held the chat window link he'd been sent by the broker, for the impending call. At about five minutes to eight, with not much time to spare, Alan nodded that he was ready, sitting directly in front of the keyboard and screen. Si and Vince pulled up a chair and sat either side of him, with Max standing behind looking over Alan's shoulder.

The tension in the room was palpable, as the next few minutes seemed to whizz by and in no time Si said to Alan, "Almost eight. You'd better open up the window using the link. Just to be clear, they can't hear or see us can they?" Alan shook his head as he clicked on the jumbled mixture of alpha numeric's for the Dark

Weblink.

The screen opened up and showed the message 'Site Not Found' on a black background which momentarily dismayed the onlookers, who thought perhaps the broker wouldn't show and everything Sir John had told them had been too good to be true. Then after twenty seconds, at precisely eight PM Vince noted, the 'Site Not Found' message disappeared leaving an entirely blank screen but now lightly framed in a box with a brief menu at the bottom and an input field space. They looked at Alan for reassurance. "We're in. Quite normal," he said, "hopefully the other user will start by saying something first, then we just type our message reply in the box and hit 'Enter' to post it to them."

A few moments later, white text appeared at the top of the screen. 'Water Spider - How are you Blackbird, do you have the Omega designs?'.

"Bloody hell," exclaimed Si, "get straight to the point don't they! How long do you need Alan to send off your Trojan?"

"I'll attach it to our first line of reply, it should be invisible," said Allen hurriedly typing in some strange looking instructions into a tiny window he'd left open in the bottom corner of the screen to control his program. Si slid his chair closer to the centre of the keyboard for better access, pushing Alan a few inches to the side. Si slowly typed in his reply and waited for Alan to give him the go-ahead before sending it, allowing the techie to attach his execute program to the message's data string. He hit 'Enter'.

'Blackbird - There's been a slight change, sorry, I wasn't able to get the designs I thought I could', appeared on the screen underneath the first message. The computer had automatically recognised them as previously entering Dark Webchat windows with Sir John's username Blackbird.

There was a pause as the other user was digesting the let-down of the message they'd just received.

Alan pointed to his smaller window, "This will hopefully give me feedback about how my Trojan is progressing, if at all. It's currently trying to find the first server on from us that this chat window is using. Once it gets past several servers I may lose contact with its progress until it returns to us."

A reply appeared on the screen. 'Water Spider - That's very disappointing, what was the problem?'.

"Great," said Max sarcastically, "the broker's probably pissed off at us already."

Si typed. 'Blackbird - Security here was changed and vastly tightened. I can't access the soft copy design files right now'.

"Let's give them a moment to stew before I tell them what we've got," said Si looking extremely tense. They were all glued to the screen and even Sir John and Sergeant Wilson had got up and were cautiously standing at the back trying to get a view of the screen as well, careful to keep their distance from the MI5 guys. Another long pause.

'Water Spider - Does that bring our business dealings to a close then?'.

Alan blurted out excitedly, making Vince jump, "The Trojan has found the first server and already got into it, it's looking for the next one!" Si typed slowly.

'Blackbird - No. The Omega is a worthy design for us to get a high price for. I am confident that I can provide a piece of its hardware, a fully functioning sample of the key component.'.

The reply was quicker this time, not allowing their concentration on the computer to drift for a second. 'Water Spider - What component?'.

Si looked to Alan, "Are you absolutely sure about this before I offer it up? You can definitely do what you mentioned to me on the way over here from Apollo?"

Alan looked pensive and anxious at the same time. He nodded. "In theory. Yes. We'll sort something anyway. Go for it."

'Blackbird - The most innovative component I can get you hopefully two samples of, is of the self-accuracy-adjusting long-range projectile. That's the most important part of the whole Omega 6500 system.'

They waited and this time the pause seemed to go on forever.

Alan blurted out, "The Trojan has just gone through two more servers!"

"How many servers are there?" asked Max.

"No idea, it'll keep going until it either gets blocked, or the encryption is too hard for it to crack, or it reaches the broker's PC. We'll probably lose contact with it soon, then we just have to wait."

A new message appeared. 'Water Spider – Are you sure you cannot get the soft copy designs, far easier to sell on?'.

Si typed his reply. 'Blackbird – The samples will be all I can get, but worth it. If you feel that won't be enough then there's nothing more I can sell you at the moment.'

"Blimey Si, that's a bit risky isn't it?" queried Vince.

"Just calling his bluff, they've surely got to want the samples." Si turned to Alan. "How much longer do you need, I think we're coming to a close soon?"

"I'm afraid I've no idea, could be loads of servers to get through. It's not given me any more updates yet."

They all moved close as the next reply appeared. 'Water Spider – Alright, I can sell the Omega 6500 projectile samples for a good price. When can you get them?'

Si looked at Alan questioningly. Alan thought quickly, he needed to do a fair amount of work if his idea was going to work for any kind of exchange. "I'll need maybe a week?" He watched as Si input his reply.

'Blackbird – I will have them in 4 days. How do I get them to you?'

"Four days! Great. When I said a week Si that means seven days!" grumbled Alan.

Alan's Trojan had amazingly managed to navigate through six different servers being used to encrypt this particular Dark Web chat window, but after the second one wasn't able to send back progress updates to Alan. The program had automatically devoted all its energy to moving forward through the network, seeking openings, breaking through access codes, trying to follow the first message Water Spider had sent. Eventually, the invisible coding successfully reached the broker's computer and was instantly able to query the geolocation data it sought. Unfortunately, the broker hadn't enabled this option, ever mindful of maintaining their secrecy. Alan's program was bounced by the broker's software when it was asked for the device's location, but this, in turn, triggered a notification on the broker's screen!

The broker had got frustrated at the unexpected way the chat conversation had gone, and that it wasn't going to be the usual simple transfer of design files over the chat. Whilst focusing on typing their next message, a small window had opened in the corner of their screen. It read simply, 'Enable Google location services?', with the usual 'OK' and 'Cancel' options to click on.

Although used to having pop-up windows disturbing their work on the PC, the broker moved their head back in puzzlement when the small alert window had appeared on their screen. They thought for a moment, and not suspecting in any way that it could possibly be any kind of hack or tracing request, clicked on the 'Cancel' button, assuming it was some kind of background app running.

Unbeknown to Alan, that was the instant his Trojan seeker program was terminated and rendered useless. With no location to gather and send back through the myriad of servers, it simply had nothing else to do and disintegrated into the ether.

Back in the basement, it felt as though there was too much going on to keep concentrating on, as another reply came back on the big screen. 'Water Spider – I will arrange a safety deposit box you can drop the samples into.'

"No, no, no, we can't do that, we'll never find out who this person is," said Si through gritted teeth in response to the last reply.

Alan was staring at his Trojan control window waiting for the next update, oblivious to the fact he would not hear anything back from his program again.

Max suggested, "Tell them you'll only hand it over personally."

Si typed. 'Blackbird – The samples are too valuable, I must

hand them over to you.'

They waited, it seemed each was holding their breath as they could have heard a pin drop in the basement room. This time the pause went on, and on. Alan started to think that perhaps the user had seen some kind of alert that his Trojan had triggered.

Si was wondering if perhaps asking for a personal exchange had pushed the broker too far. He asked Alan, "When do we know if your Trojan has been successful?"

"If it has been successful and got to the end user's device, and then got the location, assuming they use Google location, then it's got to travel all the way back to us. I've no idea really, this is a first. But if we haven't got anything back from it within the next five minutes, I doubt I'll ever hear from it again. It'll have been stopped somewhere along the line."

After over a minute, which felt like forever to the MI5 onlookers, a reply popped into the window. 'Water Spider – You will bring me the Omega 6500 projectile samples. No one else, just you. Be at the Lido jetty by the Grand Hotel Imperiale in Moltresio Lake Como Friday midday. Agree?'

The jubilations erupted in front of the computer with high fiving and back-patting all round. "We've done it. They've taken it. We're going to meet the broker. This is brilliant," celebrated Vince.

Amidst the commotion, Si put in a considered reply. 'Blackbird – Agreed. I will be there with the samples. You will make the usual safety deposit box payment after the sale in due course?'

"You're not actually intending to go are you," asked Max.

"Good God no. I'll be too easy to look up. MI5 might be Secret Intelligence Services, but most management and Thames House based staff are well known to the right organisations, and if you know where to look, the wrong ones as well." Si gazed up as if formulating a thought. "No, not me, but I was thinking we'll probably send Phil Landon, the field operative who discovered this whole thing. He managed to see the last auction for the silencer. He'd be the best person to impersonate us as the seller Blackbird. We can fill him in tomorrow."

Si was very happy, the evening seemed to have gone perfectly to plan. The next reply came in simply saying, 'Water Spider – Yes.', to his query about being paid. Si had played a good game impersonating the seller, even Sir John was impressed and seemed happy, hopeful that if MI5 could find out who the broker and even buyers were. Maybe his help would be all the more appreciated by the court and his lawyers could push harder for leniency.

They were about to consider signing off from the chat window when a new message appeared. It caught them all off guard as they each read it from the screen, in horror.

'Water Spider – For identification for when I meet you, send me your picture from your computer cam. No name, just your pic. Right now'.

They all looked at one another. "Shit!" said Si.

"Damn it! What are we going to do?" fretted Vince. "Phil Landon's not here. How do we stall for time? Tell them we'll send the picture at the next chat?"

Mild panic and indecision fell over the four of them, watched by Wilson and Sir John. "We can't do that, it'll look odd. They want it right now. We're wasting time," said Si sternly.

He quickly looked at each person for a candidate to now *be* the seller Blackbird. It couldn't be himself or Vince, nor Alan and he wasn't a field operative anyway, and too young. Looking over to Sergeant Wilson and Sir John gave him an immediate and obvious 'no'. His eyes fixed on the only remaining possible candidate to impersonate the designs thief to the broker. Max looked shocked.

"Max! You're up I'm afraid," said Si commandingly, guiding Max to the seat in front of the computer. Max had no time to protest and if honest with himself had also concluded, albeit regrettably, that he was the only person in the room that could pull it off for the picture. Si hastily instructed everyone to move well to the sides, way out of camera view. Alan told Max which keys to simultaneously press to activate the tiny camera on top of the screen in front of him to take his picture, then dived out of the way. They all watched as Max gathered himself in his seat, looked into the camera and without smiling took a single picture of himself.

Alan dashed back to the seat next to Max and brought up the photo of Max, checking there was none of the rest of them in the picture. It was clear. Just Max gazing somewhat blankly into the camera, looking a little dismayed, but it would do.

Alan asked, "Shall I send it over to them Si?"

Si looked round at everyone, then at Max. "You okay with this Max? Looks like you're going to Lake Como? I'll make sure you're supported all the way."

Max gave an angry frown but nodded his agreement. Alan attached the picture of Max to the basic reply, 'Blackbird – my pic.'

It was done. Max's heart was pounding. In a moment he'd gone from being a background observer to the online interactions, to now being thrust into the front line of another dangerous and complicated operation with MI5. He had no idea whatsoever what he'd just got himself into, and fear of the unknown was an unkind mistress.

Once more a new message appeared on the screen. They refocused. 'Water Spider – Nice picture Blackbird. See you Friday, let's catch up Wed 8PM to check all is ok.'

The following message was a new, long, jumbled link for the next scheduled chat. Sir John interjected saying, "They leave it there about twenty seconds before going, copy it quickly!"

Alan copied the link and saved it in the same folder Sir John had been using. A few moments later the screen went blank with the returning message 'Site Not Found'. Alan closed their Dark Web browser window and sat back. "Wow, that was intense." The others didn't say anything but all nodded in agreement.

"What happened to your Trojan Alan?" asked Vince.

"I guess it didn't make it through the servers. Damn it!" Alan would never know that he'd actually created possibly the first-ever Dark Web seeker trojan good enough to find the other end user's device and return. If it hadn't been stopped by the simple fact the Google location services weren't enabled the other end, it would have worked.

They all allowed themselves some quiet, satisfying contemplation over what had just occurred, before Si brought them all back down to earth. "Sir John, I'm afraid you need to go back to the station for now and we'll agree the messaging for your and Margaret's absence for the next few weeks. I suggest leave of absence due to a family matter. I'll also need you to help Vince speak with Kendrick about us picking up a couple of samples from him tomorrow, as no doubt he'll have left by now."

Turning to his four MI5 guys in the room. "I'll see you guys first thing in the morning at Thames House. We've got a lot to get through in the next few days." Placing a hand on Max's shoulder, "Appreciate you stepping up for this one Max. Looks like we're still on the Omega trail after all eh."

Max smiled at Si reluctantly, thinking to himself that being on the trail wasn't what worried him. It was where the trail would lead that he was concerned about!

12

Mateo Ricci sat in his favourite chair on the patio of his beloved detached, private lakeside villa. Enjoying another bottle of Birra Moretti beer, he gazed out at his stunning vista across the enchanting Lake Como. It was a picture-postcard view. The beautiful setting of the lake, framed almost entirely by scenic, green covered mountains including the Alps, with its microclimate, had made it a top tourist destination and resort for celebrities, the wealthy and the locals.

Thirty miles north of Milan the upside-down 'Y' shaped lake covered over fifty square miles in the Lombardy region, with its deep waters going down some 1300 feet. Picturesque villages and towns dotted themselves around the lake's edge, with traditional buildings and impressive villas vying for positions, clamouring to be as close to the water as possible. The road circumnavigating the expanse of water was narrow and traditional, forcing drivers to go slowly as they picked their way around its bends and enclaves, constantly pausing to give way to oncoming traffic. Whilst the many punctual Como ferries busily transported people up and down the lake or zigzagged from town to town on either side, lakeside properties especially with a jetty, were at a huge premium. The best way to exist and move around here, if you could afford it, was with your own boat.

With only a finite amount of land and buildings alongside the lake, and years of the trendy notion that the rich and famous all had to have a Como lakeside villa amongst their global property portfolio, many locals had long since cashed in and sold their family homes or waterside grazing land for huge sums.

Mateo had been able to buy his house from the trappings of his entrepreneurial business. The three bedroomed, two-story villa was nestled on a relatively large strip of land just up from the quaint village of Nesso, and backed onto the Strada Provincial 583 road, which eventually ended up at the popular tourist town of Bellagio. With a population of only thirteen hundred, Nesso had all the necessary amenities, shops and restaurants he needed, but also gave him the quiet privacy he placed a lot of emphasis on. His property sat alone to the north of the sleepy town, which was a deliberate choice to be away from the small Nesso ferry terminal which was situated at the southern end. He could avoid the constant inquisitive gazes from the ferry passengers coming in and out.

The electric gated driveway and car parking area provided additional security and privacy from the passing public road. The big attraction of his villa was what was at the rear, hidden out of sight and away from the road. The back of the property opened out onto a large patio and staggered lawn area leading down to the water's edge, where a concrete jetty had long since been built, for several sizeable boats to be moored alongside. The unspoiled view and lake access alone, were worth a few million euros.

Across the serene water on the other side, the lush green mountainside of Mont Generoso gently sloped down to the lake, providing an incredible backdrop. To the right in the distance was the town of Argegno nestled at the base of the foothills and to the left was the smaller town of Brienno. It was perfect here for Mateo. He loved nothing more than to sit on his patio and look across the lake, watching the various boats and ferries go by, listening to the town's church bells and feeling swathed in the security of this natural basin away from the rest of the world.

When he needed to be in town he used his large apartment in Villasanta, which was in the suburbs of Milan near to where he grew up, overlooking the Parco di Monza and its tree-shrouded Lambro River.

Mateo was mid-forties. His once athletic form had become overweight from indulging in too much good food and wine, yet his seemingly mismatched handsome face remained strong, persuasive, full of energy for life, women and money. His dark good looks, strong nose and cheekbones, with dark eyes and predominantly black wavy hair, were gifted to him by his attractive, posh British mother and roguish, strapping Italian father.

His mother was working at a large travel firm's Milan office in the days when many holidays and flights were still booked through a travel agency shop, pre-internet. Though her role was based at their head office, she often filled in at the high street agency where she loved dealing with customers directly to improve her ever more acceptable Italian speech. His father had needed to book return flights from Milan to London, and with nothing more than her home city in common, the sparks flew and they found themselves attracted to one another instantly.

It was a ying-yang relationship, they were opposites. She was from a well-off family, private English schooling, impeccable manners and diplomacy, with the ambition to succeed with hard work and performance. He on the other hand was schooled locally in Milan, at various schools due to his lack of respect for teachers. He had a poor upbringing in a large family all competing for their parent's attention and was a chancer, happy to avoid hard work and pursue quick gains.

At just four years old they sent Mateo to the James Henderson British School of Milan where he stayed for the next twelve years, mainly on the insistence of the British mother. She wanted her son to have the best of both English and Italian worlds, whilst his roots were in Milan, she felt it would be his British influence that would stand him in better stead for a successful life. He benefited from being able to speak fluent English and Italian.

But Mateo's childhood was torn between the two different orbits of his dissimilar parents, and unfortunately, over the years, he gravitated towards his darker, less impressive and somewhat spurious father figure. Mateo became indifferent to the system of education and shunned doing an apprenticeship with a big firm. He yearned for an easier path to success, which for him meant' earning easy money, often only found when risks are taken.

At the time he left school late teens and just before starting the antiquated duty of his eight-month 'naja' conscription into the Italian military, the inevitable differences between his parents finally broke down. With the excuse their son was now a man and could look after himself, they both agreed to be free of one another in the hope of each finding more compatible partners. Mateo's mother returned to London, leaving him with his father in Milan. The absence of his positive guiding influence parent now left him to fall deeper into the selfish ways of his father, who had a string of businesses, buying, selling, brokering deals, doing one-off risky jobs. The dye was now cast for Mateo.

He hated the discipline of the army but found that being thrown together with all sorts of undesirables pulling together against the system, made him friends in low places. He left the army as soon as he was allowed to and using his newfound comrades, spent a decade working for various small firms, family businesses and enterprises, mostly legal and upstanding, some not so much. Mateo found he had a talent for bringing people together, sharing in their good fortune, without committing himself one way or the other. An impartial broker, like his father sometimes seemed to be. He started taking his father's compromised advice being, 'be where there's lots of money swilling around, if you're close enough it'll always rub off on you'. Mateo became affectionately known by his friends as 'il mediatore', the middleman, the mediator. The broker.

For more than ten years Mateo brokered deals, mostly legitimate, helping with negotiations between two parties, taking escrow payments to be held until contracts had been agreed and signed, and selling expensive items like houses, jewellery or cars for sellers that didn't want to be in the limelight or preferred anonymity. Of course, for everything he did, he charged a small but reasonable commission and over the years his fees got larger and earned him millions. He was earning money from brokering other people's money and goods. His father who had by now passed away would have been proud of him. His mother preferred not to acknowledge her son seemingly following after her husband's dealings and felt her attempts to put him on the right path were wasted. They spoke on the telephone a few times a year.

Then aged forty, just as Mateo was thinking of retiring to his beloved Lake Como with his fortune, one of his 'associates' asked him to broker an arms deal. He'd had to take part payment of a dubious property sale in the form of a small warehouse full of Kalashnikov AK47 automatic rifles. Fortunately, these were one of the most reliable and desirable weapons around, favoured by everyone for their reliability and robustness. If given the option of any medium-sized gun to have in battle or on war-torn streets, one simply avoided fancy looking weapons in favour of the ones that you knew would shoot true every time, come rain or shine.

Mateo made enquiries around his network and soon found a willing buyer for the AK47's, which were duly collected by three large khaki coloured trucks and driven off up the E70 motorway to Slovenia, likely to an uncontrolled point along the two-hundred-kilometre border. Mateo was paid in US dollars cash and had doubled his money within a month. He never once touched or saw a single Kalashnikov. He felt like Christmas had come early with one of the easiest big deals he'd handled. Mateo decided to put all his semi-retirement efforts into brokering arms deals. He also did the odd rare Italian supercar deal he'd source locally and export abroad, just so he had something to show the Italian Revenue Agency for tax purposes.

Then by sheer coincidence, Mateo was contacted by one of the men he'd served his brief conscription in the army with, who had somehow heard of his abilities to broker more dubious deals under the radar. The man was one of the few to be conscripted who chose to make the army and their career and after two decades had worked his way up to the senior rank of Generale di Divisione, Divisional General of the Italian Special Operations Forces. He was about to retire and felt underwhelmed at the lack of any decent financial provision for a retiring, long-serving officer, albeit that his promotions were mainly due to his longevity and not his performance.

The Italian Army had commissioned at that time significant ground-breaking improvements to two of their less secretive pieces of equipment, being the NC4/09 bullet-proof vest and their Officine

Galileo VTG-240 thermal imaging system. Such design upgrades would not usually attract much attention or interest. However, the Divisional General had struck up a friendship recently with a General Major in the Slovakian army, where in the Western Istria region Italian was spoken fluently.

Their topic of conversation would often broach on improvements and innovations each of their militaries had just launched, and then inevitably they would try to tease out at one another any technology or improvements they were each working on. On this occasion, Mateo's conscription friend had mentioned their soon to be launched improved bullet-proof vest and thermal imaging system. Much to his surprise, the Slovakian General Major wanted a discreet and personal accomplishment of his own to impress his General with and suggested a sizeable payment in exchange for a sample of each of the items.

The Italian officer had made tentative arrangements with his Slovakian peer and wanted Mateo to handle the exchange and money collection personally as he couldn't possibly be seen to be involved. At the time Mateo simply looked upon this as another of his straightforward brokering deals, similar to those he'd done many times in the past and agreed his cut would be a very reasonable thirty per cent, three hundred thousand Euros. He went to his old comrade's country villa on the outskirts of Rome, where the Italian Army headquarters were based, and picked up the latest prototypes for the two items.

Hiding them in the spare wheel recess under the boot of his car. He did the eight-hour drive from Rome to the Austrian town of Stossau, which was about halfway in between Rome and Slovakia. He'd been instructed to meet the General Major's contact at a deserted farmhouse just outside the village of Hohenthurn.

When Mateo arrived the Slovakian contact was already waiting for him. The payment was to be made with a small bag of diamonds to the value of the agreed one million Euros, but it was clear to Mateo that the other man had had too long in possession of this valuable pouch to ponder alternative options rather than hand it over for a lousy bullet-proof vest and thermal sights. He suggested to Mateo that they shared the diamonds equally and returned to their prospective employers, claiming they'd been ambushed and the diamonds had gone.

Mateo was always open to brokering a dodgy deal, but his reputation to do what was agreed was what kept him in business as someone who could be trusted to deliver. He wasn't happy at all with the idea of splitting with the diamonds and possibly having to go on the run forevermore, especially as he knew he was already getting a third of them for his efforts, which was considerably more than the other man was getting, if anything at all. They argued and as they fronted up to one another there was a scuffle. As the Slovakian started to choke Mateo on the ground, his flailing freehand searching the floor around him for anything of assistance, found a rusty hammer. The strike was clumsy but made contact with the Slovakian's head and was enough to knock the man off him. Mateo rose to his feet ready to defend himself again, but saw the blow to his attacker take its delayed stun effect and the small splintering of the man's skull, became a lethal blow. The Slovakian died on the floor in front of Mateo.

He drove the other car into the barn and hid the two samples in a dusty, rotting wooden tool chest in the corner, took the diamonds and left. Mateo was in shock and physically shaking for the first half an hour of his drive back to Rome. During his journey, he called the Divisional General and relayed to him exactly what had happened.

By the time he duly delivered the bag of diamonds, his old friend had long since contacted the Slovakian General Major, who had surprisingly shared his misgivings about the man he'd sent to meet Mateo. With no concerns for the dead foot-soldier, he'd immediately arranged for a couple of his more trusted and loyal operatives to leave at once and go to the barn, where they would dispose of the body and car, and retrieve the two items from the toolbox.

The Italian officer had been impressed with what Mateo had

done and upon receiving the bag of diamonds from him, had spread them out on a table at his home and very roughly separated off approximately a third of the sparkling gems, pushing them across to Mateo as his payment.

Mateo celebrated his large payoff for only a few days work, but was still shaken over the unfortunate outcome of his clandestine meeting in that deserted Austrian farmhouse. He'd killed a man. He kept reminding himself it was an accident and in self-defence. He would have been strangled to death if he hadn't done something. However, he swore to himself that he would never get involved with another face-to-face transaction and would retreat to the cover of the Dark Web, from behind which he could handle any future communications and soft file transactions in the safety of anonymity. He had many millions to his name and simply didn't need to take any more personal risks to add to his already comfortable fortune.

For this reason, he had been particularly perturbed when he found himself having to agree to a face-to-face meeting with this Blackbird seller, to facilitate the sale of the Omega 6500 projectile.

As Mateo looked out across Lake Como, it was this that he was pondering. Had he done the right thing? Could there possibly be anything about this that could go dreadfully wrong? He had been encouraged by the computer selfie that Blackbird had sent him, being of a young executive-type sitting in what looked like a samples or records room and not some dodgy-looking gangster.

However, he still felt uncomfortable about having to meet up with someone, though found himself spurred on by the prize at hand. A unique high-powered sniper rifle that could almost guarantee hitting a lasered target maybe four miles away using self-accuracy adjusting bullets. That was incredible. His optimism had run away with himself and he honestly believed that he could sell something like this for maybe fifty million dollars, even with just a couple of samples of the Omega projectiles. They were the key innovative component here. Perhaps this time he'd keep more than his usual seventy per cent.

Mateo had hosted a regular open chat forum on the Dark Web which he viewed as a fishing trip, an opportunity to recruit new informers and intelligence thieves in the military or ordnance sectors. He'd found a few low-level employees snooping around the Dark Web that knew someone, who knew someone else, who could pass on the link to his chat window, where designs and intel had passed across their desks. He'd made a few quick sales mostly for much smaller numbers than he'd bother with, but remained hopeful his seller contacts might stumble on something bigger in time.

Then Blackbird came along. For no reason, Mateo had assumed this timid, cautious potential seller was American, until after the first sale he'd asked them what their nearest airport was so that he could fly in and drop off the payment for them. Once he knew it was Gatwick it confirmed he was probably dealing with a Brit. He was always careful to maintain anonymity for both himself and his seller, never tempted to pry or ask searching, give-away questions about their identity. It was merely observing two-way respect and building up trust, after all, he was expecting them to hand over design secrets and trust that he would sell them, declare the correct share for them and pay up, which he always did.

Mateo had started off gently with Blackbird, whom it became apparent had access to some impressive IP. He thought perhaps they worked for the military, or maybe the MOD and was excited when they finally sent over the specifications for a new, tougher Kevlar-carbon weave helmet. Then came the room-clearing grenade, and recently the stealth silencer. Mateo was making another fortune on top of the one he already had. He'd figured that the online sellers had no idea what value their stolen intel was worth, so would be happy with anything resembling a seven-figure sum. Mateo had been bold and for his troubles finding these items discreet international buyers, had decided to keep seventy per cent as his fee. After all, he was at the peak of his career, perhaps after a few more big deals, he would finally retire.

Mateo's Dark Webchat the previous day with Blackbird had felt different. The replies from this seller seemed more confident, he detected a slight loss of leverage and control down the encrypted transmissions between the two of them. He put it down to the apparent security changes at Blackbird's employment location, but still didn't know where that might have been. He couldn't find out which manufacturer or design firm was responsible for the weapons he'd brokered, as they weren't yet in the public domain or launched, they were still secrets.

Something told him that if he was going to put himself out and meet with this Blackbird guy to have the Omega samples handed over, he may as well line up a buyer at the same time to also be part of the meeting. If he was able to agree a direct, off-auction price in advance, the buyer could bring the full payment with them, they would all share equally the risk and the exposure of the face-to-face transaction and he would not have to bankroll anyone with the whole deal being done the same day. He'd simply take his seventy-plus per cent from the payment in diamonds and pass Blackbird their share. Then it was up to Blackbird to worry about travelling home with the diamonds, and the responsibility of the buyer to worry about travelling back with their precious Omega samples. He didn't want to be carrying around valuable samples for other people.

Mateo made up his mind, no auction for this one. He now needed a known trustworthy buyer, at least as much as one could expect from such dealings, preferably able to handle the exchange this coming Friday here at Lake Como. Someone he knew could afford this design prototype. He already had the perfect potential buyer who had been hoovering up as many new weapons designs as they could lay their hands on. They'd won the last few Dark Web chat room auctions anyway, so it seemed a waste of time to go through having to arrange everyone for another auction when he was convinced this repeat buyer would do a deal for the Omega items.

Using one of his scheduled Dark Web encrypted chats, he would pitch Omega to the repeat buyer as an exclusive one-off deal. He'd offer it to the one with the username, 'Samson'.

13

The motorcycle courier effortlessly topped a hundred and ten miles an hour on the M23 motorway coming up towards London from the Gatwick area. Although the speed limit was seventy and British drivers seemed to think up to about eighty was entirely acceptable to police, this despatch rider had an exemption to travel 'at speeds of his discretion without endangering other travellers or vehicles'.

His decades of motorbike experience and expertise allowed him to feel quite safe at over one hundred, on his new black with green accents Kawasaki Ninja H2 Carbon superbike. As a regular customer, he was one of just one hundred and twenty lucky customers to be allowed to buy the bike. The makers claimed it to be the fastest on the road when launched in 2020, with a top speed of two-hundred and fifty miles an hour. At a hundred, the four-stroke sixteen valve fuel-injected one-litre supercharged engine beneath him had so much more to give.

He was one of a handful of elite dispatch riders retained by MI5 to courier important documents, collect orders and government paperwork, take urgent briefings and reports to Downing Street or collect and deliver small samples of a variety of items. The previous day he had delivered what he believed to be some highly contentious photos to the new American Embassy building in Vauxhall Gardens overlooking the Thames. The well-sealed envelope was stamped 'To be hand-delivered unopened to POTUS', the President of the United States.

He'd started early by collecting a document from MI5 Thames House which he then took down to the Crawley police station for a Sergeant Wilson to have a Sir John Tregar sign. It was a samples release authorisation. He then went up the road to the Empire Arms complex in Charlwood where he waited until a Peter Kendrick arrived at their Apollo Designs offices.

Peter Kendrick had got into work eight thirty Monday morning still wondering what all the fuss with the police had been about the night before, but as Sir John was helping them, had finally reconciled himself it was all okay. He was then surprised to see the dispatch motorcyclist waiting for him in his office's reception when he arrived, handing him a document. He'd opened it to find a note from Sir John firstly apologising for not being in due to leave of absence regarding a personal matter, and thanking him for his help with the police investigation. Sir John then went on to ask him to hand over to the courier one fully functioning sample of the Omega 6500 projectile, along with two more projectile samples but with empty shell casings.

Peter was most reticent to hand over a complete sample prototype of this treasured, secret weapon, but realised there was no point discussing the matter with the courier. Especially as they looked quite formidable in their full black leather protective gear, boots and gloves. The man had at least removed his large black helmet. He went off to the workshop and put together the three large 'bullets' into a samples case.

About ten minutes later, Kendrick had emerged back into reception and handed over a cigar sized box to the courier, which he assumed was going off to the police somewhere. In fact it was to be delivered back to London for Si Lawson at MI5 Thames House. The forty-five-mile journey at rush hour would normally have taken over an hour and a half. The courier motorcyclist did it in just over forty minutes which was impressive, given his average speed of just under seventy included the much slower last few miles in central London. It had been made very clear to him that what was being delivered was required urgently at Thames House.

All the key players of Si Lawson's team were already in the Cyber office at MI5 Thames House including Vince, Josh, Ellie, Alan, Max and Phil Landon, who had been assigned to Si for this operation.

Si had agreed with Sir John the signed release paper for Kendrick the designer to hand over the live and dummy projectile samples. He'd also agreed to accommodate his request to tell the

samples. He'd also agreed to accommodate his request to tell the other Empire board members that Sir John needed leave for a personal matter, as Si needed both Sir John and the CPO Margaret Fallon in safe custody while this mission played out over the next week or so. They couldn't have anyone including the press, getting hold of this and scaring off the Lake Como meeting with the broker Water Spider. Margaret's procurement team would also be given a similar message regarding her absence.

Si had already thought things through and gave a quick update to them all in the meeting room. "We've got a great opportunity now with this meeting on Friday with the arms broker. Max will go to Lake Como with Phil Landon alongside for backup, but who'll keep out the way when the pickup for the meeting is done. You guys need to familiarise yourselves this week with every part of Lake Como, given the broker wants you to be at the Lido jetty in Moltrasio, I think we can safely assume they'll collect you by boat then take you off somewhere else around the lake. Phil, you need to prep for the usual long-range surveillance of Max, we don't want to lose him for this one."

Looking to Alan he continued. "Alan and I spoke yesterday about using the Omega projectiles to in theory allow Phil sight of Max's whereabouts whilst he has them. Then more importantly to be able to onward track them for when they're hopefully in the possession of the end buyer. That's the main idea here, we follow the Omega projectiles through to the end. Alan, why don't you explain what you're thinking?"

Alan cleared his throat. "We have an opportunity as Si said to use the small projectiles we're giving to the broker and then hopefully the buyer, as a tracking device."

"How can we track bullets," asked Josh.

"I'm certain that with the technology advances in covert trackers, me and the tech team here can get one into an Omega projectile." Everyone looked dubious, Alan continued regardless. "Yes, we should be getting any moment a live sample along with two empty dummy shells. They're the ones we can play around with and fit either a GPS or radio-tracking device into. We're proposing Max takes the two samples as promised on the Dark Web chat, one of them will be the real deal propelled laser adjusting one, the other will be our tracker."

"What if they want to start inspecting or dismantling the bullets," asked Ellie.

"Unlikely," said Alan. "They can only dismantle one of these in laboratory conditions."

Si chipped in. "We'll have to assume they won't, and if they do, we'll have to pray they pick the real one and not our dummy tracker. Alan, you'll need to make sure the dummy with your tracker weighs the same of the real one."

"Can you really get a tracker into that tiny shell casing?" Max wanted more reassurance.

Alan replied, "I'm pretty certain we can make it work judging by the size of the casings we saw at Apollo. They looked to be about six inches long by an inch wide. I'm also confident we can put it back together so it looks and weighs exactly the same as the real one. Size isn't the issue. The only thing I'm worried about is how much the brass shell case, or whatever it's made of, will block the transmission signal from the tracker. But we'll only find that out this week by testing it."

Max asked, "I thought GPS and mobile signals won't go through metal?"

"You're right, that's what we've got this week to figure out and overcome. But we do have a failsafe tracker we'll also install, that we know will give us complete and accurate positioning using a micro sim card and tiny battery."

"Great, problem solved, but where does that go? I can't carry it, any way you need it with the projectiles to track through to the end buyer, not on me?" said Max.

Alan nodded in agreement. "Totally. We'll put it inside a case we'll construct to hold the two projectiles. That bit's easy. However, if anyone doesn't like the case and throws it away to keep hold of just the projectiles, then that tracking idea is screwed."

Si's mobile buzzed, it was reception asking him to go down and personally collect a delivery. "I'm sending Alan, he has my authority to receive the package from the courier thanks." Alan needed no invitation to leave and excused himself excitedly, like a child wanting to rush downstairs to see their Christmas presents. The Omega projectiles had arrived.

"One last thing guys, don't forget we've got a follow-up Dark Webchat booked in for Wednesday at eight," reminded Si as everyone left the room to go about their various preparations for Max and Phil's trip.

Alan went to reception excitedly and after signing for the small parcel handed over by the courier rider, fumbled with the tape around the package. Opening it slowly he gazed at the three large projectiles neatly sitting in their foam surround. One of them had a post-it note stuck onto it saying 'REAL'. He carefully lifted each one to discover the 'real' one was far heavier than the other two. The tiny glass ends were in place so externally they looked identical, but the empty shells would allow him two attempts to play around with inserting his tracker electronics into.

Alan could now see the detail behind these amazing super-large bullets. They were six inches long by an inch in diameter, the biggest bullet he'd ever seen. Each had a small fin and four tiny rear angled facing portholes near the base of the bullet part, above the shell case, for the directional propulsion jets. He marvelled at the thought few others in the world had yet been able to hold such a unique part of weaponry history.

Alan texted Si to confirm he'd collected the three samples and all was as it should be, one real, two dummies, and that he was off back to the lab to start working out how best to insert a tracker into both a shell and either this box or another small case. He'd spend the next few days assembling and trialling various trackers that could be fitted into one of the empty shell casings. Then they would start the real challenge of inserting the devices into the shells and seeing how badly their transmission was affected by the metal casing. It wasn't going to be easy.

14

Mateo Ricci pensively looked out over the beautiful Lake Como. He knew that his greed to obtain these parts of the Omega long-range sniper system, was forcing him to compromise his rule about not meeting buyers or sellers. But something so innovative and deadly would command an unusually high price. This could make him tens of millions, so as long as he controlled the public meetup, it was worth the risk. He glanced at his hundred thousand euro Patek Philippe Nautilus watch and went inside to his office. He'd arranged a Dark webchat with his top client Samson.

Mateo's user name was chosen like so many are, on the spur of the moment. It had been mid-summer when unfortunately the insect population becomes abundant at Lake Como. He was on his boat moored to his dock, using his laptop. When prompted for a username he'd looked down at the water and closely watched a tiny water spider skating around on the surface chasing flies. And so his tag was created.

Mateo opened up the chat page and could see another user 'Samson' was already in the lobby waiting.

He typed. 'Water Spider – Thanks for joining.'

'Samson – What's this about then, is it another upcoming auction?'

'Water Spider – As you have won several auctions I wanted to give you first refusal on a very impressive new design. Interested?' Mateo was pretty sure the buyer would go for this, but there was now that moment where Samson could simply say they'd let the auction run and win it at market value.

The reply was fast. 'Samson – Of course, tell me about it!'

Mateo smirked to himself. 'Water Spider – It's a unique long-range sniper system component. Highly classified, but I can get samples of the key component.' Mateo felt that should whet the buyer's appetite enough and paused before typing the critical condition.

'Water Spider – I can't get designs, this sale is for two samples of the self-adjusting targeting long-range projectile.' Mateo waited, staring at the screen. There was a long pause.

'Samson – How long-range?'

'Water Spider – Existing sniper technology is somewhat inaccurate but can reach 2 miles. The system I have can accurately hit its lasered target at TWICE that distance.'

Mateo again frowned at the even longer pause on the screen, it took to get a reply.

'Samson – I am interested, what other components does this sniper system have?'

'Water Spider – A large, longer rifle with matching bore for the projectile and spotter's sights with laser targetting and variables analysis system, wind, temperature, distance etc. But the projectile is the key item that can only be replicated with a sample.'

'Samson - Subject to me seeing these samples, what are you suggesting for a sale?'

Mateo relished this part. The price. 'Water Spider – This will sell at auction for maybe $60m. You can have it for $50m?'

Mateo knew he was pushing his luck and plucking the number out of thin air, for something so small with no blueprints, nor accompanying rifle and sighting computer. But he felt he had the buyer now and the advantage was his. Given Samson was hoovering up all-new weapons designs, it seemed reasonable to assume they would not want anyone else to have the march on them with this particular sniper system. The reply flashed up onto his screen.

'Samson – I can go to $40m and no more.'

'Damn it!' thought Mateo, 'playing hardball are they. We'll see about that'! The reasonable ploy might have been to suggest meeting halfway at $45m, but Mateo wasn't reasonable. He hadn't made millions by meeting people halfway.

'Water Spider – As you're a regular buyer, I can go $48m.

Take it or leave it. Otherwise, I will sell off-auction to another buyer.' Mateo rolled the dice. He would agree to less if the pushback came through again, but experience told him the buyer couldn't take the risk of losing this item. Another long pause.

'Samson - $48m agreed, in diamonds, subject to inspection though. When and where?'

Mateo punched the air in celebration and immediately calculated in his mind the usual seventy per cent would earn him over thirty-three million dollars. But that would leave way too much for Blackbird. No, he would keep say forty million for himself and he could still reward Blackbird with a massive eight million. That was only fair, after all, he was doing all the work here.

Mateo typed in the instructions for the buyer Samson to come to Lake Como this Friday, alone, with the diamonds, to make the exchange. After the final chat signoff, he closed down the Dark web window, leaving no trace of the anonymous sale agreed. He sat back in his chair and looked through the patio doors onto the lake. Mateo's jubilation curtailed as he now realised that his communications with Blackbird and Samson were the easy parts. Doing deals in the safety of his beloved Como lakeside villa without having to meet anyone was a luxury. But now he would be meeting both seller and buyer for this exchange.

Had he got carried away with the size of the prize? Could he trust them both to handle a clean transaction? How would they react to having both the valuable merchandise and the diamonds in their sight? Mateo now started to wonder if perhaps he'd bitten off too much here. He knew how people could change in the presence of such wealth in front of them, there for the taking. He had a few days to think very carefully about how to play this on Friday and a couple of options were already starting to form in his mind, one reasonable and one high risk. But Mateo wasn't reasonable.

In Berlin, Leon Becker turned away from his desktop computer calm and contemplative. Satisfied with yet another weapons design purchase for his organisation and entirely relaxed about having to meet up with the broker calling themselves Water Spider. He relished the opportunities a face-to-face liaison would throw his way. Nothing phased Leon, he'd experienced too much horror to be worried about anything the normal world might throw at him.

In complete contradiction to his character, he's chosen the username Samson, not because of its biblical connotations of the man endowed with super-strength, until his love Delilah cut his hair to destroy him. His choice was far more innocent and childish. He grew up watching the German version of the American hit show Seasame Street. Sesamstrasse had a different star to the original yellow Big Bird. A bear, called Samson.

Leon was the buyer of the various ordnance that had come up for sale on the Dark web. But not for himself, he was just the frontman for a larger, more sinister organisation, the Dreizack.

This was a unique mafia collaboration between certain underworld gangs from Germany, Italy and Russia. Brokered some ten years ago by the leaders of the three outfits, who had all crossed paths earlier in life, facilitating this unheard-of international alliance between the gangland factions. The more overbearing leader was of the German mafia, hence the overarching mob name was given of Dreizack, the German meaning for tripod, representing the three gangs.

They operated from Munich to Berlin, Milan to Rome, and Moscow to St Petersburg. The usual businesses were conducted across extorsion, prostitution, gambling, loan sharking, people trafficking and blackmail. The organisation had agreed with other gangs to stay clear of the drug scene in return for being able to focus on their main and growing business, of weapons smuggling, selling, brokering and theft. With more cash than they knew what to do with, they decided to extend their ordnance sector into buying up stolen, top-secret new weapons designs. They would then either start manufacturing these if the designs were within the capabilities of their growing weapons-making expertise, or if not, resell them onto wealthy nations who were prepared to pay many times the price to jump ahead of the arms race by obtaining someones else's hard work and design.

Whilst Leon had been on the dark webchat with Water Spider, he'd had another mobile alongside his computer on the desk, with an open line to his boss. As the chat window was restricted to typed messages only, he could freely give a running commentary over his mobile to his superior on what was said and whether he could offer the prices needed to obtain the design. This explained the various pauses in his reply to Water Spider, where he was waiting for his boss to decide how to respond.

Leon Becker was your classic silent assassin. A man of few words and little complexity. He expressed himself through action, usually violent action. In his late forties with a slim athletic build just under six foot tall, of mostly sinewy muscle with straight fair hair. Leon was very fit. Whenever his schedule allowed it, he would run about ten miles and do weights early in the morning, followed by a hot, then freezing cold shower.

Leon grew up in the village of Koldingen situated alongside the River Leine, just south of Hanover in Germany. From a young age, his parents were concerned about his apparent inability to understand how others felt, or pick up on their expressions and feelings. When a doctor started to suggest the diagnosis of Empathy Deficit Disorder his mother quickly backed off, from fear of tarnishing her beloved son with the label for the rest of his life. Both German parents spoke excellent English and by the time Leon was in his teens, he could speak both languages fluently.

He had a bizarre fascination of good versus evil, cops against robbers, dictators against freedom. Indeed anything which had two grossly opposing views was of interest to him. These antitheses allowed his unfeeling, logical thinking to harshly, but often entirely logically, set out the case for justifying which position made sense. He would debate the existence of UFO's, religion, punishments for criminals, dictatorships, law and order, then also the right of criminals to prosper.

Much to his mother and father's relief, in his early twenties Leon came down on the side of good and joined the German Police.

With his unquestioning ability to follow orders, his rarely rivalled fitness levels and determination, Leon quickly worked his way up through the Landespolizei State Police. One of his superiors, Hans Meyer, quickly saw the potential Leon had to serve him as a loyal enforcer and kept him close, looking out for him on many occasions.

Hans was destined for big things, more than likely heading for a senior role in the Bundesnachrichtendienst, Germany's Federal Intelligence Service. So when Hans was promoted into the Bundespolizei Federal Police, he made certain that his protégé Leon went with him. In the Bundespolizei, Leon grew a reputation not to be trifled with, indeed avoided whenever possible, both with his police peers and also the criminal world.

Then his callous and often cruel ways got ahead of him when he was asked to interrogate a bank robber. The police had managed to capture one of three assailants, who the others left behind with a leg injury inflicted by a guard who'd shot at him. One of the fleeing men came back and shot the guard in the head. Reasonable questioning and persuasion hadn't worked and the robber was loyally protecting the names of his two friends, despite threats of taking the wrap for them, for armed robbery and murder.

Leon was asked to 'have a chat' with this criminal and try to 'persuade' him to give the other names. He started talking to the man and when met with either swearing or silence, quickly grew impatient of the standard professional, unrewarding tactics. Leon asked the other officer to leave the room, who dutifully left turning off both the in-room recording device and the CCTV from the adjoining room, not out of loyalty, but because he was afraid of Leon himself.

Now Leon was free to start getting physical with the criminal. At first, it was a punch to the abdomen, which wouldn't cause any visible bruising. The man started to explain he was forced to do the raid, that his family would be killed if he didn't do the job. But this fell on deaf ears, all Leon wanted were the names of the other two, because that's what he'd been asked to get. It got more brutal. A finger was broken, an arm almost twisted out of its socket.

Then in pure rage and frustration, Leon held the man in a chokehold standing behind him and squeezing harder and harder.

Whilst he was careful not to break the man's neck, he misjudged the delicate balance needed with his powerful arms, to only almost kill him, but release enough to keep him alive. When the poor man went limp Leon had assumed he'd merely passed out. But after a minute of trying to bring him round, it became apparent he'd choked the man to death with his powerful arm lock around his neck.

Leon's accompanying officer returned to the room and was confronted with the sight of Leon rather feebly trying to wake up the prisoner, who was clearly dead. He quickly exited raising the alarm and then chaos broke loose. Other officers rushed in, several tried to resuscitate the dead man to no avail. The senior officer removed Leon from the scene to a holding room for a statement.

Both Leon and the other officer were plunged into deep trouble. There was a full investigation, lots of interviews. The dead man's family sued the police. Things were looking bad for Leon, until his senior officer mentor Hans Meyer got involved. The man destined for the top, who had an aura of superiority and confidence about him. The man everyone knew was soon to transfer to the Federal Intelligence Service. What seemed like an open and shut case against Leon, quickly deteriorated into a regrettable death by natural causes incident while in police custody. The cleverly positioned chokehold left little evidence for the coroner to press charges for strangulation, and with no witnesses nor video, enough had been done to cast doubt on the whole sorry affair.

Whilst Leon didn't give anything away, it was generally accepted that he had killed the man, but he wouldn't be charged for it. His canny superior arranged for Leon's resignation to be accepted by the Federal Police Commission and then disappear. No one in the services kept in touch with him and for all intents and purposes, everyone forgot about the unruly, violent officer, Leon Becker.

Almost two years later, Leon had exercised his ying-yang fascinations and had started to make inroads into a different organisation. With his police knowledge and brutal history well known to the underworld, he had been recruited by the very people he once sought to put down. The Dreizack mafia.

He'd started to interest them with a few pieces of choice information about how the police operated, along with names of officials who might be corruptible. Then he was asked to prove his worth with a series of strong-arming incidents, exploitation, bribery and plain physical enforcement assignments, all of which he excelled at. His criminal bosses were impressed and congratulated themselves on their rare police turncoat find.

Then one day he happened to be hanging out with one of the gang's more nerdy guys, who invited Leon to sit with him while he engaged in an online Dark Web chat with a broker selling off innovative weapons designs. As the techy guy started, he turned to Leon to ask what username he should choose. The two of them had just been reminiscing about their favourite childhood TV programmes, so Leon had glibly suggested the username Samson after the German Sesame Street bear, not expecting the computer bod to pay attention to his sarcastic offering. But he had, Samson was chosen for their username.

Leon accompanied and closely watched his colleague through many online chats which led up to their first auction, where they won the design for a new kevlar helmet. Their Dreizack organisation masters had already lined up two overseas buyers for the helmet blueprints, at several times more than the buying price. Leon was intrigued by the simplicity of buying design soft files and just selling them on for huge profits.

Then the computer guy fell foul of his employers. They'd checked up on the transactions mechanism for other high-value sales he'd arranged and found he'd been syphoning off proceeds for his own private offshore bank account. He was called up to their St Petersburg base and then, he simply disappeared. A week later Leon heard that his body was found in the Neva River under the Big Obukhov Bridge, with his feet set into a large bucket of hardened cement. His hands hadn't even been tied, making his final struggle for life all the more desperate, yet futile.

The top Dreizack man in Berlin then asked Leon if he would be able to take over the Dark Web weapons interactions and purchases for them, to which Leon agreed, having already learned how it all worked. Leon successfully handled the next few ordnance auction wins.

Having now heard from Water Spider that the next transaction had to be in person, Leon relished getting out from behind his computer screen and back into action, with real, live bodies again. He would collect the briefcase of forty-eight million dollars worth of diamonds from his 'handler' and drive down to Lake Como on Thursday, ready for the Friday meet up. He couldn't wait. He was quite unlike most normal people who would have been apprehensive about the dangers awaiting them. Leon actually hoped there would be trouble during his Lake Como transaction.

15

Wednesday morning and the MI5 team met up in their Thames House offices. Si Lawson wanted a round-up from everyone of progress, before the next scheduled Dark Web contact with Water Spider that evening.

Phil Landon and Max had spent time familiarising themselves with Lake Como, the roads, towns, layout, nearest police stations in case of emergencies, boat and water-plane hire points, major exit routes away from the lake. They had agreed to drive there on Thursday to avoid any holdups with luggage having to be searched, as they would be carrying the two projectile samples. Also, it allowed Phil to bring with them in the car all the necessary surveillance and tracking equipment so he could provide support for Max and keep an eye on things.

Next Si turned to Alan. "How are we getting on with installing a suitable tracker in the box and bullet Alan?"

Everyone knew that this part was critical if they were to follow the Omega trail onwards from the broker to the end buyer and see where they're based.

Alan cleared his throat. "Well, this has been much harder than we thought. The bullet tracker that is. The one we've hidden in the small carry-case for the two samples was easy. It's a normal micro tracker which we'll all be able to see where it is at any time. But if they dump this box, then we're relying on the tracker we think we can get into one of the empty shell casings we've got to play around with."

Max had to ask, "Well, can you?"

Alan frowned, which was not what Max wanted to see. "Unfortunately GPS hi-power nor radio waves can penetrate out of the metal casing. What we've found is that low-frequency electromagnetic waves with longitudinal E component *can* penetrate through the metal. The lesser the frequency, the better the penetration of the waves and we can wire it up to use the metal casing as an antenna of sorts."

"What the hell does all that mean Alan?" asked Vince.

"Yes, we can get a tracker into one of the empty shells," he paused. "There's a couple of 'but's' though. Firstly the battery is going to be sealed in there along with everything else, so will probably only last three or four days."

"Okay, that's not an issue," said Si. "The buyer will have gone back to their base within a day or so I'd imagine, so fine, we'll only need a couple of days of battery life. What's the other problem?"

Alan held his hands up in advance apology, knowing what he was about to say wouldn't be ideal. "Well, because we're having to use electromagnetic radio waves, these won't be compatible to the nearest mobile phone antenna, to then be boosted into the network for us all to pick up."

"So?" said Max getting mildly frustrated with what the pending punchline would be.

"So we're only going to be able to pick up this signal, within about four or five miles from the tracker in the shell," said Alan, frowning again.

Phil Landon wasn't happy, especially as he'd be the one following Max or the samples. "What! So we've got to hang around near the broker until he then gives it to the buyer, who eventually disappears off into the sunset with our two shells. How on earth are Max and me going to follow them?"

Everyone looked back to Alan, who gathered himself and stated plainly, "You'll have to stay within five miles of those shells to keep tracking them. When they go out of range, you'll lose their signal."

Max and Phil looked at one another with matched exasperation in their expressions. Despite the following discussion, protestations and pleading for some better way with Alan, it was the best option. As Alan repeated, "You simply can't put a usual micro-tracker or sim inside a robust metal casing and expect it to transmit like a mobile phone."

Si cut through the chit chat around the room. "Right, if that's the best Alan can do, then that's what we'll work with. Firstly we'll have to hope that the broker has got the buyer to come and collect his merchandise. Given he's made us go to him at Como, there's a good chance he'll tell the buyer to collect the shells and pay him within the next forty-eight hours of meeting Max. Phil, and Max, you're just going to have to stay close to the broker, for as long as it takes until he meets up with the buyer. Once that buyer goes on the move with our shells, you guys are going to have to somehow stick with them like glue and not get further than Alan's five miles away or we lose them forever. Hopefully, we'll also have the shell case tracker working but I think we have to assume that could get discarded at any time, so stay within that five-mile zone!"

Phil looked to Max, "We should also both link up on the usual tracking apps like 'Find My Friends' so I've got you covered on that as well.

Si interjected. "No, sorry guys, too risky. If they take a look at Max's phone and see that, your cover's blown straight away. As the tracker in the case is using the GPS sim card we can all track that online from here as well. Phil, you'll have your surveillance equipment and might be able to get enough sight of the broker when they pick up Max, for us to ID them back here. Alan, have the trackers to Phil and Max latest early tomorrow morning, well before they leave for Como. Remember to ensure your tracker shell casing weighs the same as the live projectile and they look identical as well. And figure out a way of letting Max know which is the live shell and which is the tracker one okay?"

Alan nodded, "Hopefully guys we'll get the samples to you tonight."

Si continued. "Max, Phil and Vince, I suggest you meet me at Empire later say seven-thirty ready for the next eight PM dark webchat with this broker.

Having each made their way to the Charlwood site in Sussex, the four of them settled down in front of the computer in Lyndsey's basement room. At precisely eight the black screen jolted to life with the chat box and input fields.

'Water Spider – Do you have the two Omega shell samples?'

Si typed. 'Blackbird – Yes. Do you have the $48m?'

"Bloody hell boss, you're being a bit pushy aren't you!" said Vince. Si shrugged.

There was a slight pause. 'Water Spider – I've decided to do a back-to-back deal as the buyer wants to inspect the shells. They will be at the lake with payment, in diamonds. Once the deal is done you'll get your share of them.'

"Bloody hell! Looks like it's all going down possibly on the same day," exclaimed Max, again looking to Phil for a nod of reassurance Phil was concentrating on the screen though, thinking everything through himself. "The buyer will be there with us!"

"That's good, we didn't want a big gap between giving the shells to the broker and then them passing it onto the buyer," said Si. He started typing.

'Blackbird – Ok sounds good, that way I can take my payment on the day.'

'Water Spider – see you midday Friday at the Moltresio Lido jetty.'

The screen went blank seconds later with the usual 'Site Not Found' message appearing.

Max mentioned, "Don't they usually give another chat window address for the next time?"

Si reassured him, "Why would they need to, they'll see you Friday and probably sort something out with you then.

However, Max wondered if there was any finality intended to not proposing another online meetup.

Phil Landon had worked for MI5 since leaving University about fifteen years ago. He studied criminal intelligence for his degree and inspired by the fictional movie spies, had always wanted to join the

British Intelligence Services. Unfortunately, he was no James Bond.

At almost forty years old his progress through the ranks had been slow. Having spent almost all his time behind a desk, he'd progressed from basic analytics and tracking data and intel to predict crime. Next onto planning out operations to then handover to an operative who'd then put his ideas into action. For a while, he'd been assistant to one of the senior Directors, usually a holding position for greater things, but he was not thought to be of the right calibre for front line agent work and continued his desk career.

Then a few years ago, more out of pity one of his previous mentors from years back put his name forward for non-confrontational agent assignments. This meant that whilst he got the operative title he'd yearned for, he would not be put in any front line situations where he might have to face off directly with the enemy, such as criminals or terrorists. He was then given a safe assignment, being told to see what he could come up with regarding the possibility of the Dark Web being used to broker sales of secret military designs.

At five-foot-nine all those years behind a desk with little exercise had long started to take its toll, despite his high metabolism which had tricked him into thinking he'd always be slim. He now filled out his frame and sported a bit of a belly. His dark curly hair sat above a young but childish face, another facet that unfortunately compromised any maturity and gravitas he had. The thick black-rimmed spectacles which he only needed for reading, but kept them on most of the time, added to the unlikeliness of any spectacular role being forthcoming for him.

He was still a corporate man loyal to the MI5 cause and despite slow promotion and a salary he probably could have attained within a few years working for industry, he still loved the excitement. He was diligent, efficient and reliable, just a bit dull. However, this ability to be 'unnoticed', he'd argue, was an asset in this line of work.

Courting online chat rooms on the Dark Web, he eventually got introduced to someone, who pushed him onto another suspect individual and finally, he ended up being invited to Water Spider's chat room, where they were eventually offering a sort of 'jumping room grenade', the 'APaRC'. With his MI5 superior's permission, he was allowed to place one bid, the second to be submitted, safe in the knowledge that the price would far exceed his offering, but it would show him to be a potential buyer in the future.

Phil had picked up from the chats that a buyer with the username Samson had bought the previous offering, but didn't know at the time it was the Kevlar carbon helmet. He then saw Samson win the auction for the APaRC but at the time wasn't able to determine who exactly was making this device as it was so secretive. The fact that the designs were coming out of Empire Arms and Apollo Designs, at this point, continued to elude him.

However, when Water Spider advised his potential buyers of a new super-silencer design to be auctioned, Phil started making enquiries and was able to narrow it down to several possible ordnance makers including Empire. Once the broker pitched the item being sold by showing the teaser plans at the start of the auction, Phil was convinced they matched what he'd heard of the Apollo Stealth Silencer 50. He was over the moon and triumphantly reported back to his superiors back at MI5, that the source for the stolen designs being sold off was Empire Arms in Sussex.

Si Lawson was happy to give the operative a break and have him temporarily assigned to him so he could continue as part of his team. Given Max needed someone with experience to simply follow him in Italy for the rendezvous, Si so no reason why Phil Landon couldn't support Max. Phil had been calm about the whole thing, but unbeknown to Si Lawson, was incredibly excited to at last, after all those years working for MI5, be out and about on a mission!

Wednesday evening Alan had completed the installation of the GPS tracker in the small carry-case for the two projectiles, and the short distance radio wave tracker inside the dummy shell casing. Max hadn't gone back to the office after their meetup at Empire, but as Phil had, he collected the samples from Alan and got the full briefing about their use, tracking apps and ranges. They agreed the safest way to distinguish which shell was the dummy tracker, was to lightly scuff its base, so he and Max would know which was which.

Early the next morning Phil loaded up his specialist equipment into his BMW m340i tourer and set off to collect Max. His pride and joy car was deceptive in that he'd de-badged it, so for all intents and purposes it looked like your average family estate car, but with blacked-out windows around the sides and rear. This was a very fast car for the three-litre inline six-cylinder engine could produce three hundred and seventy-five brake horsepower, projecting it down the road from 0 to 60 in just four-point four seconds.

At six AM he went to collect Max from his Clapham Common home and after showing Max the Omega bullet samples and giving him a quick tour of his equipment before they set off on their day-long journey.

Phil proudly showed Max that he was ready to track and follow him for the Lake Como meet. In the rear of his BMM hidden behind the black glass and within various cases, he had long-range binoculars, a set of night vision goggles, a directional listening device, mini walkie-talkies, a camera with long-range lens, a spare mobile phone, batteries and chargers. Max was impressed and felt happy that Phil would do whatever it took to keep an eye on him.

Pointing to a small case that Phil hadn't mentioned, Max asked, "And what about this one here?"

Phil puffed up with pride as he pulled the box towards them, pausing before opening it for full dramatic effect. He opened the lid to reveal the Glock 17 handgun he'd been temporarily issued with. Hoping this would provoke some shock from Max, he was disappointed when Max nodded albeit appreciatively simply saying, "Great, I was hoping you might have a little extra backup just in case it's needed."

They joined the M20 to Folkstone, then took the Eurotunnel to Calais, down France through Reims.

"Sorry about my drama showing you the Glock," said Phil

apologetically. "I should have known that wouldn't impress you, after all, you're not a stranger to weapons and all that are you, Max?"

Max immediately realised from Phil's clumsy words, he'd likely been made aware of his long-gone past, but played along. "What do you mean?"

Phil shrugged behind the wheel and glanced at Max. "Given we're in this together I wanted to know a bit more about you. So I looked through your records. All of them. Including the Commandos. I didn't know whether to be impressed or sorry for what you went through. Must have been awful," ventured Phil.

Max stared at the road ahead, his mind flashing through images of his Marines training at Lympstone, his posting to Sierra Leone, then his shocking capture with his friend and Sergeant. And then, of course, the killing. For some strange reason, perhaps as they were indeed comrades driving towards the unknown with this Como meeting, Max felt more relaxed talking about it for the first time in two decades.

"It was quite a shock for a nineteen-year-old I can tell you," reminisced Max.

"What you did was incredibly brave Max. You deserved the Military Cross."

Max sighed. "You don't think about bravery. You don't plan anything like that. It's a matter of handling the shock of what's happening to you, being terrified, angry at the way you and your friends are being treated. Then before you have time to think about being brave or getting revenge, it's just sheer survival. It's you or them. You'd be surprised what someone is capable of under those conditions." Max returned the glance to Phil, who quickly turned his focus back onto the road, humbled by Max's words.

"How do you feel about killing those bastards now, twenty years later?" Another clumsy question from Phil.

Max shrugged. "I feel nothing." Then nodding as if agreeing with himself, "It was war. They'd murdered my best friend in front of me and were about to do the same to me and Fifty. My Sarg that is, good at hitting the bullseye in darts! They were just thugs, doing what the hell they wanted to do under the cover of some convenient cause or rebellion. War is a great excuse for psychos to be themselves."

Phil drove silently for the next few minutes, then broke the impasse. "Well we're not in any war now, we're off to lovely Lake Como," he said trying to lighten the mood. "I'm sure this meetup will go fine, then you and I can follow the samples back to the end buyer. Job done eh. Easy!"

They drove across to Strasbourg, past Basel and Lucerne, then down to Como in Italy, at the bottom of the famous lake. The trip took them over twelve hours of driving, which they shared. During the long car journey, Phil briefed Max on the two tracking devices and explained the apps he'd installed onto his mobile. Max would keep his phone with him but wouldn't have the tracker apps, for fear of them being seen if he had to hand over his mobile for some reason.

Phil reckoned that the broker likely intended to take Max north up Lake Como, as there was little else to the south of Moltrasio other than the more populated end of the lake at the town of Como. He would hopefully follow Max and the shells as best he could along the Via Regina lakeside road. The GPS tracker in the case would have unlimited range, but in the event the broker threw it away when they picked up Max, they'd worked out that their five miles range on the shells tracker would give Phil a fighting chance to stay within range, as halfway up the entire lake was Bellagio at about ten miles away.

At the end of their trip, Phil pulled into a petrol station and filled up the BMW to the brim, ready for any long chase the next day. They checked into a small guesthouse in the town of Cavallasca just outside Como and enjoyed a fabulous Italian dinner in a local Ristorante.

Five miles up the lake in his Nesso villa, Mateo Ricci was also having dinner, and he had company. He'd asked one of his trusted friends who lived on the opposite side of the lake in Brienno, to help him out for the next day or so.

Antonio Russo had lived around Lake Como all his life. He'd run a garage in nearby Lugano, a gift shop in the centre of Como and then latterly managed his own small building firm, specialising in lakeside property renovations and building work. It was through this that he'd first met Mateo, when he'd handled the various upgrading, security and building works for him at his Nesso lakeside villa years ago. They were like brothers now and had over the years built a strong and trusting friendship. Antonio had pieced together what he thought Mateo did for a living, but they'd never spoken about it directly. They had a sort of understanding. Mateo rewarded him for his discretion and had been extremely generous to Antonio, to the point of buying him his own house in Brienno. Antonio never wanted for anything and in return would do anything asked of him by Mateo.

Antonio's large frame loomed over the table they sat at, on Mateo's waterside patio. His tanned, rough and ready look was enhanced by his somewhat dirty appearance. He was always showing signs of his last job with dirt under his fingernails, or dried cement on his hands, or plaster dust in his hair. He didn't care, he was happy, he had his business and his wealthy friend Mateo as financial backup if everything went wrong.

Antonio ventured, "So what's this all about tomorrow Mateo?"

Mateo looked up from his large bowl of spaghetti, pesto and mozzarella. "I'm overseeing a transaction, a big one, with high-value items. I just want a little extra security with you being with me, that's all."

Antonio nodded with unconditional agreement. "Are you expecting any trouble? Anything I need to be aware of?"

"It should be a straightforward exchange of goods from a seller, via me, for payment from the buyer, via me," explained Mateo. "But with so much value being handed over, I don't want either of them getting ideas about perhaps dispensing with the formalities and thinking they can just take it all."

Antonio took a large swig of beer and satisfying himself with the answer, quietly nodded, "I'll come prepared anyway eh."

Mateo looked at his friend knowingly and felt reassured that he would bring a handgun with him. "Yes, come prepared. I'll pick you up at your ferry jetty say eleven-forty-five. Now let's enjoy our food then watch the Juventus game," said Mateo, offering up his beer bottle to clink together with his friend's bottle, "Salute!"

The next day Max and Phil made their way to the lake, passing the beautiful park in front of Villa Olmo, built in 1797 as a summer retreat for the aristocracy and now open to the public. They joined the water-front road Via Cernobbio and got their first water-side view of the beautiful Lake Como. The sun glistened on the calm water and they both took in the magnificent, framed vista with the bustling boats and ferries behind them at Como. Handsome villas and homes nestled alongside the water's edge then rose up the green mountainsides that cradled the entire lake. It was one of those places you immediately thought you'd like to move to and live.

The water provided a calming serenity, surrounded by its picturesque and sought after setting. Though twenty feet below the surface, the light lost its battle to penetrate further, and the hidden, dark gloom of Europe's deepest lake at over thirteen hundred feet, lay ominously below.

Through the snatched views of the lake between buildings and trees, on the opposite side, they could see the famous Como fountains of Villa Geno. They continued along the Via Regina through the town of Cernobbio, past the grand Villa d'Este hotel with its large swimming pool suspended within a floating pontoon jutting out onto the lake. With space at a premium, the owners had run out of land and cleverly extended their facilities out onto the water.

Ahead they could see the houses of Moltrasio nestled around the main water frontage with several large hotels and the ferry terminal, which usually served as the focus for each of the lakeside towns.

Phil slowed down as they spotted the Lido and then pulled

the car into the parking area of the Hotel Grand Imperiale on the opposite side of the road. It was ten to midday.

"I'll wait here until you get going on the lake to wherever it is the broker takes you and will be tracking you all the way," assured Phil.

Max frowned as he cradled the small case holding the precious two Omega 6500 projectiles. He checked he had his mobile, though suspected this might be discarded when he was collected, so had backed it up onto a spare.

Phil continued, "Remember the tracker is inside the bullet with the scuff mark on the bottom of the shell case. The clean shell is the real, live Omega round." Max gave a nod. "Before you go let me check one last time I've got you on the two trackers."

Phil opened his mobile which was in its dash cradle of the car. He'd labelled the apps 'CASE' and 'OMEGA', and as he swiped the screen from one to the other, could see the positioning pin for both in the centre of the Hotel car park.

"Spot on Max, I've got you on both trackers. I'll observe from this side of the road until you're in the boat, then follow you up the lake as closely as these poxy little roads will let me."

Max got out of the car and with a determined nod, made his way across the road. Some steps were leading down to the Lido, which he suspected had seen better times. There was a large concrete area fronting onto the lake, with a row of changing rooms behind. A concrete diving platform stood alone hopeful for use, but only three visitors were lying on sunbeds all reading. A small pizzeria café was situated to the far end, beside which Max could see the floating wooden jetty protruding out across the water about ten metres long.

He made his way over to the café, nodding to the attendant of the Lido who was aimlessly sweeping the sandy covering on the hard floor, unconcerned with Max's arrival. Max walked through the outside tables and chairs and jumped up onto the jetty. With no sign yet of any approaching boats, he slowly strolled towards the end, tightly clutching the small case holding the two precious bullet samples. He started to wonder what this Water Spider broker would look like, imagining some rough, burly ex-military type in khakis and armed to the teeth.

Phil Landon had positioned himself behind a tree at the entrance to the hotel, where he could see across the road, over the hidden Lido below and get a clear sight of the outstanding jetty, with Max at the end. He held his camera down at his side, hiding it from any passing pedestrians. He was tingling with excitement, ready for the chase with the aide of those trackers, but couldn't help thinking 'rather him than me!'.

Max scanned up and down the lake, waiting for any likely looking craft heading in his direction. At midday, he spotted an impressive speed boat coming down the centre of the expanse of water from the North end of the lake. He instinctively knew it was the broker and was conscious of a second man in the boat. He reminded himself that was to be expected though.

Mateo stood behind the steering consul of his beautiful four-hundred thousand dollar Riva Tritone motor launch, one of Italy's finest speed boats. He was part of an elite club, as only two-hundred-and-fifty-seven of this model were hand made by skilled craftsmen in the fifties and sixties. The highly polished, glossy lacquered wooden bands ran its entire eight-metre length. Behind the wrap around chrome framed windscreen, were two crème leather-covered bench seats. Antonio sat menacingly on the rear seat. The back half of the boat held the two large Chris-Craft six-cylinder engines which drove the two 177 horse powered propellors giving up to fifty kph over the water.

Mateo turned back to Antonio, "He's waiting for us on the jetty. Stay alert, but no need to say anything okay." His friend gave a slight nod and reached behind himself to check the small handgun wedged into the back of his trouser belt.

Mateo held up his mobile with the screenshot picture of Max to remind himself of what this Blackbird seller looked like again, to be sure it was him on the jetty. As he approached he could see it was indeed the same person. Mateo bristled with excitement as he saw that 'Blackbird' was holding a small case. 'The Omega bullets' he thought, 'and worth so much'.

He throttled down the powerful engines and the boat sat down into the water as it slowed. Then as he neared the jetty he adeptly shifted it briefly into reverse, just enough to precisely stop the side of the craft next to the jetty.

"Blackbird? So we meet at last," said Mateo, as he waved Max on board to sit next to him in the front.

"I assume you're Water Spider?" asked Max before venturing forward.

"Yes I am. You have the samples?"

Max held up the small case, then looked at Antonio sitting in the back. "And who's this?"

"Don't worry about my friend here," replied Mateo unconvincingly. "He won't be involved at all," he paused, "unless there are any problems."

Max quickly studied the man in the back, a large, burly lout with clumsy-looking dirt-stained hands and concluded it was unlikely he'd had any combat training and had likely dodged any conscripted military duty. From the way he sat slightly forward uncomfortably, Max also guessed he had some sort of weapon shoved into the rear of his well-worn leather belt.

His gaze returned to the man at the front, Water Spider. The broker. The man who had been obtaining all those weapons designs unknowingly from Sir John Tregar. He must have made millions. He was certainly not the military thug he'd expected. More of a desk jockey, a little overweight and exuding more confidence than he likely had. There was however an edge to him that rang alarm bells for Max, who was glad they were meeting in a public place, there was some safety in that.

Phil Landon zoomed his camera right in on both the men in the fancy boat, to the point he got a good view of them filling most of his picture frame. The digital camera was in silent mode but as he pressed the button down it took about twenty pictures within a few seconds. He'd send these over to Thames House when he had a moment later. He just needed to see which way up or down the lake they took off, before jumping into his car to follow.

Max climbed into the front and sat slowly next to Mateo, who casually reversed the Riva away from the jetty, watched by the several Lido readers. He slowly moved the throttle lever forward and the boat responded immediately, rising up as it started to gather speed on the water. As he reached the middle of the lake he swung the boat to the left and headed North up the lake away from Como, as Max and Phil had rightly assumed.

Phil ran back to his BMW and pulled out of the hotel car park to head towards the next town up the lake being Carate Urio. The Via Regina road fortuitously ran adjacent to the water's edge, so gave him a clear view of the speed boat on the lake. He looked at his mobile which was on the 'CASE' tracking app and could see the dot on the lake corresponding to the boat to his side and slightly ahead of him.

Just in front of him, an old looking farmer's truck pulled out towing a dirty trailer with small logs stacked high between metal posts. It crawled onto the road in front of him and seemed to take forever to change up a gear and get moving.

"Damn it!" shouted Phil hitting his steering wheel. "You've got to be kidding me!" He pressed his horn a couple of times and was waved at by the Italian farmer apologetically, but to no avail. The farmer continued on his journey as there was nowhere to pull in. Phil glanced over to see where the boat had got to and was dismayed to see the Riva starting to pull away from him up the lake. The tracker was still working fine. He'd have to endure the farmer's truck until it pulled off.

"Can I see the samples?" asked Mateo.

Max kept tight hold of the case whilst opening the lid to reveal the two shiny projectile shells sitting in their foam slots.

"Wow," exclaimed Mateo. "Those are quite stunning. Big aren't they."

They gave the appearance of mini rockets rather than bullets. On the outside, Mateo could see there were several things that distinguished them from standard bullets, apart from their size.

There were the small propulsion portholes just above the shell casing, the single tiny stabiliser fin on the bullet half and the small glass tip housing the laser-tracking eye. Everything else was inside the casing.

Max closed the lid. "So where are we going? I'd rather stay in public view if that's agreeable?" Max knew this broker would do what he wanted to regardless of what he said, but it was worth playing the naïve executive hoping for a safe transaction in the open.

Mateo looked ahead. "This is quite the exception my friend, meeting up like this. It won't happen again. After this sale you and I will never meet or communicate ever again, is that clear?" Not waiting for an answer, he continued. "Yes, we will stay on the lake for this meeting. It will be a snapshot deal. That means we will meet the buyer," Max hid his celebratory feeling, "they will inspect the samples, pay me, then I pay you, and we all go our separate ways."

Max played along. "What about more designs I steal for us to sell?"

Mateo sounded more irritated this time. "No more sales. No more chats on the Dark Web. Nothing. You will never come to this area ever again. Understood? You'll be rich, sort yourself out back in England and live a happy life." He forced a smile which Max felt betrayed something else. Pity. This didn't feel good to Max, but he had no options right now. He had to keep going and make the handover if they were to track the buyer. Max was hoping that Phil was following them, closely.

The farmer's truck ambled along frustrating the hell out of Phil, as he watched the gap between his position on the tracker map and that of the boat, grow larger and larger. He could see that Max was now rounding the bend in the lake two towns up from him by Torriggia and he still hadn't got to the first town of Carate Urio. Furthermore, he'd now lost actual eyesight of Max as he strained to look up the lake. He'd have to rely on the tracker app now. "Damn this bloody farmer!" He daren't press the horn again for fear the farmer's cordial response may deteriorate and have him stop altogether and get out for one of those famous, long Italian arguments and shouting.

Then as if by magic Phil saw what he wanted, the broken lensed left indicator light started flicking and just as they reached the outskirts of the town, the lumbering truck and trailer pulled off to make its way up the hillside to his smallholding. Phil sped dramatically past as soon as the gap was big enough, almost hitting an oncoming car. He was back in the chase and checked again to see Max's location, swiping across to the 'OMEGA' tracker just to check it was still in range. The dot appeared on the lake, it was still working fine. Max was three miles away. Phil needed to catch up now.

Max asked innocently, "Who's the buyer? How are they paying?"

Mateo was now getting agitated. "Chatty aren't we. You want to remain anonymous, don't you? Well so do I and so does the buyer. Let's stick with our Dark web usernames, shall we? His is Samson okay. That's all I know about him and it's best that way."

As they came level with Antonio and Mateo's hometowns of Brienno and Nesso, both men deliberately looked straight ahead, ignoring their homes both visible from the lake. Max noticed their obvious concentration forward but remained unaware of the significance of their odd behaviour. He turned to check on the back seat man and met his stare. Antonio had a steely, glazed look on his face and after a few moments, shifted uneasily in his seat. Looking back at max, there was something about this 'office worker', this 'admin clerk' Blackbird in front of him that made him uneasy. As if there was more to him than meets the eye. A hidden edge, an awareness of everything around him.

At Torriggia the waterside road joined the larger SS340 which was set back from the lake by a single row of houses with that sought after water frontage. Phil still had a good view of the lake and was closing in on Max's tracker dot on the map.

The Riva skimmed over the water and slowly arced around the next right-hand bend of the lake between the towns of Argegno and Carvagnana. Max could see the broker starting to veer towards the far left side. Just after the streamlined boat passed by Argegno, an ominous-looking black Mercedes G400 pulled up alongside the small harbour there. Amidst the variety of about twenty-five plain mostly white sailing and speed boats, the boxy, modern off-roader looked quite out of place with its black windows, towering over the handful of other bland cars parked there. A few of the locals tending to their boats strained round to take in the impressive hundred-thousand Euro SUV and after a few moments, when no one got out, returned to their cleaning or motor tinkering.

Five minutes later, Leon Becker got out of the Mercedes. He'd driven down from Germany the day before and stayed the night in Lugano, just north of Como. Water Spider had instructed him, Samson, to meet at a particular place on the lake at twelve-thirty for the transaction. He was to bring the forty-eight million dollars worth of diamonds ready for an on-the-spot deal, if he was happy with the Omega projectile samples the seller would bring.

Leon leant into the Mercedes and opened the medium-sized black briefcase to just check one more time the large velvet bag of diamonds was inside. Alongside the bag sat a bizarre-looking pair of small binoculars, but these were quite different. With a battery pack, wires and several knobs and buttons, it looked more like high-tech night-vision goggles.

Looking up to ensure no one was watching him, he picked up his trusty Heckler and Koch semi-automatic VP9 handgun, and quickly checked the magazine held its full fifteen nine millimetre rounds. He knew it did but the habit of always checking again before any 'incident' had stayed with him ever since watching another mafia thug realising he didn't have a full magazine in a firefight. The man had fired a few rounds but was then greeted by that terrible click, where the top slider of the weapon stays back revealing the empty chamber with no more rounds left. The man looked at his useless firearm, then back up at his opponent, who just smirked at him before calmly shooting him in the face.

Leon tucked the gun into its lower back holster. A rare design of straps hidden under his shirt, suspending the weapon's holster in the centre of his back just above the waist, with the grip facing to the right so he could easily grab the gun from under his jacket. Anyone doing a proper full body frisk would discover the gun, but most inexperienced people searching someone did the task quickly and usually concentrated on any pockets and under the arms. Rarely would they turn a man round and pat down the lower back.

Should his main gun ever have to be handed over, Leon also had a small Derringer Model 1 two-shot .38 ankle pistol. He mostly forgot he had this as he was so used to wearing it every day and its small, light size was of no consequence to him.

He texted his superior to confirm he was about to reach the meeting place. He then walked over to a row of four small speed boats and spoke to the proprietor who was busy cleaning the seats in one of them. Leon had contacted him several days ago and arranged to hire one of the speedboats today. After a quick briefing, he jumped in and reversed it away from the dock.

Max could make out what appeared to be a small island ahead. It was the only one of the whole of Lake Como, called Isola Comacina, just six-hundred feet or so away from the lake's edge, adjacent to the towns of Sala Comacina and Ossuccio. The island was about fifteen hundred feet in length, covered mainly in trees. At one end was a restaurant with a small wharf with boat docking. A handful of huts were dotted around, along with the remains of an old church the Basilica di Sant'Eufemia. Max was pleased they were staying in plain sight of the public. Behind him he noticed a small speedboat pull away from the town they'd just passed.

Phil had made good progress along the SS340 and was passing through Argegno as he saw Max's dot on the lake head towards the small island. He looked up and could now clearly see the Riva again. He would carry on to the next town of Sala Comacina and find the closest car park overlooking the island.

Mateo pointed to the island for Max's benefit albeit already obvious that was where he was heading. He slowed the Riva's speed and Max was conscious of the broker's friend gathering himself on the rear seat as if getting ready for 'showtime'. Max again hoped that Phil was somewhere close watching on. He should be, given both of the trackers were intact and hadn't been discarded or discovered, yet. He looked around the restaurant area as they approached the jetties to see if anyone stood out as potentially being the buyer, Samson. All looked normal with a handful of couples and a few families enjoying the amazing views from the island, walking or getting seated for lunch. This was all good. Perhaps this exchange would be straightforward, the broker would drop him back ashore and he and Phil could simply follow the Omega bullet with the buyer. Somehow Max felt it was unlikely to be that straight forward and his senses tingled as he remained on high alert.

The Riva Tritone was by far the most impressive boat to dock alongside the island and a few of the public watched them manoeuvre alongside one of the wooden jetty's. Antonio stood and jumped out as soon as he could to stop the Riva's front from bumping into the wooden structure. Mateo threw him the rope. Max immediately noticed the small handgun protruding from the back of the man's belt as he bent down to secure the boat.

Mateo gestured for Max to climb ashore. "Everything will be fine Blackbird," he said to Max in a poor effort of reassurance. "We will now wait here for the buyer to join us, then do the deal and you will be very rich, yes."

They walked across the neat concrete platform and up some steps to the restaurant area where they sat at the furthest, most secluded table. An innocent-looking waitress sauntered over and Mateo ordered four beers. Max kept the precious case on his lap rather than placing it on the table. Watching Antonio shuffling, trying to get comfortable without dropping the gun from his belt, had started to become mildly amusing to Max. His opinion of the broker's guard-man was lowering by the minute.

He glanced at Water Spider imagining him sat at his keyboard conversing with him across the Dark Web and wondered about this man's past, what he'd done to get to such a sought after criminal position of brokering weapons designs for such large sums of money. Max opened the case to reassure himself the two large bullets were in place and reminded himself that the one with the scuff on the bottom of the shell case was the dummy with the tracker inside. If he was asked to show one for any close inspection, he must hand over the other real, live sample.

Antonio nodded his head up and towards the lake to signal to Mateo that the speedboat coming across to the island may be their buyer. Mateo looked up anxiously, he hadn't, of course, met Leon Becker. When he'd asked Samson over the chat window for a screenshot to identify him, as he did with Max, Leon had merely replied, 'Piss off, I'll be there as agreed with the diamonds!'. So this harsh edge to Samson's response had worried Mateo that he likely had a 'tiger by the tail' for a buyer. It was more for this reason than being worried about the office man Blackbird, that he wanted Antonio there with his gun. Especially because of what he had planned for the transaction. He'd briefed Antonio fully that morning when he'd collected him from Brienno, on what he wanted him to do. That way his friend had no time to argue or protest.

Mateo, Antonio and Max all stared at the speedboat ploughing across the lake, which they could see from its trail in the water had come from Argegno. The slim, fit-looking man steering had fair hair and a look of determination that neither Mateo nor Max liked one bit. He then harshly swerved into the docking area and slammed the engine into reverse bringing the boat to an untidy and uncaring halt by the key side. Everything about him, his actions, his look, was violent.

Despite being broker and seller, two opposing sides in this transaction, Mateo and Max looked at one another more as a team just for a moment. Max was hoping Water Spider had this covered.

As Leon jumped adeptly out and tied up the craft, they all appreciated his efficient, athletic build. His movements were sparing, limited to only what was required, but strong and unwavering. He leant down into the boat and grabbed the briefcase. Mateo smiled. His diamonds had arrived.

Max and Antonio both looked concerned.

16

Leon strolled powerfully up to the restaurant and before Mateo could wave to him. He started making his way over to them. He'd already seen them from the lake and figured they were the broker, seller plus broker's guard. He was unconcerned with the few members of the public on this island, there were no police here, so he was clear he would do whatever he needed to do without any limitations or intervention from authorities. Not that it would have bothered him even if there were a couple of policemen sitting at the restaurant. He approached the table.

Mateo greeted him. "Samson?"

"Ja. Bist du Wasserspinne?" said Leon.

The German reply threw Mateo for a moment as he had no idea where Leon was from, but Max was mentally ticking off a box for himself, 'So the buyer's from Germany'.

Mateo beckoned him to sit. "Let's speak English, is that okay?"

Leon sat, "Yes, of course," and gave Max and Antonio a hard, overconfident gaze followed by a quick nod.

Max quickly glanced over to the land and wondered if Phil was watching.

Once Phil had entered the adjacent town of Sala Comacina he'd slowed right down as the narrow road winded its way carefully between the tall sided buildings. Looking at his map he could see there was a small off-road that appeared to give access to the water's edge, directly across from the restaurant where Max's dot had settled on the island. He came to a tiny off-slope and manoeuvred into the single road, barely wide enough for a car, called Via Enrico Prestinari. He followed it down thirty yards and it opened up into a small car park overlooking a stony beach and a clear view of the nearby island. He'd parked his BMW facing the island and quickly retrieved some of his gear from the boot. He was now set up in the front looking out through the windscreen and with a quick check using the high-powered binoculars, could see Max sitting at the table with three others.

Phil gathered up his digital camera and levelled the telescopic lens at the island, zoomed in on the trio at the table with Max and began taking photos of each of them. He could see the broker who'd collected Max with his aide and assumed the fair-haired man was the buyer Samson. He would set up the directional listening device with its antenna clamped to his front door pillar on the outside, so it had an unobstructed path to the table.

"Now that we're all gathered here, we'll continue to refer to one another by our Dark Web usernames, Water Spider, Blackbird and Samson," explained Mateo.

Leon flicked his head towards Antonio, "And who is this then?" he asked abruptly.

Antonio looked uncomfortable as Mateo replied, "This is my friend."

"Why is he here?" asked Leon mischievously.

Mateo was clear, "To ensure we conduct this deal without any issues. We may be in public gentlemen, but I assure you I won't tolerate anyone acting outside a professional transaction here."

Leon looked back to Mateo with a dismissive expression as if to say, 'Really, you think so do you?'.

Mateo moved onto what he really wanted to see. "Samson. You have the forty-eight million in diamonds?"

"Yes."

"Well can we see them please?"

Leon huffed and spun the briefcase round to face them, then carefully half opened the lid, checking that no one else was close enough to see. With his free hand, he opened the velvet bag to reveal several hundred sparkling diamonds of varying sizes. Max, Mateo and Antonio couldn't help but gaze in awe at the sight of the spectacular collection of beautiful gemstones. Leon closed the bag and the case lid.

Mateo asked, "What's the piece of kit in there?"

"You don't think I'm going to hand over these diamonds for a couple of large bullets, do you. I want to inspect them. We're paying for what's inside them after all. I need to see," said Leon. Max tensed.

Mateo spoke again. "I don't think that will show you the inside of the shells, through the metal casing that is."

Leon patted on the top of the case. "This will. It's a specially prepared low energy tomography scanner. Like a CAT scan, but better. Now show me these samples we're paying so much for?" he demanded impatiently.

Max, and Phil listening in from the shoreline, both winced. The buyer had brought something allowing him to see inside the shells. It was now down to Max to give him the live round and not the one with the tracker inside.

Mateo looked over to Max. "Can you let the buyer to see them now please?"

Max opened the case whilst reminding himself which side was the live round, but at that instant, he couldn't remember if it was the one on the right or left. He went to pick up the lefthand projectile and then noticed as he touched it, it had the faint scuff on the base. 'Damn it!' he thought.

Before he could change his choice to the correct, live round, Leon had leant over saying, "I will choose which one to examine." Max froze. Leon hesitated over the shell Max had initially gone for, then looking into Max's eyes, he stopped. He then grabbed the other shell from its foam slot and pulled back.

'Thank the Lord' thought Max. He'd taken the live round after all. Max closed the case lid hoping the buyer wouldn't want to examine both shells, in which case he was finished.

Leon, Mateo and Antonio each marvelled at the shell Leon held somewhat clumsily in his hand.

"Be careful with it, it's a live round with a high explosive charge," cautioned Max.

"I'm not stupid!" retorted Leon crossly.

The Omega round was truly an impressive thing to behold. The six-inch-long shiny casing filled Leon's large hand and glinted menacingly in the sunlight. The onlookers took in the unusual single fin on the bullet, the four tiny exhaust ports around the bullet's base and the glass tip.

Leon asked, "Explain these?" pointing at the various unique design parts.

"The shell has a massive charge to fire the bullet around four miles," advised Max. "The glass window in the tip holds the target's laser dot tracking eye, which is connected to the self accuracy chip inside. This in turn activates whichever of the four directional propulsion rockets are needed to fine-tune the bullet's path, guaranteeing a direct hit. The smooth bore grooved gun barrel and this stabiliser fin, prevents the bullet spinning so the self-accuracy system can operate with a tiny gyroscope." Max sat back pleased with his summary and added, "I'm not a technical person though, I just work in the office."

Leon and Mateo were starting to suspect this seller Blackbird perhaps had more to him than the mere corporate executive front he portrayed. So did Leon.

Phil continued to listen in whilst sending off his pictures of the men to Si and Vince back at MI5 Thames House. They would start the computers doing a facial recognition search through everything they had access to, just in case they could identify any of the three men with Max.

Leon placed the Omega shell on the table, carefully this time and retrieved his small portable scanning device, offering, "It's a bit like what they use to inspect welds and inside aeroplane panels. With the right adjustments, it should let me see inside the metal casing. He looked at Max as if to say 'this had better impress me'. Max prayed this shell sample they got from Kendrick at Apollo, was all it was cracked up to be.

Leon's scanner looked like it came out of a science fiction movie, with two eyepieces like binoculars, which then converged into a single lens at the front, similar to night-vision goggles with a headband. Attached to it were a battery pack and a cumbersome box holding all the technical parts to the scanner. On the outside were several tuning, frequency and energy dials for the user to find the right settings to see through the metal, depending on what its makeup was.

Leon now placed the shell on top of his case in front of him and turned on the scanner. It made a slight humming sound as the lights came to life. He held the two viewing pieces up to his eyes and moved the inspection lens at the front onto the Omega bullet, simultaneously starting to turn the small dials.

Max, Mateo and Antonio waited expectantly for any reaction from Leon, who continued to find the optimum settings.

"Ahh," mumbled Leon slowly, as a black and white view of the inside of the casing started to come into his view. The others didn't know whether it was a good 'Ahh' or a bad one.

"Well," said Mateo who couldn't contain himself any longer.

"I can see inside," whispered Leon. He shook his head and Max wondered if it was bad news, the wrong shell, a mixup or that Kendrick hadn't given them a fully working prototype.

Leon's reaction was however in pure wonderment, not only that the scanning device allowed him to see inside the round, but even more so at what it revealed inside. He knew a normal bullet had a load of charge powder in the shell and a solid bullet in the end. That was it. Nothing else. But this Omega projectile was indeed a work of art.

He could see a large amount of charge in the shell casing alright, as expected and explained by Max. It was what was within the projectile top part that was truly fascinating to him. There was some kind of viewing, tracking device behind the tip's glass eye. Then a solid, bullet mass of metal through which a tiny wire ran, leading to a micro-circuit board, something that resembled a small battery, then more hairline wires to four separate charge cavities. Each of these then funnelled through to the four portholes on the exterior of the casing.

"Das ist gut," said Leon as he looked up from his scanner device.

The others were relieved, none more than Max, who was now worrying that this buyer would want to examine the other shell, and get to see a lot more than he bargained for. The tracker!

"Can I see?" asked Mateo keenly, leaning forward.

"Nein! No need for you to verify this, I'm buying it, not you!"

Antonio shifted at seeing his boss and friend put down. The uneasiness wasn't lost on Leon. Max was still waiting for the request to examine the other shell and when Samson handed him back the one he'd inspected and placed his scanner back into the case, Max was utterly relieved.

"Now gentlemen, let's conclude this deal. Would you both please pass me the samples and the payment?" instructed Mateo, as was usual that all items went through the broker acting as escrow, albeit just for a few moments.

Leon pushed the briefcase with the diamonds inside, across the small table, keenly eying the others, especially Antonio. Max had placed the Omega shell back into its slot and closed the lid. He carefully put the case onto the table and also slid it slowly over towards Mateo.

The instant Mateo took possession of both cases, a handgun was quickly raised above the tabletop. Max instinctively flinched but then instantly froze as the barrel threatened him not to move. Leon surprisingly was startled and then looked furious, because he'd allowed himself to be outdrawn by the broker's aide. It was Antonio who was pointing his handgun at them both, sneering satisfyingly that this was now his part in the meeting, having taken a back seat until now.

"Scheisse!" snarled Leon, who hadn't been able to go for his own gun, but at least hadn't given away that he had one.

"What the…" started Max, but was interrupted by Mateo.

"Just calm down and sit perfectly still, both of you. If you move an inch, my friend here will put a bullet through each of your heads, right here, right now." Having annoyingly been put in his place by Leon, Mateo was now back in control and about to do what he'd never done with any of his lifetime's deals. Renege. He explained.

"Given this will be the last deal I ever broker, I kinda felt I deserved a retirement gift. A pension fund if you like. I'm sorry to tell you guys, that includes all the diamonds, and both the Omega samples, which I'll find another buyer for in due course to sell all over again."

Leon pursed his lips in defiance at Mateo. "You are dead. Both of you," looking back to Antonio, who tightened his grip on the gun.

"I'd be careful what you say, Samson. It would be far more sensible for me to kill you both, which I will, but only if you force me to," said Mateo. "I'm not a murderer, so the gifts I'm giving you both, are your lives."

Phil was both watching and listening to the proceedings and going frantic, helpless from afar to be able to do anything to help Max. He'd have to watch how this played out and hope Max, as the 'innocent office worker', wouldn't get embroiled in the quarrel.

"What happens now then?" asked Max, feeling some comradery with Leon as they were both looking into the same gun barrel.

"My friend and I are going to get into our boat and never see you again." He took a small dark metal orb from his pocket and placed it on the table. As he did so he flicked a small switch and a red light started flashing on the black metal ball. From his other pocket, he grabbed a small transmitter which he also turned on.

"This gentlemen is a mini frag grenade. Not a huge blast but the pieces of metal blown into you will be enough to either kill or maim you badly." He held up the transmitter. "This is the button that detonates the grenade." Leon looked like a caged wild animal, and with the introduction of this new device in front of them on the table, he was fighting every fibre wanting to lunge at Mateo, but stayed put. "If you get up from this table before we've gone, my friend will open fire on you and I will detonate the grenade," said Mateo, rising to leave.

"How do we know you won't kill us when you're clear?" asked Leon through gritted teeth.

Mateo gave a slight shrug. "You don't I guess. You'll just have to trust me. I don't care either way, but it's up to you if you want to live or die at this table."

Leon was not someone who would allow a foe to determine his living or dying. His nature was to take control, act, fight, so at least he would be the one deciding on his own fate. But right now he couldn't think of a way out. The broker had a simple but foolproof plan going here. Leon was fuming that he'd been taken advantage of and had handed over the diamonds, the organisation's diamonds, and not got the Omega samples. Something was going to have to happen in the next minute, for if he returned to Germany empty-handed, he'd be hunted down and killed by his mafia peers for sure.

Max could see that Samson was tensed and ready to pounce and hoped the wiry man realised he couldn't outspring a shot at him, so held his hand up to calm him. "Okay, you get to your boat, we're not doing anything."

Leon gave him a sideways glance but remained still. He had no choice. Mateo and Antonio backed away from the table and as they approached the nearest of the public seated at another table, Antonio lowered his gun and Mateo held up his transmitter to remind Max and Leon he was still in control of the grenade. They watched, quietly fuming, their minds racing to find some way to avert the possibility that the broker might indeed set off the grenade once they'd got clear.

Max looked ahead of them at the path they'd have to take to get back to their Riva docked at one of the jetties. Once through the restaurant area, they would double back towards him going down the steps which led to the boats. As he scanned the route an idea hit him, as he noticed one particular large shrub which would momentarily block the broker's view of them at the table. The two men were already nearing the top of the steps. Max had a few seconds to make up his mind and committed himself. It was the only chance they had, and whispered to Leon next to him, "Get ready to go after them!"

Leon looked at Max in astonishment. The idea that this office worker from England was telling him what to do or might have a plan, let alone be ready to initiate something, stunned him. That was ideal, as Max didn't want him doing anything until he'd made his move. Max also knew he needed to get the tracked Omega case and sample back in the buyer's hands, so he and MI5 could continue following the trail back to who Samson was working for.

Mateo and Antonio proceeded slowly down the steps, keeping their gaze on Max and Leon through the iron railings around the seating area. They approached the shrub, Max tensed and they passed out of sight behind it for a second.

Max moved with lightning speed as he picked up the frag grenade and in one movement flung it over the railing ahead of Mateo and Antonio to block their escape. Leon was momentarily perplexed as he took in what was happening. Mateo reappeared from behind the shrub to see the grenade flying through the air towards the railing. His trigger happy reaction was to press the detonation button, but by the time he'd done this and the radio wave signal was received by the grenade, it was already over the railing and about to land fifteen feet in front of them. The grenade's killing range was only six feet, but it was still going to do some damage.

There was a dull boom as the grenade exploded just before hitting the concrete, shooting small pieces of the breakaway metal casing in all directions. Everything around its epicentre instantaneously bristled with the small fragments hitting whatever the first thing was they came across. The concrete floor, the water, some of the boats nearby got peppered, the steep bank leading up to the restaurant, the trees above. Anything in its sightline received a sprinkling of metal shards.

A woman in the restaurant screamed in shock and many of the nearby visitors instinctively jumped or ducked down on hearing the bang. Luckily none of them was in the dockside area, but people now started to crane their necks and look round buildings to see what had caused the noise.

Max had pushed Leon down as he'd thrown the device, so they were on the floor and blocked from any shrapnel by the bank alongside the steps. Mateo had turned away as he'd pressed the button, just realising in time his mistake to detonate the grenade, now flying through the air in front of him. Several pieces of metal had hit him in the back, legs and an arm, with one piece grazing the side of his jawline, gouging a three-inch-long cut. But he was okay and mobile.

Antonio simply hadn't had enough time to realise what was happening and although Mateo took some of the pieces heading his way, a few still reached him. He had puncture wounds in one of his legs, several in his belly and chest, and one had ripped through his right ear. He fell down, more from shock, holding his wounds, stunned.

Within an instant, Max saw Leon scramble to his feet and sprint towards the railing. He jumped over it and whilst flying through the air, Max saw his right hand move round his side, lift his jacket and grab a handgun from its holster, in a well practised, precise move. In Leon's determination to jump straight over the railing, he hadn't had time to plan his landing and as he dropped the eight feet down, he twisted one of his ankles as it landed on the edge of one of the steps.

He was temporarily disabled, holding his gun with one hand and his ankle in the other, overly rubbing and nursing it quickly back to working order. Leon wasn't going to let anyone off this island until he had his Omega samples, and preferably also his diamonds back. He'd instinctively jumped ahead of the broker so they couldn't get to their boat, now he had them captive.

Mateo saw Leon now between him and his Riva, so quickly turned around and started to run back up the steps clutching the briefcase and Omega samples box. As he passed his friend, ignoring his wounds, he snapped at him, "Get up Antonio, quickly, follow me!"

The dazed Italian picked himself up off the floor and fighting through the stinging pains about his body, jostled after Mateo back up the steps and past the restaurant towards the trees.

Max stood up and saw them running back into the island, then cautiously approached the railing to see Leon recovering from a bad landing. He then gathered himself up and started up the steps in pursuit of the other two.

Max figured he wasn't a threat to Samson as he didn't have either the samples or the diamonds. If he'd wanted Max dead he could have shot him at the table. He decided to follow, after all his objective now was bizarrely to help get the Omega samples back with the buyer. Then assuming he was still alive, rendevous with Phil and follow him. They still needed to find out what organisation this Samson was working for.

Phil had seen the events unfold and for now, decided to continue watching to see what happened and hopefully, once Max was able to get clear, he could arrange to collect him in a boat if necessary. He wrongly assumed Max would want to get out of there.

Mateo led Antonio along a pathway then veered off into the trees. He assumed the office worker seller would flee the island as quickly as he could. But not the buyer. He didn't need to turn to check if he was in pursuit. He knew he would be, given he'd launched himself over the railing to cutoff their exit to the boat. What worried him more was that he had produced a handgun from somewhere and looked like he wanted to use it, on him.

Negotiations weren't going to be an option. He needed to lure him across the small island, then double back to the Riva and escape. Antonio was ten yards behind, so Mateo quickly dropped to one knee and opened the briefcase. He discarded the weighty scanner device and replaced it with the smaller case holding the two Omega samples. Now everything was in the one case and he had a free hand.

Antonio reached him amidst the trees looking pale, shocked and scared. Mateo grabbed the handgun from him, "You're too badly injured my friend to be effective with this, I'll protect us both. Follow me a bit further then you continue to the church ruins. I'll get back to the boat once that German passes me, then I'll collect you from the furthest side of the island okay?"

The plan seemed plausible so Antonio nodded, wincing from his wounds. The bleeding from his torso and ear had abated but he was covered in patchy bloodstains. "You need to kill that bloke Mateo, he's gone nuts. Did you see the way he jumped over the railing to get in front of us. And where did that gun come from? Sweet Mary, he's totally pissed now we've taken his samples and his damn diamonds."

Leon ran up the path but had lost sight of the two men ahead of him. The path was curvy so he couldn't see if they were far ahead on the path or whether they'd gone into hiding in the trees. He continued up the path cautiously. Whilst he didn't rate the broker's aide, a gun was a gun and he could always get off a lucky shot. Leon didn't intend to die on this poxy little island today.

Max saw Leon disappear up the path and hesitated from continuing to follow. He figured that whoever came out of this alive, would have to get back to the jetty area near the restaurant to leave by boat. He might be abandoning the two Italians to their deaths at the hands of the German, but selfishly out of all of them, he needed the buyer to stay alive with the samples. He turned and made his way back towards the restaurant and took up position in the trees overlooking the café and steps down to the boats. From there he'd see any of them before they tried to leave the island.

Mateo and Antonio reached the old church ruins. "Somehow Antonio, you need to draw the buyer across the ruins into the far trees after you."

"You're kidding!" he replied despondently.

"Don't worry, when he's in the open, I'll have him! He'll never catch up with you before I shoot him." Mateo offered his hand out to his friend. "When this is over, I'll give you five million Euros okay."

Antonio's frown showed a glimmer of satisfaction as he took

in the huge number and what it could do for him. He nodded.

"Hang on," said Mateo. He'd realised the German if given the choice, would chase the briefcase and likely not be deterred by Antonio running away. He knelt down again and opened the case. He now put the Omega samples box inside the velvet bag with the diamonds and pulled the drawstring tight. Closing the briefcase he thrust it into Antonio's hands. "Take this, and make sure he sees it!"

Antonio felt like a piece of bait and didn't fancy this at all. It was only the thought of the big payday that spurred him on again. He took the briefcase and moved over to the far side of the ruins where he waited to catch sight of Leon. Mateo found a broken wall to crouch behind, giving him a good view of the open land across the ruins from a well-concealed position. He could feel his heart pounding and thought to himself, 'This is why I promised myself never to meet the buyer and seller, what was I thinking doing all this!'.

Leon moved along the path and passed a young couple who took one look at the gun and scarpered past him with hands raised. He ignored them. The only danger on the island was that broker's aide, the scruffy, dirty bloke who said nothing, but the one with a gun. He couldn't let the samples and diamonds off the island either. He'd take them both out as they were likely sticking together anyway, easier for him.

The path opened out into a clearing in the trees revealing the broken stonework, part walls and foundations of a long since crumbled building. Leon had reached the church ruins.

Mateo and Antonio were both simultaneously aware of the German's arrival on the scene. Both were even more aware of the black gun he held out in front of him, which looked new and efficient. Mateo crouched down further and almost held his breath, as he looked down at Antonio's gun that he now held. As he studied it for the first time his heart sank. He knew enough about weapons to see that it was a Colt Cobra revolver with six rounds in the chambers. However, from the size of the rounds and bore, he realised this wasn't the classic .38, instead, it had the much smaller

.22 bullets! This, combined with the very short snub-nose barrel size, meant it was only effective if he hit a vital organ such as the heart or brain. He swore to himself. He wasn't going to get any closer to this madman, so consoled himself with having to fire off as many rounds as he could at the German, hoping at least one or several would hit their mark.

Antonio waited just long enough, then ran from the clearing towards the path at the far end, knowing he'd be seen. Leon immediately saw the movement and as he instinctively started towards him, could see it was the aide, and more importantly he was carrying the black briefcase. That was enough for him to accelerate after him, but as he still assumed Antonio had the gun as well, he ran between the stonework and walls, just in case the man ahead turned and opened fire on him.

Leon drew level with Mateo's hiding place, then once he had firmly passed by, Mateo knew it was now or never. He waited another moment fearing Samson could turn and be too close to him for comfort, then stood up from behind the wall. The German was already twenty feet away from him and seemed to be weaving amongst the ruins. Mateo raised the gun quickly and fired off all six rounds in hurried succession at Leon's back and head.

Leon was taken completely by surprise by the noise of gunshot behind him and by the time the third round was being fired, he'd dived to the ground behind a low brick foundation on a small mound. He could feel and hear bullets passing him by, closely, hitting stonework and thudding into the soil around him. He lay there with adrenalin pumping, genuinely not knowing if he'd been hit or not. His canny subconsciousness had counted six shots and immediately computed that was the full load the aide's revolver could hold. By the time he slowly raised his head, he just caught sight of the broker running back into the treeline behind him.

Unfortunately for Mateo, the accuracy of the short-barrelled revolver wasn't great beyond ten-to-fifteen feet and with the distance Leon had reached, combined with his ducking around the ruins, he hadn't much chance of a fatal shot. It would have been pure luck. But today luck was not on his side as the barrage of small bullets had whistled close to their target, but only one had cut through Leon's left shoulder muscle, which he was now feeling a soft searing pain from. He gritted his teeth, not at the discomfort, but the broker, for tricking him again, and shooting at him.

Leon's instinct was to go after him as he was no doubt heading for his boat. He checked himself and knew that first of all he had to retrieve the briefcase, then smiled at the assumption that the so-called bodyguard was now almost certainly unarmed. He set off and continued to follow Antonio, already ignoring his wounded shoulder.

Max had heard the six shots and so had all the island's visitors, who were making their way to their boats at the dockside and jetties, to get clear away from this violence and gunfire. He decided to go up the path to see what was going on.

Antonio struggled through the trees and after just a minute emerged from them at the far end of the island. He was relieved to reach the point where his friend Mateo would surely collect him in a few minutes. The six shots he'd heard must have taken care of the German buyer, but all the same, he turned around and peered into the crowded trees to make sure. He waited a few moments. Nothing. He took a deep sigh of relief, turned to face the lake and slowly sat down on the grass to rest his weary, wounded body. His torn ear hurt like hell and the wound to his belly had stopped bleeding, but had a twitching, sharp pain inside that he suspected would need urgent attention once they got ashore.

He felt quite surreal sitting there with grenade injuries, the meeting, being chased, the money he'd soon get. All on this Como island he'd visited his whole life, played on, had dates on, celebrations, parties and sunsets. He was conscious of several boats coming round both sides of the island and guessing it was the public fleeing from the mayhem they created, eagerly scanned left and right in the hope one of the approaching boats being Mateo.

Without hearing a sound, purely his sixth sense tingling, Antonio felt something or someone behind him. The moment he turned around he realised the dark figure emerging from the treeline was that of the German buyer, looking determined as ever. Antonio's heart almost stopped right then and there. His whole body felt weak and he thought he'd faint on the spot. Unfortunately, he didn't.

Leon held the Heckler and Koch out in front of him as he purposefully walked towards Antonio, who simply froze, and gulped. Any chance of talking his way out of it evaporated as he reminded himself there was nothing inside the briefcase. All he could think of saying was, "Per favore? Per favore?" he pleaded. He looked straight into the German's eyes and knew he was finished.

Antonio managed to start that millisecond thought of his life, flashing by, a montage of events over his decades. He was even conscious of the flash from the German's gun barrel, but his instant death came before hearing the sound of the gun being fired.

The bullet hit Antonio in the centre of his forehead and passed out the back of his skull almost cleanly, creating a small splash in the water behind. He slumped onto the grass half over the briefcase he still clutched.

Leon knew he didn't have time to talk to the man before shooting, he simply wanted the briefcase and didn't need any wasted time talking or negotiating. He just wanted the contents and then return to the dockside after the broker, fast. He stood over Antonio's body for a moment of satisfaction, then grabbed his briefcase back from the man's dead grasp. As soon as he tugged it away he knew something was wrong. It didn't feel heavy enough to hold the diamonds, the scanner goggles and maybe even the samples box. He knelt and fumbled to open it, half knowing what to expect.

As the lid rose, his heart burnt with rage. The empty case mocked up at him, but not for long. Leon was up and running immediately. He had to get back to the boats and stop the broker from escaping. He sprinted, fast, along the pathway around the side of the trees. Oblivious now of his ankle and shoulder wounds. He had to retrieve the Omega samples.

In addition to this, his superiors had made it very clear to him, there was another objective he must fulfil. Surprisingly not the diamonds, these would only be a bonus if he came away with them still in his possession, but not essential. Leon Becker could only achieve his other priority, if the seller Blackbird hadn't already left the island. The seller, the corporate executive with access to weapons designs, was also part of his assignment. Leon had already figured out the athletic, modest man, who saved them from the frag grenade, likely had more to him than sitting at a desk all day and wasn't underestimating the difficulty he faced.

He needed to find Max as well. Then he needed to keep him near, and keep him alive.

17

Max was making his way slowly along the path when he heard the long strides on the shingle ahead of someone running towards him. He quickly dodged into the trees and waited. Moments later he quietly watched as Samson the German buyer ran by, still holding his gun. But he didn't appear to have the briefcase and wasn't carrying anything else.

Max figured that with the first six shots being fired and then after a gap, another single, deliberate shot, one or both of the broker and his aide were dead. As the broker's bodyguard had the gun, at least when Max had seen them last, he thought maybe the broker was dead and his friend had all the gear and was being chased by Samson back to the boats.

Max felt like calling out to the German, but thought better of it. For now, he would double back to the jetties and see if he caught up with anyone.

Mateo clutched the black velvet bag with the diamonds and Omega samples case inside. He'd heard that single shot and knew his friend Antonio must have died at the hands of the buyer at that moment. Terror and grief had pushed him along making his way back through the trees, unknowingly avoiding Max on the pathway and had reached the now deserted restaurant area. Just a single staff member looked out cautiously from behind the kitchen entrance, then disappeared as they saw Mateo, still holding the revolver and sporting his blood-stained wounds from the grenade.

Mateo shuffled past the seating area and made his way down the steps, reliving the pain of being hit several times by his frag grenade. As he reached the dockside he could see there were only three boats left, thankfully his Riva Tritone, Samson's speedboat and one other motorboat, presumably the restaurant manager's. As he fumbled for his keys whilst proceeding down the steps, he was shocked to notice behind him two men coming from different directions. Max reappeared from the treeline behind the restaurant, paused when he saw Mateo, then started to run his way. Then at the same time, Leon came into sight on the pathway on the far side of the seating area.

"Bastardi!" cried Mateo, as he hastened towards his Riva. He thought maybe Max had left the island and Leon was still at the far end, but hadn't accounted for Leon's pace running back. Adrenalin spurred him onto the jetty where he flicked the rope mooring loose as he jumped into his boat. He slotted in the key, gunned the engines and in one move, pushed the lever full forward accelerating the launch towards the bank, then turning full lock away and out onto the lake.

Max and Leon converged at the top of the steps, much to Leon's surprise and delight in seeing the seller again. 'Perfect' he thought.

However, they were too late to stop the broker who was now out of range for Leon to shoot him accurately. Leon started moving again saying to Max, "Come with me! Let's get your diamonds and my samples!" pointing at his speedboat.

Max knew he had to follow so also set off down the steps. Leon untied his rope and they both got in. Leon abruptly started it up and reversed out from the jetty, then thrusting it into forward full throttle, lurched off in the trail left by the other boat.

Mateo had gone round the island out of loyalty to his friend, just in case he was waiting to be collected. As he rounded the far end, his eyes scanned the waters edge for him but then noticed a slumped figure on top of the grassy bank, with the briefcase discarded nearby. His heart sank, but the reality of the life and death chase he was now in, brought him back quickly as he became conscious of another boat speeding alongside the island after him. He powered up and the strong Riva dug into the water, raising its nose up and gathering speed quickly.

Leon and Max came round the island in time to see Mateo heading up the lake towards the peninsula where the famous Villa del Balbianello proudly sat. Despite the powerful twin engines of the Riva, it was a larger and heavier boat with a sizable hull water displacement and drag. Leon's speedboat only had one efficient outboard motor, but the craft was significantly smaller and lighter, skimming across the top of the water it was nippy and easily manoeuvred, so was managing to match the bigger boat ahead.

Leon knew that if he could keep the boat on flat water and not hit any wake waves, he could slowly gain on the Riva. Leon also sat down and gestured Max to do the same, to reduce the slight drag caused by them both standing higher than the small, ineffective windscreen.

Max could see this guy knew his stuff, but all the same ventured, "He still has a gun!"

Leon smirked back and held up his Heckler and Koch. "He's got a useless revolver, and he's had his six shots. Let's hope he hasn't had a chance to reload eh!"

"What happened back at the island?" asked Max tentatively.

"No-one double-crosses me," sneered Leon. "They took my diamonds and my Omega samples, and were going to kill us with that grenade." Max thought for a moment he might even get a thank you for saving this man's life. No. "I got the bodyguard, but they'd switched the gear. He now has it all," nodding to the boat some fifty yards ahead of them.

When they'd all made their way back to the boats, Phil Landon watching, had then got his car back onto the lake road and guessing they'd go up-lake, was already following the tracker dots whilst driving along the Via Statale towards the next town of Lenno.

Max could clearly see the broker in front of them, repeatedly turning to check their distance from him. They were slowly closing the gap between them. They started passing Ferries and other boats going about their normal business, with passengers looking curiously at the two boats racing menacingly at high speed.

"What are we going to do when we catch up with him?" asked Max.

"We can't let him get to one of the larger towns like Bellagio, we need to take him out on the water." Leon was determined. "When I get closer, I shoot him, pull alongside and get the bag off him."

"I don't think you should do any shooting in the middle of the lake. Too many onlookers and the Polizia water patrol's will probably have been alerted by now after the shooting on the island." Max had an idea that might just save the broker's life. "Get alongside, hold up your gun but don't shoot and I'll jump over and persuade him to just hand it over rather than you kill him?" Max realised it sounded a little feeble and assumed the broker hadn't reloaded his gun, but it was his last chance to get the broker alive for MI5 who would want to question him more about the history of his dealings.

Leon shook his head. "You're too soft." But he didn't want to attract any more attention and knew once they were being chased by the Lake Polizia high powered boats, the game was probably up for them. Leon reluctantly agreed. "Okay. Don't try to speed off once you get the bag, or I *will* shoot."

Max nodded and stood up in readiness to make the jump. Leon had now got them within about twenty yards behind, dodging in and out of the Riva's wake trail. He waited to see if the broker would turn and shoot, but he didn't, so convinced he still had no more rounds, started to draw closer.

Mateo could see they were trying to draw alongside, so started to weave about trying to throw off the smaller speedboat, but it was far more responsive than his larger boat and matched his turns and swerves easily. During the dodging and avoidance tactics, the two boats began to veer away from the lake's centre and were now heading towards the town of San Giovanni, just below the tourist hot spot of Bellagio.

Leon levelled his gun at the broker and shouted, "Halt!", and although Mateo slowed a little he kept going. Leon closed in again and Max put his foot up on the edge of their boat ready to jump across to the Riva. The two boats clashed together but they weren't quite close enough, then as Leon throttled up their speedboat lunged over a wake wave and was momentarily almost alongside the Riva.

Max jumped, hurling himself onto the large padded lounging platform at the rear over the engines, behind the seating cockpit. Leon's boat bounced away again as he fought with the throttle lever and steering wheel. Mateo kept going, whilst realising Max was now onboard. Max could see the black velvet bag on the front passenger seat and cried out to Mateo through the spray of the water, "Just let me have the bag, and he won't shoot you! Don't be a fool!"

Mateo was nobody's fool and had risked too much for this bag of goodies. Driven on by blind anger and greed, he continued trying to shake off the other boat making it hard for Leon to aim his gun.

Max climbed onto the rear bench seat to try one last time to appease the broker, but Mateo then made a mistake. He pulled out the revolver which had no live rounds left in it, thinking it would scare Max into submission. Max's instincts from the Commando's and his martial arts training of years ago kicked in, and without thinking he swiped Mateo's wrist sending the revolver flying off into the water. In the same move, he followed up with a disabling punch to the side of Mateo's face, dislodging one of his teeth and sending him reeling towards the edge of the cabin area.

The two boats were now fast approaching the shoreline where a long row of boulders had been placed, behind which there was a small promenade. There were a few people casually strolling along the pathway by the water's edge, now looking up at the two approaching boats in consternation and surprise. People started to pull back or freeze in shock at the likely crash to follow.

Leon saw the oncoming rocks and swerved away. Max held out his hand to Mateo as he teetered on the edge of falling over the side. He looked at the bag, held out his hand to grab it, but then as the boat rocked on another wave, lost his balance and went out into the water.

Max looked up just in time to see the Riva was going to hit the rocks, but couldn't reach the throttle lever or steering wheel. He held onto the seat in front of him and braced himself.

Fortunately, the sheer size and momentum of the large boat

carried it over the first smooth boulder taking off some of the speed. It then glanced another before wedging itself to a stop between several more rocks. There was a sheering and splintering sound from underneath the Riva, as the uncompromising rocks tore into the boat's hull. Despite the boat coming to a more cushioned halt grinding over the boulders, Max ended up on his side in the footwell of the front seats. He gathered himself and was okay apart from a few bashes from the tumble.

The black bag was on the floor beside him. He opened it up and sure enough, the diamonds and the Omega samples case were all intact inside.

The engines of the Riva were still running, so Max turned off the ignition then looked up ahead of him. The onlookers had all retreated well back or run off both ways from the walkway except one old local, who remained seated on a bench some yards back. The elderly man sat there shaking his head at Max disapprovingly, thinking, 'Bloody tourists!'.

Max turned his head to locate the broker in the water and immediately spotted him thrashing around about twenty yards out. He then saw Samson in the speedboat and held up the bag, shaking it and nodding, to confirm the goods were inside and all was well. But as he celebrated their success, Max could see Samson turning the boat towards the broker, at first he assumed it was to pick him up. The boat continued at speed and it suddenly dawned on Max that the German wasn't going back to collect the man, he was going to run him over!

Max protested, shouting, "No! Pick him up!"

Leon heard him but ignored him. It was time to get his revenge on the broker who'd threatened to kill him and stolen his diamonds and samples. He adjusted the boat's line and pushed the lever forward, so the centre of the boat's bow would hit the flailing man's head. It wasn't the hull he knew would finish him off. It was what would follow, at the rear of the speedboat.

Mateo had gathered himself in the water and was looking around getting his bearings and about to start swimming for the shore. Then, like Max, he first thought the speedboat was turning to collect him, but as it got faster and started to line up exactly with him, he realised what was happening. His instinct was to dive down, but he didn't have enough time to make the move as the boat homed in on him fast. Before he managed to cry out, the apex of the boat's underside gave him a heavy glancing blow half knocking him out and sprawling him out just under the water's surface.

A moment later the real threat reached him. The speedboat's four steel propeller blades were spinning at over fifty revolutions per second and passed across Mateo's belly unwaveringly, like a hot knife through butter. The six-inch-wide groove furrowed through him exposed his torn stomach and intestines, then from the propellers passing suction, dragged much of his organs out into the water. It took several seconds for Mateo to lose consciousness and die.

A female onlooker screamed from the end of the promenade. Leon turned the boat around and retraced his wake slowing the boat right down as if checking he'd finished the man off. He arrived at a large red staining in the water just in time to see Mateo's ripped body sink, then enveloped into the water's gloom. Unconcerned he looked up to Max who was still in the damaged Riva on the rocks. He shuffled the speedboat alongside the back of the Tritone launch and waved for Max to climb back in.

Phil had pulled over next to the water's edge just below the town of Tremezzo, directly opposite the boat antics. He'd watched through his binoculars as Max had jumped onto the Riva, then struggled with the broker falling out, crashing into the rocks, followed by Samson's merciless running-over of the hapless man in the water. The rubber eye-pieces were pressed into his eye sockets in horror as he watched events unfold. He was impressed with Max's agility and taking on the broker and more importantly he had the bag and the buyer Samson was still in play. He remained helpless on the other side of the lake, but would continue to track and follow Max and the samples. He wondered what would happen now as he saw Samson beckoning for Max to come back into the speedboat.

Max hesitated but knew he needed to reunite the buyer with the Omega samples. He also had to get away from the damaged boat and preferably away from Samson and back to Phil. He clambered across the leather padding on top of the engines and nimbly jumped back into the boat with Leon.

"We go back to my car at Argegno, I give you your share of the diamonds and we part company, yes?" announced Leon. "You did well my friend." Leon was more certain than ever, having watched this supposed office executive handle himself, that there was a lot more to this seller Blackbird than met the eye. For now though, he just needed Max to stay with him.

Max shrugged his shoulders and Leon accelerated away from the Riva on the rocks and back down the lake. No more was said as they skimmed over the water retracing their route from the island. As they rounded the bend in the lake by the Villa del Balbianello, they could see a Polizia boat just disappearing behind the other side of the island where the docking jetties were, so continued down the middle of the lake out of sight of the Police. Max thought about the body of the hapless bodyguard and suspected he was well out of his depth today. Both he and their broker friend had bitten off more than they could chew, especially with this violent madman next to him driving the boat, who seemed to have no empathy or concern for others.

Max's deliberations led to him asking himself why Samson was looking out for him, why he didn't just do away with him as well. Maybe he'd garnered some valuable loyalty points when he saved him from the broker's frag grenade. Perhaps that one move was just enough for the buyer to spare his life. Something just didn't quite feel right. What else could he do though? He'd have to go along with this, and just maybe Samson would give him a handful of the diamonds and be on his way, presumably back to Germany. Phil could then pick him up and they could follow the trackers, both of which seemed intact and find out where this buyer was from, or more importantly who he worked for.

Phil was racing back down the Via Regina lakeside road,

following the two dots both together and could see Max seemed okay alongside the buyer. He was cautious to keep some distance between them, as he'd figured that they were going to put ashore soon and it looked like it would be on his side of the lake.

Leon headed straight for his small harbour at Argegno where he'd parked his Mercedes. The hire attendant acknowledged the boat's arrival with a friendly wave to Leon, which was ignored. He shuffled the boat alongside a jetty and they both got out with Leon grabbing hold of the bag before Max could gather it up.

"I'm the black one," Leon said, pointing towards the Mercedes G400.

Max couldn't help thinking, 'Of course you are, German car, large off-roader, black with blacked-out windows all round!'.

Max looked back at the island and could now just make out about five armed police around the restaurant area, likely being given the story by the manager there. Some pointing was followed by a couple of the police heading off up the pathway.

"Let's get on with this eh," he suggested, "this whole area will be swamped with police once they figure out what's happened on the island and link it with the inevitable witness reports of the broker's demise."

Leon opened his car and gestured for Max to get in the passenger side which he did. Before getting in himself he went to the rear and quickly fumbled around with something in the back, then came round the side and got in. max noticed the edge to him had returned and suddenly wanted to make this final exchange as fast as possible and leave. He was very conscious that no one could see them inside the car with its jet black tinted windows.

Leon firstly took out the Omega case, placed it on his lap and opened it up. Both of them were somewhat relieved to see the two large projectiles sitting safely in their slots, unaffected by the days events. Leon picked one up and Max immediately noticed the scuff on the base of the casing, he had the tracker sample. Leon marvelled again at its design, which was identical to its real, live partner in the box. Alan back at MI5 had ensured that after all its components were installed, the tracker dummy round matched the weight of its real companion, using of all things, fishing line lead weights set into fast-drying glue.

"Quite a beauty," said Leon. "Do you think it really can hit a lasered target at four miles?" he asked.

"That's what the specs and designer claimed," replied Max feigning ignorance.

"What company do you work for, Blackbird?" pushed Leon.

"I can't possibly say, you understand."

"It's a weapons design firm yes?"

Max gave a 'probably' shrug.

"So will you have access to more designs in the future?" This was the key question for Leon. Before acting on his second assignment, he wanted to check he wouldn't be wasting his time. His eyes wavered from the shiny Omega bullet and met Max's, watching for any flicker of a lie to this crucial question.

Max immediately calculated that if he said he wouldn't be able to get any more designs, then why should this buyer let him live. He was just another witness then. Without missing a beat, he replied confidently. "Yes. As and when things become available in our records department, I can access them." Leon looked curious.

Max remembered how they'd had to pretend they couldn't get the soft copy designs for the Omega rifle and before Leon could ask him, he continued, "Of course I'm going to have to find a workaround to the new security they started just before I got the Omega samples." Leon's suspicious look faded to acceptance and intrigue.

"So now Water Spider the broker has gone," he paused, "would you be interested in selling your designs to me directly, for more of these." He dug his hand into the diamonds and raised it up, full of the sparkling stones which momentarily mesmerised both of them with their beauty, and high value.

Max was already ahead of Leon so confidently stated, "Yes. That sounds great. Give me some way of contacting you, let me have some of those diamonds, and I'll be gone." It was a hopeful statement which he didn't think for a moment Samson would agree to.

Phil had by now parked up-road from the harbour and had hurriedly got out his directional listening device. He could see from the tracker dots which were accurate to a few feet, that Max and Samson were inside the most obvious car being the black Mercedes. He aimed the small antenna wand at the car and tuned its sensitivity, straining to hear something in his headphones. All he got was a dull, muffled whisper which was unintelligible. The device required a clear, unobstructed line of sight to the people talking and with the hushed conversation taking place behind the closed windows of the Mercedes, Phil couldn't hear what was being said.

He cursed, took some pictures of the car, then transferred these to his mobile along with the earlier photos of the boats and the men meeting on the island. With all the chasing going on, this was the first time since dropping off Max that he'd had a chance to sort out the photos for Thames House. He hurriedly sent them all over to Vince at MI5 with the message, 'max met broker and bodyguard, then met buyer at island, big fall out, bodyguard likely dead, broker dead, max with buyer, diamonds and Omega samples, will continue to follow and call soon'. Phil sat back and watched through his binoculars again.

Leon poured the handful of diamonds back into the bag. "I have a better idea and I'll give you more of these diamonds," he said tantalisingly.

"I'm listening," said Max playing along, not wanting to disagree or cut the conversation short. He wanted to see where Samson would take this.

"Come with me back to Germany. Meet my boss and seal the deal. You give your designs directly to us, and we'll pay you twice what you've been getting from Water Spider!" Leon looked up again at Max inquisitively searching for a reaction in his eyes.

Max hid his thought process which had just gone into turmoil. 'Go with him to Germany? He could, he'd find out where this all led, Phil would surely follow them, but was it a kidnap trap or did they simply want to indoctrinate him fully into their organisation, whatever that was?'. Max surmised he was better off rejoining Phil and following Samson and the trackers from a distance, so he could report back everything to Si at MI5.

"I'm happy to work with you directly, but no need to meet your boss. Give me a contact and my share of the diamonds and I'll be on my way now." Max met Leon's stare which he could see was turning into an incredulous, dissatisfied fog. Not good.

Leon snapped out of it and laughed off Max's finality with his last comment. "Okay, okay, whatever you want Mister Blackbird." He leant across Max and opened the glove compartment in the dash, taking out a small cloth bag holding his sunglasses. "Here we are, a bag for your diamonds," he announced. He opened the black velvet bag again and grabbed a hearty handful of the precious stones and funnelled them into the smaller bag cupping his hand. "I'd say you have about seven to ten million dollars in there. You take this while I write down a contact number you can reach me on," said Leon.

But he had no intention of handing over any such number. He sat back into his driver's seat and then held out the bag of diamonds in front of Max, above his knees. As Max went to take the bag Leon deliberately fumbled it, dropping it into Max's footwell.

"Sorry," he apologised casually.

Max instinctively leant forward in the tight space and reached down to pick up the bag, having to lower his head almost onto his knees to grab it, when he suddenly realised what was happening. It was too late.

Leon had retrieved something from his door compartment. With Max's head at its lowest point, he felt Samson's large, strong hand clamp down on the back of his neck, harshly thrusting his head down further, momentarily immobilising him in a hunched squat position. He felt the scratch on the side of his neck and a pin-prick penetrate inwards, just before his adrenalin kicked in to lash out with an arm.

"What the …." Max couldn't even finish his curse.

The potent cocktail consisting mainly of benzodiazepine went straight to the brain and knocked him clean unconscious within seconds. Leon kept his hold on Max's neck, pushing down for a while longer, feeling for any resistance or muscular movement. Max was still. Satisfied the drug had done its job, Leon hauled Max back up into his seat and held him upright with his safety belt strapped in. He would have him in the front so he could keep an eye on him. He wouldn't be seen as the front door windows were also blacked out.

He frisked Max and found his mobile phone. Giving it a cursory glance, he then opened it up and extracted both the sim card which he snapped in two and the battery. He then threw the phone, battery and card pieces into the water by the car.

Phil was watching and at this point knew something was up. He wanted to rush in like the cavalry with his gun, but that would ruin the mission. He may have liked having the gun, but wasn't really up for confronting this nasty buyer bloke and having to use it. He held fast knowing he must continue to follow the Omega samples and the buyer. He knew Max was still in the car so he'd have to hope Max had maybe just been knocked out with the butt of the man's gun or something. He checked the tracker dots were still working fine.

Leon's boss had been quite clear about his secondary assignment. He was to bring this seller Blackbird back to Germany with him, to be questioned about other designs he might have access to and be made an offer he couldn't refuse. To sell all future designs he stole to the Dreizack mafia only. They would continue to make him a rich man, but they wanted exclusivity. If they had some 'quality' time with him, they could understand who he was, what firm he worked for and what the designs pipeline looked like. After which they'd release him back to England to get on with his corporate job and weapon designs espionage and theft. For them.

Leon was told to try to get Blackbird to come back to Germany with him voluntarily if possible. Far easier to transport a willing, conscious person who would do as they're told. But if that failed, then Leon's orders were to use the drugs and bring him in anyway, unconscious for the car journey if that's what had to be done. Unfortunately, Max had made that choice when he insisted on taking his share of the diamonds and then leaving.

Leon made a call on his mobile. "Boss. I met Water Spider the broker who had a bodyguard and then also met Blackbird the seller. The broker tried to scam us and take the diamonds and the Omega samples."

"You're kidding," said the voice on the other end. "You've not lost them have you?" the man's voice asked sternly.

"No boss. I've got the diamonds and samples back with me. The broker and bodyguard are both dead now."

"Good. Good. And what about Blackbird?"

"He's with me back in my car. I tried to give him the option to come quietly but he wanted to leave."

"So what happened then?"

"Don't worry, I used the drugs, he'll be out cold for the whole journey I reckon," said Leon with some pride, pleased he'd got everything done expected of him and killed a couple of people as a bonus.

"Well done Leon. I can always rely on you," said the other voice. "Get back up here to the safe-house lab I told you about, so we can have a closer look at the Omega samples and have a chat with our friendly seller Blackbird."

Leon asked, "He's out cold boss, what about the border checks?"

"Leave that with me, I'll tell you which control gates to go through in plenty of time," said the voice confidently. "You've got a long ten-hour drive back up here to Berlin, are you okay to do it with only fuel stops?"

"No problem boss, hopefully, I'll be there by midnight."

Back at MI5 Thames House, Vince received the message and pictures from Phil Landon. He printed them out and went into Si's office.

"Ah Vince, I hoped you'd have an update for me," said Si,

"how's Max and Phil getting on in Como? I've been looking at the Omega case tracker. It went from the Lido to that island, then up the lake and back to Argegno where it's at now!"

Vince laid out all the pictures from which he'd deduced which person was the broker, buyer and bodyguard. He'd labelled them for his boss. He read out Phil's message.

"Good God, what the hell's being going on there," said Si. "Two dead! But you think Max is okay? What does he mean 'max with buyer'?"

"I'm not sure, but if there was a problem I'm sure Phil would alert us or move in to help. He seems happy to continue watching and will follow them wherever they go," surmised Vince. "I've already got the team working on the photo ID's of the three men and the buyer's car, Phil's got us some pretty good photos."

"Yes, good, I want to know everything about these characters ASAP, let's try and see what we're dealing with here shall we." Si wanted to cover all options. "Make sure you utilise every database we have access to, ours with MI6's, each of the various European countries police records, Interpol, hell throw in the US agencies as well. The photo-matching software should be able to give us some information about these guys. Passports, driving licenses, employment records, military, CCTV, web and social media, something will have caught them. Tell me when you have anything so we can update Phil?"

Vince was excited. "Two deaths aside, we've got Max with the buyer and Phil following. This could go our way."

"Steady on Vince," cautioned Si. "I suspect we've still got a way to go yet and we're relying on Phil to support Max however things turn out."

Vince's phone buzzed, it was another clipped message from Phil Landon. He showed Si. It said, 'buyer on the move with Max. following'.

Si looked up at Vince. "Let's see where the Omega trail takes us now?"

18

Phil Landon watched the black Mercedes G400 pull out of the small harbour car park, with Max inside. It turned down the road back towards Como and he let it get out of sight before starting up his BMW to follow. Checking his OMEGA and CASE tracker apps he could see their dot ahead of him.

Inside the black off-roader, Max was out for the count, lying back in the front passenger seat slightly slumped against the side of the seat and the door pillar. Behind the black one-way glass, no-one could see him and even if they could have, would have assumed the passenger was having an innocent knap.

Leon had his phone in its cradle and was following his sat-nav back to Berlin. The estimated one-thousand kilometre journey time said '10 hours and 12 minutes'. He settled himself back into his seat, pleased with how things had gone. He had been surprised by the broker thinking he could run off with the samples and the diamonds. That had caught him out momentarily and when Blackbird had disposed of the frag grenade and saved them, a glimmer of appreciation had registered with him, briefly. He envisioned the bodyguard's eyes when he'd shot him and revelled in that special power one experiences that moment you literally have someone's life in your hands, to decide on.

He recalled thinking Blackbird had likely fled the island, and then the luck he'd felt when he'd bumped into him again. How fortuitous. But then wondered why he hadn't got out of there, with all the shots being fired, wouldn't you want to get away as fast as you could. He pondered for a while feeling he was maybe missing something, why this seller Blackbird had hung around, stayed with him. Maybe he just wanted his diamonds. He gave up trying to play detective. His boss could ask the questions and find out everything about the man next to him.

He turned on the radio and soon turned away from the lake. Within a minute he was driving under an innocuous sign above the road, alongside cafes and shops, saying 'Confine di Stato – Svizzera CH'. They'd crossed the border from Italy to Switzerland in the blink of an eye. No checks, no passport, not even a sign of any police. The old Customs House in the centre of the road lay dormant, with its 'Dogana' sign above barely noticeable. Leon thought how easy it was in some places to pass from country to country, while in others you could be stopped, arrested or shot for trying, remembering the Berlin Wall.

In no time he joined the A2 at Chiasso and would drive from the very bottom of Switzerland to the top of the country, where he would briefly pass through the corner of Austria before entering Germany. It was these two border crossings that were known for doing frequent, random spot checks on cars as they passed by the Customs buildings in the centre of the road.

A mile behind Leon was the BMW being driven by Phil Landon. Although the tracker in the samples case was online and could be seen on his app from any distance, Phil was mindful that if the case should get discarded, he needed to be within about five miles of them for the tracker inside the Omega dummy bullet to work. He'd stay within a few miles of them if possible and dutifully followed the path of Leon's Mercedes.

At MI5 Thames House some information had come back to Vince already, from the photos he'd circulated to the various analytics teams. Vince took it into Si.

"I think we may have found our buyer Samson," reported Vince cautiously. He knew that identifying photos wasn't an exact science, but was pretty confident nonetheless.

"Let's have a look then?" said Si Lawson leaning forward to get a close look at the documents Vince placed in front of him on the desk.

Vince explained. "Here are the three men that met with Max on the island in Lake Como," pointing to each one. "This guy here, who later on pulls a gun out, appears to be the broker's bodyguard or something. We've not got anything on him yet suggesting he's not got much in the way of records or form. Probably just a mate of the broker, an amateur." Si focused on the next one, unconcerned they hadn't got his name yet and trusting they would eventually. As more pieces of the jigsaw fell into place, most things got revealed in the end.

Vince continued. "Then we have our broker, Water Spider. Here he is," pointing at him driving his Riva boat then sitting at the restaurant table.

"Not what I expected, but they never are eh?" commented Si looking at the overweight Italian.

"I'm sure we'll get his name soon, but as usual it's a bit slower with our Italian counterparts. Nothing's urgent, lots of process, all a big deal for them. We did our own check on the boat registration and came to a dead-end with a false ownership name and address. They don't really care about boat documentation over there. Or anything much else to be honest." Vince was quite disparaging about the comparatively lax processes and diligence of the various Italian authorities, which he felt wouldn't pass muster against the governance and standards of the mighty MI5.

"Alright, let's not be too harsh on our friends," countered Si professionally. "Now give me the good news?"

Vince pointed out the last man with pictures of him in the speedboat arriving, sitting at the table, then chasing around with a handgun.

Si asked, "What on earth went on there? Looks like the gunfight at the OK Corral for Christ's sake? Have we had a full report yet from Landon?"

"Not yet sir but expecting one anytime now as he appears to be following Max and this buyer, so they're back on the road. He should have a chance to call in, but we don't want to disturb anything by initiating a call ourselves." Vince turned back to the photos laid out like a movie storyboard.

"It seems from the pictures, they met at this restaurant on the island. The buyer inspected the samples, all okay. Then the bodyguard pulls a gun and he and the broker try to leave with the samples and payment. Then it looks like there's some kind of small explosion near the dockside and everyone starts chasing one another back into and around the island."

"Good God, it's like a movie!" said Si. "What about all this then," he said pointing at more pictures.

"We think Max and the buyer then chase the broker up the lake. Max boards the other boat and fights him. Max and the boat crash, he's okay though."

"And the broker?"

"Well, it would appear he drowns in the lake." Vince paused. "There is this picture of the buyer heading towards him, but probably not to pick him up given the wake behind him. He looks like he's going pretty fast. I suspect he got run down and is dead."

"Good God," exclaimed Si. "Thank heavens Max is alright after that lot. Crikey, bit of an action man after all eh! So to the buyer's identity?"

"Our Samson character, the buyer, is called Leon Becker we believe," pronounced Vince finally.

"And how did he come up in the search?" asked Si, always curious as to criminal's backgrounds and how they became what they are now.

"Ex-Police!" said Vince.

"What?"

"Can you believe it? Leon Becker was a German policeman, in the Landespolizei State Police. That's how we were able to get a match so fast, I couldn't believe it," said Vince proudly.

Si surmised, "So we've got a dodgy cop gone rogue have we?"

"Not quite Sir, there's more," said Vince. "Our Leon Becker gets promoted into the Bundespolizei Federal Police so must have something about him and then just a few years back, he resigns!"

"Why would he do that?"

"The information suggests that it may be linked to a well-publicised death of a suspect in police custody around the same time he resigns. We'll get more info soon, but that's my guess at this point."

Si pondered. "Okay, great we have his name and interesting he was German Police." He looked up to Vince. "But after all that, we still don't know why he's acting as the weapons designs buyer. More importantly, we don't know who he's doing this for. There's no way he's acting alone, especially with all the money involved with buyer these designs. We've got to find out what organisation he's fronting for. They're the people we're after Vince."

Vince nodded in agreement. "Well, it's a good thing we still have Max and Phil on the case."

"Indeed. Let's see where this Leon Becker takes us now. Tell me as soon as you hear from Phil?" said Si nodding for Vince to leave as he picked out a large folder from his desk drawer.

Si Lawson had over the years collaborated with many of his counterparts across the globe in other country's intelligence services. Sharing operations, exchanging information to help one another, meeting at cooperative conferences and passing on vital intel had all served to develop an impressive network of high ranking contacts for Si. Now he had Leon Becker's name, he immediately thought of one of his contacts, now holding a very senior position within the Bundesnachrichtendienst, Germany's Federal Intelligence Service. He found the details he was looking for, hesitated to compose himself on how to pitch the call, then picked up his phone.

The other end picked up sounding clipped and slightly irritable, "Ja, Meyer."

Si swung into his happy greeting mode. "Hello, is that Hans Meyer? It's Si Lawson calling, from England, MI5."

There was a pause on the line as Hans immediately signalled for the six staff in his meeting room to leave at once. The BND team leads had been giving their boss his weekly security operations briefing. This was usually sacrosanct and never to be disturbed, but a rare call from British Intelligence trumped the usual meeting's protocol.

"Si Lawson, my goodness. How are you? How long's it been, must be a few years since we spoke on that awful terrorist plot you MI5 guys uncovered for us." Hans had likewise immediately changed from being annoyed at the interruption in his meeting, to excitedly pleased to hear from an old acquaintance abroad. "To what do I owe the pleasure of this call?" Both men knew this wasn't an informal catchup between old friends, it was always business.

Si jumped right in. "Well, it's just a quickie really. A certain Leon Becker…" Hans' attention peaked at once, "has come onto my radar. Your country's low-level ID search cooperation confirmed to us he was with your regional then federal police. I just wondered if you'd ever come across him?"

Despite Si's innocent question, Hans could feel the tension inside him rocket and had to compose himself before replying nonchalantly. "The name does ring a bell. I've had thousands of staff in my various departments over the years." Then casually he asked, "Why? What's this Mister Becker done that warrants your attention?"

The question hung there for a moment before Si answered vaguely, "Oh nothing serious, just some potential corporate espionage we're looking into, being Cyber, that's why it came across my desk. His involvement at this time is only inferred." Si didn't want to give too much away at this point, given he had two of his agents Max and Phil with Leon who being German, may well be heading back to his homeland right now. The last thing he wanted was the locals taking over the operation. He brought the question back, "So does he ring any bells for you Hans?"

Hans was canny enough to know that as Leon had been with their police, if MI5 hadn't got his file by now they would have very soon, so there was no point in pretending to know nothing. He played along. "Leon Becker, yes, I thought the name sounded familiar. He was an excellent officer but was on duty when an armed robber being questioned, sadly passed away in police custody. He was cleared but his career was ruined, so he left the police. It was in the papers here." Si detected Hans was being tentative with his version, so pushed again, carefully.

"And what's he been doing since leaving the force?"

Hans replied faster this time. "I really have no idea, you can't expect me to keep track of everyone all the time. He was cleared, his choice if he resigns, after that he's no concern of mine."

Si could tell he'd reached the edge of his counterpart's patience on this call and didn't want to unduly put the senior official on the spot anymore. Something was up, but this call wasn't the place to push his luck. He needed more intel from Phil Landon. Hans' political mind was racing though. If things were closing in on Leon he needed to pave the way for a little more confusion.

"Okay, well thank you for your time Hans, I'll be in touch if our investigations come up with anything tangible that's worth sharing," Si was keen to end the call now.

Hans added, "There is just one thing I should mention, in the spirit of full collaboration."

"What's that?" said Si, keen to hear anything more.

"Well it's probably nothing," said Hans tentatively, "but I did hear on the grapevine that your Mister Becker may have got himself involved with one of the underworld gangs." Hans was hedging his bets now.

"Really. Which one?" asked Si keenly.

"Possibly the Dreizack mafia I'm afraid."

"Oh!" said Si ruefully. Si was aware of this infamous organisation, spread across various European countries and that one of their growing business lines could be that of the weapons business, but not yet confirmed though. "So he's gone rogue and working for the opposition eh?"

"It is only what I've heard, it's not verified I should add," clarified Hans.

Both men on the call knew that the other undoubtedly had more information they weren't sharing, but that was the way it got played when the top Intelligence staff were trying to ascertain how much everyone else knew. Then they could decide what intel they could, or should give up.

"Well thanks for that, interesting. I'll revert if anything more comes to light," promised Si.

"No problem at all Si, always happy to help whenever we can. Do keep me updated please, as soon as you know more. He's one of ours after all. Goodbye."

Si thought the last comment strange and he hung up. Did Hans mean 'one of ours' because Leon Becker was a German, or was he referring to his past service in the Police? Surely not given the guy's now potentially working for one of the growing Mafia's renowned for harsh punishments on those who tried to cross them. Either way, the implication at the end was crystal clear to Si. The inference was very much, 'you've got one foot in my territory, so be careful how you tread!'.

Hans Meyer sat back in his chair and sighed as he looked out of the window overlooking the Chausseestrasse road in the Berlin district of Mitte. The massive high security, monolithic, imposing building was opened in 2019 by Chancellor Angela Merkel, when the Bundesnachrichtendienst moved in from their previous base in Munich. The Federal Intelligence Service is one of the largest in the world with over seven thousand staff globally, mostly based in this building and forming the largest part of the German Intelligence community. Within the BND, also known simply as 'The Organization', various departments operate including crime, technology, weapons, terrorism, military intelligence, security and intelligence services.

Hans headed up the directorate known as TW comprising Proliferation, ABC-Waffen, Wehrtechnik, meaning international arms trade, atomic, biological and chemical weapons, and defence technologies.

He was a small figure at only five-foot-seven inches tall, but what he lacked in height and stature, he made up for in character and determination. His political and management skills were legendary and accompanied by an unwavering, committed passion in what he did and what he wanted, was a force to be reckoned with. When

Hans Meyer walked into the room, staff sat up, and shut up.

He rose up through the ranks with his leadership manoeuvrability skills. He impressed and persuaded superiors and those with influence. He left his peers behind in a daze of confusion or reprimand of jobs that should have been done better. He had no patience for fools, nor people who opposed his aims and views, and would never forget both those who helped him, nor those who challenged him. He was a larger than life figure in the Federal Intelligence Service and had the ear of the BND President, the Minister of Special Affairs and the Chancellor.

Several years ago when his protégé Leon Becker had followed him from his regional posting into the Federal Police, Hans was planning a secret operation to infiltrate one of the fastest growing criminal organisations in Germany. But this mafia also operated across two other countries, Italy and Russia. They were called the Dreizack.

When Leon had his unfortunate incident with the armed robber suspect in the police cells, Hans took the opportunity of jumping on the perfect background cover story for his unorthodox follower, to release him from duty by telling him to publicly resign from the police. Hans arranged for Leon to continue being paid on a covert operations payroll and go into hiding for a year. Then they would start their operation to infiltrate the Dreizack mafia using Leon in the role of the disgruntled ex-policeman wanting payback and turning against his previous employer.

Leon's misdemeanours and ruthlessness soon came to the attention of the mafia and over a period of time, tests, jobs and growing trust in him, he was accepted by them. Whilst he had his superior in the criminal gang, he also had another boss. Hans Meyer.

However, Hans was worried. He didn't like one bit that Leon had somehow hit the radar of the infamous MI5, an organisation not to be trifled with despite their public fair-play British stiff upper lip persona. Once they had a whiff of intel on anything dubious, they would close in until all was revealed, and stopped if dangerous, illegal or nefarious in any way. The Dreizack were a dangerous, criminal organisation who were repeatedly breaking the law and threatening international disruption across the borders they operated across. They also specialised in arms espionage, theft and dealing, and that was right in the middle of his BND responsibility and he couldn't be humiliated by any upsets caused by them. He would have to work fast now.

Hans picked up his phone and made a call to a colleague of his, who headed up the Bundeszollverwaltung. Also known as Zoll, the German Federal Customs Service.

"Franz, it's Hans Meyer here." He'd known this man some years and was influential in his latest promotion to this senior appointment, so was direct. "I have an operative passing through a couple of your border control posts in the next five hours or so. I need you to ensure he is not stopped, for any reason. Is that clear?"

"Of course," came the obedient reply. "Which customs points?"

"The first is by the town of Kriessern, where the Zollstrasse crosses over the Rhine from Switzerland to Austria. Use your influence to sort that one out with whoever is in charge there. The second is likely to be the Weidach customs office at Zollamt Horbranz-Autobahn, passing from Austria into Germany. Clear?"

Franz was compliant. "Yes Sir. The operative and car please?"

"You don't need his name, just let his car through," barked Hans. "It's a black Mercedes G400!"

19

Leon checked again that Max was out cold. The journey had been straightforward so far and he was already approaching the first border control point near the northerly Swiss town of Kriessern. He peeled off the E43 and drove up to the border control, comprising of an office in the centre of the road and a small building to the side for the customs staff. There were only a couple of cars ahead waiting to be waved through and as he drew to the front, the Swiss customs officer had either been briefed or was not bothering doing any close checks and simply waved him through with barely a glance.

He crossed over the Rhine and pulled up in a queue of five cars waiting for the Austrian border staff to make whatever random checks they felt like doing. Leon noticed an over-diligent officer walking around the cars, talking to the drivers and asking for ID. This didn't feel right. The man looked too keen. Leon reached for his handgun to instinctively check it was beside him inside the centre consul compartment. He was next in line.

The officer waved the car in front through then turned his full attention to Leon's ominous-looking black Mercedes. He had a glint in his eye as he circled round to Leon's driver's door and gesticulated for him to wind down the window. Leon obliged but only lowered the dark glass allowing a few inches view so he could make eye contact with the man, now peering in.

"ID please?" he demanded, but was then distracted upon seeing Max slumped in the passenger seat. "Your friend, is he okay?" he asked curtly.

Leon readied himself. "He's just sleeping, don't wake him."

At that moment another officer came dashing out of the nearby office hut shouting to his colleague by Leon's door. "Elias, Elias!" Leon was about to grab his gun. "Just stop a moment. I'll take this one okay. You deal with the next one!"

The senior officer hurriedly waved Elias away from the Mercedes, who was trying to protest. "But Sir, I was just..."

"Nevermind. I've got this one!"

"But the passenger! He looks..."

"Enough! Go to the next car." He turned back to Leon. "I'm sorry for my fellow officer. I only just got a message from my superior. You may pass through," he offered, standing aside whilst peering at Max inquisitively.

Leon relaxed, put his window up and drove on.

Phil Landon was about two miles behind, still with both tracker dots showing the car ahead.

Less than fifteen minutes later Leon was coming up on the final customs checkpoint at Zollamt Horbranz-Autobahn in Weidach where he would pass from Austria back into Germany. It was around four PM and he could see two short lines of vehicles slowing at the customs centre. There were more officers about this time and it appeared as though they were waving through most of the cars, but then randomly picking out others to be taken into their check-lane to the side for closer examination.

Leon hoped that this time the directive from above had got through to the right person, he didn't relish having a problem with the German authorities. He moved to the front of the line and scrutinised the officer dealing with the car ahead. He had that canny look about him. Professional, officious, but loyal. The man looked up and saw the black G400 approach, he looked straight through the windscreen at Leon... then nodded deferentially and calmly waved him by, moving his attention immediately to the next car behind. Once Leon had passed he glanced back in his mirror and noticed the officer lean his head down to his radio attached to his lapel and say something. The man was merely confirming to his boss that 'the black Merc is through as instructed'.

Leon felt happier being back on his country's turf again. He knew from his time in the Police how complicated things could get when a criminal was caught outside their own country's jurisdiction.

Whilst travelling, Phil Landon had called Vince and given a

full and detailed report of everything. The MI5 team were now fully up to date, though Si Lawson had expressed concerns.

"I'm worried about Max's welfare and state of health. Do we even know if he's still alive?" Si asked. "I need confirmation."

He'd had an idea that was proposed to Phil. With a bit of luck, the Mercedes would be stopping soon to refuel. Phil hadn't been happy about the instruction, as he didn't want to jeopardise breaking his cover. He wanted to keep following the buyer from a safe and unnoticed distance, but he would follow Si's request.

Before Si rang off, he added, "Oh yes Phil, just a piece of intel for you about this Samson buyer you're following. His name is Leon Becker. We got that from identifying your Como photographs. He's ex-German Police, left a few years ago. My contact there thinks he might now be involved with the Dreizack mafia. They're infiltrating the weapons and arms dealing business, so just be careful. I suspect he's quite an unsavoury chap, well you've already seen that for yourself haven't you. Be careful. Anything you need a steer on, if you get the time to call me, just ask. Our priority is Max, over and above confirming who Leon Becker works for, or the samples, or the diamonds."

Since the call, he'd made good progress in his sporty BMW and was now within about a mile of the tracker dots. He'd also been conscious for a while of the big car's need to refuel soon and closely watched his map app for any deviation of the dot ahead.

As they approached Kleinkellmunz, without warning the dot veered off the main highway and pulled into a fuel station. Phil's excitement and also anxiety rose a notch as he raced to the same petrol stop. By the time he arrived at the forecourt, he could see the buyer Leon just finishing filling up the large black off-roader, so he pulled his BMW into the bay alongside, he needed to refuel himself anyway. He watched Leon closely as he strode into the large shop to settle his fuel bill and could see there was a blind spot he'd have to walk past along an aisle of high shelves.

Phil quickly got out of his car and hovered, pretending to fumble with his keys, to get the timing right to coincide with the moment Leon would briefly disappear. Then, Leon was gone, behind the shelves. Phil darted over to the Mercedes and as he passed in front of the bonnet, he focused on the passenger through the windscreen. He could see Max, slumped back in his seat which had been slightly reclined to keep him laid back. He was motionless but there was no sign of any struggle, no bruises or blood stains. And then, he saw Max's chest rise and fall as he took in a deeper breath during his deep sleep.

He'd pushed his luck enough, hovering there in front of the car and continued to the rubber glove dispenser beside the Mercedes. Unbeknown to Phil, Leon had come back into view and had made a cursory glance back out to his car to check all was well. He stopped for a second, seeing another traveller pulling out a couple of rubber gloves to keep your hands clean when refuelling, then walk back to their BMW near to his Mercedes. Leon studied the man for a second. All seemed fine and thought even if he had looked into his car he either wouldn't have seen anything in the darkness or if he did, he'd just see a sleeping passenger. He let it go and paid.

Phil's heart was racing and he was conscious of Leon coming back out to his car next to him. He put his head down and concentrated on the filler nozzle filling up the BMW's fuel tank. As it clicked 'full' and he'd replaced the nozzle, by the time he turned to head for the shop, thankfully the black Merc was pulling away. Leon hadn't even seen his face close up nor challenged him. Phil eagerly paid and jumped back into his car, both to continue following, but also keen to report back to Vince and Si that he'd managed to do as Si had suggested and although Max was likely drugged, he appeared to be alive and 'undamaged'.

The hours rolled by as both cars proceeded along the A7 past Ulm, Nuremberg and up past Hof. As they came towards Leipzig, Leon took a call, from his superior.

"It's come to my attention that the operation might have attracted interest from an unfriendly party. I can't have anything tracing all this back to me or the organisation. Did you search the seller Blackbird?"

Leon was horrified that anyone could have been aware of what had only happened earlier that day in Como and connected it with him already. "Yes, I searched him, all he had was his mobile. Battery, sim and phone all discarded," he reported efficiently.

"You don't still have the briefcase, that could have been bugged for instance by the broker when he took it from you?"

"No, the case was discarded on the island."

"Could the broker have put something in with the diamonds? In the bag?"

Leon kicked himself. He hadn't thought of that, nor fully inspected the velvet bag he'd taken back. "It's possible. I'll search the bag in the next layby," he promised, cross with himself.

"What else did you take possession of?"

"Only the two Omega samples of course."

"Are the two bullets loose… or in a box of some kind?"

This time Leon felt stupid. Inadequate. Angrier. He met the question head-on though. "The two bullets are both in a small case, in their foam slots. But I will search this as well when I stop!"

"Come straight to the meetup location in Berlin, the lab technicians will be waiting to reverse engineer the Omega samples. Also, I want the seller intact! He could be valuable to us in the future." The other caller hung up, leaving Leon feeling like a chastised schoolboy being admonished by the headteacher and told he might still get expelled later.

"Scheisse! Arschloch!" he swore at himself out loud in the car, hitting the steering wheel. He concentrated on the right of the road ahead, eager to use the next stopping layby to find out if there was anything to worry about after the call. Within five minutes he saw a rest point and swerved in, skidding the car to a stop behind a worried-looking couple parked up having a sandwich in an old Audi.

Leon grabbed the black velvet bag and set aside the Omega samples box first, then thrust his hand into the bag, deeply, moving it all around the precious gems, searching with his fingers. Then he lifted up the inside of the fabric bag to check if anything had been affixed into it. Nothing. Just forty-eight million dollars worth of diamonds.

He then turned his attention to the Omega samples case. Opening it up he carefully placed the two projectiles into the centre consul tray, then angrily ripped out the foam from both the base and the lid. Again nothing. Then his keen eyes saw a tiny raised section of the inner fabric covering of the base. It was just visible and seemed to show the outline of something underneath. Using his fingernail he lifted the corner of the stuck down material enough to grasp it, then tore it away from its glued position in the box.

The small, neat, paper-thin circuit board with power cell, transmitter and micro sim card revealed itself!

"You've got to be kidding me!"

As Leon put two and two together he realised that the man sleeping quietly next to him must have been responsible, or surely known about this device. He was now furious at this seller Blackbird. He wanted to quietly strangle the life out of him right there in that layby, while he was unconscious. But then he thought just maybe the seller might not have known about it. Perhaps it was planted there by the company he'd stolen it from. Either way, his instructions were clear, deliver the seller intact!

He broke up the sim card and circuitry and threw it out the window. Then sent a text to his handler saying, 'Trace device found in samples box, destroyed, all good now, proceeding to lab'.

At that moment Vince back at MI5 and Phil who had deliberately passed the layby Leon was in, both saw the tracking dot on their maps labelled 'CASE' disappear. They knew at once Samson must have either discovered the tracing device or preferably just decided to throw away the samples box and keep hold of the Omega bullets. Vince updated Si Lawson.

Phil continued slowly up the carriageway and pulled into the next layby point to wait for the buyer to pass him. He was now painfully aware that he *had* to stay within four to five miles of the Mercedes now, otherwise he could lose Max, the buyer and the samples. He waited patiently with his gaze fixed on the dot on his map. Then as the tracker GPS inside the dummy bullet refreshed itself, the dot started to move again, back onto the A9 from the layby.

Phil waited to let the dot pass him by then quickly pulled out of his layby in time to see the black G400 in the distance. He would now keep just out of sight and continue following at less than a mile back now, he simply couldn't risk losing them.

They proceeded along the A9 past Wittenberg and eventually the A9 turned into the A10. Phil could see the dot ahead appear to turn off the main motorway at Michendorf, on the outskirts of Berlin and proceed along an off-road. He followed closely behind, also pulling off away from the A115 which headed north to Berlin and onto the smaller road towards the town of Ludwigsfelde. He thought they must be getting near their destination and was about to call Vince, when to his horror, the dot on the map veered north! He realised that the G400 had in fact stayed on the main motorway to Berlin all along, but because the slip road passed underneath the A115 it looked as though he'd turned off.

Phil swore and frantically turned his head around trying to see if there was any way of turning around, but to no avail as it was a one-way filter road. He sped up knowing he might have a chance of rejoining the A115 further up and still be within his five-mile signal range of them. He watched the misleading dot continue north and wondered if they might turn off to Potsdam up ahead or continue further into the City of Berlin.

He raced to follow the quickest route around the countryside and rejoin the main road Max was being taken along. Constantly watching to see where the dot was, spurred him on to drive faster. He reached a junction and turned left, then at the next junction left again, doubling back towards the fast-moving dot which had just passed the turning for Potsdam. At least he knew it was more than likely now they were heading into the centre of Berlin.

Phil proceeded along the L40 road past Guterfelde and could just see the main road ahead he so badly needed to rejoin, when the cars in front of him started braking.

"Oh come on, not now! The motorway's right in front of us!"

he cried out loud.

About eight cars ahead, Phil could see there'd been some sort of minor collision, with several cars stopped in the road with bumps to the sides, front and rear. 'Why do they just stop in the middle of the road and not simply pull into the side so we can all pass!' thought Phil angrily. He craned his head to see if there was any way past the confusion, but the road was completely blocked.

Desperate not to lose the fast disappearing dot on his map, Phil grabbed his phone and got out, striding towards the puzzled looking drivers ahead. He quickly opened his translate app and spoke into the mic, "Please move your cars to the side, I have an emergency!". The software dutifully gave him the German translation which he shouted out loud to the gathering group of travellers.

His accent was terrible, but because he spoke with such determination and urgency, amazingly people started to get back into their cars and begin to pull them off the main road and onto the hard-shoulder.

Phil was surprised but wasn't going to hang about to thank them. He ran back to his BMW and just as enough of the cars parted, he raced through the first gap that opened up allowing him through. He could see the main road he wanted to join ahead and cancelled the translation app to bring up the 'OMEGA' location map again.

To his utter horror, the all-important dot, had gone! He frantically scrolled across the map screen hoping it would reappear. It didn't.

Just over five miles away up the motorway, Leon continued towards his nearing destination, oblivious that his pursuer had been delayed just long enough for the tracker inside the dummy bullet to pass out of range. He checked his passenger who was just starting to stir occasionally. Max was slowly coming round from the drug-induced sleep.

Phil's mobile rang. It was Si Lawson calling for an update. He wasn't going to be happy to hear from Phil that he'd lost the buyer, and Max.

20

Leon continued along the A115 deeper into central Berlin, passing by the Grunewald forest. He made a quick call and said simply, "Five minutes away, meet me outside." He rounded the junctions at Witzleben and turned onto the A2 which led to the Brandenburg Gate three miles ahead. Halfway to the famous archways, he turned off at the Tiergarten roundabout, in the centre of which stood the impressive two-hundred and twenty-foot high Siegessaule Victory Column, commemorating the 1873 Prussian victory. On the top of the column the golden coloured thirty-five-tonne bronze sculpture of Victoria, the Roman goddess of victory, looked down on the passing traffic.

He then turned into Tiergartenstrasse where many countries have their Embassy's situated, overlooking the lush greenery of the park opposite. A little way along this road Leon finally pulled up alongside a plain building, just hidden from the main road behind the Austrian Embassy. A military-looking man waited on the pavement, constantly looking around to check no one was approaching them.

It was almost midnight and the streets and buildings were deserted. Max was now coming round and starting to mutter, "Where am I?" and "What's happening?"

The burly man came over to the car and Leon unlocked the doors telling him to "Get him inside quickly." Max was unceremoniously dragged out of the Mercedes and helped to his feet, before then being propped up and taken to some steps leading down to a lower level entrance door. Leon placed his Heckler gun into its hidden back holster, grabbed the bag with the diamonds and samples and followed them inside.

There were no CCTV cameras, nor heavy deadlocked doors, nor barred windows. This safe-house had been hastily commandeered by the organisation's superiors. It resembled an empty flat or small office. Despite the humble frontage and entrance, once inside, the rooms opened out and revealed a surprisingly large width and depth to the basement floor space. The front door opened into a large room which followed through to a corridor, off which several other rooms lay and then another larger room at the end. In addition to the door guard, Leon and Max, there were two others coming from the far end room, Ben and Anna, both wearing white coats looking like doctors.

Their room had been converted into a mini laboratory that afternoon as Leon drove up from Como, with boxes of specialised kit and machines being delivered and set up. They were both highly qualified weapons technology designers, whose job it was to inspect, photograph, measure, open, test and dissect the Omega bullet samples. They would reverse engineer the prototypes and build a new set of design blueprints from the hardware examples they now longed to see. From that, they would later work out the specifications of the rifle required to fire these super-sized bullets, the scope and the systems control box and laser sighting. They could all be made by enhancing technology already available. It all just needed piecing together, around the valuable samples they now had.

Ben bustled forward ignoring the man they'd brought in looking a little groggy, who was now coming round. "Well then, let's have a look at these Omega samples shall we?" He held out his hands like an expectant child wanting a present.

Leon dug into the velvet bag and produced the samples box. Anna leaned over Ben's shoulder as he slowly opened the lid revealing the two shiny, huge shells. "Ahh, look at those Anna. They are truly beautiful aren't they. See here," he pointed to the four tiny propulsion ports, "these are the self-targeting rocket adjusters!"

Anna pointed to the ends. "Look at these, they actually have tiny eyes on the tips!"

"The directional laser tracker lens," added Ben. The two experts marvelled at the design and sheer brashness of the invention, overcoming the challenges of a four-mile range self-adjusting sniper projectile. "This will jump our program right to the top of the pile." Ben examined the small fin of one of the bullets.

Leon snapped them out of their gushing admiration. "Alright you two, enough! Get on and start doing what you're here for," pointing to the corridor and their room at the far end. They both carefully exited, cradling the Omega samples case like a newborn baby.

Leon glanced at the guard-man who quickly got the hint and grabbed a couple of seats for him and Max to sit on, then retreated to the corner chair where he continued reading his newspaper. The low key safe-house with no real security and just one guard to support Leon, was a reflection of their understanding that Blackbird the seller, was just a plain, normal office executive. They weren't expecting any trouble from such a civilian, though Leon's respect for Max had increased throughout the morning's events on the island and boats.

Max was now fully conscious, with a headache, and could speak for the first time since being knocked out cold.

"What the hell did you give me?" looking at Leon in a somewhat disappointed manner.

Leon shrugged, "Who cares! I gave you a chance to come here willingly."

"Where is *here*? And can I have some water?"

The guard-man got up and went to the kitchen for a glass of water for Max, before Leon could shoot him another glance this time.

"We'll wait for my boss. You can do all the yapping you want then. If it was up to me you'd be dead on the island, but you might have some use to us I gather," sneered Leon.

"You seem to have forgotten that *I* saved *your* life on that island! Remember, the frag grenade?" fought back Max sarcastically, rubbing his forehead.

The guard came back into the room having heard what Max said and Leon looked embarrassed, that this man might have saved *his* life!

"Hardly. I was about to throw it away myself!"

"Yeah right!" challenged Max, who was irritable and in no mood to play the fool right now.

Leon knew he should wait for his boss, but couldn't help himself, so continued. "What's with the tracker in the box then eh?"

Max played dumb. "What tracker? I've no idea what you're talking about."

"Anyway, I destroyed it!" said Leon triumphantly.

Max shrugged as if he neither knew what Leon was referring to, nor cared. However, he hoped that the tracker in the dummy sample had still allowed Phil to follow them. He was hopeful they weren't intending to kill him given he'd been brought here alive, but didn't relish the idea of meeting this thug's boss. 'Where the hell are you Phil!', he thought to himself.

"What in God's name do you mean 'you've lost them'!" Si Lawson was on the phone with Phil Landon and he wasn't happy.

"I'm sorry Si. After the Omega tracker dropped out I've been right on their tail to stay in range, but then the map sent me off down a sliproad when the Merc had gone straight on," explained Phil rather pathetically, "then there was a traffic accident and delay, so unfortunately..."

Si interjected. "They must have headed into Berlin. So get yourself back to the British Embassy there immediately and we'll figure out what to do next. Be on standby though," demanded Si.

Phil was still on the A115 at Dreilinden and swiped his 'OMEGA' tracker map aside to then open up his normal SatNav ap, punching in the Embassy. The map directed him off the junction he was just approaching and up the B1. This would take him past the suburbs of Zehlendorf, Steglitz and Schoneberg, before bringing him out by the British Embassy near the Brandenburg Gate.

"Damn it!" The long day's stress of watching over Max, helplessly seeing events unfold on the island, worry about Max's health, then closely, but not too closely, follow that bloody Mercedes for ten hours, was all taking its toll on the inexperienced field agent. Phil felt stressed. Having lost Max he also felt like he'd let down the side and Si the boss wasn't happy with him. Had he just messed up the chance to prove himself and get promoted? "Shit!"

Ben and Anna had started to meticulously examine the two Omega samples in their make-shift laboratory. Ben had fortunately chosen the live sample round and was preparing the advanced scanner ready to begin mapping out everything inside the shell. Anna had picked the dummy projectile, still with the tracker inside, to note the dimensions and analyse the metal content makeup.

In the front room, Max reminded himself that he was playing the part of a greedy executive stealing designs from his arms company employer.

"You said earlier your organisation seems to have a use for me. What's that then?" he asked Leon.

Leon was reticent to get into a discussion his boss was likely to want to have, but acquiesced momentarily. "As I asked earlier at Como, you've been getting access to all these weapons designs. You'll be able to get more won't you? For us."

"Sure, but what's in it for me?"

Leon smirked. "Don't worry, you'll be paid. Might even get some of these," he held up the bag of diamonds again, "if you play your cards right. You bloody office desk jockey's, you're all the same. Just out for yourself, and money. Never have enough do you?"

Max shook his head. "You're getting leading-edge, unique, unseen weapons designs and technology. Probably selling it on for many times what you give me. I'd say you're getting a bargain!"

Leon stood up, almost to attention and for a moment Max wondered what on earth had spooked him. He then realised someone was coming down the steps to their basement apartment. The guard in the corner now also stood up. Max remained seated as the door opened and a figure moved out of the dark night outside into the light of the room.

The man nodded to Leon and the guard who both started to relax again, then set his gaze upon Max.

"Well, well, well. The infamous seller we've been buying all this gear from. Blackbird eh." To Max's surprise, the man held out a hand. Max shook it cautiously. The guard in the corner quickly gave up his chair and placed it by the new arrival, then shuffled back into the corner and perched on the small table there.

"I'm sorry about the way you've been brought here. Hopefully, you're feeling okay now, but I was quite insistent that Leon here made sure you did me the courtesy of a meeting, after all the money we've spent with you and the broker fellow." He waited for Max to reply.

Max was conscious that this was the first time he'd been given the buyers name, Leon, assuming it was his real name. He felt there was no harm in giving up his own name, they were all far too committed to worry about such things now.

"I would have preferred some explanation and a lighter touch, but I guess I'm fine now. You can call me Max. Seems silly we were still on usernames doesn't it?" offered Max.

"Good. Excellent," the man said, but didn't offer up his own name yet. "As I'm sure you've gathered by now, I represent the organisation that's been buying these designs you've been stealing, then selling via the broker."

"What organisation is that may I ask?"

"We're glamourously known as the Dreizack."

Max shrugged, he had no idea who or what that was. The man elaborated.

"Silly really, but it refers to a three-legged being, rather like a tripod. We operate a mafia across Italy, Germany and Russia. One of our fastest-growing parts of the 'business' shall we say, is that of weapons design and arms dealing. Hence our keen interest in you Max. Someone who can offer us a future pipeline of designs."

Max feigned a shocked look and the man turned his attention to Leon, "Have Ben and Anna got the samples? Started working on them?"

Leon nodded towards the other room, "They have. Seemed very pleased when they saw the bullets!"

"The diamonds?"

Leon pointed to the black velvet bag. "All here."

The man gave a glint of satisfaction. "You okay? No-one followed you here?"

"No chance anyone would know where we are now boss."

Phil Landon was still fuming over the events of the day and losing his precious buyer and Max. He was driving up the B1 past Schoneberg and was now just minutes away from the British Embassy which he could see ahead on the map. No longer needing the satnav he closed it down on his phone, revealing the icon for the 'OMEGA' tracker, waiting on standby to be reopened or closed down.

He touched the icon out of sheer desperation. The map opened up showing the area he was travelling through in Berlin. No dot was visible. His heart sank. Then just as he was about to swipe the map off his screen in anger, the application refreshed itself and detected the signal from the tiny tracker inside the dummy Omega shell that Anna was now measuring. The dot reappeared on the map!

Phil did a double-take disbelievingly staring at the screen. "Oh my God. It can't be. You beautiful thing!"

Having driven back into the five-mile range of the tracking signal, the map showed the dot about 1.3 miles ahead of Phil's route, just behind the Austrian Embassy on Tiergartenstrasse.

"Jesus. This is it! My chance to sort out this mess!" Adrenalin and nervous excitement surged through Phil's body. His mind raced ahead of himself thinking through lots of scenarios, what kind of building the dot was coming from, how Max was, who else was there, were they armed. Of course they'd be armed. Phil reminded himself of the gun he had in the rear of the car. 'Shit! I might actually have to use it!' he vexed.

Phil knew he should immediately call this into Si and Vince at MI5 Thames House, probably request local backup, take more instructions. No. He wanted to sort this out himself, besides, no time for long explanations, he'd be there in a minute and his mind was playing havoc now with all the 'what if's'. He knew the Omega samples would be where the dot was. He also assumed Max would be there as well. But he found that he couldn't help wondering about whether or not something else might be there. The thought kept pushing its way past his concern for Max and the bullets. What had happened to all those diamonds!

Ben and Anna were progressing with their study of the two samples, making notes, taking careful measurements, analysing the makeup of the outer metals of both the bullet end and the shell casing. Ben had already set up his larger, more powerful scanning device and was excited to get his first look into the inside of this amazing Omega prototype projectile. Once they had completely photographed, measured and drawn out the whole of the internal parts, they would then remove the upper bullet part of the round from its lower shell casing holding the main charge. They could then further dissect the electronic parts in the 'bullet' half including the eye, wiring, circuitry, mini-gyroscope, control system and propulsion adjuster boosts with their separate charge cavities.

The man in charge leant back in his chair. "So Max, I'm offering you the opportunity to continue selling your weapons designs, to us, exclusively of course?"

"Payment?" asked Max.

"We will better whatever the broker was giving you, I suspect probably only ten-to-twenty per cent. We'll give you a third of a decent market valuation for each item. In diamonds. Or indeed transfer to an offshore account. Or gold. Whatever you want," he offered.

In the lab, Ben marvelled at the inside view of the projectile.

Max could see how normal people could so easily be tempted to the dark side, when such criminal organisations had access to large amounts of readily available wealth, in whatever form one fancied. He gathered his thoughts on where he wanted to lead the conversation.

The man continued. "You can appreciate that I wanted us to

have this chat, to make a deal, in person. One has to look the other in the eye when committing oneself to such an enormous agreement. Trust is everything wouldn't you agree?"

"And what if I want to make those two samples you have, my last deal. Take my share of the diamonds and call it a day? I don't suppose that's an option is it?" Max asked, still trying to assess how this could go if things turned against him. His senses were now closely monitoring everyone in the room and movement down the corridor from the two lab people.

Anna had finished taking measurements and brought her dummy shell over to the scanner. Ben looked up from his eye-pieces and said, "Ah, the other one. Let's have a look at this as well!"

The boss man frowned and shook his head disapprovingly. Leon seemed to perk up with the hint that the negotiation might deteriorate.

"I think we've gone beyond that point Max. I've come here personally in good faith. I'd prefer we all part as friends and partners. Then we go home and I'll arrange for you to get back to England," looking at his watch, it was twelve-thirty AM, "this lovely Saturday morning."

Max knew he had to go along with all this and before he could agree, the man added, "This is a once only offer Max. You understand that when you agree, which I sincerely hope you're about to, you must never do anything to betray that trust I've spoken of. If this meeting comes back to any of us, if you go to your authorities, if you betray us in any way," he paused, seemingly regretful at having to state the obvious, "then Leon here, or another the same as Leon, will find you, and kill you!"

There was ever such a faint sound from outside. Possibly just someone walking nearby on the pavement above. The boss looked at an unconcerned Leon, who in turn flicked his head to the guard in the corner to go and have a look. He rose off the table, nonchalantly exited the front door and closed it behind him. They could hear him going up the several steps to street level.

Max replied. "Then we have a deal," and held out his hand.

From the lab room along the corridor, they heard Ben shouting inexplicably, "Nein! Nein!" They looked round in bewilderment and then came some clarification as to what had distressed the technician so abruptly, having looked into the dummy shell. He yelled out, "Ein versteckter tracker!"

The boss looked at Leon, then back towards Ben, shouting, "What the hell do you mean there's a hidden tracker?"

Having seen the scan of the dubious, harmless contents, Ben cracked open the shell parting the top half bullet from the lower shell case, revealing the tiny device inside. He shouted back, "One of these shells is a dummy, it's got some kind of tracking device inside it!"

At that very moment, the door opened. It was the guard, looking calm but stilted as he walked back inside, slowly.

The boss and Leon were thrown into momentary confusion, with Ben shouting his revelations about the tracker, their realisation things had gone sour on them, and now the shock of noticing that another person was entering the room hidden behind their guard.

A Glock 17 handgun revealed itself from behind the hapless man and was now pointing at them. Phil Landon was holding it.

His face was determined but belied a twitchy hype about him. Having been near the top of the steps wondering what to do, the decision was made for him as the guard came up the stairs. He'd simply raised his gun, put his finger to his lips and waved the man to go back down and into the apartment, with him following closely behind.

In the confusion, Max lunged himself towards Leon and the one thing he knew could cause a problem, having seen Leon retrieve it when he'd jumped down to the dockside on the island.

Max landed a disabling punch right into the centre of Leon's stomach, winding him for just a second. He continued round to Leon's side, lifted up his jacket to reveal the weapon and grabbed the Heckler and Koch out of his centre-back holster. Max quickly moved away from Leon who was already absorbing the stomach blow and straightening up again.

Ben came rushing down the corridor and into the room, closely followed by Anna, holding the broken dummy shell showing the small tracking device. He froze as he was greeted by the change in circumstances before him. His three German colleagues were now being held at gunpoint by the groggy seller and a new person.

The boss was about to speak, but Phil took control. "Just shut up and everyone calm down," he demanded, gripping the handgun more tightly to show his resolve.

Leon sneered at Max, who himself held the gun tightly, levelling it with Leon's head from several metres away.

Max spoke. "Phil! For crying out loud. Where the hell have you been?" he panted.

Phil didn't take his eyes off the guard and man in front of him. "Long story Max. But I'm here now. Just in time by the sounds of it!"

21

"Can someone tell me what's going on here?" demanded the boss, with a face on him like thunder, flicking an angry look at both Leon and the guard.

Phil pulled the small handgun out of the belt holster of the guard then pushed him forward by pressing his gun into his back. "Over there, all five of you, against the wall." Ben and Anna obediently bustled alongside the others as they backed up against the same long wall. "Cover them, Max," asked Phil, who then disassembled the top slider part of the guard's gun, emptied the chamber and all the rounds in the magazine and threw the lot into the far corner of the room. He returned his concentration to his own gun.

Phil turned to Anna. "You. Have you got any strong gaffer or duct tape? You must have back there somewhere."

Anna quickly nodded and disappeared down the corridor to fetch it.

Phil shouted after her, "Anything funny and I start shooting everyone, I've got a very twitchy trigger finger right now!"

The boss tried again, more calmly this time. "Please. This must be a misunderstanding. Who are you and what do you want with us?"

Phil looked to Max for a nod to reply, before Max asked him, "You have called this in haven't you? Backup?"

Phil looked away from Max back to the others, but his not wanting to reply to Max was enough to give him the hint that he had not called this in yet!

Phil spoke. "We're both with British Intelligence Services. MI5 to be precise."

"What!" exclaimed Leon, looking at Max, "you, MI5. I knew there was something about you. You're no desk jockey are you?"

The boss spoke next. "But I thought you are Blackbird. The seller of the designs. Water Spider the broker would have checked you out. This must be a terrible mistake, let me sort this out," as he reached inside his jacket for his phone.

Phil shouted. "Hold it right there. Each of you, take out your mobiles, just using your thumb and forefinger, very slowly. Throw your phones at my feet. Now!"

Anna shook her head. "I don't have a mobile with me here." Phil nodded irritably. They each drew out their mobile phone and tossed it over to Phil. Last to throw it over was the guard, who just as he looked like he was throwing it at Phil's feet, quickly accelerated the arc of his arm and chucked the device straight at Phil's face. At the same time, he lunged forward at him in an attempt to grab Phil's gun.

Phil swung his gun upwards to deflect the phone coming at him and clumsily pulled the trigger firing a round off up into the ceiling, splintering through the plasterboard and wooden joists. The lunging man just managed to get a hand onto Phil's gun, when there was another shot fired, this time the bang was accompanied with a softer thud. Max's round passed through the upper side torso of the guard and out through the middle of his shoulder blade, shattering it with excruciating pain.

The man's intended grip on Phil's gun crumpled instantly as he continued his lunge, but to the floor, writhing in agony from his shoulder wound. Phil staggered back away from him and re-aligned his aim at the others, who were too shocked to react. Only Leon had managed to get himself ready to make a move, but Max's gun was immediately trained back on him after the shot was fired.

Now Max had Leon's full respect, but the anger and hatred inside were at boiling point and Max could see Leon was practically bursting at the seams to have a go himself.

Max looked to Phil. "I've got them covered. For God's sake, smash their phones or the sim cards, then tie their hands behind their backs with the tape. Do it well." Phil hesitated. "Move!" cried Max, trying to snap Phil out of it. He pulled himself together and went through the four mobiles one by one, opting to smash them on the ground with the handle of his Glock, quicker than fiddling about extracting tiny sim cards.

"All of you kneel down, slowly!" Phil ordered, as he gave his gun to Max to hold. He then set about binding each of them in turn, apologising to the wounded guard as he still bound him as well.

Max spoke. "Alright. So who do you really work for?"

The boss replied. "I've already told you. We're with the Dreikack. You realise you're both dead after this don't you?"

"Not a wise thing to tell someone pointing a gun at your head is it?" replied Max dismissively.

"Look, I'll tell you what," the man continued, "you two just leave us here, right now, we won't move for ten minutes," pausing for dramatic effect, "and take the bag of diamonds!" Phil's interest rose as he looked up for a reaction from Max. "Come on, you get the forty-eight million and we won't come after you?"

Max was conscious of the look on Phil's face as he finished binding them and realised that Phil was actually hoping he'd consider their offer, to take the diamonds. But was that for MI5... or himself?

Phil returned to Max and retrieved his handgun from him. Max said, "Phil, I assume you've got your phone? Do the mug shots."

Phil pulled out his mobile and went down the row of five Germans pressing his camera button several times in front of each of them, to ensure getting at least one good head and shoulders photo.

Max went on. "We will be taking the diamonds thank you." The man looked pleased that maybe a deal had been struck to save them. "And we'll also take back our Omega sample." The boss's relief turned back to incredulity and anger. Max looked at Phil, "Go get the Omega round from the lab back there, and make sure it has the clean base and not the scuffed one." He gestured towards the dummy shell in Ben's hand. "That one, you can keep. As a memento!"

Leon couldn't contain himself and started swearing at Max. The boss looked as though he was trying to think of something clever to save the day. The guard was out of action, moaning from the pain. His bleeding had already stopped and no vital organs or blood vessels had been hit, Max had aimed well under the circumstances. Ben and Anna were still confused about everything, not knowing all the details and simply wishing they wouldn't be hurt in any way.

Phil returned proudly with the clean, live Omega round and held it up for Max to share in the victory. He then went across the room and gathered up the black velvet bag. He opened it up to put the round inside and was stopped in his tracks for just a moment, upon laying his eyes on the bag full of beautiful, sparkling gemstones for the first time.

"So that's what almost fifty million looks like in diamonds," Phil marvelled. "I can kinda see what all the fuss was about today, jees!" He dropped in the shell and pulled the drawstring tight.

"Can you put the tape over their mouths as well," Max asked Phil, who obliged.

Just before the tape went on, Leon managed to get out one final threat. "Mister Max, Blackbird, MI5 man, whoever the hell you are. I will come after you. You know that don't you!" The tape completely sealed off his mouth.

"Not today you won't," said Max, "but when you do, I'll be waiting!"

Next was their leader. "Last chance Max. We can all get away with no repercussions, I promise you…" the tape went on.

"Now that you've all quite finished, we'll be on our way," said Max. "I'll hold you to your offer of not moving for ten minutes." The man and Leon started angrily mumbling behind their taped mouths.

Max and Phil edged back towards the door and slipped outside and up the steps.

"Where's your car Phil?" asked Max.

"It's just around the corner," pointing away from the park.

They trotted down the street. It was one AM and all was quiet, just the odd car passing by. As Phil rounded the corner of a building he stopped in his tracks, then cautiously backed up behind the brickwork to Max who'd immediately stopped himself as well.

"Shit!" whispered Phil. There's a goddamn policeman checking out my BMW!"

"Why?"

"I don't know," said Phil, "it is the middle of the night, I parked up on a deserted road all by itself and we're right in the Embassies district. What do we do?"

"We've got to get to our Embassy, that's the only safe place for us right now. It's not far, let's double back then go through the park, more cover, less people," said Max.

Once Max and Phil were out of sight having left the apartment, Leon was up on his feet, hurriedly looking around the room for something sharp or with a strong corner to it. Nothing. He disappeared down the corridor and went into one of the adjoining rooms which had a heating radiator against the wall. He backed himself up to it and hooked the tape wrapped tightly around his wrists over the metal valve on the top end. Then with all his weight and a push from his powerful legs, he managed to tear the tape freeing his hands. He fell heavily onto the floor on his chest, but his anger compensated for any minor discomforts or injuries. He was on a mission now having been humiliated by this Max MI5 agent.

He ran back to the others and undid their tapes, starting with his boss. Once they were all freed, the lead man instructed Leon.

"We'll sort things here. You go!" waving him away. "Leon. You find them and get back the Omega round and diamonds."

Leon looked quizzical as if saying, 'Is that all?'.

"And obviously stop those two escaping!" Leon headed for the door. "We can't have any witnesses!" Leon was striding up the steps and just heard his boss shout, "And get his phone!"

He cautiously ran down the road away from Tiergartenstrasse, rightly thinking it was unlikely the other MI5 agent would have parked up on such a busy road. Turning the corner he saw the same policeman standing by a parked BMW. Leon stopped quickly. The last thing he needed right now was a long conversation with this policeman about what he was doing at one AM running around the streets of Berlin.

Before he backed up round the corner out of sight, he had at least been given hope the chase was still on. The boldly displayed British number plates on the BMW told him that the two Brits he was after hadn't been able to escape in their car. They were on foot. In his city. Leon instantly knew that they had to head for their British Embassy and the most direct and out-of-sight route, was through the Tiergarten park.

Phil and Max had passed back by the apartment from the other side of the road, crossed Tiergartenstrasse and just disappeared into the trees of the park, as Leon had emerged up the steps onto the street, then gone in the opposite direction to them.

They were both trotting at a steady pace, one which Max suspected Phil wouldn't be able to sustain for too long, but they needed to get some distance from the apartment. They had an inkling that the taped wrists would be overcome soon, but felt convinced they wouldn't be able to muster much backup or support at this time of the night.

Phil started to fumble for his phone to get directions.

"Forget that, no time," said Max. "The Embassy is at the far eastern end of the park, just behind the Brandenburg Gate and the Jewish Memorial. We keep going in this direction we'll hit the end of the park soon, it's probably only three-quarters of a mile."

The park was almost deserted, though they did see one person walking their dog, probably an insomniac, so Max said to Phil, "Better put these away in case we're spotted by a civi!" gesturing to their handguns. Phil felt a bit more exposed without the gun in his hand, but returned it to its belt holster all the same. He wondered what had happened back at the apartment, 'they're bound to have got free from that tape by now' he thought.

They made their way along one of the paths and passed over onto a small island with the statue of Luisen Denkmal a Prussian royal. Her stony face seemed to mock their plight as they crossed her gaze and left her water surrounded memorial, back into the park.

At the apartment Anna had gone back into the lab room and eagerly returned with her mobile, handing it deferentially to the man in charge. "I lied!" she said simply.

"Good girl Anna," the short man said enthusiastically. He punched in a number.

"Luis? Is that you?"

"Yes, who the hell is this? Do you realise what time it is for crying out loud!"

"This is Hans Meyer!" said the boss in the apartment!

"What? Oh! Herr Meyer! My goodness, I didn't realise it was you, I'm so sorry. How can I help you?" said the other man on the line apologetically, sitting upright in bed.

"You'll have a couple of your men in the Brandenburg Gate area at this time won't you?" said Hans.

"Probably a handful at a stretch. Why?"

"I need a favour Luis. A big one. I'll owe you. I need you to call each of them, immediately! Let me explain why," directed Hans.

Max and Phil continued down the path set about a hundred metres back from the Tiergarten road, so they had plenty of cover from passers-by on the main street.

Leon was jogging at a good pace, aided by his daily runs and fitness. He knew the park well and wanting to avoid a cat and mouse hunt, had decided to run along Tiergartenstrasse which led into Lennestrasse road in the hope of then heading them off ahead. There was a large area of open ground near to the Jewish Memorial, where Leon would have a good view of most of the paths leading in the direction of the British Embassy. He would try to get ahead of them and figure out what to do if he saw them once he got in position.

Phil was starting to tire and slow up behind Max, who turned around and went back over to Phil to gee him along. Just ahead he could see an open space where the Skulpturengruppe was, the global stone project, with five stone arrangements symbolising love, peace, hope, awakening and forgiveness.

Phil was bent over, gasping for breath as Max approached him. "Come on Phil, we're almost there. Once we get to that Embassy we're home dry."

Phil slowly straightened up and it was then, to Max's astonishment, he could see the Glock pointing straight at him.

"Sorry old chap," said Phil, seemingly not out of breath at all. "I don't think I'll be coming to the Embassy with you after all!"

"What on earth are you talking about, it's just over there." Max composed himself, feeling the handgun he took from Leon was still lodged in the back of his belt. "Why are you pointing your gun at me Phil, you need to put that down! What is it you want?"

Phil sighed, then slightly raised the black velvet bag. "I've got everything I want right here! Forty-eight million in diamonds. With that amount I can do whatever I want. I can disappear in some hot, sunny country and live like a king." He nodded at Max's rear. "Take out your gun. With thumb and finger. Slowly."

"Phil, listen to me. Come back to the Embassy with me and we'll forget all about this." Max was trying to be assuring, but felt his words were falling on deaf ears as he handed over his gun. "Stay with me. You'll be a hero, get promoted, more fieldwork. This'll be a real win for you."

"I'm sorry Max, really I am. But this bag is simply too much temptation all wrapped up in a once in a lifetime opportunity." He took Max's gun and started to pull away from him. "You go now Max, I'll be just fine."

Max quickly threw in one last plea as Phil was leaving. "Phil. At least let me have the Omega sample. It's useless to you. We've worked so hard for that damn thing. Let me take it in with me?"

Phil hesitated and pondered for a moment. "You're right, I don't need it." He took it from the bag, "Here, you have it," and tossed it over to Max who carefully caught it.

"Thanks, Phil," said Max. He could almost empathise with the man. How easy it was for a weaker-minded person to be completely changed in character by the temptation of so much life-changing wealth. Phil got further away and before he disappeared into the gloomy night, Max said softly, "Be careful!" Phil just heard Max utter something but couldn't make out what he'd said. He started trotting again, northwards.

Max put the Omega round into his pocket and made his way around the perimeter of the open space the ornamental stones lay in. He then realised that Phil had his mobile with him, and it was on that phone the mug shots of the guys back at the apartment were on. 'Damn it! Bang goes the evidence'.

He suddenly became conscious of hushed, light footsteps in the distance, moving fast. Someone running. Could be a jogger? Not at this hour surely? Max felt a shot of adrenalin surge through him as the fears he'd had ever since entering the park looked like they could become reality. 'Could that really be Leon?' he thought. "Shit!"

The quick steps were still a way off to the side of him. With no gun, he felt this was now maybe a straightforward sprint to the finish line. He set off accelerating as quickly as he could. Cutting across the open ground, he put himself further away from the runner who must now be well behind him. Max continued into the last area of trees past the Goethe Denkmal monument and rejoined another pathway heading in the direction he needed.

Leon had been running towards the open ground and was just too late to intercept the two MI5 men, who had just separated. However, he heard someone suddenly running fast and could just make out a figure crossing the open space past the stones. It was Max. Leon was already running, so easily picked up his pace and headed towards where he thought Max would emerge from the park treeline onto the road.

Ten seconds later, Max reached the edge of the park and with little traffic, kept running across the four lanes of the Evertstrasse. To his left, some five hundred feet up the road he could see the Brandenburg Gate highlighted in the dark sky. Having crossed over he kept on running into the midst of the first area he found himself in, the incredible five-acre Jewish Holocaust Memorial.

Built in 2004, there were two-thousand seven-hundred and eleven stelae smoothed concrete slabs perfectly aligned in varying heights across the site. With fifty-four columns and eighty-seven rows of rectangle slabs varying from eight inches tall up to a massive fifteen and a half feet high, the site provided a rabbit warren maze of cover. Max headed straight into the centre where the land dipped down, twisting occasionally between the slabs to change his path. He was conscious of the runner behind him already crossing the road.

Leon cursed to himself as he helplessly watched Max a small distance in front of him cross the Evertstrasse and disappear into the forest of slabs. He still assumed Max had his Heckler gun so whilst he headed down one of the lower aisles enabling him to make up some more distance quickly, he was mindful not to get too close to Max's approximate location. Leon hunched down and starting moving more cautiously towards where he thought Max was. He continued trying to skirt around the southern part of the site, knowing that Max would probably want to exit on the far side nearest where the British Embassy was in Wilhelmstrasse just two roads away.

Max ducked behind a large slab and now also crept from one to the next. As long as they weren't both in the same aisle and he kept low, it would be hard to see one another. The cat and mouse hunt began, but neither was sure if they were the cat, or the mouse. Keeping low he deliberately didn't look up over the slabs to see where Leon might be. If he could see Leon, then Leon could see him and he still had maybe three-hundred long and dangerous feet to get to safety.

Just up the road, Phil Landon emerged from the north-easterly corner of the Tiergarten park, right opposite the famous Brandenburg Gate. Another Prussian monument, completed in 1791 under the orders of King Frederick William II, symbolising peace after a Batavian revolution. Above the two rows each of six large columns, sat the Quadriga, with Victoria the goddess of victory triumphantly riding her chariot pulled by four horses. Atop of her standard was an eagle above an oak leaves wreath encircling an iron cross, symbols since used frequently in German history.

This magnificent monument had witnessed so much beneath its gaze including use by only the Prussian royal family, ceremonies and triumphant processions by among others, Adolf Hitler and his Nazis. It mostly survived the second world war fighting and bombing and watched on as the Berlin Wall was hastily erected in 1961, then dramatically taken down in 1989.

Phil planned to find a small hotel somewhere in the city and lie low for a few days to let the dust settle. He'd written off returning to his abandoned BMW and ever going home to England again. He could hire a car and drive down to Serbia, out of the European Union and then fly from Belgrade airport to either Indonesia or South America, he hadn't decided which yet.

He was trying to look calm and blend in with the odd nighttime stroller, but with his Glock in its holster, the Heckler he'd got back from Max in his jacket and a medium-sized black velvet bag full of diamonds too big to conceal, he looked far from blending in innocently.

As he came to the edge of the Ebertstrasse road he immediately became aware of several figures in his peripheral vision. One to his far-left coming along the Simsonweg path from the park towards the Gate and the other to his right walking away from the Gate down the other opposite side of the road towards the Jewish Memorial. Both of them were dark blue uniformed German Policemen.

The three of them all looked at one another at the same time. Phil was too far out in the open to avoid them now and his stomach churned with anxiety. What were the chances of stumbling across not one, but two police officers in the middle of the night, both in this area.

Phil had no idea that these officers were two of several who had been called by their superior and told to circulate the roads near the British Embassy. Hans Meyer had demanded that the officers apprehend two foreign agents trying to flee with critically sensitive German intel. He'd ordered that they should preferably be detained for him, but if there was any likelihood of them escaping, then they were to be shot as both were believed to be armed and dangerous.

The two policemen looked at Phil curiously and as the stares were exchanged, they quickly realised this man was up to no good and could be one of the fleeing agents they were to find and stop.

The nearest policeman started to walk across the road and with his hand now lowered towards his gun at his side, shouted out to Phil, "Halt!"

This was the cue for the other policeman to start running towards them from his more distant position, also joining in with the shouting, "Halt! Hande hoch!"

With two impressive looking large uniformed officials both moving at him, both shouting orders as they went, Phil was terrified. He knew the best thing to do was to simply put his hands up in the air as requested, but the bag full of diamonds in his hand, his future fortune, reminded him of what was at stake here. He ran.

Phil ran across the road between the two nearing officers towards the arches of the Brandenburg columns. As he did so he swapped the bag into his left hand and pulled out his Glock with his right hand, quickly turning to each of the chasing men to assess how close they might get to him and whether or not he could outrun them. His brain instantly returned the calculation that they would catch up with him within moments.

At the sight of the man running from them, pulling out a gun, both officers had drawn their handguns as they ran. Neither of them felt inclined to try talking down this agent, this spy, when he was waving a gun at them. They had their orders. They could use their discretion on apprehending, or shooting.

The officer from the park fired the first shot at Phil, which passed his arm by inches and took a small chunk out of one of the historic columns with a puff of fragments.

Phil instinctively returned fire at the officer and although running and twisting round to try to aim, got off a lucky round piercing the sleeve of the man's jacket and gouging a wound into his forearm. The man cried out and was momentarily slowed, until seconds later he'd assessed the pain and figured it was a glancing blow and he could continue the chase.

Phil came to the monument and as he passed through, could see the Berlin Fernsehturm Tower with its round observation sphere in the distance, beckoning him to fight for freedom. It was the last thing Phil Landon saw.

He was conscious of an instantaneous bite in his back and a strange wave of pain inside him, as something tiny jumped from his chest. Then nothing.

The policeman nearest to him had seen that the British agent was heading between the columns and had slowed down to take time to aim and fire just one, accurate shot at the man. Firing at the largest part of his target, the centre of his back, the bullet had pierced through Phil's upper latissimus dorsi back muscle and clipped the right atrium of his heart, tearing it open and useless. It then smashed through his sternum chest bone and out the front of Phil's shirt.

Phil's momentum carried him through the Gate and he fell flat on his front on the edge of the Pariser Platz, dead. His gun clattered along the floor ahead of him and as the velvet bag hit the ground with such force, many of the stunning diamonds inside were released, sprinkling across the cold, damp stones. Millions of dollars worth of diamonds splayed out under the Brandenburg Gate.

The two policemen converged at Phil's body and stopped to look down at their quarry. The diamonds twinkled up at them both tantalisingly. A fortune the two officers could only dream of. However, they knew better than to even wonder about the 'what if's' of having such wealth. One of them started to gather up each of the gems back into the bag, while the other got onto his radio to update their superior, who reminded them to stay alert. There was still one other fugitive somewhere in the area.

Max and Leon both heard the three shots coming from a short

distance up the road in the vicinity of the Brandenburg Gate. They also both knew it could only be because Phil Landon had encountered trouble, or police. 'Had he been shot? Or had he managed to get by?'

Max knew the British Embassy was only one block to his north-east and the most direct route would be to go to the top of the memorial site and right and along the Behrenstrasse road. But he could see that most of the memorial slabs in that far corner were lower in height, barely above waist level. If he went that way he'd be seen by Leon well before he was able to make a run for it.

Then to further add to his thinking, just before Max turned away and back to planning a different route out of the memorial, he noticed a policeman come into view in that top far corner. He was strolling watchfully, purposefully. He was clearly waiting and looking for someone. Max knew that the lead man from the apartment would likely have some of the police in his pocket and having got free as Max knew they would, realised that he must have called upon them to search for him and Phil.

'Damn it! So close but so far!" he thought with gritted teeth.

He would have to move to the bottom corner of the site, at least there the blocks in the ground were still quite high. He picked his way in that direction, unaware he was getting closer to where Leon was.

Leon was crouched down behind one of the mid-sized slabs with his hand on the ground next to his right ankle. He'd known since leaving the apartment he still had one ace card left to play. He pushed aside the bottom of his trouser hem and firmly grasped the small two-shot model 1 Derringer pistol. The two barrels, one on top of the other, were only three inches long, so provided little in the way of long-range or accuracy, but at close quarters the .38 slugs could be disabling, even lethal. Having expected Phil to also bind their ankles together back at the apartment and discover his trusty hidden backup, he was elated when only their wrists had been taped up.

Leon tentatively peered around the side of the slab, keeping his head low to the ground. He had a clear view right up that aisle to the far end of the site and likewise, the same uninterrupted line of sight across the other aisle he was in.

At that moment something caught his eye. Whilst staring north up the row of slabs, something moved across his side view. As he turned his head he just took in Max disappearing across that aisle moving to the south-easterly corner. Leon quickly moved through the stelae in the same direction to get ahead of Max for a shot as he passed level with him again. He took up position just as Max came into view again. Leon fired.

Max was only five slab lengths away which appeared quite near to Leon, but their distance apart was still some fifty feet. Max moving, confusing shadows cast by the concrete monoliths, along with his tiny Derringer, all played their part of just slightly compromising Leon's aim and ability to pinpoint a shot at his target.

The bullet whizzed across Max's shoulder, tearing the fabric of his jacket. Max felt it pass him, completely out of the blue, milliseconds before hearing the sound of the gunshot to his right.

Max was jolted with surprise and filled with an instant adrenalin rush from the terror of realising he'd been shot at. He started sprinting, heading for the Hannah-Arendt-Strass road adjacent to the bottom of the large Memorial site.

Leon cursed as he saw Max continue on after firing his shot. He got up and was running immediately after him. He still couldn't get too close though. His Derringer was no match for his old Heckler and Koch that he still assumed Max had.

Max sprinted along the open road, passing a sole car whose driver peered through their windscreen looking most perturbed at the sight of two men running down the centre of the road, with the chaser holding a small handgun.

As he ran the one block, Max could see a policeman far ahead of him on the same road coming his way. The officer saw Max and Leon, stopped in surprise, then with no further delay, started running in Max's direction, drawing his gun at the same time and shouting, "Halt!"

Max reached the Wilhelmstrasse road and knowing the British Embassy was only a block away, veered left. He could now see it ahead. The large Union Jack flag protruded out over the pedestrianised road, from amongst the bizarre blue angular and rounded purple design features of the Embassy frontage. Max ran through the waist-high robust steel retractable bollards shouting out, "Guards! Guards! Britsh Agent being chased!" It was all he could think of yelling under the circumstances.

The chasing German policeman drew level with Leon who yelled at him, "Use your gun! Shoot him! Don't let him get away!"

The policeman fired a shot at Max, but missing, the bullet went smashing into the Embassy's steel barred gates set into the fifteen-foot high walls. It pinged as it ricocheted off the metal and then smashed into the glass entrance panels set further back from the gates.

At the bollards, the German police officer slowed, then stopped running altogether. The closed-off part of this road was unofficially known to be the British Embassy turf and no orders from above were going to persuade him to continue firing at a British agent who was effectively on British soil.

Leon swore at him as he ran by, continuing to chase Max. He had one round left in his Derringer and having seen that Max had not produced the handgun he'd thought he still had, was sprinting to get close enough for one last kill shot. British turf or not didn't concern him, he wanted payback. He wanted to win, impress his boss and show this Max guy he was better than him.

Max could see yet another German police officer appear at the far end of Wilhelmstrass and pull out his gun. It was one of the two who'd chased Phil Landon down at the Gate. He'd heard Leon's shot at the Memorial so had gone to cover the top end of the Embassy's access road. But like the other policeman, he watched helplessly from where he was, not daring to take another step with his gun drawn.

More because of the German policeman's shot hitting the Embassy's reception panel, than from Max shouting, the sole British armed police officer on duty in the entrance area, came out of the opened gates. He was immediately met with the sight of Max bearing down on him, again shouting, "I'm a British agent. They're armed! Don't let them shoot us!"

The many, many hours of training the armed police office had endured over the years, had prepared him for this moment, where he had to assess and then act. He looked at the sight in front of him and with an instant glance read the whole scenario. He could see the Brit claiming to be an agent was unarmed and being chased. The man behind him was tearing towards the Embassy entrance now holding up a small handgun, pointing directly at him and the fleeing agent.

Max briefly crossed the officer's line of sight to Leon, as he went to lunge through the entrance gates. As Leon was about to shoot at Max, he saw the armed policeman holding a lowered Heckler and Koch MP5 machine gun. As Max passed across him he blocked his view of the policeman for a second. Then as Max cleared the armed officer, Leon was confronted with a raised MP5 pointing at him and his aimed Derringer.

Leon's eyes met the armed officer's for a fraction of a second. The trigger was squeezed.

Before Leon could exert the slight force needed to fire off his one round at Max's back, the single tap of the policeman's trigger had sprayed twelve rounds into Leon's torso, mincing most of his vital organs.

Leon's body was instantly rendered lifeless and twisted sideways as it fell, pushed by the force of the impacting bullets. He slumped onto the pavement in front of the Embassy's entrance, at the feet of the armed police officer, still pointing his MP5 at his body.

22

Later that day, at MI5 Thames House, Vince popped his head around Si Lawson's door. "He's back."

As soon as Max had gathered himself having got to the safety of the British Embassy in Berlin, at around two-thirty AM he'd called Si Lawson. Max gave him a complete briefing of everything he remembered since Phil Landon had dropped him off at the Moltrasio Lido jetty where he'd been collected by the broker. The whole island meeting, the broker trying to take both the samples and the diamonds, running around the island, the boat chase and going back to the buyer's car. Then waking up in Berlin, events at the apartment, Phil rescuing him then leaving with the diamonds and finally the chase through Berlin back to the Embassy. Si had listened with intrigue, peppering Max's outline of events with quick questions.

After a few well-placed calls between English and German government ministers, Max had been granted 'emergency safe passage'. After catching a few hours sleep in Berlin, he was escorted by an Embassy official to the airport and onto a plane back to London Heathrow where he was met by an MI5 driver and brought to Thames House.

"Send him in," said Si Lawson as he watched Max walk through the MI5 Cyberteam offices, getting a standing round of applause from the rest of the twelve strong team.

"Max! Thank God you're okay. Wow, you've been through a lot in the last day haven't you!" gushed Si heartily greeting him.

"Next time you offer me up to masquerade as an international weapons design thief and deal with the mafia!" said Max, "perhaps give me a little bit more warning eh!"

"Indeed my friend," said Si, "and probably also better backup by the sounds of it! We're still waiting to hear any news on

Phil Landon from German authorities."

Max produced from his pocket the remaining shiny Omega projectile live round and carefully laid it on the desktop in front of Si. "There you go Si, live shell intact, safely home!"

"Peter Kendrick will be pleased," noted Si.

Vince added, "Such a lot of fuss, over such a tiny thing!"

They all took a seat as Si recounted their conclusions. "Thanks to you Max, we've successfully managed to follow the Omega trail from thief and seller and broker to buyer. With the pictures Phil took at the lake, we've just got some photo ID's back of the broker and his mate. Water Spider was a chap called Mateo Ricci. Known to Italian authorities but never prosecuted. Made a career out of fixing, arranging and brokering deals, earning many tens of millions no doubt."

"And his friend with the gun?" asked Max.

"Just a local guy, Antonio Russo, nothing notable, builder, probably just a mate providing some backup," said Vince.

"Now to our enforcer chap, the one that tried to kill you in Berlin," started Si.

Max reminisced. "Yeah, a right nasty piece of work!"

Si continued. "Leon Becker. Can you believe it, Max, he was ex-German police, local then Federal. After some incident where he likely killed a suspect, he left the police, then a few years later according to my 'oppo' in Berlin, turns up playing for the other side, working for this large underworld organisation. Likely as an assassin, enforcer, heavy hand and then amongst all that, their Dark Web buyer Samson!"

"Yeah, what about this Dreizack bunch? They're the buyers right?" asked Max.

"It seems they are. Large setup across Italy, Germany and Russia, nasty mob. Among the usual dodgy dealings, they're known for expanding their weapons manufacturing and arms dealing lines of business. They have the money, so getting hold of these new designs from Empire gave them a boost to the top of the pile as ordnance sellers."

"It's a shame Phil's phone took the mugshots of them all at the apartment, would have been good to get the identity of the lead man there," mused Max.

"Well, Phil Landon may have a change of heart and come back to us, with his mobile and the photos," offered Vince trying to be positive.

Max chuckled, "I suspect he's either been shot or captured last night. Or maybe even already sitting on some beach counting his money, far, far away."

Si was reminded, "Talking about Phil Landon, I put a call into my contact over in their Federal Intelligence Service very early this morning, to see what had come up their end and explain what's been going on over there."

"What did they have to say about the whole thing, and me being chased through Berlin by an armed madman?" asked Max.

"Middle of the night," replied Si, "he was unobtainable. I think I'll try him again. Can you guys give me a minute?" Vince and Max went back out into the main offices and closed the door.

Si dialled the number and after a few rings, rather than being put through to a receptionist service, it picked up. "Hans Meyer!" announced the curt voice.

"Hans," said Si. "I'm so glad I've caught you. Got a moment? It's Si Lawson. MI5."

"Oh yes, Si. Hello, how are you? I'm sorry I missed your call earlier," said Hans. "I've been meaning to call you back, sorry, so busy."

Si spoke. "You remember my call recently, about a Leon Becker? Well, there's been a lot of things going on in the last day or so I need to talk to you about. I'm assuming you must have heard about the incident outside our Embassy in the early hours of this morning?"

There was a slight pause before Hans replied. "Yes, of course, and I need to speak with you as well. Quite a lot to talk about it seems." Another pause. "Listen Si, I think it would be best to have a 'ghost meeting'. Just you and me. I can be in London in three hours or so?"

Now Si knew it was serious, but only suspected the great Hans Meyer was paying him the courtesy of a face-to-face meeting to tell him Phil Landon was being held by them, or possibly dead? The rare use of such so-called 'ghost meetings' meant the discussion was to be off the record, unauthorised, unsanctioned, no notes nor minutes to be taken, no record of the conversation, everything totally confidential and without prejudice. Such a meeting would never have taken place, so to say.

"Oh, okay, I thought we could just.... but fine. Let's meet up at the old place, Hyde Park Corner, shall we say three PM this afternoon?" suggested Si pensively.

"Perfect," said Hans, "usual ghost meeting rules, one bodyguard, everything off the record, yes?"

"Hans, you're making this sound very serious, anything I need to know in advance?"

"Usual rules Si, I'll see you later."

Hans and his minder took one of the several private jets the German Intelligence Service had at their disposal day and night, from Berlin Brandenburg airport. He landed at Heathrow just after two, giving his driver plenty of time to do the fourteen-mile, forty-minute journey into central London. Like so many capital's airports, it always amused him it was called London Heathrow, then it still took ages to get into the actual centre.

Si Lawson requested an armed MI5 agent to drive him to the meeting. It was normal for each senior official to have just one, armed bodyguard for protection giving equalled assurance of nothing being tried outside of the rules of the special rendezvous. Protocol also inferred that when one of them had requested a 'ghost' meetup, the senior intelligence officers attending should not tell anyone of their meeting. However, it was known throughout the upper echelons that one other person should be notified, again just a precaution in case something untoward were to happen.

At half-past two Si waved for Vince his deputy to pop into

his office.

"Vince, you know what a ghost meeting is don't you?"

"I've never had one boss, but know about the unwritten laws of a confidential meeting, yes."

"Remember I mentioned earlier I was waiting for some news on the whole Berlin thing with Max from my oppo," said Si. Vince nodded. "Well he's requested such a meeting with me, I'm off there now. I need to tell you, you know, just in case."

Vince looked worried.

"No cause for concern, but I must tell someone where I'm going. His name is Hans Meyer. He's a senior guy in the German Federal Intelligence Service, section TW. He heads up their weapons and defence."

"Oh, right, so this whole weapons design theft thing by one of his local mafia's is happening on his turf," said Vince. "That can't be good for him can it?"

"I think not. But I'm hoping he'll have news about Phil Landon and how we'll both keep the Como and Berlin body counts under wraps. It could be a massive PR disaster for both of us if it all gets out, if it hasn't already," hoped Si. "See you later then."

Hyde Park Corner was an ideal place for such meetings. It was a very public, safe location, being a three and a half acre pedestrianised memorial roundabout. The prestigious Park Lane was above, Belgravia below and to its sides Hyde Park, Green Park and the edge of the Buckingham Palace estate. Because it is surrounded by three lanes of London's busiest, constant traffic, with six streets converging there, sightseers rarely ventured onto its hallowed turf.

Designed in the 1820s, in its centre sits the large Wellington Triumphal Arch, named after the original statue that sat above it. After sixty years this was replaced by the quadriga sculpture depicting Nike, the winged goddess of victory, descending on the chariot of war, holding a laurel wreath symbolizing victory and honour. Over the years, surrounding the central arch, a statue of the Duke of Wellington was built, along with war memorials for Australia, New Zealand, the Machine Gun Corps and the Royal

Artillery.

Si's driver took the short route up Vauxhall Bridge Road then Grosvenor Place road and at Hyde Park corner, turner into the wide-open Apsley Way pedestrianised path that passed through the site. He parked up by the Royal Artillery memorial and they both got out. Any passing police checking the plates would quickly find out the car was registered to the United Kingdon Government and wouldn't bother challenging it being parked there.

Hans' driver had pulled in on the opposite end of the site and watched Si's car arrive. The plates showing '159 D 401' would immediately tell any inquisitive Metropolitan policeman this was a diplomatic car belonging to Germany and not to be approached unless in danger or committing a serious crime. Hans got out and waited to catch Si's eye, before then giving him a brief wave.

The two intelligence officials made their way towards one another, each with their armed wards keeping some distance behind them. Following their instincts and training, the guards were both looking around constantly, assessing for any threats that could endanger their valued leaders, checking out pedestrians and tourists, then each other.

Si Lawson and Hans Meyer met perfectly below the Wellington Arch in the centre of the site and shook hands. After exchanging pleasantries they began slowly walking around the outskirts of the area.

"I was intrigued by your request for a 'ghost' meeting Hans, and appreciate you flying over today. What's it all about then?" opened Si.

"You mentioned to me some days ago when you called," said Hans, "that you were looking into some corporate espionage, and that the name of Leon Becker had come up. Can you now tell me anything more about that Si?"

Si had hoped to get a bit more information on what this was about, as opposed to being questioned himself. He was happy to take the high ground though, hoping in the fullness of time he'd get to the detail of events with Hans, so might as well start now with good intentions.

"Well Hans, we came across quite a serious and disturbing issue."

Hans interjected sympathetically. "Those are the kind of issues you and I have to deal with eh."

"Quite so. We discovered that someone, or some organisation, was buying stolen weapons blueprints from one of our largest and most innovative ordnance design firms here in England."

"Awful," tutted Hans. "I hope you caught the thief responsible?"

"We did, of course, and are dealing with that through the usual channels. Business espionage is one thing and I wouldn't get overly involved with that these days. But when it involves stealing and selling our country's military designs and secrets, then it's a big deal that goes right to the top here!"

Hans nodded in agreement. "You've caught the thief, so what's the problem?"

"Come on Hans, you're playing coy with me today, I'm not sure either of us have the time for that do we?" snapped Si.

"My apologies Si, old habits and all that," conceded Hans. "I'm guessing this is linked to you name-checking our Leon Becker is it?" Hans knew full well that the MI5 agent he'd met called Max must have told Si all about the Como and Berlin events.

"It does. Bluntly, Leon Becker, from Germany, ex-police I gather, was the buyer of these stolen designs! Via a broker in Italy, whom Becker killed." Si let that hang in the air, and so did Hans before responding. He needed to choose his next words carefully.

"Interesting," said Hans, pondering. "After you called I was advised that Leon Becker, who indeed was in our Federal Police, had left after some incident and we gather joined one of the mafia's operating in Germany." Now it was the turn of Hans to start offering up some information he knew would come out sooner or later. "It's the Dreizack bunch, whom I'm familiar with as they're growing their weapons business which falls right into my BND remit. They're a real pain in the neck. Can you imagine how embarrassing this could be for me Si, for us, one of my own policemen defects to the underworld and from what you've said, was buying up your stolen designs for the Dreizack! Terrible!" shaking his head.

Si clarified, "So you're saying the real buyers of our arms info were the Dreizack mafia, fronted online by this Leon Becker?"

"Of course," agreed Hans eagerly.

Back at MI5 Thames House, the temptation had been eating away at Vince. He knew that what Si had told him about his ghost meeting with his oppo was confidential and only to be used if anything went wrong. He was extremely loyal to Si, and really just wanted to make sure he would be ok. It wouldn't be snooping. He simply had to look up this Hans Meyer character and see what he was all about, this high-up German intelligence officer.

He casually looked around the room. Everyone was busy with their work and no one looked as though they were approaching his desk area. Knowing his search path history would be stored somewhere, but only looked at if there was some issue, he logged into the European database of Government staff, then another login gave him access to staff within the Bundesnachrichtendienst, Germany's Federal Intelligence Service.

Vince typed into the search box, 'Hans Meyer' and hit the 'Enter' button. Immediately a high-level profile page appeared on his screen. At the top was a head and shoulders photograph of the man, alongside which were his basic stats, date of birth, height, weight, town of birth, marital status. Then underneath was a longer bulleted summary of his previous and current roles, notable operations, awards and so on. Nothing confidential, but a lot more than what you'd find with a Google search.

Vince was drawn to Hans' name at the top being highlighted in a red background, which denoted that this staff member was 'IMPORTANT' and held a senior position immediately below the Head Minister in charge of their Intelligence Service.

"What the hell have you got there!" exclaimed Max loudly from his desk some fifteen feet behind Vince's.

Vince literally jumped in his seat. "Bloody hell Max, you gave me a fright!"

Max was staring at Vince's screen and continued to do so as he skirted around his desk and came over.

"What is that you're looking at," demanded Max.

Vince tried to quieten him down holding his finger to his lips. "Shhhhh, please Max, not so loud. What's the problem?"

"That guy on your screen. Where did you get that from? Who is he?" asked Max again.

"Look, don't worry about it, Max. I just wanted to check on someone Si's meeting up with."

"What! Si's meeting one of the bosses of the Dreizack German mafia?" said Max, quite alarmed.

"What do you mean, Dreizack mafia?" said Vince, confused, but starting to figure something was up here.

Max now sounded angry. Not at Vince. At the mugshot staring at them from the screen. "That's the bloody leader that had me brought to Berlin to meet! The mafia boss who wanted to enlist me to sell them all future designs!"

Vince sighed, now convinced Max had mistaken the picture. "No, no, no. It can't possibly be, Max, you've got the wrong person. This is Si's oppo in the German Intelligence Service! He's a senior guy there. Not some criminal!"

"Oh my God Vince. It's him! I was in the apartment with him just last night, in fact just this morning. I'd know him from anywhere!"

His look finally told Vince he wasn't mistaken at all. "Okay, Max. Blimey, we've got to tell the boss!"

"Call him then, they'll have started their meeting by now won't they, I've got to talk to him," said Max.

Vince looked apologetic, shaking his head. "Si won't answer me. It's one of those weird meets where calls shouldn't really be taken or made."

"Vince, we've got to tell him, he could be in danger. Who will he accept a call from?" insisted Max.

Vince shrugged. "The only person he'd answer I guess would be his boss. The MI5 Deputy Director General!"

"Print out this profile and let's get up there right now to see him," Max ordered, pulling Vince out of his chair.

"We can't just walk in and expect to see the DDG!"

"Well that's what we're gonna bloody do!" said Max.

Si was relieved that some pieces of the jigsaw were starting to reveal themselves. "That does seem to make sense, that the Dreizack would want to muscle in on any new arms coming to the black market," said Si. "The corporate thief had made contact with a Dark Web broker who was auctioning them off online and Leon Becker was winning every sale."

"That's good we've managed to clear that up," said Hans with obvious relief. "My team can work with yours on the details and let's hope I can then close the net on this mafia bunch. We can't have them buying up your arms designs, can we? Glad it's sorted."

Just then Si Lawson's mobile buzzed inside his pocket. Both of them looked surprised at the intrusion, but Si grabbed it saying, "I'm so sorry, let me just turn this off."

He glanced at the screen as he was about to power it down, then stopped himself. It showed him, 'Incoming call – DDG'.

Si turned to Hans apologetically. "Sorry again Hans, it's the one caller I have to take. My boss. Just give me a moment please," and he broke away from Hans and walked off in another direction.

"Yes, Guv?" answered Si, wondering what on earth his boss could possibly need from him.

"Yes, it's me Si. Can you listen carefully for just twenty seconds, I'll be quick?" said the DDG.

"Of course." Si was now concerned about what the DDG was about to say, he sounded very serious.

"I've got your lads in with me, Vince and Max. Seems they looked up Hans Meyer, the BND chap you're having your ghost meet with. Max has identified his picture as being the lead person fronting the supposed Dreizack mafia buying your arms designs. He was forced to meet him in Berlin. Si, there's no way he's mafia for Christ's sake. He's the bloody BND head of their TW section. Be careful okay?"

The words his Deputy Director General had uttered completely floored Si, but he managed to mumble out his response of, "Understood," before they both hung up.

Si ideally needed a seat for a moment, but quickly composed himself before turning round to face Hans and rejoin him. His head was spinning with permutations of what could be happening and none of them was good.

"All okay I hope?" joshed Hans, trying to make light of what was surely an important call.

Si didn't have enough time to play clever or think tactics with this one, so he just said what he was thinking. "No Hans. I'm afraid everything is not okay!"

Hans was acutely aware of Si's change in look, voice tone and demeanour. He instantly knew everything was different now, because of whatever someone had just told him on that damn call.

"Whatever do you mean Si," he said pathetically. "I was about to tell you that I'll sort out that mess with Leon Becker chasing one of your guys to your Embassy. Awful business! Your man's okay I gather, just as well your Embassy guard shot him. I'll make sure there are no issues with all that Si, don't worry."

Both men knew that Hans was on the ropes now and what he'd just offered up wasn't going to fix everything that easily.

Si walked up to Hans, right into his personal space. "My man Max, who I believe you know, has identified you from your little meeting with him in the Berlin apartment." Hans continued to look puzzled. "Why don't you tell me what's going on?"

"As I've said," Hans was losing his calm, authoritative tone, which alerted his bodyguard who tried to tune in more closely now. "Leon Becker was in my force and when he got into trouble, well alright I admit, I made him resign so I could get him into the Dreizack, undercover. This mafia was causing me all sorts of problems, I needed one of my best men in there, feeding me intel so

I could bring them down. They were operating across my jurisdiction, making a mockery of my country's weapons intelligence service."

The explanation seemed plausible, but Si thought back to the pretty thorough debrief that Max had already given him in the early hours of the morning, after events in Berlin had unfolded.

"But Hans, that doesn't explain why you were there at this apartment last night. You presumably told Leon to bring Max all the way from Como to see you. You took possession of the Omega samples and had your lab guys start reverse-engineering the designs, and you tried to convince my man, who you thought was the blueprints thief, to sell you all future designs?"

Despite being surrounded by the busy traffic, that was the moment neither of them heard anything. They were each lost in their own realisation that the game was up. Hans quickly looked round to check how close his armed escort was and catching sight of that all-important 'D' in the centre of his car's plates, renewed his air of authority once more.

"Si. I think we've reached that point where the facts might have momentarily overtaken me it seems." Hans tried to reason with Si. "Let's you and me sort out this mess together, we don't want an international incident with us in the middle of it all do we?"

"This mess as you put it, is your creation Hans, not mine!"

"Come, come Si," Hans was more defiant. "You have Max back and your Omega sample. I however, have lost one of my best men in Leon, I've lost the Omega, and I've also lost about fifty million in diamonds! I'd say my offer to call it quits is a generous one wouldn't you?"

"Yes, that reminds me, on the subject of *your* diamonds. Have you really lost them? What happened to my other agent, a Phil Landon? Do you have him?"

Hans sighed. "We do have him. It seems he was doing a runner from us, and even from your Max, with the diamonds. He started shooting at police, so that was only going to end one way I'm afraid." Si looked at him, wanting to hear him say the words. Hans finally did. "He's dead. Quite ironic I gather. Under the Brandenburg Gate. Yes, we have the diamonds back. The headlines wouldn't exactly look good, would they? 'MI5 agent tries to steal mafia diamonds!'"

Whilst Hans had been speaking, Si had used the time to also fully compute what this all meant. The conclusion was even more outlandish than all the other events put together. His overwhelming realisation of the frightening fact gave him a shiver down his spine.

Si spoke with determination. "The biggest problem we have Hans comes back to who the real buyer is of these stolen designs. The British Government simply cannot tolerate what is effectively arms trading of our secret designs. Are you actually working for the Dreizack?"

"Don't give me that British Government speech shit Si," interrupted Hans crossly.

Si went on. "I'm clear that you do not work for the Dreizack mafia, yet it is you who via Leon bought the designs and wanted the Omega samples and future blueprints. You're acting on behalf of the German Intelligence Service for Christ's sake!"

"I tell you that Leon was buying the designs for the Dreizack," insisted Hans. Then with another turn of arrogance, "You know what, it doesn't matter anyway now, so yes, Leon also then passed the designs to me as well, for my TW team!"

Si was incredulous. "Good God Hans! You were using your undercover plant in the mafia, to buy the weapons designs not just for them, but for you and the BND as well! Your Government!"

"I think this meeting is over Si. My team will liaise with yours to return your agent's body. We'll keep Leon's death outside your Embassy under wraps. You've got Max and the sample. We should call it quits. In fact, I insist!" said Hans aggressively. "Farewell Si," and turning, he began walking back towards his guard and the car.

Si signalled his armed agent who immediately came over to them with his left hand on his jacket lapel, showing he was ready to draw out his gun.

Hans looked round to his guard who dramatically ran over to his side and also hovered his hand across his jacket.

"Calm down Si, you don't want to do that," insisted Hans holding his arm up.

"You're on *my* soil here," said Si with conviction, "I'm going to have to ask you to come in with me so we can sort this out, it's got too serious Hans."

"Come with you?" Hans repeated indignantly. "You're joking aren't you? We're going to get in our car, go to the airport and fly home in our private jet, and no one's stopping us. Not even you Si!"

The MI5 agent foolishly drew his gun, which immediately prompted the German guard to do the same. They ended up in a standoff with Hans and Si waving their hands for everyone to calm down, and the two guards both pointing at one another threateningly.

Si appealed to them, looking at the bodyguard next to Hans. "Put down your gun soldier. You're in Britain now, we don't take kindly to foreigners waving a gun around at us!" With no signal from Hans to lower his weapon, the man stood firm. "Hans. I'm asking you to come in with me to sort this out properly. Now *I'm* insisting!"

Hans stared at Si defiantly. "You can't make me do anything Si. You know I have diplomatic immunity!"

The words hung in the air. Si immediately knew he was right. He couldn't do anything because of this bizarre and often misplaced immunity foreign diplomats and high ranking officials were granted. Hans backed up a little, then once he was satisfied that Si had accepted his declaration of immunity, he turned and walked quickly to his car, closely followed by his guard walking backwards.

Si called after him. "Hans. We can't leave it like this. We cannot have a so-called friendly power thinking they can rob us of our country's military designs and get away with it!"

Hans didn't turn round as he replied. "That's above even our pay grades. Let it be Si, you won't like what you stir up. I'll fight you all the way!" He waved to his escort to hurry back to their car, where he finally put away his gun as he climbed in.

Si stood there, gritting his teeth and watched as Hans was driven away and disappeared into the London traffic, heading back to Heathrow airport.

"Get me back to the office," he ordered his agent, as they quickly returned to their car.

In the rear seat, Si dialled up the contact number saying 'DDG'.

Within the hour, Hans Meyer was taking off in the 'company jet' from Heathrow. He sat back in the large leather chair onboard and was grateful to be getting out of England and on his way back to the safety of his motherland. He was satisfied with his performance at the meeting with his counterpart. He understood Si's frustration over him pulling out his immunity card, but also at what he would now get away with. Yes Si was angry, but Hans knew he'd get over it and in a couple of days, they'd be sorting things out on the phone, quelling worries from their respective governments and life would go on. It would all be just another tiny blip along the never-ending journey of keeping international relations on an even keel.

Towards the end of the flight, the captain came out of the cockpit and approached Hans. "Sir. I thought you should know we've been asked to pull up at one of the hangers nearer the main airport, rather than our usual hanger space further away."

"Why on earth do we need to do that? The car will be waiting at the normal dropoff point won't it?" asked Hans.

The pilot shrugged, "I'm sorry Sir, that's what I've been told. Just thought you should know." He returned to the front of the plane.

Hans didn't think anything more of it. They often got diverted around the Berlin airport runways and disembarkment gates and hangers, depending on other flight schedules and how busy the airport was at any one time. He settled back in his chair and felt reassured as the plane soon touched down on the runway. 'Home at last', he thought, 'what a damn awful couple of days it's been!'.

From the North runway, the jet taxied along several of the

many intermingling runway lanes and headed for the corner of the airfield nearest to Terminal One, where other smaller business jets regularly dropped off or collected their VIP passengers. Hans was looking out of his window as the plane started to slow down, when he was aware of a group of people coming into view just ahead of them. They were standing where the plane looked like it would come to a halt.

Hans' canny senses were tingling and not in a good way. This didn't feel right. He shouted out to the cockpit, "What's happening, please? Who's the entourage on the tarmac for?"

The pilot didn't reply. Hans got out of his seat just as the plane came to a stop and before he could get into the cockpit to challenge the pilot again, the flight crewman was already opening the automatic door. With the steps neatly unfolding ahead of him, Hans tentatively looked out.

He was immediately horrified at the sight in front of him. There were four suited men and three armed uniformed Policemen with guns drawn, all staring at him as he ventured onto the top step. Standing ahead of the group was an older, stern-looking gentleman Hans now recognised.

"Good God, Finn? Finn Schneider? What in hell's name is going on here?"

Finn Schneider was the Head of the German Bundeskriminalamt BKA, the Federal Criminal Police Office, which included the 'police of the police'. When instructed from on high about a misdemeanour within the BND, he had authority over everyone in the organisation.

"I haven't seen you in years my old friend!" said Hans nervously.

The older man's expression remained frozen as he spoke. "I'm not your friend today, I'm sorry Hans. You're under arrest!"

Si Lawson had been tied up in meetings around London and Thames House for the remainder of the day and it was late when he finally returned to his office. He had hoped all of his team would have gone home by now, but as he expected, two of them were still at their desks. Max and Vince weren't going anywhere until they'd seen him. They were dying to ask what had happened during the rest of the afternoon, since persuading the DDG to call him.

Si walked past them, "Come on you two, follow me, I expect you'd like to know what's been going on?"

They scurried behind him into his office.

"Firstly thank you, Max," started Si, "for taking on this assignment, with your usual professionalism and resolve, no matter what was thrown at you. What a great job you did and thank you both for getting together after you'd identified Hans and somehow managing to see the DDG without an appointment. Incidentally, how did you get to see him?"

Vince looked at Max, then offered up, "It was Max's idea boss. We went up there and he told Chuck his PA that if we didn't get in immediately, then he'd have to explain why we failed to break a German Intelligence and mafia ring, stealing Britain's military design secrets!"

Si chuckled. "Heavy, but true I guess. I'd loved to have seen Chuck's stuck up little face when you laid that on him!"

"He went right over to the Guv's door and told us to go straight in, much to the DDG's bewilderment," added Max. "He was great though. Listened carefully, asked what level of certainty I had, to which I said one-hundred per cent. He got all the facts, then made the call to you. Impressive."

"Yes, he is. Well, thanks to that piece of intel and me getting it during my meet with Hans, I was able to challenge and pin him with not acting on behalf of the Dreizack, but can you believe, potentially buying up these designs for the German Intelligence Service. He was using the mafia as his front!"

"How did he take it all?"

"He as good as admitted it, claimed immunity when I asked him to come in with me, then scampered back off to the airport, telling me to stick it!" said Si feigning being insulted.

"Any news on Phil Landon boss?" asked Vince.

"Yes, unfortunately," regretted Si. After he took the diamonds and left Max in the park, he ran into a couple of policemen, part of the bunch in the area looking for you two, likely briefed by Hans to stop you both. The shots you heard Max were a bit of a to and fro between them and Phil. Phil came off worse. Hans told me he was shot under the Brandenburg Gate. They retrieved their diamonds from him. We'll get his body returned in the next few days for his family."

"Poor sod," quipped Vince.

Max added, "Yeah, he did follow me for twelve hours and break up the little party at the apartment, saving me from heavens knows what."

"Agree," said Si, "but the temptation of all that money was just too much for the man. Shame. As they say, the devil catches many souls in a golden net."

"So after Hans took off, what then?" asked Vince eagerly.

"I got straight on the phone to the DDG and we both agreed, ghost meeting and immunity aside, we couldn't let Germany take the mick and just buy up our military designs without repercussions. And so the calls up the chain started. The DDG spoke with the Director General, who then spoke to the Home Secretary, who in turn agreed we needed to take action at the highest level. So they ran it all past the PM, who then, all credit where credit's due, called the German Chancellor, explained the whole sorry affair and demanded action." Si paused for breath.

Max and Vince chorused together impatiently, "Yes? Then what?"

"The Chancellor came back to the PM within ten minutes stating that their Federal Intelligence Service had no such sanctioned operation to misappropriate British designs. *Apparently,* Hans Meyer had acted alone and out of self-advancement. The excuse if you can call it that, was his own TW section of the BND needed to come up with more and better innovations. So when his guy Leon Becker, genuinely undercover with the Dreizack, stumbled across the Dark Web designs pipeline, Hans decided to also have a copy of each weapon blueprints for his own department's kudos. If anything went wrong, he'd blame it on the mafia and Leon."

"Oh my God," whispered Max. "So he was buying the designs for the German Intelligence, they just didn't know he was getting his wonderful new ideas from us!"

"Yes," confirmed Si. "Though that's what their Chancellor has said and I'm sure will stick with forevermore. I guess we'll never truly know if the German Intelligence Services were ripping us off, or just Hans."

"So what will happen to him?" asked Max.

"I gather the wily fox had a reception committee waiting for him when he got off his jet in Berlin this evening. They arrested him on the spot. They've promised to try him, it'll likely be a closed court-martial of sorts. However, with all the intel he could spill as leverage, he'll negotiate a deal and they'll probably tuck him away under guarded supervision in a mansion somewhere for the rest of his life. Or just possibly, they won't want to risk him talking in later years, embarrassing them," Si paused, "and he'll simply disappear!"

"If they do a deal as you say," said Vince feeling short-changed, "you mean he'll get a payoff and retire happily ever after?"

"Someone like Hans Meyer doesn't need any more money, I'm sure he's a multi-millionaire already. No, it's being fired, in disgrace and losing all that hard-fought authority, that's what will punish him. Without power, he's nothing. He lives to work, direct, lead and manipulate people. That's what he'll miss, every single day until his death."

They were silent for a few moments, each thinking about the events of the last week, the subterfuge required, the dangers and risks taken, the four deaths and the unbelievable outcome. Then Max offered out his hand in the middle of the three of them. "We did it boss." Si and Vince reached out and held Max's hand as a team.

Si agreed. "We found the end of the Omega trail!"

THE END

Max Sargent Corporate Espionage Mystery Thrillers

available in the series by the author BEN COLT

can be read in any order

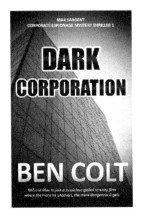 

ABOUT THE AUTHOR

BEN COLT

He grew up in the house previously owned by notorious British-Soviet double-agent Kim Philby.

A senior executive of three decades in the corporate world, having been a management consultant and Chief Procurement Officer for many big brand companies in various industries.

Most of his roles had a global remit, which took him around the world on business to many different countries and cities.

His procurement teams had a privileged role in firms, with unquestioned business-wide access and control of large spends, suppliers and intellectual property.

His extensive procurement and management experience gives him first-hand insight of the potential for corporate corruption and espionage, to quickly become dangerous.

www.BenColt.com

Printed in Great Britain
by Amazon

17718011R00169